KU-276-521

THE GREAT PUSH

TO

MARGARET

If we forget the Fairies,
  And tread upon their rings,
God will perchance forget us,
  And think of other things.

When we forget you, Fairies,
  Who guard our spirits' light:
God will forget the morrow,
  And Day forget the Night.

THE GREAT PUSH

An Episode of the Great War

PATRICK MacGILL

Introduction by Brian D. Osborne

Birlinn

This edition published in 2000 by

Birlinn Limited
8 Canongate Venture
5 New Street
Edinburgh EH8 8BH

© Patrick MacGill

All rights reserved.
No part of this publication may be reproduced, stored,
or transmitted in any form, or by any means, electronic,
mechanical, photocopying, recording or otherwise, without
the express written permission of the publisher.

ISBN 1 84158 036 8

Originally published by Herbert Jenkins

Subsequently published by Caliban Books
17 South Hill Park Gardens
London, NW3
1984

British Library Cataloguing-in-Publication Data

A catalogue record for this book is available from
the British Library

The publisher acknowledges subsidy from

THE SCOTTISH ARTS COUNCIL

towards the publication of this book

Typeset in Stempel Garamond by Brinnoven, Livingston
Printed and bound in Great Britain by Cox & Wyman Ltd, Reading

CONTENTS

INTRODUCTION

In August 1914, at the outbreak of the Great War, Patrick MacGill had already won considerable fame as the 'navvy-poet' and as the author of *Children of the Dead End* which had appeared earlier that year. This was the thinly fictionalised and vivid account of his early life in Donegal, his coming to Scotland as a potato picker, his life as a tramp, the hardships of work as a railway permanent-way labourer and his experiences as a navvy at the great Kinlochleven hydroelectric construction camp. Dermod Flynn, the central character of *Children of the Dead End*, is Patrick MacGill, or at least is as much of Patrick MacGill as MacGill wanted his readers to know. MacGill had escaped from the common lodging house and the navvy's bivouac by his self-taught skill as a writer when his sketches from the construction camp and reviews of his first collection of poetry had found him a post as a writer on the *Daily Express*.

Earlier, in that last summer of peace, he had returned to Glasgow from his new, and perhaps somewhat improbable, position at the heart of the Anglican Establishment as secretary and librarian at St George's Chapel, Windsor (he was after all a scantily educated Irish Catholic), to research the background for what would be his second and equally successful and sensational novel, *The Rat-Pit*. This is the harrowing account of the life and death of Dermod's youthful love, Norah Ryan, in the lodging-houses and slum tenements of Glasgow. MacGill's work in the cloisters of Windsor, helping Canon John Dalton, the Steward of St George's Chapel and a domestic chaplain to the King, translate Latin manuscripts seems light years away from the grim bleakness of Norah Flynn's existence and the experiences that Dermod Flynn/Patrick MacGill had shared with her.

On 11 September 1914 MacGill volunteered for military

service at Chelsea Barracks London. He was, as he wrote himself, one who had:

> . . . no special yearning towards military life, but who joined the army after war was declared.

Like many Irishmen of the day MacGill saw no difficulty in enlisting in the army of what some of his countrymen saw as an occupying, colonial power. Lord Esher, the President of the County of London Territorial Association, writing in the fore-word to another of MacGill's wartime novels, said:

> You had much to give us. The rare experiences of your boyhood, your talents, your brilliant hopes for the future. Upon all these the Western hills and loughs of your native Donegal seemed to have a prior claim. But you gave them to London and our London Territorials. It was an example and a symbol.

As a healthy young man of twenty-four years and six months, hardened by years of physical work in Scotland and standing five foot ten and a half inches tall and with a 41-inch chest, he was readily accepted for service in the 2nd Battalion of the London Irish. Rifleman MacGill, Regimental Number 3008, was sent for basic training to the White City Stadium and then to St Albans. After training he was posted to the 1st Battalion of the same regiment and crossed to France to serve on the Western Front, where, he boasted, he and the Colonel were the only two real Irishmen in the Battalion – a somewhat hyperbolic statement, to judge from the number of Irish names that MacGill introduces into his novel.

Just as MacGill had put his navvying experience to good use in his first novel, so he was to use his army service to create a series of successful autobiographical novels which catered for the public demand for personal accounts of the war. The first of these was *The Amateur Army*, published in 1915, which gave his personal account of how a young civilian was transformed by basic training into a 'finished fighter'. Perhaps somewhat naive in its style and tone, *The Amateur Army* had its origins in a series of articles MacGill wrote during his early months of service and it is naturally untempered by the realities of warfare. The novel was well-received, the *Daily Telegraph* noting that it gave:

> . . . many vivid pictures of the incidents and humours attending the transformation of a citizen into a soldier.

There are certainly very obvious differences between *The Amateur Army* and his later war novels. What however they do share is MacGill's vivid descriptive power.

MacGill had clearly shared in the wave of patriotic zeal which led so many young men of every class and condition to rush to join up in time to take part in a war which was, in the popular view, going to 'be over by Christmas'. *The Amateur Army* (and the title is irresistibly British and very much of the period) was described by MacGill as:

> ... the most democratic army in history; where Oxford under-graduate and farm labourer, cockney and peer's son lost their identity and their caste in a vast war machine. I learned that Tommy Atkins, no matter from what class he was recruited, is immortal.

A year's service experience, however, led him, perhaps more realistically, to reflect in *The Red Horizon*, that:

> ... the public school clique and the board school clique live each in a separate world, and the line of demarcation between them is sharply drawn.

Both *The Red Horizon* and *The Great Push* give an unvarnished, private soldier's account of war at the sharp end, of the confusion and horrors of war, and of the forces that enable ordinary men to perform extraordinary deeds. Just as in his earlier novels MacGill had written with the insight and actuality which comes from hard-earned living experience rather than from library research, so, in these wartime novels, he puts the 256 days he spent on active service in France to good effect. We get a graphic, insider's, description of the realities of trench warfare and its impact on both the soldier and on the marvellously resilient, but often forgotten, French civilian population around whose homes, farms and factories the horrors of total war raged. MacGill writes in *The Great Push*:

> ... at Cuinchy I saw an ancient woman selling *café-au-lait* at four sous a cup in the jumble of bricks which was once her home. When the cow which supplied the milk was shot in the stomach the woman still persisted in selling coffee, *café noir*, at three sous a cup.

If heroic and suffering France was, in MacGill's words:

> . . . the Phoenix that rises resplendent from her ashes; France
> that will live for ever because she has suffered . . .

then the ordinary British soldier is equally long-suffering
and heroic. In a passage which foreshadows the notion of
the British Expeditionary Force as 'Lions led by Donkeys', a
concept attributed to the German General Max Hoffman, he
writes:

> We, soldiers, are part of the Army, the British Army, which
> will be remembered in days to come, not by a figurehead, as
> the fighters of Waterloo are remembered by Wellington, but
> as an army mighty in deed, prowess and endurance; an army
> which outshone its figureheads.

By the period of *The Great Push*, the days immediately
before the Battle of Loos, MacGill has become a stretcher-
bearer, still with the London Irish. This changed role, in
the front line but excused many of the routine duties of his
comrades, clearly gave MacGill time to observe, to think and
to write. He tells us in his Introduction that the book was
sketched out in the field and even gives the precise times and
places where two of the sections were actually written.

This immediacy of experience was surely one of the reasons
for the enormous success of MacGill's wartime novels and for
their interest today. Although they are presented as novels,
The Amateur Army, *The Red Horizon* and *The Great Push*
are intensely autobiographical. Patrick MacGill is the central
figure; in these novels we do not even have the thin disguise
of a 'Dermod Flynn' character interposing between experience
and the reader. Contemporary critics recognised that here there
was something different, something far removed from the flag-
waving, jingoistic novels which had naturally proliferated to fill
the market. A critic in *Punch* reflected a common perception:

> Nothing so absolutely absorbing and so awful as *The Great
> Push* has, in the way of war literature, crossed my path since
> August, 1914. It penetrates into one's very vitals, not because it
> tells of wonderful hairs-breadth escapes or tremendous deeds
> of valour, but because it emphasises the grimness and unutter-
> able pathos of modern war.

MacGill does actually tell of hairs-breadth escapes and
tremendous deeds of valour but the horror and grimness of

war is the prevailing message which most readers will take from this book.

MacGill's first book had been a collection of poetry, *Gleanings from a Navvy's Scrap Book*, and the chapters of *The Big Push* are prefaced with verses from his poetry, which he later collected in *Soldier Songs*. He carries over into his fiction a poetic pen and a poet's eye for detail. Describing the scene on a road behind the front line, a road which had been subject to heavy German shelling, he writes of 'dead Highlanders with their white legs showing wan in the moonlight' and the image of young recruits who had not been wearing the kilt long enough to have their legs darkened by sun and wind is both vivid and moving.

The differing perspectives of the front-line soldier and the civilian, safe at home, are well captured by MacGill. One of his characters, Pryor, reflects on the German soldiers, that:

> We have no particular hatred for the men across the way . . .

but that at home:

> Good Heavens! you should hear the men past military age revile the Hun. If they were here we couldn't keep them from getting over the top to have a smack at the foe. And the women! If they were out here, they would just simply tear the Germans to pieces.

MacGill and his comrades carry on doing their duty, suffering and dying, but questioning the processes by which 'a war to end wars' is fought. MacGill says:

> No one likes this job, but we all endure it as means towards an end.

However he also goes on, with more bitterness, to remark:

> Did you see the dead and wounded to-day, the men groaning and shrieking, the bombs flung down into cellars, the blood-stained bayonets, the gouging and the gruelling; all those things are means towards creating peace in a disordered world.

It would be hard for a reader of *The Great Push* to believe in what the English war-poet Wilfred Owen called 'the old lie':

> My friend, you would not tell with such high zest
> To children ardent for some desperate glory,

The old lie: *Dulce et decorum est*
Pro patria mori.

There is, in truth, very little that is sweet and proper in the deaths that the men of the London Irish see, share, inflict and suffer. The corpses MacGill sees are:

. . . crucifixes fashioned from decaying flesh wrapped in khaki.

The body of the dead soldier lying in No Man's Land is an outcast.

Worms feasted on its entrails, slugs trailed silverily over its face, and lean rats gnawed at its flesh.

The question of which fatherland he was running the risk of dying for does not seem to have been one that very greatly exercised MacGill. The 'Irish Question', which had dogged British politics for more than half a century, and which would find violent form in the Dublin Easter Rising of April 1916, never seemed high on either the civilian or the military MacGill's agenda. His early novels were filled more with a class-based bitterness against exploitative clergy, greedy employers and rack-renting landlords than with any nationalistic fervour. In his first collection of poems he had written:

I sing of them,
The underworld, the great oppressed,
Befooled of parson, priest and king

and there seems every reason to believe that, as a socialist, he considered the socio-economic relationships of society of more significance to the ordinary man and woman than the niceties of forms of government.

The images of *The Great Push* are sharp and vivid, as are the insights into what makes men risk their life for abstractions like 'democracy', 'fatherland' or 'duty'. The musing of Private Felan who finds himself alone between the lines:

I can't take a trench by myself. Shall I go back? If I do some may call me a coward. Oh, damn it! I'll go forward.

has the ring of truth about it, as has the scene, near the end of the book, where MacGill and his comrades, short of rations, at last receive bread only to find that the loaf is red. When he asks how this had come about he is told:

The bloke as was carryin' it got 'it in the chest. The rations fell all round 'im and 'e fell top of 'em. That's why the loaf is red. We were very hungry, and hungry men are not fastidious. We made a good meal.

MacGill was gassed in an action on 14 October 1915, an incident which later caused him some health problems and which brought him before a medical board at the end of the war claiming a pension for nervous debility caused by military service and lung problems. A temporary payment was made but no permanent disability was found. This medical board and its associated paperwork has resulted in some basic records of MacGill's military service surviving in the Public Record Office. The gas incident was evidently not serious enough to take him out of service because MacGill was wounded in the right arm at the battle of Loos on 28 October 1915. This injury was what the soldiers of the day would have described as 'a Blighty wound' and he was invalided home.

While on sick leave in London he married, on 27 November, Margaret Gibbons, a romantic novelist and grandniece of Cardinal James Gibbons of Baltimore.

Press reports of his wedding suggested that, after a honeymoon in Devon, he was going to rejoin his regiment but MacGill never again served overseas. In March 1917 he was transferred to the Middlesex Regiment, and was thereafter posted to the Labour Corps, the Gloucestershire Regiment and various holding units in the London area. He continued to write, with a fourth war novel, *The Brown Brethren*, following in 1917. This was not in the autobiographical vein of *The Red Horizon* and *The Great Push*, although still informed by his personal experiences of the Western Front. He also published *Soldiers Songs* in 1916 and *The Diggers: The Australians in France* in 1919. It may well be that the military authorities thought MacGill was of more use to the war effort as a writer than as a stretcher-bearer. In the 1918 and 1919 editions of *Who's Who* he is described as being in the Intelligence Department of the War Office. However exact details of his military employment after November 1915 do not survive – the War Office records, including most of the soldiers' records from the First World War, were destroyed in the London Blitz in September 1940 and only the note of his service medal entitlement and the records of his medical board survive.

MacGill, after the war, continued for some years to be a prolific and successful commercial novelist although he never perhaps quite achieved the acclaim that his first books enjoyed. In *Moleskin Joe*, published in 1923, he went back, with some success, to the setting of *Children of the Dead End*. In 1920 he went on an international lecture tour, and in 1930 diversified into the theatre with a play, *Suspense*, which was staged at the Duke of York's Theatre in London in April 1930. This drama was based on an incident from the First World War but seems to have been of only limited success. The critic of *The Times* noted that:

> At the end of Mr MacGill's play there are five minutes so good that all seems grey when compared with them.

but complained of an earlier lack of narrative tension.

Suspense was later filmed and MacGill moved with his wife and three daughters to the United States, probably in the hopes of pursuing a writing career in Hollywood. However this does not seem to have been a successful endeavour and, although he had a bit-part in Noel Coward's 1932 film *Cavalcade*, there is no evidence of much success in the United States. It was, of course, the period of the Great Depression and perhaps not the most propitious time to seek a new career. MacGill later moved to Florida and continued to write for a few years – his last novel, *Helen Spenser*, was published in 1937. Ill health marred his later years and he died in Miami on Saturday 23rd November 1963. His death was not reported in British newspapers such as *The Times* or *The Glasgow Herald* – partly because he had been silent as an author for so many years, and doubtless also because the news of the assassination of President John F. Kennedy, on 22 November, preoccupied editors at the time.

He is buried in Fall River, Massachusetts, the home of his daughter Patricia.

Brian D. Osborne
January 2000

FOREWORD

The justice of the cause which endeavours to achieve its object by the murdering and maiming of mankind is apt to be doubted by a man who has come through a bayonet charge. The dead lying on the fields seem to ask, 'Why has this been done to us? Why have you done it, brothers? What purpose has it served?' The battle-line is a secret world, a world of curses. The guilty secrecy of war is shrouded in lies, and shielded by bloodstained swords; to know it you must be one of those who wage it, a party to dark and mysterious orgies of carnage. War is the purge of repleted kingdoms, needing a close place for its operations.

I have tried in this book to give, as far as I am allowed, an account of an attack in which I took part. Practically the whole book was written in the scene of action, and the chapter dealing with our night at Les Brebis, prior to the Big Push, was written in the trench between midnight and dawn of September the 25th; the concluding chapter in the hospital at Versailles two days after I had been wounded at Loos.

PATRICK MACGILL

CHAPTER I

IN THE ADVANCE TRENCHES

Now when we take the cobbled road
We often took before,
Our thoughts are with the hearty lads
Who tread that way no more.

Oh! boys upon the level fields,
If you could call to mind
The wine of Café Pierre le Blanc
You wouldn't stay behind.

But when we leave the trench at night,
And stagger 'neath our load,
Grey, silent ghosts as light as air
Come with us down the road.

And when we sit us down to drink
You sit beside us too,
And drink at Café Pierre le Blanc
As once you used to do.

The Company marched from the village of Les Brebis at night-fall; the moon, waning a little at one of its corners, shone brightly amidst the stars in the east, and under it, behind the German lines, a burning mine threw a flame, salmon pink and wreathed in smoke, into the air. Our Company was sadly thinned now, it had cast off many – so many of its men at Cuinchy, Givenchy, and Vermelles. At each of these places there are graves of the London Irish boys who have been killed in action.

We marched through a world of slag heaps and chimney stacks, the moonlight flowing down the sides of the former like mist, the smoke stood up from the latter straight as the chimneys themselves. The whirr of machinery in the mine could be heard, and the creaking wagon wheels on an adjoining railway spoke out in a low, monotonous clank the half strangled message of labour.

Our way lay up a hill; at the top we came into full view of the night of battle, the bursting shells up by Souchez, the flash of rifles by the village of Vermelles, the long white searchlights near Lens, and the star-shells, red, green and electric-white, rioting in a splendid blaze of colour over the decay, death and pity of the firing line. We could hear the dull thud of shells bursting in the fields and the sharp explosion they made amidst the masonry of deserted homes; you feel glad that the homes are deserted, and you hope that if any soldiers are billeted there they are in the safe protection of the cellars.

The road by which we marched was lined with houses all in various stages of collapse, some with merely a few tiles shot out of the roofs, others levelled to the ground. Some of the buildings were still peopled; at one home a woman was putting up the shutters and we could see some children drinking coffee from little tin mugs inside near the door; the garret of the house was blown in, the rafters stuck up over the tiles like long, accusing fingers, charging all who passed by with the mischief which had happened. The cats were crooning love songs on the roofs, and stray dogs slunk from the roadway as we approached. In the villages, with the natives gone and the laughter dead, there are always to be found stray dogs and love-making cats. The cats raise their primordial, instinctive yowl in villages raked with artillery fire, and poor lone dogs often cry at night to the moon, and their plaint is full of longing.

We marched down the reverse slope of the hill in silence. At the end of the road was the village; our firing trench fringed the outer row of houses. Two months before an impudent red chimney stack stood high in air here; but humbled now, it had fallen upon itself, and its own bricks lay still as sandbags at its base, a forgotten ghost with blurred outlines, it brooded, a stricken giant.

The long road down the hill was a tedious, deceptive way; it took a deal of marching to make the village. Bill Teake growled. 'One would think the place was tied to a string,' he grumbled, 'and some one pullin' it away.'

We were going to dig a sap out from the front trench towards the German lines; we drew our spades and shovels for the work from the Engineers' store at the rear and made our way into the labyrinth of trenches. Men were at their posts on the fire positions, their balaclava helmets resting on their ears, their bayonets gleaming bright in the moonshine, their hands close to their rifle barrels. Sleepers lay stretched out on the banquette with their overcoats over their heads and bodies. Out on the front the Engineers had already taped out the night's work; our battalion had to dig some two hundred and fifty yards of trench three feet wide and six feet deep before dawn, and the work had to be performed with all possible dispatch. Rumour spoke of thrilling days ahead; and men spoke of a big push which was shortly to take place. Between the lines there are no slackers; the safety of a man so often depends upon the dexterous handling of his spade; the deeper a man digs, the better is his shelter from bullet and bomb; the spade is the key to safety.

The men set to work eagerly, one picked up the earth with a spade and a mate shovelled the loose stuff out over the meadow. The grass, very long now and tapering tall as the props that held the web of wire entanglements in air, shook gently backwards and forwards as the slight breezes caught it. The night was wonderfully calm and peaceful; it seemed as if heaven and earth held no threat for the men who delved in the alleys of war.

Out ahead lay the German trenches. I could discern their line of sandbags winding over the meadows and losing itself for a moment when it disappeared behind the ruins of a farmhouse – a favourite resort of the enemy snipers, until our artillery blew the place to atoms. Silent and full of mystery as it lay there in the moonlight, the place had a strange fascination for me. How interesting it would be to go out there beyond our most advanced outpost and have a peep at the place all by myself. Being a stretcher-bearer there was no necessity for me to dig; my work began when my mates ceased their labours and fell wounded.

Out in front of me lay a line of barbed wire entanglements. 'Our wire?' I asked the Engineer.

'No – the Germans',' he answered.

I noticed a path through it, and I took my way to the other side. Behind me I could heard the thud of picks and the sharp, rasping sound of shovels digging into the earth, and now and again the whispered words of command passing from lip to lip. The long grass impeded my movements, tripping me as I walked, and lurking shell-holes caught me twice by the foot and flung me to the ground. Twenty yards out from the wire I noticed in front of me something moving on the ground, wriggling, as I thought, towards the enemy's line. I threw myself flat and watched. There was no mistaking it now; it was a man, belly flat on the ground, moving off from our lines. Being a non-combatant I had no rifle, no weapon to defend myself with if attacked. I wriggled back a few yards, then got to my feet, re-crossed the line of wires and found a company-sergeant-major speaking to an officer.

'There's somebody out there lying on the ground,' I said. 'A man moving off towards the German trenches.'

The three of us went off together and approached the figure on the ground, which had hardly changed its position since I last saw it. It was dressed in khaki, the dark barrel of a rifle stretched out in front. I saw stripes on a khaki sleeve . . .

'One of a covering-party?' asked the sergeant-major.

'That's right,' came the answer from the grass, and a white face looked up at us.

'Quiet?' asked the S.M.

'Nothing doing,' said the voice from the ground. 'It's cold lying here, though. We've been out for four hours.'

'I did not think that the covering-party was so far out,' said the officer, and the two men returned to their company.

I sat in the long grass with the watcher; he was the sergeant in command of the covering party.

'Are your party out digging?' he asked.

'Yes, out behind us,' I answered. 'Is the covering-party a large one?'

'About fifty of us,' said the sergeant.

'They've all got orders to shoot on sight when they see anything suspicious. Do you hear the Germans at work out there?'

I listened; from the right front came the sound of hammering.

'They're putting up barbed wire entanglements and digging a sap,' said the sergeant. 'Both sides are working and none are fighting. I must have another smoke,' said the sergeant.

'But it's dangerous to strike a light here,' I said.

'Not in this way,' said the sergeant, drawing a cigarette and a patent flint tinder-lighter from his pocket. Over a hole newly dug in the earth, as if with a bayonet, the sergeant leant, lit the cigarette in its little dug-out, hiding the glow with his hand.

'Do you smoke?' he asked.

'Yes, I smoke,' and the man gave me a cigarette.

It was so very quiet lying there. The grasses nodded together, whispering to one another. To speak of the grasses whispering during the day is merely a sweet idea; but God! they do whisper at night. The ancients called the winds the Unseen Multitude; the grasses are long, tapering fingers laid on the lips of the winds. 'Hush!' the night whispers. 'Hush!' breathes the world. The grasses touch your ears, saying sleepily, 'Hush! be quiet!'

At the end of half an hour I ventured to go nearer the German lines. The sergeant told me to be careful and not to go too close to the enemy's trenches or working parties. 'And mind your own covering-party when you're coming in,' said the sergeant. 'They may slip you a bullet or two if you're unlucky.'

Absurd silvery shadows chased one another up and down the entanglement props. In front, behind the German lines, I could hear sounds of railway wagons being shunted, and the clank of rails being unloaded. The enemy's transports were busy; they clattered along the roads, and now and again the neighing of horses came to my ears. On my right a working party was out; the clank of hammers filled the air. The Germans were strengthening their wire entanglements; the barbs stuck out, I could see them in front of me, waiting to rip our men if ever we dared to charge. I had a feeling of horror for a moment. Then, having one more look round, I went back, got through the line of outposts, and came up to our working party, which was deep in the earth already. Shovels and picks were rising and falling, and long lines of black clay bulked up on either side of the trench.

I took off my coat, got hold of a mate's idle shovel, and began to work.

'That my shovel?' said Bill Teake.

'Yes, I'm going to do a little,' I answered. 'It would never do much lying on the slope.'

'I suppose it wouldn't,' he answered. 'Will you keep it goin' for a spell?'

'I'll do a little bit with it,' I answered. 'You've got to go to the back of the trenches if you're wanting to smoke.'

'That's where I'm goin',' Bill replied. ''Ave yer got any matches?'

I handed him a box and bent to my work. It was quite easy to make headway; the clay was crisp and brittle, and the pick went in easily, making very little sound. M'Crone, one of our section, was working three paces ahead, shattering a square foot of earth at every blow of his instrument.

'It's very quiet here,' he said. 'I suppose they won't fire on us, having their own party out. By Jove, I'm sweating at this.'

'When does the shift come to an end?' I asked.

'At dawn,' came the reply. He rubbed the perspiration from his brow as he spoke. 'The nights are growing longer,' he said, 'and it will soon be winter again. It *will* be cold then.'

As he spoke we heard the sound of rifle firing out by the German wires. Half a dozen shots were fired, then followed a long moment of silent suspense.

'There's something doing,' said Pryor, leaning on his pick. 'I wonder what it is.'

Five minutes afterwards a sergeant and two men came in from listening patrol and reported to our officer.

'We've just encountered a strong German patrol between the lines,' said the sergeant. 'We exchanged shots with them and then withdrew. We have no casualties, but the Germans have one man out of action, shot through the stomach.'

'How do you know it went through his stomach?' asked the officer.

'In this way,' said the sergeant. 'When we fired one of the Germans (we were quite close to them) put his hands across his stomach and fell to the ground yellin' "Mein Gutt! Mein Gutt!"'

'So it did get 'im in the guts then,' said Bill Teake, when he heard of the incident.

'You fool!' exclaimed Pryor. 'It was "My God" that the German said.'

'But Pat 'as just told me that the German said "Mine Gut,"' Bill protested.

'Well, "Mein Gott" (the Germans pronounce "Gott" like "Gutt" on a dark night) is the same as "My God",' said Pryor.

'Well, any'ow, that's just wot the Allymongs would say,' Bill muttered. 'It's just like them to call God Almighty nicknames.'

When dawn showed pale yellow in a cold sky, and stars were fading in the west, we packed up and took our way out and marched back to Nouex-les-Mines, there to rest for a day or two.

CHAPTER 2

OUT FROM NOUEX-LES-MINES

Every soldier to his trade –
Trigger sure and bayonet keen –
But we go forth to use a spade
Marching out from Nouex-les-Mines.

As I was sitting in the Café Pierre le Blanc helping Bill Teake, my Cockney mate, to finish a bottle of vin rouge, a snub-nosed soldier with thin lips who sat at a table opposite leant towards me and asked:

'Are you MacGill, the feller that writes?'

'Yes,' I answered.

'Thought I twigged yer from the photo of yer phiz in the papers,' said the man with the snub nose, as he turned to his mates who were illustrating a previous fight in lines of beer representing trenches on the table.

'See!' he said to them, 'I knew 'im the moment I clapped my eyes on 'im.'

'Hold your tongue,' one of the men, a ginger-headed fellow, who had his trigger finger deep in beer, made answer. Then the dripping finger rose slowly and was placed carefully on the table.

'This,' said Carrots, 'is Richebourg, this drop of beer is the German trench, and these are our lines. Our regiment crossed at this point and made for this one, but somehow or another we missed our objective. Just another drop of beer and I'll show you where we got to; it was – Blimey! where's that bloomin' beer? 'Oo the 'ell! – Oh! it's Gilhooley!'

I had never seen Gilhooley before, but I had often heard talk of him. Gilhooley was an Irishman and fought in an English regiment; he was notorious for his mad escapades, his daredevil pranks, and his wild fearlessness. Now he was opposite to me, drinking a mate's beer, big, broad-shouldered, ungainly Gilhooley.

The first impression the sight of him gave me was one of almost irresistible strength; I felt that if he caught a man around the waist with his hand he could, if he wished it, squeeze him to death. He was clumsily built, but an air of placid confidence in his own strength gave his figure a certain grace of its own. His eyes glowed brightly under heavy brows, his jowl thrust forward aggressively seemed to challenge all upon whom he fixed his gaze. It looked as if vast passions hidden in the man were thirsting to break free and rout everything. Gilhooley was a dangerous man to cross. Report had it that he was a bomber, and a master in this branch of warfare. Stories were told about him how he went over to the German trenches near Vermelles at dusk every day for a fortnight, and on each visit flung half a dozen bombs into the enemy's midst. Then he sauntered back to his own lines and reported to an officer, saying, 'By Jasus! I got them out of it!'

Once, when a German sniper potting at our trenches in Vermelles picked off a few of our men, an exasperated English subaltern gripped a Webley revolver and clambered over the parapet.

'I'm going to stop that damned sniper,' said the young officer. 'I'm going to earn the V.C. Who's coming along with me?'

'I'm with you,' said Gilhooley, scrambling lazily out into the open with a couple of pet bombs in his hand. 'By Jasus! we'll get him out of it!'

The two men went forward for about twenty yards, when the officer fell with a bullet through his head. Gilhooley turned round and called back, 'Any other officer wantin' to earn the V.C.?'

There was no reply: Gilhooley sauntered back, waited in the trench till dusk, when he went across to the sniper's abode with a bomb and 'got him out of it'.

A calamity occurred a few days later. The irrepressible Irishman was fooling with a bomb in the trench when it fell and exploded. Two soldiers were wounded, and Gilhooley went off to the Hospital at X with a metal reminder of his discrepancy wedged in the soft of his thigh. There he saw Colonel Z, or 'Up-you-go-and-the-best-of -luck', as Colonel Z is known to the rank and file of the B.E.F.

The hospital at X is a comfortable place, and the men are

in no hurry to leave there for the trenches; but when Colonel Z pronounces them fit they must hasten to the fighting line again.

Four men accompanied Gilhooley when he was considered fit for further fight. The five appeared before the Colonel.

'How do you feel?' the Colonel asked the first man.

'Not well at all,' was the answer. 'I can't eat 'ardly nuffink.'

'That's the sort of man required up there,' Colonel Z answered. 'So up you go and the best of luck.'

'How far can you see?' the Colonel asked the next man, who had complained that his eyesight was bad.

'Only about fifty yards,' was the answer.

'Your regiment is in trenches barely twenty-five yards from those of the enemy,' the Colonel told him. 'So up you go, and the best of luck.'

'Off you go and find the man who wounded you,' the third soldier was told; the fourth man confessed that he had never killed a German.

'*You* had better double up,' said the Colonel. 'It's time you killed one.'

It came to Gilhooley's turn.

'How many men have you killed?' he was asked.

'In and out about fifty,' was Gilhooley's answer.

'Make it a hundred then,' said the Colonel; 'and up you go, and the best of luck.'

'By Jasus! I'll get fifty more out of it in no time,' said Gilhooley, and on the following day he sauntered into the Café Pierre le Blanc in Nouex-les-Mines, drank another man's beer, and sat down on a chair at the table where four glasses filled to the brim stood sparkling in the lamplight.

Gilhooley, penniless and thirsty, had an unrivalled capacity for storing beer in his person.

'Back again, Gilhooley?' someone remarked in a diffident voice.

'Back again!' said Gilhooley wearily, putting his hand in the pocket of his tunic and taking out a little round object about the size of a penny inkpot.

'I hear there's going to be a big push shortly,' he muttered. 'This,' he said, holding the bomb between trigger finger and thumb, 'will go bang into the enemy's trenches next charge.'

A dozen horror-stricken eyes gazed at the bomb for a second, and the soldiers in the café remembered how Gilhooley once, in a moment of distraction, forgot that a fuse was lighted, then followed a hurried rush, and the café was almost deserted by the occupants. Gilhooley smiled wearily, replaced the bomb in his pocket, and set himself the task of draining the beer glasses.

My momentary thrill of terror died away when the bomb disappeared, and, leaving Bill, I approached the Wild Man's table and sat down.

'Gilhooley?' I said.

'Eh, what is it?' he interjected.

'Will you have a drink with me?' I hurried to inquire. 'Something better than this beer for a change. Shall we try champagne?'

'Yes, we'll try it,' he said sarcastically, and a queer smile hovered about his eyes. Somehow I had a guilty sense of doing a mean action . . . I called to Bill.

'Come on, matey,' I said.

Bill approached the table and sat down. I called for a bottle of champagne.

'This is Gilhooley, Bill,' I said to my mate. 'He's the bomber we've heard so much about.'

'I suppose ye'll want to know everythin' about me now, seein' ye've asked me to take a drop of champagne,' said Gilhooley, his voice rising. 'Damn yer champagne. You think I'm a bloomin' alligator in the Zoo, d'ye? Give me a bun and I'll do anythin' ye want me to.'

'That men should want to speak to you is merely due to your fame,' I said. 'In the dim recesses of the trenches men speak of your exploits with bated breath –'

'What the devil are ye talkin' about?' asked Gilhooley.

'About you,' I said.

He burst out laughing at this and clinked glasses with me when we drank, but he seemed to forget Bill.

For the rest of the evening he was in high good humour, and before leaving he brought out his bomb and showed that it was only a dummy one, harmless as an egg-shell.

'But let me get half a dozen sergeants round a rum jar and out comes this bomb!' said Gilhooley. 'Then they fly like hell and I get a double tot of rum.'

'It's a damned good idea,' I said. 'What is he wanting?' I pointed at the military policeman who had just poked his head through the café door. He looked round the room, taking stock of the occupants.

'All men of the London Irish must report to their companies at once,' he shouted.

'There's somethin' on the blurry boards again,' said Bill Teake. 'I suppose we've got to get up to the trenches tonight. We were up last night diggin',' he said to Gilhooley.

Gilhooley shrugged his shoulders, took a stump of a cigarette from behind his ear and lit it.

'Take care of yourselves,' he said as he went out.

At half-past nine we marched out of Nouex-les-Mines bound for the trenches where we had to continue the digging which we had started the night before.

The brigade holding the firing line told us that the enemy were registering their range during the day, and the objective was the trench which we had dug on the previous night ... Then we knew that the work before us was fraught with danger; we would certainly be shelled when operations started. In single file, with rifles and picks over their shoulders, the boys went out into the perilous space between the lines. The night was grey with rain; not a star was visible in the drab expanse of cloudy sky, and the wet oozed from sandbag and dug-out; the trench itself was sodden, and slush squirted about the boots that shuffled along; it was a miserable night. One of our men returned to the post occupied by the stretcher-bearers; he had become suddenly unwell with a violent pain in his stomach. We took him back to the nearest dressing-station and there he was put into an Engineers' wagon which was returning to the village in which our regiment was quartered.

Returning, I went out into the open between the lines. Our men were working across the front, little dark, blurred figures in the rainy greyness, picks and shovels were rising and falling, and lumps of earth were being flung out on to the grass. The enemy were already shelling on the left, the white flash of shrapnel and the red, lurid flames of bursting concussion shells lit up the night. So far the missiles were either falling short or overshooting their mark, and nobody had been touched. I just got to our company when the enemy began to shell it. There was a hurried flop to earth in the newly-dug holes, and I was immediately down flat on my face on top of several prostrate figures, a shrapnel burst in front, and a hail of singing bullets dug into the earth all round. A concussion shell raced past overhead and broke into splinters by the fire trench, several of the pieces whizzing back as far as the working party.

There followed a hail of shells, flash on flash, and explosion after explosion over our heads; the moment was a ticklish one, and I longed for the comparative safety of the fire trench. Why had I come out? I should have stopped with the other stretcher-bearers. But what did it matter. I was in no greater danger than any of my mates; what they had to stick I could stick, for the moment at least.

The shelling subsided as suddenly as it had begun. I got up again to find my attention directed towards something in front; a dark figure kneeling on the ground. I went forward and found a dead soldier, a Frenchman, a mere skeleton with the flesh eaten away from his face, leaning forward on his entrenching tool over a little hole that he had dug in the ground months before.

A tragedy was there, one of the sorrowful sights of war. The man, no doubt, had been in a charge – the French made a bayonet attack across this ground in the early part of last winter –and had been wounded. Immediately he was struck he got out his entrenching tool and endeavoured to dig himself in. A few shovelsful of earth were scooped out when a bullet struck him, and he leaned forward on his entrenching tool, dead. Thus I found him; and the picture in the grey night was one of a dead man resting for a moment as he dug his own grave.

'See that dead man?' I said to one of the digging party.

'H'm! there are hundreds of them lying here,' was the answer, given almost indifferently. 'I had to throw four to one side before I could start digging!'

I went back to the stretcher-bearers again; the men of my own company were standing under a shrapnel-proof bomb store, smoking and humming ragtime in low, monotonous voices. Music-hall melodies are so melancholy at times, so full of pathos, especially on a wet night under shell fire.

'Where are the other stretcher-bearers?' I asked.

'They've gone out to the front to their companies,' I was told. 'Some of their men have been hit.'

'Badly?'

'No one knows,' was the answer. 'Are our boys all right?'

'As far as I could see they're safe; but they're getting shelled in an unhealthy manner.'

'They've left off firing now,' said one of my mates. 'You should've seen the splinters coming in here a minute ago, pit!

pit! plop! on the sandbags. It's beastly out in the open.'

A man came running along the trench, stumbled into our shelter, and sat down on a sandbag.

'You're the London Irish?' he asked.

'Stretcher-bearers,' I said. 'Have you been out?'

'My God! I have,' he answered, ''Tisn't half a do, either. A shell comes over and down I flops in the trench. My mate was standing on the parapet and down he fell atop of me. God! 'twasn't half a squeeze; I thought I was burst like a bubble.

' "Git off, matey," I yells, "I'm squeezed to death!"

' "Squeezed to death," them was my words. But he didn't move, and something warm and sloppy ran down my face. It turned me sick . . . I wriggled out from under and had a look . . . He was dead, with half his head blown away . . . Your boys are sticking to the work out there; just going on with the job as if nothing was amiss. When is the whole damned thing to come to a finish?'

A momentary lull followed, and a million sparks fluttered earthwards from a galaxy of searching star-shells.

'Why are such beautiful lights used in the killing of men?' I asked myself. Above in the quiet the gods were meditating, then, losing patience, they again burst into irrevocable rage, seeking, as it seemed, some obscure and fierce retribution.

The shells were loosened again; there was no escape from their frightful vitality, they crushed, burrowed, exterminated; obstacles were broken down, and men's lives were flicked out like flies off a window pane. A dug-out flew skywards, and the roof beams fell in the trench at our feet. We crouched under the bomb-shelter, mute, pale, hesitating. Oh! the terrible anxiety of men who wait passively for something to take place and always fearing the worst!

'Stretcher-bearers at the double!'

We met him, crawling in on all fours like a beetle, the first case that came under our care. We dressed a stomach wound in the dug-out, and gave the boy two morphia tablets . . . He sank into unconsciousness and never recovered. His grave is out behind the church of Loos-Gohelle, and his cap hangs on the arm of the cross that marks his sleeping place. A man had the calf of his right leg blown away; he died from shock; another got a bullet through his skull, another . . . But why enumerate how young lives were hurled away from young bodies? . . .

On the field of death, the shells, in colossal joy, chorused

their terrible harmonies, making the heavens sonorous with
their wanton and unbridled frenzy; star-shells, which seemed
at times to be fixed on the ceiling of the sky, oscillated in
a dazzling whirl of red and green – and men died . . . We
remained in the trenches the next day. They were very quiet,
and we lay at ease in our dug-outs, read week-old papers,
wrote letters and took turns on sentry-go. On our front lay
a dull brown, monotonous level and two red-brick villages,
Loos and Hulluch. Our barbed-wire entanglement, twisted
and shell-scarred, showed countless rusty spikes which stuck
out ominous and forbidding. A dead German hung on a wire
prop, his feet caught in a *cheval de frise*, the skin of his face
peeling away from his bones, and his hand clutching the wire
as if for support. He had been out there for many months, a
foolhardy foe who got a bullet through his head when examin-
ing our defences.

Here, in this salient, the war had its routine and habits, everything was done with regimental precision, and men followed
the trade of arms as clerks follow their profession: to each man
was allocated his post, he worked a certain number of hours,
slept at stated times, had breakfast at dawn, lunch at noon, and
tea at four. The ration parties called on the cave-dwellers with
the promptitude of the butcher and baker, who attend to the
needs of the villa-dwellers.

The postmen called at the dug-outs when dusk was settling,
and delivered letters and parcels. Letter-boxes were placed in
the parados walls and the hours of collection written upon
them in pencil or chalk. Concerts were held in the big dug-outs,
and little supper parties were fashionable when parcels were
bulky. Tea was drunk in the open, the soldiers ate at looted
tables, spread outside the dug-out doors. Over the 'Savoy' a
picture of the Mother of Perpetual Succour was to be seen and
the boys who lived there swore that it brought them good luck;
they always won at Banker and Brag. All shaved daily and
washed with perfumed soaps.

The artillery exchanged shots every morning just to keep
the guns clean. Sometimes a rifle shot might be heard, and we
would ask, 'Who is firing at the birds on the wire entanglements?' The days were peaceful then, but now all was different.
The temper of the salient had changed.

In the distance we could see Lens, a mining town with many
large chimneys, one of which was almost hidden in its own

smoke. No doubt the Germans were working the coal mines. Loos looked quite small, there was a big slag-heap on its right, and on its left was a windmill with shattered wings. We had been shelling the village persistently for days, and, though it was not battered as Philosophé and Maroc were battered, many big, ugly rents and fractures were showing on the red-brick houses.

But it stood its beating well; it takes a lot of strafing to bring down even a jerry-built village. Houses built for a few hundred francs in times of peace, cost thousands of pounds to demolish in days of war. I suppose war is the most costly means of destruction.

Rumours flew about daily. Men spoke of a big push ahead, fixed the date for the great charge, and, as proof of their gossip, pointed at innumerable guns and wagons of shell which came through Les Brebis and Nouex-les-Mines daily. Even the Germans got wind of our activities, and in front of the blue-black slag-heap on the right of Loos they placed a large white board with the question written fair in big, black letters:

WHEN IS THE BIG PUSH COMING OFF?
WE ARE WAITING.

A well-directed shell blew the board to pieces ten minutes after it was put up.

I had a very nice dug-out in these trenches. It burrowed into the chalk, and its walls were as white as snow. When the candle was lit in the twilight, the most wonderfully soft shadows rustled over the roof and walls. The shadow of an elbow of chalk sticking out in the wall over my bed looked like the beak of a great formless vulture. On a closer examination I found that I had mistaken a wide-diffused bloodstain for a shadow. A man had come into the place once and he died there; his death was written in red on the wall.

I named the dug-out 'The Last House in the World'. Was it not? It was the last tenanted house in our world.

Over the parapet of the trench was the Unknown with its mysteries deep as those of the grave.

CHAPTER 3

PREPARATIONS FOR LOOS

'Death will give us all a clean sheet'
– Dudley Pryor.

We, the London Irish Rifles, know Les Brebis well, know every café and *estaminet*, every street and corner, every house, broken or sound, every washerwoman, wineshop matron, handy cook, and pretty girl. Time after time we have returned from the trenches to our old billet to find the good housewife up and waiting for us. She was a lank woman, made and clothed anyhow. Her garments looked as if they had been put on with a pitchfork. Her eyes protruded from their sockets, and one felt that if her tightly strained eyelids relaxed their grip for a moment the eyes would roll out on the floor. Her upper teeth protruded, and the point of her receding chin had lost itself somewhere in the hollow of her neck. Her pendant breasts hung flabbily, and it was a miracle how her youngest child, Gustave, a tot of seven months, could find any sustenance there. She had three children, who prattled all through the peaceful hours of the day. When the enemy shelled Les Brebis the children were bundled down into the cellar, and the mother went out to pick percussion caps from the streets. These she sold to officers going home on leave. The value of the percussion cap was fixed by the damage which the shell had done. A shell which fell on Les Brebis school and killed many men was picked up by this good woman, and at the present moment it is in my possession. We nicknamed this woman 'Joan of Arc'.

We had a delightful billet in this woman's house. We came in from war to find a big fire in the stove and basins of hot, steaming *café-au-lait* on the table. If we returned from duty dripping wet through the rain, lines were hung across from wall to wall, and we knew that morning would find our muddy clothes warm and dry. The woman would count our number as we entered. One less than when we left! The missing man wore spectacles. She remembered him and all his mannerisms. He used to nurse her little baby boy, Gustave, and play games with the mite's toes. What had happened to him? He was killed by a shell, we told her. On the road to the trenches he was hit. Then a mist gathered in the woman's eyes, and two tears rolled down her cheeks. We drank our *café-au-lait*.

'Combien, madam?'

'Souvenir,' was the reply through sobs, and we thanked her for the kindness. Upstairs we bundled into our room, and threw our equipment down on the clean wooden floor, lit a candle and undressed. All wet clothes were flung downstairs, where the woman would hang them up to dry. Everything was the same here as when we left; save where the last regiment had, in a moment of inspiration, chronicled its deeds in verse on the wall. Pryor, the lance-corporal, read the poem aloud to us:

> *Gentlemen, the Guards,*
> *When the brick fields they took*
> *The Germans took the hook*
> *And left the Gentlemen in charge.*

The soldiers who came and went voiced their griefs on this wall, but in latrine language and Rabelaisian humour. Here were three proverbs written in a shaky hand:

> *The Army pays good money, but little of it.*
> *In the Army you are sertin to receive what you get.*
> *The wages of sin and a soldier is death.*

Under these was a couplet written by a fatalist:

> *I don't care if the Germans come,*
> *If I have an extra tot of rum.*

Names of men were scrawled everywhere on the wall, from roof to floor. Why have some men this desire to scrawl their names on every white surface they see, I often wonder? One of my mates, who wondered as I did, finally found expression in verse, which glared forth accusingly from the midst of the riot of names in the room:

> *A man's ambition must be small*
> *Who writes his name upon this wall,*

And well he does deserve his pay
A measly, mucky bob a day.

The woman never seemed to mind this scribbling on the
wall; in Les Brebis they have to put up with worse than this.
The house of which I speak is the nearest inhabited one to the
firing line. Half the houses in the street are blown down, and
every ruin has its tragedy. The natives are gradually getting
thinned out by the weapons of war. The people refuse to quit
their homes. This woman has a sister in Nouex-les-Mines, a
town five kilometres further away from the firing line, but she
refused to go there. 'The people of Nouex-les-Mines are no
good,' she told us. 'I would not be where they are. Nobody can
trust them.'

The history of Les Brebis must, if written, be written in
blood. The washerwoman who washed our shirts could tell
stories of adventure that would eclipse tales of romance as the
sun eclipses a brazier. Honesty and fortitude are the predomi-
nant traits of the Frenchwoman.

Once I gave the washerwoman my cardigan jacket to
wash, and immediately afterwards we were ordered off to
the trenches. When we left the firing line we went back to
Nouex-les-Mines. A month passed before the regiment got to
Les Brebis again. The washerwoman called at my billet and
brought back the cardigan jacket, also a franc piece which she
had found in the pocket. On the day following the woman
was washing her baby at a pump in the street and a shell blew
her head off. Pieces of the child were picked up a hundred
yards away. The washerwoman's second husband (she had been
married twice) was away at the war; all that remained in the
household now was a daughter whom Pryor, with his nick-
naming craze, dubbed 'Mercédès'.

But here in Les Brebis, amidst death and desolation, wont
and use held their sway. The cataclysm of a continent had
not changed the ways and manners of the villagers, they took
things phlegmatically, with fatalistic calm. The children played
in the gutters of the streets, lovers met beneath the stars
and told the story of ancient passion, the miser hoarded his
money, the preacher spoke to his Sunday congregation, and
the plate was handed round for the worshippers' sous, men
and women died natural deaths, children were born, females
chattered at the street pumps and circulated rumours about

their neighbours . . . All this when wagons of shells passed through the streets all day and big guns travelled up nearer the lines every night. Never had Les Brebis known such traffic. Horses, limbers and guns, guns, limbers and horses going and coming from dawn to dusk and from dusk to dawn. From their emplacements in every spinney and every hollow in the fields the guns spoke earnestly and continuously. Never had guns voiced such a threat before. They were everywhere; could there be room for another in all the spaces of Les Brebis and our front line? It was impossible to believe it, but still they came up, monsters with a mysterious air of detachment perched on limbers with caterpillar wheels, little field guns that flashed metallic glints to the café lamps, squat trench howitzers on steel platforms impassive as toads . . .

The coming and passing was a grand poem, and the poem found expression in clanging and rattle in the streets of Les Brebis through the days and nights of August and September, 1915. For us, we worked in our little ways, dug advanced trenches under shell fire in a field where four thousand dead Frenchmen were wasting to clay. These men had charged last winter and fell to maxim and rifle fire; over their bodies we were to charge presently and take Loos and the trenches behind. The London Irish were to cross the top in the first line of attack, so the rumour said.

One evening, when dusk was settling in the streets, when ruined houses assumed fantastic shapes, and spirits seemed to be lurking in the shattered piles, we went up the streets of Les Brebis on our way to the trenches. Over by the church of Les Brebis, the spire of which was sharply defined in the clear air, the shells were bursting and the smoke of the explosions curled above the red roofs of the houses. The enemy was bombarding the road ahead, and the wounded were being carried back to the dressing stations. We met many stretchers on the road. The church of Bully-Grenay had been hit, and a barn near the church had been blown in on top of a platoon of soldiers which occupied it. We had to pass the church. The whole battalion seemed to be very nervous, and a presentiment of something evil seemed to fill the minds of the men. The mood was not of common occurrence, but this unaccountable depression permeates whole bodies of men at times.

We marched in silence, hardly daring to breathe. Ahead, under a hurricane of shell, Bully-Grenay was withering to earth. The night itself was dark and subdued, not a breeze stirred in the poplars which lined the long, straight road. Now and again, when a star-shell flamed over the firing line, we caught a glimpse of Bully-Grenay, huddled and helpless, its houses battered, its church riven, its chimneys fractured and lacerated. We dreaded passing the church; the cobbles on the roadway there were red with the blood of men.

We got into the village, which was deserted even by the soldiery; the civil population had left the place weeks ago. We reached the church, and there, arm in arm, we encountered a French soldier and a young girl. They took very little notice of us, they were deep in sweet confidences which only the young can exchange. The maiden was 'Mercédès'. The sight was good; it was as a tonic to us. A load seemed to have been lifted off our shoulders, and we experienced a light and airy sensation of heart. We reached the trenches without mishap, and set about our work. The enemy spotted us digging a new sap, and he began to shell with more than usual vigour. We were rather unlucky, for four of our men were killed and nine or ten got wounded.

Night after night we went up to the trenches and performed our various duties.

Keeps and redoubts were strengthened and four machine guns were placed where only one stood before. Always while we worked the artillery on both sides conducted a loud-voiced argument; concussion shells played havoc with masonry, and shrapnel shells flung their deadly freight on roads where the transports hurried, and where the long-eared mules sweated in the traces of the limbers of war. We spoke of the big work ahead, but up till the evening preceding Saturday, September 25, we were not aware of the part which we had to play in the forthcoming event. An hour before dusk our officer read instructions, and outlined the plan of the main attack, which would start at dawn on the following day, September 25, 1915.

In co-operation with an offensive movement by the 10th French Army on our right, the 1st and 4th Army Corps were to attack the enemy from a point opposite Bully-Grenay on the south to the La Bassée Canal on the north. We had dug the assembly trenches on our right opposite Bully-Grenay; that was to be the starting point for the 4th Corps – our Corps. Our Division, the 47th London, would lead the attack of the 4th Army Corps, and the London Irish would be the first in the fight. Our objective was the second German trench which lay just in front of Loos village and a mile away from our own first line trench. Every movement of the operations had been carefully planned, and nothing was left to chance. Never had we as many guns as now, and these guns had been bombarding the enemy's positions almost incessantly for ten days. Smoke bombs would be used. The thick fumes resulting from their explosion between the lines would cover our advance. At five o'clock all our guns, great and small, would open up a heavy fire. Our aircraft had located most of the enemy's batteries, and our heavy guns would be trained on these until they put them out of action. Five minutes past six our guns would lengthen their range and shell the enemy's reserves, and at the same moment our regiment would get clear of the trenches and advance in four lines in extended order with a second's interval between the lines. The advance must be made in silence at a steady pace.

Stretcher-bearers had to cross with their companies; none of the attacking party must deal with the men who fell out on the way across. A party would be detailed out to attend to the wounded who fell near the assembly trenches . . . The attack had been planned with such intelligent foresight that our casualties would be very few. The job before us was quite easy and simple.

'What do you think of it?' I asked my mate, Bill Teake. 'I think a bottle of champagne would be very nice.'

'Just what I thought myself,' said Bill. 'I see Dudley Pryor is off to the café already. I've no money. I'm pore as a mummy.'

'You got paid yesterday,' I said with a laugh. 'You get poor very quickly.'

An embarrassed smile fluttered around his lips.

'A man gets pore 'cordin' to no rule,' he replied. 'Leastways, I do.'

'Well, I've got a lot of francs,' I said. 'We may as well spend it.'

'You're damned right,' he answered. 'Maybe, we'll not 'ave a chance to –'

'It doesn't matter a damn whether –'

'The officer says it will be an easy job. I don't know the –'

He paused. We understood things half spoken.

'Champagne?' I hinted.

'Nothing like champagne,' said Bill.

CHAPTER 4

BEFORE THE CHARGE

Before I joined the Army
I lived in Donegal,
Where every night the Fairies,
Would hold their carnival.

But now I'm out in Flanders,
Where men like wheat-ears fall,
And it's Death and not the Fairies
Who is holding carnival.

I poked my head through the upper window of our billet and looked down the street. An ominous calm brooded over the village, the trees which lined the streets stood immovable in the darkness, with lone shadows clinging to the trunks. On my right, across a little rise, was the firing line. In the near distance was the village of Bully-Grenay, roofless and tenantless, and further off was Philosophé, the hamlet with its dark-blue slag-heap bulking large against the horizon. Souchez in the hills was as usual active; a heavy artillery engagement was in progress. White and lurid splashes of flame dabbed at the sky, and the smoke, rising from the ground, paled in the higher air; but the breeze blowing away from me carried the tumult and thunder far from my ears. I looked on a conflict without sound; a furious fight seen but unheard.

A coal-heap near the village stood, colossal and threatening; an engine shunted a long row of wagons along the railway line which fringed Les Brebis. In a pit by the mine a big gun began to speak loudly, and the echo of its voice palpitated through the room and dislodged a tile from the roof ... My mind was suddenly permeated by a feeling of proximity to the enemy. He whom we were going to attack at dawn seemed to be very close to me. I could almost feel his presence in the room. At dawn I might deprive him of life and he might deprive me of mine. Two beings give life to a man, but one can deprive him of it. Which is the greater mystery? Birth or death? They who are responsible for the first may take pleasure, but who can glory in the second? . . . To kill a man . . . To feel for ever after the deed that you have deprived a fellow being of life!

'We're beginning to strafe again,' said Pryor, coming to my side as a second reverberation shook the house. 'It doesn't matter. I've got a bottle of champagne and a box of cigars.'

'I've got a bottle as well,' I said.

'There'll be a hell of a do tomorrow,' said Pryor.

'I suppose there will,' I replied. 'The officer said that our job will be quite an easy one.'

'H'm!' said Pryor.

I looked down at the street and saw Bill Teake.

'There's Bill down there,' I remarked. 'He's singing a song. Listen.'

> *'I like your smile,*
> *I like your style,*
> *I like your soft blue dreamy eyes –'*

'There's passion in that voice,' I said. 'Has he fallen in love again?'

A cork went plunk! from a bottle behind me, and Pryor from the shadows of the room answered, 'Oh, yes! He's in love again; the girl next door is his fancy now.'

'Oh, so it seems,' I said. 'She's out at the pump now and Bill is edging up to her as quietly as if he were going to loot a chicken off its perch.'

Bill is a boy for the girls; he finds a new love at every billet. His fresh flame was a squat stump of a Millet girl in short petticoats and stout sabots. Her eyes were a deep black, her teeth very white. She was a comfortable, good-natured girl, 'a big 'andful of love,' as he said himself, but she was not very good-looking.

Bill sidled up to her side and fixed an earnest gaze on the water falling from the pump; then he nudged the girl in the hip with a playful hand and ran his fingers over the back of her neck.

'Allez vous en!' she cried, but otherwise made no attempt to resist Bill's advances.

'Allez voos ong yerself!' said Bill, and burst into song again.

> *'She's the pretty little girl from Nowhere,*
> *Nowhere at all.*
> *She's the –'*

He was unable to resist the temptation any longer, and he clasped the girl round the waist and planted a kiss on her cheek. The maiden did not relish this familiarity. Stooping down she placed her hand in the pail, raised a handful of water and flung it in Bill's face. The Cockney retired crestfallen and spluttering, and a few minutes afterwards he entered the room.

'Yes, I think that there are no women on earth to equal them,' said Pryor to me, deep in a pre-arranged conversation. 'They have a grace of their own and a coyness which I admire. I don't think that any women are like the women of France.'

''Oo?' asked Bill Teake, sitting down on the floor.

'Pat and I are talking about the French girls,' said Pryor. 'They're splendid.'

'H'm!' grunted Bill in a colourless voice.

'Not much humbug about them,' I remarked.

'I prefer English gals,' said Bill. 'They can make a joke and take one. As for the French gals, ugh!'

'But they're not all alike,' I said. 'Some may resent advances in the street, and show a temper when they're kissed over a pump.'

'The water from the Les Brebis pumps is very cold,' said Pryor.

We could not see Bill's face in the darkness, but we could almost feel our companion squirm.

''Ave yer got some champagne, Pryor?' he asked with studied indifference. 'My froat's like sandpaper.'

'Plenty of champagne, matey,' said Pryor in a repentant voice. 'We're all going to get drunk tonight. Are you?'

'Course I am,' said Bill. 'It's very comfy to 'ave a drop of champagne.'

'More comfy than a kiss even,' said Pryor.

As he spoke the door was shoved inwards and our corporal entered. For a moment he stood there without speaking, his long, lank form darkly outlined against the half light.

'Well, corporal?' said Pryor interrogatively.

'Why don't you light a candle?' asked the corporal. 'I thought that we were going to get one another's addresses.'

'So we were,' I said, as if just remembering a decision arrived at a few hours previously. But I had it in my mind all the time.

Bill lit a candle and placed it on the floor while I covered up the window with a ground sheet. The window looked out on the firing line three kilometres away, and the light, if uncovered, might be seen by the enemy. I glanced down the street and saw boys in khaki strolling aimlessly about, their cigarettes glowing . . . The star-shells rose in the sky out behind Bully-Grenay, and again I had that feeling of the enemy's presence which was mine a few moments before.

Kore, another of our section, returned from a neighbouring café, a thoughtful look in his dark eyes and a certain irresolution in his movements. His delicate nostrils and pale lips quivered nervously, betraying doubt and a little fear of the work ahead at dawn. Under his arm he carried a bottle of champagne which he placed on the floor beside the candle. Sighing a little, he lay down at full length on the floor, not before he brushed the dust aside with a newspaper. Kore was very neat and took great pride in his uniform, which fitted him like an eyelid.

Felan and M'Crone came in together, arm in arm. The latter was in a state of subdued excitement; his whole body shook as if he were in fever; when he spoke his voice was highly pitched and unnatural, a sign that he was under the strain of great nervous tension. Felan looked very much at ease, though now and again he fumbled with the pockets of his tunic, buttoning and unbuttoning the flaps and digging his hands into his pockets as if for something which was not there. He had no cause for alarm; he was the company cook and, according to regulations, would not cross in the charge.

'Blimey! you're not 'arf a lucky dawg!' said Bill, glancing at Felan. 'I wish I was the cook tomorrow.'

'I almost wish I was myself.'

'Wot d'yer mean?'

'Do you expect an Irishman is going to cook bully-beef when his regiment goes over the top?' asked Felan. 'For shame!'

We rose, all of us, shook him solemnly by the hand, and wished him luck.

'Now, what about the addresses?' asked Kore. 'It's time we wrote them down.'

'It's as well to get it over,' I said, but no one stirred. We viewed the job with distrust. By doing it we reconciled ourselves to a dread inevitable; the writing of these addresses seemed to be the only thing that stood between us and death. If we could only put it off for another, little while . . .

'We'll 'ave a drink to 'elp us,' said Bill, and a cork went plonk! The bottle was handed round, and each of us, except the corporal, drank in turn until the bottle was emptied. The corporal was a teetotaller.

'Now we'll begin,' I said. The wine had given me strength. 'If I'm killed write to — and —, tell them that my death was sudden – easy.'

'That's the thing to tell them,' said the corporal. 'It's always best to tell them at home that death was sudden and painless. It's not much of a consolation, but –'

He paused.

'It's the only thing one can do,' said Felan.

'I've nobody to write to,' said Pryor, when his turn came. 'There's a Miss —. But what the devil does it matter! I've nobody to write to, nobody that cares a damn what becomes of me,' he concluded. 'At least I'm not like Bill,' he added.

'And who will I write to for you, Bill?' I asked.

Bill scratched his little white potato of a nose, puckered his lips, and became thoughtful. I suddenly realised that Bill was very dear to me.

'Not afraid, matey?' I asked.

'Naw,' he answered in a thoughtful voice.

'A man has only to die once, anyhow,' said Felan.

'Greedy! 'Ow many times d'yer want ter die?' asked Bill. 'But I s'pose if a man 'ad nine lives like a cat 'e wouldn't mind dyin' once.'

'But suppose,' said Pryor.

'S'pose,' muttered Bill. 'Well, if it 'as got to be it can't be 'elped . . . I'm not goin' to give any address to anybody,' he said. 'I'm goin' to 'ave a drink.'

We were all seated on the floor round the candle which was stuck in the neck of an empty champagne bottle. The candle flickered faintly, and the light made feeble fight with the shadows in the corners. The room was full of the aromatic flavour of Turkish cigarettes and choice cigars, for money was spent that evening with the recklessness of men going out to die. Teake handed round a fresh bottle of champagne and I gulped down a mighty mouthful. My shadow, flung by the candle on the white wall, was a grotesque caricature, my nose stretched out like a beak, and a monstrous bottle was tilted on demoniac lips. Pryor pointed at it with his trigger finger, laughed, and rose to give a quotation from Omar, forgot the quotation, and sat down again. Kore was giving his home address to the corporal, Bill's hand trembled as he raised a match to his cigar. Pryor was on his feet again, handsome Pryor, with a college education.

'What does death matter?' he said. 'It's as natural to die as it is to be born, and perhaps the former is the easier event of the two. We have no remembrance of birth and will carry no remembrance of death across the bourne from which there is no return. Do you know what Epictetus said about death, Bill?'

'Wot regiment was 'e in?' asked Bill.

'He has been dead for some eighteen hundred years.'

'Oh! Blimey!'

'Epictetus said, "Where death is I am not, where death is not I am",' Pryor continued. 'Death will give us all a clean sheet. If the sergeant who issues short rum rations dies on the field of honour (don't drink all the champagne, Bill) we'll talk of him when he's gone as a damned good fellow, but alive we've got to borrow epithets from Bill's vocabulary of vituperation to speak of the aforesaid non-commissioned abomination.'

'Is 'e callin' me names, Pat?' Bill asked me.

I did not answer for the moment, for Bill was undergoing a strange transformation. His head was increasing in size, swelling up until it almost filled the entire room. His little potato of a nose assumed fantastic dimensions. The other occupants of the room diminished in bulk and receded into far distances. I tried to attract Pryor's attention to the phenomenon, but the youth receding with the others was now balancing a champagne bottle on his nose, entirely oblivious of his surroundings.

'Be quiet, Bill,' I said, speaking with difficulty. 'Hold your tongue!'

I began to feel drowsy, but another mouthful of champagne renewed vitality in my body. With this feeling came a certain indifference towards the morrow. I must confess that up to now I had a vague distrust of my actions in the work ahead. My normal self revolted at the thought of the coming dawn; the experiences of my life had not prepared me for one day of savage and ruthless butchery. Tomorrow I had to go forth prepared to do much that I disliked . . . I had another sip of wine; we were at the last bottle now.

Pryor looked out of the window, raising the blind so that little light shone out into the darkness.

'A Scottish division are passing through the street, in silence, their kilts swinging,' he said. 'My God! it does look fine.' He arranged the blind again and sat down. Bill was cutting a sultana cake in neat portions and handing them round.

'Come, Felan, and sing a song,' said M'Crone.

'My voice is no good now,' said Felan, but by his way of speaking, we knew that he would oblige.

'Now, Felan, come along!' we chorused.

Felan wiped his lips with the back of his hand, took a cigar between his fingers and thumb and put it out by rubbing the lighted end against his trousers. Then he placed the cigar behind his ear.

'Well, what will I sing?' he asked.

'Any damned thing,' said Bill.

' "The Trumpeter", and we'll all help,' said Kore.

Felan leant against the wall, thrust his head back, closed his eyes, stuck the thumb of his right hand into a buttonhole of his tunic and began his song.

His voice, rather hoarse, but very pleasant, faltered a little at first, but was gradually permeated by a note of deepest feeling, and a strange, unwonted passion surged through the melody. Felan was pouring his soul into the song. A moment ago the singer was one with us; now he gave himself up to the song, and the whole lonely romance of war, its pity and its pain, swept through the building and held us in its spell. Kore's mobile nostrils quivered. M'Crone shook as if with ague. We all listened, enraptured, our eyes shut as the singer's were, to the voice that quivered through the smoky room. I could not help feeling that Felan himself listened to his own song, as something which was no part of him, but which affected him strangely.

> *Trumpeter, what are you sounding now?*
> *Is it the call I'm seeking?*
> *Lucky for you if you hear it all*
> *For my trumpet's but faintly speaking –*
> *I'm calling 'em home. Come home! Come home!*
> *Tread light o'er the dead in the valley,*

Who are lying around
Face down to the ground,
And they can't hear –

Felan broke down suddenly, and, coming across the floor, he entered the circle and sat down.

''Twas too high for me,' he muttered huskily. 'My voice has gone to the dogs . . . One time –'

Then he relapsed into silence. None of us spoke, but we were aware that Felan knew how much his song had moved us.

'Have another drink,' said Pryor suddenly, in a thick voice. ' "Look not upon the wine when it is red",' he quoted. 'But there'll be something redder than wine tomorrow!'

'I wish we fought wiv bladders on sticks; it would be more to my taste,' said Bill Teake.

'Ye're not having a drop at all, corporal,' said M'Crone. 'Have a sup; it's grand stuff.'

The corporal shook his head. He sat on the floor with his back against the wall, his hands under his thighs. He had a blunt nose with wide nostrils, and his grey, contemplative eyes kept roving slowly round the circle as if he were puzzling over our fate in the charge tomorrow.

'I don't drink,' he said. 'If I can't do without it now after keeping off it so long, I'm not much good.'

'Yer don't know wot's good for yer,' said Bill, gazing regretfully at the last halfbottle. 'There's nuffink like fizz. My ole man's a devil fer 'is suds; so'm I.'

The conversation became riotous, questions and replies got mixed and jumbled. 'I suppose we'll get to the front trench anyhow; maybe to the second. But we'll get flung back from that.' 'Wish we'd another bloomin' bottle of fizz.' 'S'pose our guns will not lift their range quick enough when we advance. We'll have any amount of casualties with our own shells.' 'The sergeant says that our objective is the crucifix in Loos churchyard.' 'Imagine killing men right up to the foot of the Cross . . .'

Our red-headed platoon sergeant appeared at the top of the stairs, his hair lurid in the candle light.

'Enjoying yourselves, boys?' he asked, with paternal solicitude. The sergeant's heart was in his platoon.

''Avin' a bit of a frisky,' said Bill. 'Will yer 'ave a drop?'

'I don't mind,' said the sergeant. He spoke almost in a whisper, and something seemed to be gripping at his throat.

He put the bottle to his lips and paused for a moment.

'Good luck to us all!' he said, and drank.

'We're due to leave in fifteen minutes,' he told us. 'Be ready when you hear the whistle blown in the street. Have a smoke now, for no pipes or cigarettes are to be lit on the march.'

He paused for a moment, then, wiping his moustache with the back of his hand, he clattered downstairs.

The night was calm and full of enchantment. The sky hung low and was covered with a greyish haze. We marched past Les Brebis Church up a long street where most of the houses were levelled to the ground.

Ahead the star-shells rioted in a blaze of colour, and a few rifles were snapping viciously out by Hohenzollern Redoubt, and a building on fire flared lurid against the eastern sky. Apart from that silence and suspense, the world waited breathlessly for some great event. The big guns lurked on their emplacements, and now and again we passed a dark-blue muzzle peeping out from its cover, sentinel, as it seemed, over the neatly piled stack of shells which would furnish it with its feed at dawn.

At the fringe of Bully-Grenay we left the road and followed a straggling path across the level fields where telephone wires had fallen down and lay in wait to trip unwary feet. Always the whispers were coming down the line: 'Mind the wires!' 'Mind the shell-holes!' 'Gunpit on the left. Keep clear.' 'Mind the dead mule on the right', etc.

Again we got to the road where it runs into the village of Maroc. A church stood at the entrance and it was in a wonderful state of preservation. Just as we halted for a moment on the roadway the enemy sent a solitary shell across which struck the steeple squarely, turning it round, but failing to overthrow it.

'A damned good shot,' said Pryor approvingly.

CHAPTER 5

OVER THE TOP

Was it only yesterday
Lusty comrades marched away?
Now they're covered up with clay.
Hearty comrades these have been,
But no more will they be seen
Drinking wine at Nouex-les-Mines.

A brazier glowed on the floor of the trench and I saw fantastic figures in the red blaze; the interior of a vast church lit up with a myriad candles, and dark figures kneeling in prayer in front of their plaster saints. The edifice was an enchanted Fairyland, a poem of striking contrasts in light and shade. I peered over the top. The air blazed with star-shells, and Loos in front stood out like a splendid dawn. A row of impassive faces, sleep-heavy they looked, lined our parapet; bayonets, silver-spired, stood up over the sandbags; the dark bays, the recessed dug-outs with their khaki-clad occupants dimly defined in the light of little candles took on fantastic shapes.

From the North Sea to the Alps stretched a line of men who could, if they so desired, clasp one another's hands all the way along. A joke which makes men laugh at Ypres at dawn may be told on sentry-go at Souchez by dusk, and the laugh which accompanies it ripples through the long, deep trenches of Cuinchy, the breastworks of Richebourg and the chalk alleys of Vermelles until it breaks itself like a summer wave against the traverse where England ends and France begins.

Many of our men were asleep, and maybe dreaming. What were their dreams? . . . I could hear faint, indescribable rustlings as the winds loitered across the levels in front; a light shrapnel shell burst, and its smoke quivered in the radiant light of the star-shells. Showers and sparks fell from high up and died away as they fell. Like lives of men, I thought, and again that feeling of proximity to the enemy surged through me.

A boy came along the trench carrying a football under his arm. 'What are you going to do with that?' I asked.

'It's some idea, this,' he said with a laugh. 'We're going to kick it across into the German trench.'

'It *is* some idea,' I said. 'What are our chances of victory in the game?'

'The playing will tell,' he answered enigmatically. 'It's about four o'clock now,' he added, paused and became thoughtful. The mention of the hour suggested something to him . . .

I could now hear the scattered crackling of guns as they called to one another saying: 'It's time to be up and doing!' The brazen monsters of many a secret emplacement were registering their range, rivalry in their voices. For a little the cock-crowing of artillery went on, then suddenly a thousand roosts became alive and voluble, each losing its own particular sound as all united in one grand concert of fury. The orchestra of war swelled in an incessant fanfare of dizzy harmony. Floating, stuttering, whistling, screaming and thundering the clamorous voices belched into a rich gamut of passion which shook the grey heavens. The sharp, zigzagging sounds of high velocity shells cut through the pandemonium like forked lightning, and far away, as it seemed, sounding like a distant breakwater the big missiles from caterpillar howitzers lumbered through the higher deeps of the sky. The brazen lips of death cajoled, threatened, whispered, whistled, laughed and sung: here were the sinister and sullen voices of destruction, the sublime and stupendous paean of power intermixed in sonorous clamour and magnificent vibration.

Felan came out into the trench. He had been asleep in his dug-out. 'I can't make tea now,' he said, fumbling with his mess-tin.

'We'll soon have to get over the top. Murdagh, Nobby Byrne and Corporal Clancy are here,' he remarked.

'They are in hospital,' I said.

'They were,' said Felan; 'but the hospitals have been cleared out to make room for men wounded in the charge. The three boys were ordered to go further back to be out of the way, but they asked to be allowed to join in the charge, and they are here now.'

He paused for a moment. 'Good luck to you, Pat,' he said

with a strange catch in his voice. 'I hope you get through all right.'

A heavy rifle fire was opened by the Germans and the bullets snapped viciously at our sandbags. Such little things bullets seemed in the midst of all the pandemonium! But bigger stuff was coming. Twenty yards away a shell dropped on a dug-out and sandbags and occupants whirled up in mid-air. The call for stretcher-bearers came to my bay, and I rushed round the traverse towards the spot where help was required accompanied by two others. A shrapnel shell burst overhead and the man in front of me fell. I bent to lift him, but he stumbled to his feet. The concussion had knocked him down; he was little the worse for his accident, but he felt a bit shaken. The other stretcher-bearer was bleeding at the cheek and temple, and I took him back to a sound dug-out and dressed his wound. He was in great pain, but very brave, and when another stricken boy came in he set about dressing him. I went outside into the trench. A perfect hurricane of shells was coming across, concussion shells that whirled the sandbags broadcast and shrapnel that burst high in air and shot their freight to earth with resistless precipitancy; bombs whirled in air and burst when they found earth with an ear-splitting clatter. 'Out in the open!' I muttered and tried not to think too clearly of what would happen when we got out there.

It was now grey day, hazy and moist, and the thick clouds of pale yellow smoke curled high in space and curtained the dawn off from the scene of war. The word was passed along. 'London Irish lead on to assembly trench.' The assembly trench was in front, and there the scaling ladders were placed against the parapet, ready steps to death, as someone remarked. I had a view of the men swarming up the ladders when I got there, their bayonets held in steady hands, and at a little distance off a football swinging by its whang from a bayonet standard.

The company were soon out in the open marching forward. The enemy's guns were busy, and the rifle and maxim bullets ripped the sandbags. The infantry fire was wild but of slight intensity. The enemy could not see the attacking party. But, judging by the row, it was hard to think that men could weather the leaden storm in the open.

The big guns were not so vehement now, our artillery had no doubt played havoc with the hostile batteries . . . I went to the foot of a ladder and got hold of a rung. A soldier in front was clambering across. Suddenly he dropped backwards and bore me to the ground; the bullet caught him in the forehead. I got to my feet to find a stranger in grey uniform coming down the ladder. He reached the floor of the trench, put up his hands when I looked at him and cried in a weak, imploring voice, 'Kamerad! Kamerad!'

'A German!' I said to my mate.

'H'm! h'm!' he answered.

I flung my stretcher over the parapet, and, followed by my comrade stretcher-bearer, I clambered up the ladder and went over the top.

CHAPTER 6

ACROSS THE OPEN

The firefly lamps were lighted yet,
As we crossed the top of the parapet,
But the East grew pale to another fire,
As our bayonets gleamed by the foeman's wire.
And the Eastern sky was gold and grey,
And under our feet the dead men lay,
As we entered Loos in the morning.

The moment had come when it was unwise to think. The country round Loos was like a sponge; the god of war had stamped with his foot on it, and thousands of men, armed, ready to kill, were squirted out on to the level, barren fields of danger. To dwell for a moment on the novel position of being standing where a thousand deaths swept by, missing you by a mere hair's breadth, would be sheer folly. There on the open field of death my life was out of my keeping, but the sensation of fear never entered my being. There was so much simplicity and so little effort in doing what I had done, in doing what eight hundred comrades had done, that I felt I could carry through the work before me with as much credit as my code of self-respect required. The maxims went crackle like dry brushwood under the feet of a marching host. A bullet passed very close to my face like a sharp, sudden breath; a second hit the ground in front, flicked up a little shower of dust, and ricochetted to the left, hitting the earth many times before it found a resting place. The air was vicious with bullets; a million invisible birds flicked their wings very close to my face. Ahead the clouds of smoke, sluggish low-lying fog, and fumes of bursting shells, thick in volume, receded towards the German trenches, and formed a striking background for the soldiers who were marching up a low slope towards the enemy's parapet, which the smoke still hid from view. There was no haste in the forward move, every step was taken with regimental precision, and twice on the way across the Irish boys halted for a moment to correct their alignment. Only at a point on the right there was some confusion and a little irregularity. Were the men wavering? No fear! The boys on the right were dribbling the elusive football towards the German trench.

Raising the stretcher, my mate and I went forward. For the next few minutes I was conscious of many things. A slight rain was falling; the smoke and fumes I saw had drifted back, exposing a dark streak on the field of green, the enemy's trench. A little distance away from me three men hurried forward, and two of them carried a box of rifle ammunition. One of the bearers fell flat to earth, his two mates halted for a moment, looked at the stricken boy, and seemed to puzzle at something. Then they caught hold of the box hangers and rushed forward. The man on the ground raised himself on his elbow and looked after his mates, then sank down again to the wet ground. Another soldier came crawling towards us on his belly, looking for all the world like a gigantic lobster which had escaped from its basket. His lower lip was cut clean to the chin and hanging apart; blood welled through the muddy khaki trousers where they covered the hips.

I recognised the fellow.

'Much hurt, matey?' I asked.

'I'll manage to get in,' he said.

'Shall I put a dressing on?' I inquired.

'I'll manage to get into our own trench,' he stammered, spitting the blood from his lips. 'There are others out at the wires. S— has caught it bad. Try and get him in, Pat.'

'Right, old man,' I said, as he crawled off. 'Good luck.'

My cap was blown off my head as if by a violent gust of wind, and it dropped on the ground. I put it on again, and at that moment a shell burst near at hand and a dozen splinters sung by my ear. I walked forward with a steady step.

'What took my cap off?' I asked myself. 'It went away just as if it was caught in a breeze. God!' I muttered, in a burst of realisation, 'it was that shell passing.' I breathed very deeply, my blood rushed down to my toes and an airy sensation filled my body. Then the stretcher dragged.

'Lift the damned thing up,' I called to my mate over my shoulder. There was no reply. I looked round to find him gone, either mixed up in a whooping rush of kilted Highlanders, who had lost their objective and were now charging parallel to their own trench, or perhaps he got killed ... How strange that the Highlanders could not charge in silence, I thought, and then recollected that most of my boyhood friends, Donegal lads, were in Scottish regiments ... I placed my stretcher on my shoulder, walked forward towards a bank of smoke which seemed to be standing stationary, and came across our platoon sergeant and part of his company.

'Are we going wrong, or are the Jocks wrong?' he asked his men, then shouted, 'Lie flat, boys, for a minute, until we see where we are. There's a big crucifix in Loos churchyard, and we've got to draw on that.'

The men threw themselves flat; the sergeant went down on one knee and leant forward on his rifle, his hands on the bayonet standard, the fingers pointing upwards and the palms pressed close to the sword which was covered with rust ... How hard it would be to draw it from a dead body! ... The sergeant seemed to be kneeling in prayer ... In front the cloud cleared away, and the black crucifix standing over the graves of Loos became revealed.

'Advance, boys!' said the sergeant. 'Steady on to the foot of the Cross and rip the swine out of their trenches.'

The Irish went forward ...

A boy sat on the ground bleeding at the shoulder and knee.

'You've got hit,' I said.

'In a few places,' he answered, in a very matter-of-fact voice. 'I want to get into a shell-hole.'

'I'll try and get you into one,' I said. 'But I want someone to help me. Hi! you there! Come and give me a hand.'

I spoke to a man who sat on the rim of a crater near at hand. His eyes, set close in a white, ghastly face, stared tensely at me.

He sat in a crouching position, his head thrust forward, his right hand gripping tightly at a mud-stained rifle. Presumably he was a bit shaken and was afraid to advance further.

'Help me to get this fellow into a shellhole,' I called. 'He can't move.'

There was no answer.

'Come along,' I cried, and then it was suddenly borne to me that the man was dead. I dragged the wounded boy into the crater and dressed his wounds.

A shell struck the ground in front, burrowed, and failed to explode.

'Thank Heaven!' I muttered, and hurried ahead. Men and pieces of men were lying all over the place. A leg, an arm, then again a leg, cut off at the hip. A finely formed leg, the latter, gracefully putteed. A dummy leg in a tailor's window could not be more graceful. It might be X; he was an artist in dress, a Beau Brummel in khaki. Fifty yards further along I found the rest of X . . .

The harrowing sight was repellent, antagonistic to my mind. The tortured things lying at my feet were symbols of insecurity, ominous reminders of danger from which no discretion could save a man. My soul was barren of pity; fear went down into the innermost parts of me, fear for myself. The dead and dying lay all around me; I felt a vague obligation to the latter; they must be carried out. But why should I trouble! Where could I begin? Everything was so far apart. I was too puny to start my labours in such a derelict world. The difficulty of accommodating myself to an old task under new conditions was enormous.

A figure in grey, a massive block of Bavarian bone and muscle, came running towards me, his arms in air, and Bill Teake following him with a long bayonet.

'A prisoner!' yelled the boy on seeing me. ' "Kamerad! Kamerad !" 'e shouted when I came up. Blimey! I couldn't stab 'im, so I took 'im prisoner. It's not 'arf a barney! . . . 'Ave yer got a fag ter spare?'

The Cockney came to a halt, reached for a cigarette, and lit it.

The German stood still, panting like a dog.

'Double! Fritz, double!' shouted the boy, sending a little puff of smoke through his nose. 'Over to our trench you go! Grease along if yer don't want a bayonet in your –'

They rushed off, the German with hands in air, and Bill behind with his bayonet perilously close to the prisoner. There was something amusing in the incident, and I could not refrain from laughing. Then I got a whiff from a German gas-bomb which exploded near me, and I began spluttering and coughing. The irritation, only momentary, was succeeded by a strange humour. I felt as if walking on air, my head got light, and it was with difficulty that I kept my feet on earth. It would be so easy to rise into space and float away. The sensation was a delightful one; I felt so pleased with myself, with everything. A wounded man lay on the ground, clawing the earth with frenzied fingers. In a vague way, I remembered some ancient law which ordained me to assist a stricken man. But I could not do so now, the action would clog my buoyancy and that delightful feeling of freedom which permeated my being. Another soldier whom I recognised, even at a distance, by his pink-and-white bald pate, so often a subject for our jokes, reeled over the blood-stained earth, his eyes almost bursting from their sockets.

'You look bad,' I said to him with a smile.

He stared at me drunkenly, but did not answer.

A man, mother-naked, raced round in a circle, laughing boisterously. The rags that would class him as a friend or foe were gone, and I could not tell whether he was an Englishman or a German. As I watched him an impartial bullet went through his forehead, and he fell headlong to the earth. The sight sobered me and I regained my normal self.

Up near the German wire I found our Company postman sitting in a shell-hole, a bullet in his leg below the knee, and an unlighted cigarette in his mouth.

'You're the man I want,' he shouted, on seeing me. And I fumbled in my haversack for bandages.

'No dressing for me, yet,' he said with a smile. 'There are others needing help more than I. What I want is a match.'

As I handed him my match box a big high explosive shell flew over our heads and dropped fifty yards away in a little hollow where seven or eight figures in khaki lay prostrate, faces to the ground. The shell burst and the wounded and dead rose slowly into air to a height of six or seven yards and dropped slowly again, looking for all the world like puppets worked by wires.

'This,' said the postman, who had observed the incident, 'is a solution of a question which diplomacy could not settle, I suppose. The last argument of kings is a damned sorry business.'

By the German barbed wire entanglements were the shambles of war. Here our men were seen by the enemy for the first time that morning. Up till then the foe had fired erratically through the oncoming curtain of smoke; but when the cloud cleared away, the attackers were seen advancing, picking their way through the wires which had been cut to little pieces by our bombardment.

The Irish were now met with harrying rifle fire, deadly petrol bombs and hand grenades. Here I came across dead, dying and sorely wounded; lives maimed and finished, and all the romance and roving that makes up the life of a soldier gone for ever. Here, too, I saw, bullet-riddled, against one of the spider webs known as *chevaux de frise*, a limp lump of pliable leather, the football which the boys had kicked across the field.

I came across Flannery lying close to a barbed wire support, one arm round it as if in embrace. He was a clumsily built fellow, with queer bushy eyebrows and a short, squat nose. His bearing was never soldierly, but on a march he could bear any burden and stick the job when more alert men fell out. He always bore himself however with a certain grace, due, perhaps, to a placid belief in his own strength. He never made friends; a being apart, he led a solitary life. Now he lay close to earth hugging an entanglement prop, and dying.

There was something savage in the expression of his face as he looked slowly round, like an ox under a yoke, on my approach. I knelt down beside him and cut his tunic with my scissors where a burnt hole clotted with blood showed under the kidney. A splinter of shell had torn part of the man's side away. All hope was lost for the poor soul.

'In much pain, chummy?' I asked.

'Ah, Christ! yes, Pat,' he answered. 'Wife and two kiddies, too. Are we getting the best of it?'

I did not know how the fight was progressing, but I had seen a line of bayonets drawing near to the second trench out by Loos.

'Winning all along,' I answered.

'That's good,' he said. 'Is there any hope for me?'

'Of course there is, matey,' I lied. 'You have two of these morphia tablets and lie quiet. We'll take you in after a while, and you'll be back in England in two or three days' time.'

I placed the morphia under his tongue and he closed his eyes as if going to sleep. Then, with an effort, he tried to get up and gripped the wire support with such vigour that it came clean out of the ground. His legs shot out from under him, and, muttering something about rations being fit for pigs and not for men, he fell back and died.

The fighting was not over in the front trench yet, the first two companies had gone ahead, the other two companies were taking possession here. A sturdy Bavarian in shirt and pants was standing on a banquette with his bayonet over the parapet, and a determined look in his eyes. He had already done for two of our men as they tried to cross, but now his rifle seemed to be unloaded and he waited. Standing there amidst his dead countrymen he formed a striking figure. A bullet from one of our rifles would have ended his career speedily, but no one seemed to want to fire that shot. There was a moment of suspense, broken only when the monstrous futility of resistance became apparent to him, and he threw down his rifle and put up his hands, shouting 'Kamerad! kamerad!' I don't know what became of him afterwards, other events claimed my attention.

Four boys rushed up, panting under the machine gun and ammunition belts which they carried. One got hit and fell to the ground, the maxim tripod which he carried fell on top of him. The remainder of the party came to a halt.

'Lift the tripod and come along,' his mates shouted to one another.

'Who's goin' to carry it?' asked a little fellow with a box of ammunition.

'You,' came the answer.

'Some other one must carry it,' said the little fellow. 'I've the heaviest burden.'

'You've not,' one answered. 'Get the blurry thing on your shoulder.'

'Blurry yourself!' said the little fellow. 'Someone else carry the thing. Marney can carry it?'

'I'm not a damned fool!' said Marney. 'It can stick there 'fore I take it across.'

'Not much good goin' over without it,' said the little fellow.

I left them there wrangling: the extra weight would have made no appreciable difference to any of them.

It was interesting to see how the events of the morning had changed the nature of the boys. Mild-mannered youths who had spent their working hours of civil life in scratching with inky pens on white paper, and their hours of relaxation in cutting capers on roller skates and helping dainty maidens to teas and ices, became possessed of mad Berserker rage and ungovernable fury. Now that their work was war the blood-stained bayonet gave them play in which they seemed to glory.

'Here's one that I've just done in,' I heard M'Crone shout,

looking approvingly at a dead German. 'That's five of the bloody swine now.'

M'Crone's mother never sends her son any money lest he gets into the evil habit of smoking cigarettes. He is of a religious turn of mind and delights in singing hymns, his favourite being, 'There is a green hill far away'. I never heard him swear before, but at Loos his language would make a navvy in a Saturday night taproom green with envy. M'Crone was not lacking in courage. I have seen him wait for death with untroubled front in a shell-harried trench, and now, inflicting pain on others, he was a fiend personified; such transformations are of common occurrence on the field of honour.

The German trench had suffered severely from our fire; parapets were blown in, and at places the trench was full to the level of the ground with sandbags and earth. Wreckage was strewn all over the place, rifles, twisted distortions of shapeless metal, caught by high-velocity shells, machine guns smashed to atoms, bomb-proof shelters broken to pieces like houses of cards; giants had been at work of destruction in a delicately fashioned nursery.

On the reverse slope of the parapet broken tins, rusty swords, muddy equipments, wicked-looking coils of barbed-wire and discarded articles of clothing were scattered about pell-mell. I noticed an unexploded shell perched on a sandbag, cocking a perky nose in air, and beside it was a battered helmet, the brass glory of its regal eagle dimmed with trench mud and wrecked with many a bullet . . .

I had a clear personal impression of man's ingenuity for destruction when my eyes looked on the German front line where our dead lay in peace with their fallen enemies on the parapet. At the bottom of the trench the dead lay thick, and our boys, engaged in building a new parapet, were heaping the sandbags on the dead men and consolidating the captured position.

CHAPTER 7

GERMANS AT LOOS

'Some'ow a dyin' Alleymong don't seem a real Alleymong; you ain't able to 'ate 'im as you ought.'
— Bill Teake's Philosophy.

From the day I left England up till the dawn of September 25th I never met a German, and I had spent seven months in France. At night when out on working-parties I saw figures moving out by the enemy trenches, mere shadows that came into view when an ephemeral constellation of star-shells held the heavens. We never fired at these shadows, and they never fired at us; it is unwise to break the tacit truces of the trenches. The first real live German I saw was the one who blundered down the ladder into our trench, the second raced towards our trenches with Bill Teake following at his heels, uttering threats and vowing that he would stab the prisoner if he did not double in a manner approved of by the most exacting sergeant-major.

Of those who are England's enemies I know, even now, very little. I cannot well pass judgement on a nation through seeing distorted lumps of clotting and mangled flesh pounded into the muddy floor of a trench, or strewn broadcast on the reverse slopes of a shell-scarred parapet. The enemy suffered as we did, yelled with pain when his wounds prompted him, forgot perhaps in the insane combat some of the nicer tenets of chivalry. After all, war is an approved licence for brotherly mutilation, its aims are sanctioned, only the means towards its end are disputed. It is a sad and sorry business from start to finish, from diplomacy that begets it to the Te Deums that rise to God in thanksgiving for victory obtained.

In the first German trench there were dozens of dead, the trench was literally piled with lifeless bodies in ugly grey uniforms. Curiosity prompted me to look into the famous German dug-outs. They were remarkable constructions, caves leading into the bowels of the earth, some of them capable of holding a whole platoon of soldiers. These big dugouts had stairs leading down to the main chamber and steps leading out. In one I counted forty-seven steps leading down from the floor of the trench to the roof of the shelter. No shell made was capable of piercing these constructions, but a bomb flung downstairs . . .

I looked into a pretentious dug-out as I was going along the trench. This one, the floor of which was barely two feet below the level of the trench floor, must have been an officer's. It was sumptuously furnished, a curtained bed with a white coverlet stood in one corner. Near the door was a stove and a scuttle of coal. In another corner stood a table, and on it was a half bottle of wine, three glasses, a box of cigars, and a vase of flowers. These things I noticed later; what I saw first on entering was a wounded German lying across the bed, his head against the wall and his feet on the floor. His right arm was almost severed at the shoulder.

I entered and gazed at him. There was a look of mute appeal in his eyes, and for some reason I felt ashamed of myself for having intruded on the privacy of a dying man. There come times when a man on the field of battle should be left alone to his own thoughts. I loosened my water-bottle from its holder and by sign inquired if he wanted a drink. He nodded, and I placed the bottle to his lips.

'Sprechen Anglais?' I inquired, and he shook his head.

I took my bottle of morphia tablets from my pocket and explained to him as well as I was able what the bottle contained, and he permitted me to place two under his tongue. When rummaging in my pocket I happened to bring out my rosary beads and he noticed them. He spoke and I guessed that he was inquiring if I was a Catholic.

I nodded assent.

He fumbled with his left hand in his tunic pocket and brought out a little mud-stained booklet and handed it to me. I noticed that the volume was a prayer-book. By his signs I concluded that he wanted me to keep it.

I turned to leave, but he called me back and pointed to his trousers pocket as if he wanted me to bring something out of it. I put in my hand and drew out a little leather packet from which the muzzle of a revolver peeped forth. This I put in my pocket. He feared that if some of our men found this in his possession his life might be a few hours shorter than it really would be if he were left to die in peace. I could see that he required me to do something further for him. Raising his left hand with difficulty (I now saw that blood was flowing down the wrist) he pointed at his tunic pocket, and I put my hand in there. A clasp-knife, a few buttons, a piece of string and a photo were all that the pocket contained. The photograph showed a man, whom I saw was the soldier, a woman and a little child seated at a table. I put it in his hand, and with brilliant eyes and set teeth he raised his head to look at it . . .

I went outside. M'Crone was coming along the trench with a bomb in his hand.

'Any of them in that dug-out?' he asked me.

'One,' I replied.

'Then I'll give him this,' M'Crone shouted. His gestures were violent, and his indifference to personal danger as shown in his loud laughter was somewhat exaggerated. As long as he had something to do he was all right, but a moment's thought would crumple him up like a wet rag.

'I've done in seven of them already,' he shouted.

'The one in here is dying,' I said. 'Leave him alone.'

M'Crone went to the dug-out door, looked curiously in, then walked away.

Behind the German trench I found one of our boys slowly recovering from an attack of gas. Beside him lay a revolver, a mere toy of a thing, and touching him was a German with a bullet in his temple. The boy told me an interesting story as I propped him up in a sitting position against a couple of discarded equipments.

'I tripped up, and over I went,' he said. 'I came to slowly, and was conscious of many things 'fore I had the power to move my hands or feet. What do you think was happenin'? There was a bloomin' German sniper under cover pottin' at our boys, and that cover was a bundle of warm, livin' flesh; the blighter's cover was me! "If I get my hand in my pocket," I says to myself, "I'll get my revolver and blow the beggar's brains out." '

'Blow out his brains with that!' I said, looking at the weapon. 'You might as well try to blow out his brains with a pinch of snuff!'

'That's all you know!' said the boy. 'Anyway, I got my hand into my pocket, it crawled in like a snake, and I got the little pet out. And the German was pot-pottin' all the time. Then I fetched the weapon up, stuck the muzzle plunk against the man's head and pulled the trigger twice. He didn't half kick up a row. See if the two bullets have gone through one hole, Pat.'

'They have,' I told him.

'I knew it,' he answered. 'Ah! it's an easy job to kill a man. You just rush at him and you see his eyes and nothin' else. There's a mist over the trench. You shove your bayonet forward and it sticks in something soft and almost gets dragged out of your hands. Then you get annoyed because you can't pull it back easy. That's all that happens and you've killed a man . . . How much water have you got?'

A German youth of seventeen or eighteen with a magnificent helmet on his head and a red cross on his arm was working in the centre of a square formed by four of his dead countrymen, digging a grave. The sweat stood out on his forehead, and from time to time he cast an uneasy glance about him.

'What are you doing there?' I asked.

'Digging a grave for these,' he said, in good English, pointing a shaky finger at the prostrate figures. 'I suppose I'll be put in it myself,' he added.

'Why?' I inquired.

'Oh! you English shoot all prisoners.'

'You're a fool, Fritz,' said M'Crone, approaching him. 'We're not going to do you any harm. Look, I've brought you something to eat.'

He handed the boy a piece of cake, but the young Bavarian shook his head. He was trembling with terror, and the shovel shook in his hands. Fifteen minutes later when I passed that way carrying in a wounded man, I saw M'Crone and the young Bavarian sitting on the brink of the grave smoking cigarettes and laughing heartily over some joke.

Prisoners were going down towards M— across the open. Prisoners are always taken across the open in bulk with as small an escort as possible. I saw a mob of two hundred go along, their hands in the air, and stern Tommies marching on flank and at rear. The party was a mixed one. Some of the prisoners were strong, sturdy youngsters of nineteen or twenty, others were old men, war-weary and dejected. A few were thin, weedy creatures, but others were massive blocks of bone and muscle, well set-up and brimful of energy even in their degrading plight.

Now and again queer assortments of these came along. One man was taken prisoner in a cellar on the outskirts of Loos. Our men discovered him asleep in a bed, pulled him out and found that he was enjoying a decent, civilised slumber. He came down to M— as he was taken prisoner, his sole clothing being a pair of stockings, a shirt and an identity disc. Four big Highlanders, massive of shoulder and leg, escorted a puny, spectacled youth along the rim of the trench, and following them came a diminutive Cockney with a massive helmet on his head, the sole escort for twelve gigantic Bavarian Grenadiers. The Cockney had now only one enemy, he was the man who offered to help him at his work.

I came across a crumpled figure of a man in grey, dead in a shell-crater. One arm was bent under him, the other stretched forward almost touching a photograph of a woman and three little children. I placed the photograph under the edge of the man's tunic.

Near him lay another Bavarian, an old man, deeply wrinkled and white haired, and wounded through the chest. He was trembling all over like a wounded bird, but his eyes were calm and they looked beyond the tumult and turmoil of the battlefield into some secret world that only the dying can see. A rosary was in the man's hand and his lips were mumbling something: he was telling his beads. He took no notice of me. Across the level at this point came a large party of prisoners amidst a storm of shells. The German gunners had shortened their range and were now shelling the ground occupied by their troops an hour previous. Callous, indifferent destruction! The oncoming prisoners were Germans – as men they were of no use to us; it would cost our country money and men to keep and feed them. They were Germans, but of no further use to Germany; they were her pawns in a game of war and now useless in the play. As if to illustrate this, a shell from a German gun dropped in the midst of the batch and pieces of the abject party whirled in air. The gun which had destroyed them had acted as their guardian for months. It was a frantic mother slaying her helpless brood.

The stretcher-bearer sees all the horror of war written in blood and tears on the shell-riven battlefield. The wounded man, thank heaven! has only his own pain to endure, although the most extreme agony which flesh is heir to is written large on the field of fight.

Several times that day I asked myself the question, 'Why are all soldiers not allowed to carry morphia?' How much pain it would save! How many pangs of pain might morphia alleviate! How often would it give that rest and quiet which a man requires when an excited heart persists in pumping blood out through an open wound! In the East morphia is known as 'the gift of God'; on the field of battle the gift of God should not be denied to men in great pain. It would be well indeed if all soldiers were taught first aid before a sergeant-major teaches them the art of forming fours on the parade ground.

CHAPTER 8

HOW MY COMRADES FARED

Seven supple lads and clean
Sat down to drink one night,
Sat down to drink at Nouex-les-Mines,
Then went away to fight.

Seven supple lads and clean
Are finished with the fight;
But only three at Nouex-les-Mines
Sit down to drink tonight.

Felan went up the ladder of the assembly trench with a lighted cigarette in his mouth. Out on the open his first feeling was one of disappointment; to start with, the charge was as dull as a church parade. Felan, although orders were given to the contrary, expected a wild, whooping forward rush, but the men stepped out soberly, with the pious decision of ancient ladies going to church. In front the curtain of smoke receded, but the air stunk with its pungent odour still. A little valley formed by the caprice of the breeze opened in the fumes and its far end disclosed the enemy's wire entanglements. Felan walked through the valley for a distance of five yards, then he glanced to his right and found that there was nobody in sight there. Pryor had disappeared.

'Here, Bill, we've lost connection!' he cried, turning to his left. But his words were wasted on air; he was alone in his little glen, and invisible birds flicked angry wings close to his ears. His first inclination was to turn back, not through fear, but with a desire to make inquiries.

'I can't take a trench by myself,' he muttered. 'Shall I go back? If I do so some may call me a coward. Oh, damn it! I'll go forward.'

He felt afraid now, but his fear was not that which makes a man run away; he was attracted towards that which engendered the fear as an urchin attracted towards a wasps' nest longs to poke the hive and annoy its occupants.

'Suppose I get killed now and see nothing,' he said to himself. 'Where is Bill, and Pryor, and the others?'

He reached the enemy's wire, tripped, and fell headlong. He got to his feet again and took stock of the space in front. There was the German trench, sure enough, with its rows of dirty sandbags, a machine-gun emplacement and a maxim peeping furtively through the loophole. A big, bearded German was adjusting the range of the weapon. He looked at Felan, Felan looked at him and tightened his grip on his rifle.

'You –!' said Felan, and just made one step forward when something 'hit him all over', as he said afterwards. He dropped out of the world of conscious things.

A stretcher-bearer found him some twenty minutes later and placed him in a shell-hole, after removing his equipment, which he placed on the rim of the crater.

Felan returned to a conscious life that was tense with agony. Pain gripped at the innermost parts of his being. 'I cannot stand this,' he yelled. 'God Almighty, it's hell!'

He felt as if somebody was shoving a red-hot bar of iron through his chest. Unable to move, he lay still, feeling the bar getting shoved further and further in. For a moment he had a glimpse of his rifle lying on the ground near him and he tried to reach it. But the unsuccessful effort cost him much, and he became unconscious again.

A shell bursting near his hand shook him into reality, and splinters whizzed by his head. He raised himself upwards, hoping to get killed outright. He was unsuccessful. Again his eyes rested on his rifle.

'If God would give me strength to get it into my hand,' he muttered. 'Lying here like a rat in a trap and I've seen nothing. Not a run for my money . . . I suppose all the boys are dead. Lucky fellows if they die easy . . . I've seen nothing only one German, and he done for me. I wish the bullet had gone through my head.'

He looked at his equipment, at the bayonet scabbard lying limply under the haversack. The water-bottle hung over the rim of the shell-hole. 'Full of rum, the bottle is, and I'm so dry. I wish I could get hold of it. I was a damned fool ever to join the Army . . . My God! I wish I was dead,' said Felan.

The minutes passed by like a long grey thread unwinding itself slowly from some invisible ball, and the pain bit deeper into the boy. Vivid remembrances of long-past events flashed across his mind and fled away like telegraph poles seen by passengers in an express train. Then he lost consciousness again.

About eleven o'clock in the morning I found a stretcher-bearer whose mate had been wounded, and he helped me to carry a wounded man into our original front trench. On our way across I heard somebody calling 'Pat! Pat!' I looked round and saw a man crawling in on his hands and knees, his head almost touching the ground. He called to me, but he did not look in my direction. But I recognised the voice: the corporal was calling. I went across to him.

'Wounded?' I asked.

'Yes, Pat,' he answered, and, turning over, he sat down. His face was very white.

'You should not have crawled in,' I muttered. 'It's only wearing you out; and it's not very healthy here.'

'Oh, I wanted to get away from this hell,' he said.

'It's very foolish,' I replied. 'Let me see your wound.'

I dressed the wound and gave the corporal two morphia tablets and put two blue crosses on his face. This would tell those who might come his way later that morphia had been given.

'Lie down,' I said. 'When the man whom we're carrying is safely in, we'll come back for you.'

I left him. In the trench were many wounded lying on the floor and on the fire-steps. A soldier was lying face downwards, groaning. A muddy ground-sheet was placed over his shoulders. I raised the sheet and found that his wound was not dressed.

'Painful, matey?' I asked.

'Oh, it's old Pat,' muttered the man.

'Who are you?' I asked, for I did not recognise the voice.

'You don't know me!' said the man, surprise in his tones.

He turned a queer, puckered face half round, but I did not recognise him even then; pain had so distorted his countenance.

'No,' I replied. 'Who are you?'

'Felan,' he replied.

'My God!' I cried, then hurriedly, 'I'll dress your wound.

You'll get carried in to the dressing-station directly.'

'It's about time,' said Felan wearily. 'I've been out a couple of days . . . Is there no R.A.M.C.?'

I dressed Felan's wound, returned, and looked for the corporal, but I could not find him. Someone must have carried him in, I thought.

Kore had got to the German barbed-wire entanglement when he breathed in a mouthful of smoke which almost choked him at first, and afterwards instilled him with a certain placid confidence in everything. He came to a leisurely halt and looked around him. In front, a platoon of the 20th London Regiment, losing its objective, crossed parallel to the enemy's trench. Then he saw a youth who was with him at school, and he shouted to him. The youth stopped; Kore came up and the boys shook hands, leant on their rifles, and began to talk of old times when a machine gun played about their ears. Both got hit.

M'Crone disappeared; he was never seen by any of his regiment after the 25th.

The four men were reported as killed in the casualty list.

CHAPTER 9

AT LOOS

The wages of sin and a soldier is death.
– Trench Proverb.

For long I had looked on Loos from a distance, had seen the red-brick houses huddled together brooding under the shade of the massive Twin Towers, the giant sentinels of the German stronghold. Between me and the village lurked a thousand rifles and death-dealing maxims; out in the open no understanding could preserve a man from annihilation, luck alone could save him.

On September 25 I lived in the village. By night a ruined village has a certain character of its own, the demolition of war seems to give each broken wall a consciousness of dignity and worth; the moonlight ripples over the chimneys, and sheaves of shadow lurk in every nook and corner. But by day, with its broken, jerry-built houses, the village has no relieving features, it is merely a heap of broken bricks, rubble and mud. Some day, when ivy and lichen grow up the walls and cover green the litter that was Loos, a quaint, historical air may be given to the scene, but now it showed nothing but a depressing sameness of latchless doors, hingeless shutters, destruction and decay. Gone was all the fascinating, pathetic melancholy of the night when we took possession, but such might be expected: the dead is out of keeping with the day.

I was deep in thought as I stood at the door of the dressing-station, the first in Loos, and at the moment, the only one. The second German trench, the trench that was the enemy's at dawn, ran across the bottom of the street, and our boys were busy there heaping sandbags on the parapet. A dozen men with loaded rifles stood in the dressing-station on guard, and watchful eyes scanned the streets, looking for the enemy who were still in hiding in the cellars or sniping from the upper stories of houses untouched by shell-fire. Down in our cellar the wounded and dying lay: by night, if they lived till then, we would carry them across the open to the dressing-station of Maroc. To venture across now, when the big guns chorused a fanfare of fury on the levels, would have been madness.

I went to the door and looked up the street; it was totally deserted; a dead mule and several khaki-clad figures lay on the pavement, and vicious bullets kicked up showers of sparks on the cobblestones. I could not tell where they were fired from . . . A voice called my name and I turned round to see a head peep over the trench where it crossed the road. My mate, Bill Teake, was speaking.

'Come 'ere!' he called. 'There's some doin's goin' to take place.'

I rushed across the open road where a machine gun from a hill on the right was sending its messages with shrewish persistence, and tumbled into the trench at my mate's side.

'What are the doings?' I asked.

'The word 'as been passed along that a German observation balloon is going up over Lens an' we're goin' to shell it,' said Bill.

'I can't see the blurry thing nohow,' he added.

I looked towards Lens, and saw the town pencilled reddish in the morning light with several defiant chimney stacks standing in air. One of these was smoking, which showed that the enemy was still working it.

I saw the balloon rise over the town. It was a massive banana-like construction with ends pointing downwards, and it climbed slowly up the heavens. At that moment our gunners greeted it with a salvo of shrapnel and struck it, as far as I could judge.

It wriggled for a moment, like a big feather caught in a drift of air, then disappeared with startling suddenness.

'A neat shot,' I said to Bill, who was now engaged on the task of looking for the snappy maxim shrew that tapped impatiently on the sandbagged parapet.

'I think it's up there,' he said, pointing to the crest where three or four red-tiled houses snuggled in the cover of a spinney. 'It's in one of them big 'ouses, bet yer. If I find it I'll get the artillery to blow the place to blazes!' he concluded, with an air of finality.

I went back to the dressing-station and found the men on guard in a state of tense excitement. They had seen a German cross the street two hundred yards up, and a red-haired youth, Ginger Turley, who had fired at the man, vowed that he had hit him.

'I saw 'im fall,' said Ginger. 'Then 'e crawled into a 'ouse on 'ands and knees.'

''E was only shammin',' said the corporal of the guard. 'Nobody can be up to these 'ere Allemongs.'

'I 'it 'im,' said Ginger heatedly. 'Couldn't miss a man at two 'undred and me gettin' proficiency pay for good shootin' at S'nalbans [St Albans].'

A man at the door suddenly uttered a loud yell.

'Get yer 'ipes,' he yelled. 'Quick! Grease out of it and get into the scrap. There's 'undreds of 'em up the streets. Come on! Come out of it! We'll give the swine socks!'

He rushed into the street, raised his rifle to his shoulder and fired two rounds. Then he raced up the street shouting, with the guard following. I looked out.

The men in khaki were rushing on a mob of some fifty or sixty Germans who advanced to meet them with trembling arms raised over their heads, signifying in their manner that they wished to surrender. I had seen many Germans surrender that morning and always noticed that their uplifted arms shook as if stricken with palsy. I suppose they feared what might befall them when they fell into our hands.

With hands still in air and escorted by our boys they filed past the door of the dressing-station. All but one man, who was wounded in the jaw.

'This is a case for you, Pat,' said the corporal of the guard, and beckoned to the wounded German to come indoors.

He was an ungainly man, and his clothes clung to his body like rags to a scarecrow. His tunic was ripped in several places, and a mountain of Loos mud clung to his trousers. His face was an interesting one, his eyes, blue and frank, seemed full of preoccupation that put death out of reckoning.

'Sprechen Anglais?' I asked, floundering in the mud of Franco-German interrogation. He shook his head; the bullet had blown away part of the man's jaw and he could not speak.

I dressed his wound in silence, an ugly, ghastly wound it looked, one that he would hardly recover from. As I worked with the bandages he brought out a little mirror, gazed for a moment at his face in the glass, and shook his head sadly. He put the mirror back in his pocket, but after a second he drew it out again and made a second inspection of his wound.

The dressing done, I inquired by signs if he wanted to sleep; there was still some room in the cellar. He pointed his finger at his tunic over the breast and I saw a hole there that looked as if made by a red-hot poker. I cut the clothes off the man with my scissors and discovered that the bullet which went through the man's jaw had also gone through his chest. He was bleeding freely at the back near the spine and in front over the heart . . . The man brought out his mirror again, and, standing with his back to a shattered looking-glass that still remained in the building, he examined his wound after the manner of a barber who shows his customer the back of his head by use of a mirror . . . Again the German shook his head sadly. I felt sorry for the man. My stock of bandages had run short, and Ginger Turley, who had received a parcel of underclothing a few days before, brought out a new shirt from his haversack, and tearing it into strips, he handed me sufficient cloth for a bandage.

'Poor bloke!' muttered Turley, blushing a little as if ashamed of the kind action. 'I suppose it was my shot, too. 'E must be the feller that went crawlin' into the buildin'.'

'Not necessarily,' I said, hoping to comfort Ginger.

'It was my shot that did it, sure enough,' Ginger persisted. 'I couldn't miss at two 'undred yards, not if I tried.'

One of the men was looking at a little book, somewhat similar to the pay-book we carry on active service, which fell from the German's pocket.

'Bavarian!' read the man with the book, and fixed a look of interrogation on the wounded man, who nodded.

'Musician?' asked the man, who divined that certain German words stated that the Bavarian was a musician in civil life.

A sad look crept into the prisoner's eyes. He raised his hands and held them a little distance from his lips and moved his fingers rapidly; then he curved his left arm and drew his right slowly backward and forward across in front of his body.

We understood; he played the flute and violin. Ginger Turley loves ragtime and is a master of the mouth-organ; and now having met a brother artist in such a woeful plight, Ginger's feelings overcame him, and two tears gathered in his eyes.

'I wish I wasn't such a good shot,' he muttered.

We wrapped the German up in a few rags, and since he wanted to follow his comrades, who left under escort, we allowed him to go. Ten minutes later, Bill Teake poked his little white potato of a nose round the door.

'I've found 'im out,' he said, and his voice was full of enthusiasm.

'Who have you found out?' I asked.

'That bloomin' machine gun,' Bill answered. 'I saw a little puff of smoke at one of the winders of a 'ouse up in the spinney. I kept my eye on that 'ere winder. Ev'ry time I seed a puff of smoke, over comes a bullet. I told the officer, and he 'phones down to the artillery. There's goin' to be some doin's. Come on, Pat, and see the fun.'

It was too good to miss. Both of us scurried across the road and took up a position in the trench from which we could get a good view of the spinney.

'That 'ouse there,' said Bill, pointing to the red-brick building bordering a slag-heap known as "The Double Crassier" which tailed to a thin point near the village of Maroc. 'There! see at the winder on the left a puff of smoke.'

A bullet hit the sandbag at my side. I looked at the house indicated by Bill and saw a wisp of pale smoke trail up from one of the lower windows towards the roof.

'The machine gun's there, sure enough,' I said.

Then a bigger gun spoke; a shell whizzed through the air and raised a cloud of black dust from the rim of the slag-heap.

'More to the left, you bounders, more to the left!' yelled Bill.

He could not have been more intent on the work if he were the gunner engaged upon the task of demolition.

The second shot crept nearer and a shrub uprooted whirled in air.

'That's the ticket!' yelled Bill, clapping his hands. 'Come, gunner, get the bounder next time!'

The gunner got him with the next shot which struck the building fair in the centre and smashed it to pieces.

'That was a damned good one,' said Bill approvingly. 'The bloomin' gun is out of action now for the duration of war. Have you seen that bloke?'

Bill Teake pointed at a dead German who lay on the crest of the parados, his hands doubled under him, and his jaw bound with a bloodstained dressing.

'He just got killed a minute ago,' said Bill. 'He jumped across the trench when the machine gun copped 'im and 'e went down flop!'

'I've just dressed his wounds,' I said.

'He'll need no dressin' now,' said Bill, and added compassionately, 'Poor devil! S'pose 'e's 'ad someone as cared for 'im.'

I thought of home and hoped to send a letter along to Maroc with a wounded man presently. From there letters would be forwarded. I had a lead pencil in my pocket, but I had no envelope.

'I'll give you a half-franc for a green envelope,' I said, and Bill Teake took from his pocket the green envelope, which needed no regimental censure, but was liable to examination at the Base.

''Arf-franc and five fags,' he said, speaking with the studied indifference of a fishwife making a bargain.

'Half a franc and two fags,' I answered.

''Arf a franc and four fags,' he said.

'Three fags,' I ventured.

'Done,' said Bill, and added, 'I've now sold the bloomin' line of communication between myself and my ole man for a few coppers and three meesly fags.'

'What's your old man's profession, Bill?' I asked.

''Is wot?'

'His trade?'

'Yer don't know my ole man, Pat?' he inquired. 'Everybody knows 'im. 'E 'as as good a reputation as old times. Yer must 'ave seen him in the Strand wiv 'is shiny buttons, burnished like gold in a jooler's winder, carryin' a board wiv "Globe Metal Polish" on it.'

'Oh!' I said with a laugh.

'But 'e's a devil for 'is suds 'e is –'

'What are suds?' I asked.

'Beer,' said Bill. 'E can 'old more'n any man in Lunnon, more'n the chucker-out at "The Cat and Mustard Pot" boozer in W— Road even. Yer should see the chucker-out an' my ole man comin' 'ome on Saturday night. They keep themselves steady by rollin' in opposite directions.'

'Men with good reputations don't roll home inebriated,' I said. 'Excessive alcoholic dissipation is utterly repugnant to dignified humanity.'

'Wot!'

'Is your father a churchgoer?' I asked.

'Not 'im,' said Bill. ''E don't believe that one can go to 'eaven by climbin' up a church steeple. 'E's a good man, that's wot 'e is. 'E works 'ard when 'e's workin', 'e can use 'is fives wiv anyone, 'e can take a drink or leave it, but 'e prefers takin' it. Nobody can take a rise out o' 'im fer 'e knows 'is place, an' that's more'n some people do.'

'Bill, did you kill any Germans this morning?' I asked.

'Maybe I did,' Bill answered, 'and maybe I didn't. I saw one bloke, an Allemong, in the front trench laughin' like 'ell. "I'll make yer laugh," I said to 'im, and shoved my bayonet at 'is bread basket. Then I seed 'is foot; it was right off at the ankle. I left 'im alone. After that I 'ad a barney. I was goin' round a traverse and right in front of me was a Boche, eight foot 'igh or more. Oh! 'e 'ad a bayonet as long as 'imself, and a beard as long as 'is bayonet.'

'What did you do?'

'Oh! I retreated,' said Bill. 'Then I met four of the Jocks, they 'ad bombs. I told them wot I seen an' they went up with me to the place. The Boche saw us and 'e rushed inter a dug-out. One of the Jocks threw a bomb, and bang! –'

'Have you seen Kore?' I asked.

'No, I didn't see 'im at all,' Bill answered. 'I was mad for a while. Then I saw a lot of Alleymongs rush into a dug-out. "Gor-blimey!" I said to the Jocks, "we'll give 'em 'ell," and I caught 'old of a German bomb, one o' them kind where you pull the string out and this sets the fuse goin'. I coiled the string round my fingers and pulled. But I couldn't loosen the string. It was a go! I 'eld out my arm with the bomb 'angin'. "Take it off!" I yelled to the Jocks. Yer should see them run off. There was no good in me runnin'. Blimey! I didn't 'arf feel bad. Talk about a cold sweat; I sweated icicles! And there was the damned bomb 'angin' from my 'and and me thinkin' it was goin' to burst. But it didn't; I 'adn't pulled the string out far enough.

'And that's Loos,' he went on, standing on the fire-step and looking up the road. 'It's bashed about a lot. There's 'ardly a 'ouse standin'. And that's the Tower Bridge,' he added, looking fixedly at the Twin Towers that stood scarred but unbroken over Loos coal mine.

'There was a sniper up there this mornin',' he told me. ''E

didn't 'arf cause some trouble. Knocked out dozens of our fellers. 'E was brought down at last by a bomb.'

He laughed as he spoke, then became silent. For fully five minutes there was not a word spoken.

I approached the parapet stealthily and looked up the street of Loos, a solemn, shell-scarred, mysterious street where the dead lay amidst the broken tiles. Were all those brown bundles dead men? Some of them maybe were still dying; clutching at life with vicious energy. A bundle lay near me, a soldier in khaki with his hat gone. I could see his close, compact, shiny curls which seemed to have been glued on to his skull. Clambering up the parapet I reached forward and turned him round and saw his face. It was leaden-hued and dull; the wan and almost colourless eyes fixed on me in a vague and glassy stare, the jaw dropped sullenly, and the tongue hung out. Dead . . . And up the street, down in the cellars, at the base of the Twin Towers, they were dying. How futile it was to trouble about one when thousands needed help. Where should I begin? Who should I help first? Any help I might be able to give seemed so useless. I had been at work all the morning dressing the wounded, but there were so many. I was a mere child emptying the sea with a tablespoon. I crawled into the trench again to find Bill still looking over the parapet. This annoyed me. Why, I could not tell.

'What are you looking at?' I asked.

There was no answer. I looked along the trench and saw that all the men were looking towards the enemy's line; watching, as it seemed, for something to take place. None knew what the next moment would bring forth. The expectant mood was prevalent. All were waiting.

Up the road some houses were still peopled with Germans, and snipers were potting at us with malicious persistency, but behind the parapet we were practically immune from danger. As we looked a soldier appeared round the bend of the trench, the light of battle in his eyes and his body festooned with bombs.

'It's dangerous to go up the centre of the street,' I called to him as he came to a halt beside me and looked up the village.

'Bend down,' I said. 'Your head is over the parapet.' I recognised the man. He was Gilhooley the bomber.

'What does it matter?' he muttered. 'I want to get at them . . . Oh! I know yer face . . . D'ye mind the champagne at Nouex-les-Mines . . . These bombs are real ones, me boy . . . Do you know where the snipers are?'

'There's one up there,' I said, raising my head and pointing to a large house on the left of the road near the Twin Towers. 'I saw the smoke of his rifle when he fired at me a while ago.'

'Then he must get what he's lookin' for,' said Gilhooley, tightening his belt of bombs, and, clutching his rifle, rushed out into the roadway. 'By Jasus! I'll get him out of it!'

I raised my head and watched, fascinated. With prodigious strides Gilhooley raced up the street, his rifle clutched tightly in his hand. Suddenly he paused, as if in thought, and his rifle went clattering across the cobbles. Then he sank slowly to the ground, kicking out a little with his legs. The bullet had hit him in the jaw and it came out through the back of his neck . . .

I could hear the wounded crying and moaning somewhere near, or perhaps far away. A low, lazy breeze slouched up from the field which we had crossed that morning, and sound travelled far. The enemy snipers on Hulluch copse were busy, and probably the dying were being hit again. Some of them desired it, the slow process of dying on the open field of war is so dreadful . . . A den of guns, somewhere near Lens, became voluble, and a monstrous fanfare of fury echoed in the heavens. The livid sky seemed to pull itself up as if to be out of the way; under it the cavalcades of war ran riot. A chorus of screeches and yells rose trembling and whirling in air, snatching at each other like the snarling and barking of angry dogs.

Bill stood motionless, looking at the enemy's line, his gaze concentrated on a single point; in his eyes there was a tense, troubled expression, as if he was calculating a sum which he could not get right. Now and again he would shake his head as if trying to throw something off and address a remark to the man next him, who did not seem to hear. Probably he was asleep. In the midst of artillery tumult some men are overcome with languor and drop asleep as they stand. On the other hand, many get excited, burst into song and laugh boisterously at most commonplace incidents.

Amidst the riot, an undertone of pain became more persistent than ever. The levels where the wounded lay were raked with shrapnel that burst viciously in air and struck the blood stained earth with spiteful vigour.

The cry for stretcher-bearers came down the trench, and I

hurried off to attend to the stricken. I met him crawling along on all fours, looking like an ungainly lobster that has escaped from a basket. A bullet had hit the man in the back and he was in great pain; so much in pain that when I was binding his wound he raised his fist and hit me in the face.

'I'm sorry,' he muttered, a moment afterwards. 'I didn't mean it, but, my God! this is hell!'

'You'll have to lie here,' I said, when I put the bandage on. 'You'll get carried out at night when we can cross the open.'

'I'm going now,' he said. 'I want to go now. I must get away. You'll let me go, won't you, Pat?'

'You'll be killed before you're ten yards across the open,' I said. 'Better wait till tonight.'

'Does the trench lead out?' he asked.

'It probably leads to the front trench which the Germans occupied this morning,' I said.

'Well, if we get there it will be a step nearer the dressing-station, anyway,' said the wounded boy. 'Take me away from here, do please.'

'Can you stand upright?'

'I'll try,' he answered, and half weeping and half laughing, he got to his feet. 'I'll be able to walk down,' he muttered.

We set off. I walked in front, urging the men ahead to make way for a wounded man. No order meets with such quick obedience as 'Make way for wounded'.

All the way from Loos to the churchyard which the trench fringes and where the bones of the dead stick out through the parapet, the trench was in fairly good order; beyond that was the dumping ground of death.

The enemy in their endeavour to escape from the Irish that morning crowded the trench like sheep in a lane-way, and it was here that the bayonet, rifle-butt and bomb found them. Now they lay six deep in places . . . One bare-headed man lay across the parapet, his hand grasping his rifle, his face torn to shreds with rifle bullets. One of his own countrymen, hidden in Hulluch copse, was still sniping at the dead thing, believing it to be an English soldier. Such is the irony of war. The wounded man ambled painfully behind me, grunting and groaning. Sometimes he stopped for a moment, leant against the side of the trench and swore for several seconds. Then he muttered a word of apology and followed me in silence. When we came to the places where the dead lay six deep we had to crawl across them on our hands and knees. To raise our heads over the parapet would be courting quick death. We would become part of that demolition of blood and flesh that was necessary for our victory. In front of us a crowd of civilians, old men, women and children, was crawling and stumbling over the dead bodies. A little boy was eating the contents of a bully-beef tin with great relish, and the ancient female who accompanied him crossed herself whenever she stumbled across a prostrate German. The civilians were leaving Loos.

On either side we could hear the wounded making moan, their cry was like the yelping of drowning puppies. But the man who was with me seemed unconscious of his surroundings; seldom even did he notice the dead on the floor of the trench; he walked over them unconcernedly.

I managed to bring him down to the dressing-station. When we arrived he sat on a seat and cried like a child.

CHAPTER 10

A NIGHT IN LOOS

Never see good in an enemy until you have defeated him!
— War Proverb.

Twilight softened the gaunt corners of the ruined houses, and sheaves of shadows cowered in unfathomable corners. A wine shop, gashed and fractured, said 'hush!' to us as we passed; the shell-holed streets gaped at the indifferent, unconcerned sky.

'See the streets are yawning,' I said to my mate, Bill Teake.

'That's because they're bored,' he replied.

'Bill,' I said, 'what do you mean by bored?'

'They've holes in them,' he answered. 'Why d'yer arst me?'

'I wanted to know if you were trying to make a pun,' I said. 'That's all.'

Bill grunted, and a moment's silence ensued.

'Suppose it were made known to you, Bill,' I said, 'that for the rest of your natural life this was all you could look forward to, dull hours of waiting in the trenches, sleep in sodden dug-outs, eternal gun-firing and innumerable bayonet-charges; what would you do?'

'Wot would I do?' said Bill, coming to a halt in the middle of the street. 'This is wot I'd do,' he said with decision. 'I'd put a round in the breech, lay my 'ead on the muzzle of my 'ipe, and reach down and pull the blurry trigger. Wot would you do?'

'I should become very brave,' I replied.

'I see wot yer mean,' said Bill. 'Ye'd be up to the Victoria Cross caper, and run yer nose into danger every time yer got a chance.'

'You may be right,' I replied. 'No one likes this job, but we all endure it as a means towards an end.'

'Flat!' I yelled, flopping to the ground and dragging Bill with me, as a shell burst on a house up the street and flung a thousand splinters round our heads. For a few seconds we cowered in the mud, then rose to our feet again.

'There are means by which we are going to end war,' I said. 'Did you see the dead and wounded today, the men groaning and shrieking, the bombs flung down into cellars, the bloodstained bayonets, the gouging and the gruelling; all those things are means towards creating peace in a disordered world.'

The unrest which precedes night made itself felt in Loos. Crows made their way homeward, cleaving the air with weary wings; a tottering wall fell on the street with a melancholy clatter, and a joist creaked near at hand, yearning, as it seemed, to break free from its shattered neighbours. A lone wind rustled down the street, weeping over the fallen bricks, and crooning across barricades and machine-gun emplacements. The greyish-white evening sky cast a vivid pallor over the Twin Towers, which stood out sharply defined against the lurid glow of a fire in Lens.

All around Loos lay the world of trenches, secret streets, sepulchral towns, houses whose chimneys scarcely reached the level of the earth, crooked alleys, bayonet-circled squares, and lonely graveyards where dead soldiers lay in the silent sleep that wakens to no earthly réveillé.

The night fell. The world behind the German lines was lighted up with a white glow, the clouds seemed afire, and ran with a flame that was not red and had no glare. The tint was pale, and it trailed over Lens and the spinneys near the town, and spread trembling over the levels. White as a winding sheet, it looked like a fire of frost, vast and wide diffused. Every object in Loos seemed to loose its reality, a spectral glimmer hung over the ruins, and the walls were no more than outlines. The Twin Towers was a tracery of silver and enchanted fairy construction that the sun at dawn might melt away, the barbed-wire entanglements (those in front of the second German trench had not been touched by our artillery) were fancies in gossamer. The world was an enchanted poem of contrasts of shadow and shine, of nooks and corners black as ebony, and prominent objects that shone with a spiritual glow. Men coming down the street bearing stretchers or carrying rations were phantoms, the men stooping low over the earth digging holes for their dead comrades were as ghostly as that which they buried. I lived in a strange world – a world of dreams and illusions.

Where am I? I asked myself. Am I here? Do I exist? Where are the boys who marched with me from Les Brebis last night? I had looked on them during the day, seeing them as I had never seen them before, lying in silent and unquestioning peace, close to the yearning earth. Never again should I hear them sing in the musty barns near Givenchy; never again would we drink red wine together in Café Pierre le Blanc, Nouex-les-Mines . . .

Bill Teake went back to his duties in the trench and left me. A soldier came down the street and halted opposite.

'What's that light, soldier?' he asked me.

'I'm sure I don't know,' I answered.

'I hear it's an ammunition depot afire in Lens,' said the man. 'Our shells hit it, and their blurry bullets have copped me now,' he muttered, dropping on the roadway and crawling towards the shelter of the wall on his belly.

'Where are you hit?' I asked, helping him into the ruins of the *estaminet* – my dressing-station.

'In the leg,' he answered, 'just below the knee. It was when I was speaking to you about the ammunition depot on fire. "Our shells hit it," I said, and just then something went siss! through my calf. "Their blurry bullets have copped me now," I said, didn't I?'

'You did,' I answered, laying my electric torch on the table and placing the wounded man on the floor. I ripped open his trousers and found the wound; the bullet had gone through the calf.

'Can you use your foot?' I asked, and he moved his boot up and down.

'No fracture,' I told him. 'You're all right for blighty, matey.'

One of my mates who was sleeping in a cellar came up at that moment.

'Still dressing wounded, Pat?' he asked.

'I just got wounded a minute ago,' said the man on the floor as I fumbled about with a first field dressing. 'I was speaking to Pat about the fire at Lens, and I told him that our shells hit it, "and a blurry bullet has copped me now," I said, when I felt something go siss! through my leg.'

'Lucky dog,' said the man on the stair head. 'I'd give fifteen pounds for your wound.'

'Nothing doing,' said the man on the floor with a laugh.

'When can I get down to the dressing-station?' he asked.

'Now, if you can walk,' I told him. 'If you're to be carried I shall need three other men; the mud is knee deep on the road to Maroc.'

'I'll see if I can walk,' said the man, and tried to rise to his feet. The effort was futile, he collapsed like a wet rag. Fifteen minutes later four of us left Loos bearing a stretcher on our shoulders, and trudged across the fields to the main road and into the crush of war traffic, hideously incongruous in the pale light of the quiet night.

The night was quiet, for sounds that might make for riot were muffled by the mud. The limbers' wheels were mud to the axles, the mules drew their legs slowly out of muck almost reaching their bellies. Motor ambulances, wheeled stretchers, ammunition wagons, gun carriages, limbers, water-carts, mules, horses and men going up dragged their sluggish way through the mud on one side of the road; mules, horses and men, water-carts, limbers, gun carriages, ammunition wagons, wheeled stretchers and motor ambulances coming down moved slowly along the other side. Every man had that calm and assured indifference that comes with ordinary everyday life. Each was full of his own work, preoccupied with his toil, he was lost to the world around him. For the driver of the cart that we followed, a problem had to be worked out. The problem was this: how could he bring his mules and vehicles into Maroc and bring up a second load, then pilot his animals through mud and fire into Les Brebis before dawn; feed himself and his mules (when he got into safety), drink a glass or two of wine (if he had the money to pay for it), and wrap himself in his blanket and get to sleep in decent time for a good day's rest. Thus would he finish his night of work if the gods were kind. But they were not.

A momentary stoppage, and the mules stood stiffly in the mud, the offside wheeler twitching a long, restless ear. The driver lay back in his seat, resigned to the delay. I could see his whip in air, his face turned to the east where the blazing star-shells lit the line of battle. A machine gun spoke from Hill 70, and a dozen searching bullets whizzed about our heads. The driver uttered a sharp, infantile yell like a snared rabbit, leant sideways, and fell down on the roadway. The mule with the twitching ear dropped on top of the man and kicked out wildly with its hind legs.

'Cut the 'oss out' yelled someone from the top of a neighbouring wagon, and three or four soldiers rushed to the rescue, pulled the driver clear, and felt his heart.

'Dead,' one said, dodging to avoid the hoofs of the wounded mule. 'The bullet 'as caught the poor cove in the forehead . . . Well, it's all over now, and there's nothing to be done.'

'Shoot the mule,' someone suggested. 'It's kicking its mate in the belly . . . Also put the dead man out of the roadway. 'E'll get mixed with the wheels.'

Someone procured a rifle, placed the muzzle close to the animal's ear, and fired. The mule stretched its hind legs lazily out and ceased its struggles. Movement was resumed ahead, and dodging round the dead man, we continued our journey through the mud. It was difficult to make headway, our legs were knee-deep in slush, and the monstrous futility of shoving our way through wearied us beyond telling. Only at rare intervals could we lift our feet clear of the ground and walk in comparative ease for a few moments. Now and again a machine gun opened on the moving throng, and bullets hummed by perilously close to our ears. The stretcher was a dead weight on us, and the poles cut into our shoulders.

The Scottish had charged across the road in the morning, and hundreds had come to grief. They were lying everywhere, out on the fields, by the roadside, and in the roadway mixed up with the mud. The driver who had been killed a moment ago was so preoccupied with his task that he had no time for any other work but his own. We were all like him. We had one job to do and that job took up our whole attention until it was completed. That was why our party did not put down our stretcher on the road and raise the dead from the mud; we walked over them.

How cold they looked, the kilted lads lying on their backs in the open, their legs, bare from knee to hip, white and ghostly in the wan light of the blazing ammunition depot at Lens.

Mud on the roadway, reaching to the axles of the limber wheels, dead men on the roadside, horses and mules tugging and straining at the creaking vehicles, wounded men on the stretchers; that was the picture of the night, and on we trudged, moving atoms of a pattern that kept continually repeating itself.

The mutilated and maimed who still lay out in the open called plaintively for succour. 'For God's sake bring me away from here,' a voice called. 'I've been lying out this last four days.' The man who spoke had been out since dawn, but periods of unconsciousness had disordered his count of time, and every conscious moment was an eternity of suffering.

We arrived at Q—instead of Maroc, having missed the right turning. The village was crowded with men; a perfect village it was, with every house standing, though the civilian population had long since gone to other places. Two shells, monstrous twelve-inch terrors, that failed to explode, lay on the pavement at the entrance. We went past these gingerly, as ladies in dainty clothing might pass a fouling post, and carried our burden down the streets to the dressing-station. Outside the door were dozens of stretchers, and on each a stricken soldier, quiet and resigned, who gazed into the cheerless and unconcerned sky as if trying to find some deadened hope.

A Scottish regiment relieved from the trenches stood round a steaming dixie of tea, each man with a mess-tin in his hand. I approached the Jocks.

'Any tea to spare?' I asked one.

'Aye, mon, of course there's a drappie goin',' he answered, and handed me the mess-tin from which he had been drinking.

'How did you fare today?' I asked.

'There's a wheen o' us left yet,' he replied with a solemn smile. 'A dozen dixies of tea would nae gang far among us yesterday; but wi' one dixie the noo, we've some to spare . . . Wha' d'ye belong tae?' he asked.

'The London Irish,' I told him.

''Twas your fellows that kicked the futba' across the field?'

'Yes.'

'Into the German trench?'

'Not so far,' I told the man. 'A bullet hit the ball by the barbed-wire entanglements; I saw it lying there during the day.'

''Twas the maddest thing I've ever heard o',' said the Jock. 'Hae ye lost many men?'

'A good number,' I replied.

'I suppose ye did,' said the man, but by his voice, I knew that he was not in the least interested in our losses; not even in the issue of battle. In fact, few of us knew of the importance of the events in which we took part, and cared as little. If I asked one of our boys at that moment what were his thoughts he would answer, if he spoke truly: 'I wonder when we're going to

get relieved', or 'I hope we're going to get a month's rest when
we get out.' Soldiers always speak of 'we'; the individual is
submerged in his regiment. We, soldiers, are part of the Army,
the British Army, which will be remembered in days to come,
not by a figurehead, as the fighters of Waterloo are remembered by Wellington, but as an army mighty in deed, prowess
and endurance; an army which outshone its figureheads.

I went back to the dressing-station. Our wounded man
was inside, and a young doctor was busy putting on a fresh
dressing. The soldier was narrating the story of his wound.

'I was speaking to a stretcher-bearer about the ammunition
depot afire in Lens,' he was saying. ' "Our shells hit it, and
their bloomin' bullets 'ave copped me now," I said, when something went siss! through my leg.'

The man gazed round at the door and saw me.

'Wasn't that what I said, Pat?' he asked.

'Yes,' I answered.' You said that their *blooming* bullets had
copped you.'

CHAPTER II

LOOS

The dead men lay on the cellar stair,
Toll of the bomb that found them there;
In the streets men fell as a bullock drops,
Sniped from the fringe of Hulluch copse.
And stiff in khaki the boys were laid –
Food of the bullet and hand-grenade –
This we saw when the charge was done,
And the East grew pale to the rising sun
In the town of Loos in the morning.

A rim of grey clouds clustered thick on the horizon as if hiding some wonderful secret from the eyes of men. Above my head the stars were twinkling, a soft breeze swung over the open, and moist gusts caught me in the face as I picked my way carefully through the still figures in brown and grey that lay all over the stony face of the level lands. A spinney on the right was wrapped in shadow, and when, for a moment, I stood to listen, vague whispers and secret rustlings could be heard all around. The hour before the dawn was full of wonder, the world in which I moved was pregnant with mystery. 'Who are these?' I asked myself as I looked at the still figures in khaki. 'Where is the life, the vitality of yesterday's dawn; the fire of eager eyes, the mad pulsing of roving blood, and the great heart of young adventure? Has the roving, the vitality and the fire come to this; gone out like sparks from a star-shell falling in a pond? What are these things here? What am I? What is the purpose served by all this demolition and waste?' Like a child in the dark I put myself the question, but there was no answer. The stars wheel on their courses over the dance of death and the feast of joy, ever the same.

I walked up to the church by the trench through the graveyard where the white bones stuck out through the parapet. A pale mist gathered round the broken headstones and crept along the bushes of the fence. The Twin Towers stood in air – moody, apathetic, regardless of the shrapnel incense that the guns wafted against the lean girders. Sparrows twittered in the field, and a crow broke clumsily away from the branches in the spinney. A limber jolted along the road near me creaking and rumbling. On! driver, on! Get to Les Brebis before the dawn, and luck be with you! If the enemy sees you! On! On! I knew that he hurried; that one eye was on the east where the sky was flushing a faint crimson, and the other on the road in front where the dead mules grew more distinct and where the faces of the dead men showed more clearly.

At that moment the enemy began to shell the road and the trench running parallel to it. I slipped into the shelter and waited. The transport came nearer, rolling and rumbling; the shrapnel burst violently. I cowered close to the parapet and I had a vivid mental picture of the driver leaning forward on the neck of his mule, his teeth set, his breath coming in short, sudden gasps. 'Christ! am I going to get out of it?' he must have said. 'Will dawn find me at Les Brebis?'

Something shot clumsily through the air and went plop! against the parados.

'Heavens! it's all up with me!' I said, and waited for the explosion. But there was none. I looked round and saw a leg on the floor of the trench, the leg of the transport driver, with its leg-iron shining like silver. The man's boot was almost worn through in the sole, and the upper was gashed as if with a knife. I'm sure it must have let in the wet . . . And the man was alive a moment ago! The mule was still clattering along, I could hear the rumble of the wagon . . . The firing ceased, and I went out in the open again.

I walked on the rim of the parapet and gazed into the dark streak of trench where the shadows clustered round traverse and dug-out door. In one bay a brazier was burning, and a bent figure of a man leant over a mess-tin of bubbling tea. All at once he straightened himself and looked up at me.

'Pat MacGill?' he queried.

'A good guess,' I answered. 'You're making breakfast early.'

'A drop of tea on a cold morning goes down well,' he answered. 'Will you have a drop? I've milk and a sultana cake.'

'How did you come by that?' I asked.

'In a dead man's pack,' he told me, as he emptied part of the contents of the tin into a tin mug and handed it up.

The tea was excellent. A breeze swept over the parapet and ushered in the dawn. My heart fluttered like a bird; it was so happy, so wonderful to be alive, drinking tea from a sooty mess-tin on the parapet of the trench held by the enemy yesterday.

'It's quiet at present,' I said.

'It'll soon not be quiet,' said the man in the trench, busy now with a rasher of bacon which he was frying on his mess-tin lid. 'Where have you come from?'

'I've been all over the place,' I said. 'Maroc, and along that way. You should see the road to Maroc. Muck to the knees; limbers, carts, wagons, guns, stretchers, and God knows what! going up and down. Dead and dying mules; bare-legged Jocks flat in the mud and wheels going across them. I'll never forget it.'

'Nobody that has been through this will ever forget it,' said the man in the trench. 'I've seen more sights than enough. But nothing disturbs me now. I remember a year ago if I saw a man getting knocked down I'd run a mile; I never saw a dead person till I came here. Will you have a bit of bacon and fried bread?'

'Thanks,' I answered, reaching down for the food. 'It's very good of you.'

'Don't mention it, Pat,' he said, blushing as if ashamed of his kindness.' 'Maybe, it'll be my turn to come to you next time I'm hungry. Any word of when we're getting relieved?'

'I don't hear anything,' I said. 'Shortly, I hope. Many of your mates killed?' I asked.

'Many of them indeed,' he replied. 'Old L went west the moment he crossed the top. He had only one kick at the ball. A bullet caught him in the belly. I heard him say "A foul; a blurry foul!" as he went all in a heap. He was a sticker! Did you see him out there?'

He pointed a thumb to the field in rear.

'There are so many,' I replied. 'I did not come across him.'

'And then B, D, and R went,' said the man in the trench. 'B with a petrol bomb, D with shrapnel, and R with a bayonet wound. Some of the Bavarians made a damned good fight for it . . .'

Round the traverse a voice rose in song, a trembling, resonant voice, and we guessed that sleep was still heavy in the eyes of the singer:

There's a silver lining through the dark clouds shining,
We'll turn the dark cloud inside out till the boys come home.

'Ah! it will be a glad day and a sorrowful day when the boys come home,' said the man in the trench, handing me a piece of sultana cake. 'The children will be cheering, the men will be cheering, the women – some of them. One woman will say: "There's my boy, doesn't he look well in uniform?" Then another will say: "Two boys I had, *they're* not here–" '

I saw a tear glisten on the cheek of the boy below me, and something seemed to have caught in his throat. His mood craved privacy, I could tell that by the dumb appeal in his eyes.

'Good luck, matey,' I mumbled, and walked away. The singer looked up as I was passing.

'Mornin', Pat,' he said. 'How goes it?'

'Not at all bad,' I answered.

'Have you seen W.?' asked the singer.

'I've been talking to him for the last twenty minutes,' I said. 'He has given me half his breakfast.'

'I suppose he couldn't sleep last night,' said the singer, cutting splinters of wood for the morning fire. 'You've heard that his brother was killed yesterday morning?'

'Oh!' I muttered. 'No, I heard nothing about it until now.'

The dawn glowed crimson, streaks of red shot through the clouds to eastwards and touched the bowl of sky overhead with fingers of flame. From the dug-outs came the sound of sleepy voices, and a soldier out in open trench was cleaning his bayonet. A thin white fog lay close to the ground, and through it I could see the dead boys in khaki clinging, as it were, to the earth. I could see a long way round. Behind was the village where the wounded were dressed; how blurred it looked with its shell-scarred chimneys in air like the fingers of a wounded hand held up to a doctor. The chimneys, dun-tinted and lonely, stood silent above the mist, and here and there a tree which seemed to have been ejected from the brotherhood of its kind stood out in the open all alone. The smoke of many fires curled over the line of trenches. Behind the parapets lay many dead; they had fallen in the trench and their comrades had flung them out into the open. It was sad to see them there; yesterday or the day before their supple legs were strong for a long march; today –

A shell burst dangerously near, and I went into the trench; the Germans were fumbling for their objective. Our artillery, as yet quiet, was making preparations for an anticipated German counter-attack, and back from our trench to Les Brebis, every spinney concealed a battery, every tree a gun, and every broken wall an ammunition depot. The dawning sun showed the terror of war quiet in gay disguise; the blue-grey, long-nosed guns hidden in orchards where the apples lingered late, the howitzers under golden-fringed leaves, the metallic glint on the weapons' muzzles; the gunners asleep in adjacent dug-outs, their blankets tied tightly around their bodies, their heads resting on heavy shells, fit pillows for the men whose work dealt in death and destruction. The sleepers husbanded their energy for trying labour, the shells seemed to be saving their fury for more sure destruction. All our men were looking forward to a heavy day's work.

I went back to the dressing-station in Loos. The street outside, pitted with shell-holes, showed a sullen face to the leaden sky. The dead lay in the gutters, on the pavement, at the door-steps; the quick in the trenches were now consolidating our position, strengthening the trench which we had taken from the Germans. Two soldiers on guard stood at the door of the dressing-station. I dressed a few wounds and lit a cigarette.

'What's up with that fool?' said a voice at the door, and I turned to the man who spoke.

'Who?' I inquired.

'Come and see,' said the man at the door. I looked up the street and saw one of our boys standing in the roadway and the smoke of a concussion shell coiling round his body. It was Bill Teake. He looked round, noticed us, and I could see a smile flower broadly on his face. He made a step towards us, halted and said something that sounded like 'Yook! yook!' Then he took another step forward and shot out his hand as if playing bowls.

'He's going mad?' I muttered. 'Bill, what are you doing?' I cried to him.

'Yook! Yook! Yook!' he answered in a coaxing voice.

'A bullet will give you yook! yook! directly,' I cried. 'Get under cover and don't be a fool.'

'Yook! Yook!'

Then a shell took a neighbouring chimney away and a truckful of bricks assorted itself on the roadway in Bill's neighbourhood. Out of the smother of dust and lime a fowl, a long-necked black hen, fluttered into the air and flew towards our shelter. On the road in front it alighted and wobbled its head from one side to another in a cursory inspection of its position. Bill Teake came racing down the road.

'Don't frighten it away!' he yelled. 'Don't shout. I want that 'en. It's my own 'en. I discovered it. Yook! Yook! Yook!'

He sobered his pace and approached the hen with cautious steps. The fowl was now standing on one leg, the other leg drawn up under its wing, its head in listening position, and its attitude betokened extreme dejection. It looked for all the world like Bill when he peers down the neck of a rum jar and finds the jar empty.

'Not a word now,' said Teake, fixing one eye on me and another on the hen. 'I must get my feelers on this 'ere cackler. It was up there sittin' atop of a dead Jock when I sees it . . . Yook! Yook! That's wot you must say to a bloomin' 'en w'en yer wants ter nab it . . . Yook! Yook! Yook!'

He threw a crumb to the fowl. The hen picked it up, swallowed it, and hopped off for a little distance. Then it drew one leg up under its wing and assumed a look of philosophic calm.

'Clever hen!' I said.

'Damned ungrateful fraud!' said Bill angrily. 'I've given it 'arf my iron rations. If it wasn't that I might miss it I'd fling a bully-beef tin at it.'

'Where's your rifle?' I inquired.

'Left it in the trench,' Bill replied. 'I just came out to look for sooveneers. This is the only sooveneer I seen. Yook! Yook! I'll sooveneer yer, yer swine. Don't yer understand yer own language?'

The hen made a noise like a chuckling frog.

'Yes, yer may uck! uck!' cried Bill, apostrophising the fowl. 'I'll soon stop yer uck! uck! yer one-legged von Kluck! Where's a rifle to spare?'

I handed him a spare rifle which belonged to a man who had been shot outside the door that morning.

'Loaded?' asked Bill.

'Loaded,' I lied.

The Cockney lay down on the roadway, stretched the rifle

out in front, took steady aim, and pulled the trigger. A slight click was the only response.

'That's a dirty trick,' he growled, as we roared with laughter. 'A bloomin' Alleymong wouldn't do a thing like that.'

So saying he pulled the bolt back, jerked a cartridge from the magazine, shoved a round into the breech and fired. The fowl fluttered in agony for a moment, then fell in a heap on the roadway. Bill handed the rifle back to me.

'I'll cook that 'en tonight,' he said, with studied slowness. 'It'll make a fine feed. 'En well cooked can't be beaten, and I'm damned if you'll get one bone to pick!'

'Bill!' I protested.

'Givin' me a hipe as wasn't loaded and sayin' it was,' he muttered sullenly.

'I haven't eaten a morsel of hen since you pinched one at Mazingarbe,' I said. 'You remember that. 'Twas a damned smart piece of work.'

A glow of pride suffused his face.

'Well, if there's any to spare tonight I'll let you know,' said my mate. 'Now I'm off.'

'There's a machine gun playing on the road,' I called to him, as he strolled off towards the trench with the hen under his arm. 'You'd better double along.'

He broke into a run, but suddenly stopped right in the centre of the danger zone. I could hear the bullets rapping on the cobblestones.

'I'll tell yer when the feed's ready, Pat,' he called back. 'You can 'ave 'arf the 'en for supper.'

Then he slid off and disappeared over the rim of the trench.

CHAPTER 12

RETREAT

There's a battery snug in the spinney,
A French 'seventy-five' in the mine,
A big 'nine-point-two' in the village,
Three miles to the rear of the line.
The gunners will clean them at dawning,
And slumber beside them all day,
But the guns chant a chorus at sunset,
And then you should hear what they say.

The hour was one o'clock in the afternoon, and a slight rain was now falling. A dug-out in the bay leant wearily forward on its props; the floor of the trench, foul with blood and accumulated dirt, showed a weary face to the sky. A breeze had sprung up, and the watcher who looked over the parapet was met in the face with a soft, wet gust laden with rain swept off the grassy spot in front . . . A gaunt willow peeped over the sandbags and looked timorously down at us. All the sandbags were perforated by machine-gun fire, a new gun was hidden on the rise on our right, but none of our observers could locate its position. On the evening before it had accounted for eighty-seven casualties; from the door of a house in Loos I had seen our men, who had attempted to cross the street, wiped out like flies.

Very heavy fighting had been going on in the front line to the east of Hill 70 all through the morning. Several bomb attacks were made by the enemy, and all were repulsed. For the men in the front line trench the time was very trying. They had been subject to continual bomb attacks since the morning before.

''Ow long 'ave we been 'ere?' asked Bill Teake, as he removed a clot of dirt from the foresight guard of his rifle. 'I've lost all count of time.'

'Not such a length of time,' I told him.

'Time's long a-passin'' 'ere,' said Bill, leaning his head against the muddy parados. 'Gawd, I'd like to be back in Les Brebis drinkin' beer, or 'avin' a bit of a kip for a change. When I go back to blighty I'll go to bed and I'll not get up for umpty-eleven months.'

'We may get relieved tomorrow night,' I said.

'Tomorrow'll be another day nearer the day we get relieved, any'ow,' said Bill sarcastically. 'And another day nearer the end of the war,' he added.

'I'm sick of it,' he muttered, after a short silence. 'I wish the damned war was blurry well finished. It gives me the pip. Curse the war! Curse everyone and everything! If the Alley-mongs would come over now, I'd not lift my blurry 'ipe. I'd surrender; that's wot I'd do. Curse . . . Damn . . . Blast . . .'

I slipped to the wet floor of the trench asleep and lay there, only to awaken ten minutes later. I awoke with a start; some-body jumping over the parapet had planted his feet on my stomach. I rose from the soft earth and looked round. A kilted soldier was standing in the trench, an awkward smile on his face and one of his knees bleeding. Bill, who was awake, was gazing at the kiltie with wide open eyes.

The machine gun was speaking from the enemy's line, a shrewish tang in its voice, and little spurts of dirt flicked from our sandbags shot into the trench.

Bill's eyes looked so large that they surprised me; I had never seen him look in such a way before. What was happening? Several soldiers belonging to strange regiments were in our trench now; they were jumping over the parapet in from the open. One man I noticed was a nigger in khaki . . .

'They're all from the front trench,' said Bill in a whisper of mysterious significance, and a disagreeable sensation stirred in my being.

'That means,' I said, and paused.

'It means that the Allemongs are gettin' the best of it,' said Bill, displaying an unusual interest in the action of his rifle. 'They say the 21st and 24th Division are retreating from ''ill 70. Too 'ot up there. It's goin' to be a blurry row 'ere,' he muttered. 'But we're goin' to stick 'ere, wotever 'appens. No damned runnin' away with us!'

The trench was now crowded with strangers, and others were coming in. The field in front of our line was covered with figures running towards us. Some crouched as they ran, some tottered and fell; three or four crawled on their bellies, and many dropped down and lay where they fell.

The machine gun swept the field, and a vicious hail of shrapnel swept impartially over the quick, the wounded and the dead. A man raced up to the parapet which curved the bay in which I stood, a look of terror on his face. There he stood a moment, a timorous foot on a sandbag, calculating the distance of the jump . . . He dropped in, a bullet wound showing on the back of his tunic, and lay prostrate, face upwards on the floor of the trench. A second man jumped in on the face of the stricken man.

I hastened to help, but the newcomers pressed forward and pushed me along the trench. No heed was taken of the wounded man.

'Back! Get back!' yelled a chorus of voices. 'We've got to retire.'

''Oo the blurry 'ell said that?' I heard Bill Teake thunder. 'If ye're not goin' to fight, get out of this 'ere place and die in the fields. Runnin' away, yer blasted cowards!'

No one seemed to heed him. The cry of 'Back! Back!' redoubled in violence. 'We've got orders to retire! We must get back at once!' was the shout. 'Make way there, let us get by.'

It was almost impossible to stem the tide which swept up the trench towards Loos Road where the road leaves the village. I had a fleeting glimpse of one of our men rising on the fire position and gazing over the parapet. Even as he looked a bullet hit him in the face, and he dropped back, clawing at the air with his fingers . . . Men still crowded in from the front, jumping on the struggling crush in the trench . . . In front of me was a stranger, and in front of him was Rifleman Pryor, trying to press back against the oncoming men. A bullet ricochetted off a sandbag and hit the stranger on the shoulder and he fell face downwards to the floor. I bent to lift the wounded fellow and got pushed on top of him.

'Can you help him?' Pryor asked.

'If you can keep the crowd back,' I muttered, getting to my feet and endeavouring to raise the fallen man.

Pryor pulled a revolver from his pocket, levelled it at the man behind me and shouted: 'If you come another step further I'll put a bullet through your head.'

This sobered the soldier at the rear, who steadied himself by placing his hand against the traverse. Then he called to those who followed, 'Get back! there's a wounded man on the floor of the trench.'

A momentary halt ensued. Pryor and I gripped the wounded man, raised him on the parapet and pushed him into a shell-hole behind the sandbags. Lying flat on the ground up there I dressed the man's wounds. Pryor sat beside me, fully exposed to the enemy's fire, his revolver in his hand.

'Down, Pryor,' I said several times. 'You'll get hit.'

'Oh, my time hasn't come yet,' he said. 'I'll not be done in this time, anyway. Fighting is going on in the front trench yet, and dozens of men are racing this way. Many of them are falling. I think some of our boys are firing at them, mistaking them for Germans . . . Here's our colonel coming along the trench.'

The colonel was in the trench when I got back there, exhorting his men to stand and make a fight of it. 'Keep your backs to the walls, boys,' he said, 'and fight to the last.'

The Irish had their back to the wall, no man deserted his post. The regiment at the moment was the backbone of the Loos front; if the boys wavered and broke, the thousands of lives that were given to make the victory of Loos would have been lost in vain. Intrepid little Bill Teake, who was going to surrender to the first German whom he met, stood on the banquette, his jaw thrust forward determinedly and the light of battle in his eyes. Now and again he turned round and apostrophised the soldiers who had fallen back from the front line.

'Runnin' away!' he yelled. 'Ugh! Get back again and make a fight of it. Go for the Alleymongs just like you's go for rum rations.'

The machine gun on the hill peppered Loos Road and dozens dropped there. The trench crossing the road was not more than a few feet deep at any time, and a wagon which had fallen in when crossing a hastily-constructed bridge the night before, now blocked the way. To pass across the men had to get up on the road, and here the machine gun found them; and all round the wagon bleeding bodies were lying three deep.

A young officer of the — Regiment, whose men were carried away in the stampede, stood on the road with a Webley revolver in his hand and tried to urge his followers back to the front trench. 'It's all a mistake,' he shouted. 'The Germans did not advance. The order to retire was a false one. Back again; boys,

get back. Now, get back for the regiment's sake. If you don't
we'll be branded with shame. Come now, make a stand and I'll
lead you back again.'

Almost simultaneously a dozen bullets hit him and he fell,
his revolver still in his hand. Bill Teake procured the revolver
at dusk . . .

Our guns came suddenly into play and a hell-riot of artillery broke forth. Guns of all calibres were brought into work,
and all spoke earnestly, madly, the 4.2s in the emplacement
immediately to rear, the 9.2s back at Maroc, and our big giants,
the caterpillar howitzers, away behind further still. Gigantic
shells swung over our heads, laughing, moaning, whistling,
hooting, yelling. We could see them passing high up in air,
looking for all the world like beer bottles flung from a juggler's
hand. The messengers of death came from everywhere and
seemed to be everywhere.

The spinney on the spur was churned, shivered, blown to
pieces. Trees uprooted rose twenty yards in the air, paused for
a moment to take a look round, as it were, when at the zenith
of their flight, then sank slowly, lazily to earth as if selecting a
spot to rest upon. Two red-brick cottages with terra-cotta tiles
which snuggled amidst the trees were struck simultaneously,
and they went up in little pieces, save where one rafter rose
hurriedly over the smoke and swayed, a clearly defined black
line, in mid-air. Coming down abruptly it found a resting place
on the branches of the trees. One of the cottages held a German
gun and gunners . . . Smoke, dust, lyddite fumes robed the
autumn-tinted trees on the crest, the concussion shells burst
into lurid flame, the shrapnel shells puffed high in air, and
their white, ghostly smoke paled into the overcast heavens.

The retreat was stopped for a moment. The — Regiment
recovered its nerve and fifty or sixty men rushed back. Our
boys cheered . . . But the renewed vitality was short-lived. A
hail of shrapnel caught the party in the field and many of them
fell. The nigger whom I had noticed earlier came running back,
his teeth chattering, and flung himself into the trench. He lay
on the floor and refused to move until Bill Teake gave him a
playful prod with a bayonet. Our guns now spoke boisterously,
and the German trenches on the hill were being blown to little
pieces. Dug-outs were rioting, piecemeal, in air, parapets were
crumbling hurriedly in and burying the men in the trench,
bombs spun lazily in air, and the big caterpillar howitzers

flung their projectiles across with a loud whoop of tumult. Our thousand and one guns were bellowing their terrible anthem of hate.

Pryor stood on the fire-step, his bayonet in one hand, an open tin of bully-beef in the other.

'There's no damned attack on at all,' he said. 'A fresh English regiment came up and the — got orders to retire for a few hundred yards to make way for them. Then there was some confusion, a telephone wire got broken, the retirement became a retreat. A strategic retreat, of course,' said Pryor sarcastically, and pointed at the broken wagon on the Loos Road. 'A strategic retreat,' he muttered, and munched a piece of beef which he lifted from the tin with his fingers.

The spinney on which we had gazed so often now retained its unity no longer, the brick houses were gone; the lyddite clouds took on strange forms amidst the greenery, glided towards one another in a graceful waltz, bowed, touched tips, retired and paled away, weary as it seemed of their fantastic dance. Other smoke bands of ashen hue intermixed with ragged, bilious-yellow fragments of cloud rose in the air and disappeared in the leaden atmosphere. Little wisps of vapour like feathers of some gigantic bird detached themselves from the horrible, diffused glare of bursting explosives, floated towards our parapet, and the fumes of poisonous gases caused us to gasp for breath. The shapelessness of Destruction reigned on the hill, a fitting accompaniment to the background of cloudy sky, dull, dark and wan.

Strange contrasts were evoked on the crest, monstrous heads rose over the spinney, elephants bearing ships, Vikings, bearded and savage, beings grotesque and gigantic took shape in the smoke and lyddite fumes.

The terrible assault continued without truce, interruption or respite; our guns scattered broadcast with prodigal indifference their apparently inexhaustible resources of murder and terror. The essence of the bombardment was in the furious succession of its blows. In the clamour and tumult was the crash and uproar of a vast bubbling cauldron forged and heated by the gods in ungodly fury.

The enemy would reply presently. Through the uproar I could hear the premonitory whispering of his guns regulating their range and feeling for an objective. A concussion shell whistled across the traverse in which I stood and in futile rage dashed itself to pieces on the level field behind. Another followed, crying like a child in pain, and finished its short, drunken career by burrowing into the red clay of the parados where it failed to explode. It passed close to my head, and fear went down into the innermost parts of me and held me for a moment . . . A dozen shells passed over in the next few moments, rushing ahead as if they were pursued by something terrible, and burst in the open a hundred yards away. Then a livid flash lit a near dug-out; lumps of earth, a dozen beams and several sandbags changed their locality, and a man was killed by concussion. When the body was examined no trace of a wound could be seen. Up the street of Loos was a clatter and tumult. A house was flung to earth, making a noise like a statue falling downstairs in a giant's castle; iron girders at the coalmine were wrenched and tortured, and the churchyard that bordered our trench had the remnants of its headstones flung about and its oft muddled graves dug anew by the shells.

The temporary bridge across the trench where it intersected the road, made the night before to allow ammunition limbers to pass, was blown sky high, and two men who sheltered under it were killed. Earth, splinters of wood and bits of masonry were flung into the trench, and it was wise on our part to lie on the floor or press close to the parapet. One man, who was chattering a little, tried to sing, but became silent when a comrade advised him 'to hold his row; if the Germans heard the noise they might begin shelling'.

The gods were thundering. At times the sound dwarfed me into such infinitesimal littleness that a feeling of security was engendered. In the midst of such an uproar and tumult, I thought that the gods, bent though they were upon destruction, would leave such a little atom as myself untouched. This for a while would give me a self-satisfying confidence in my own invulnerability.

At other times my being swelled to the grand chorus. I was one with it, at home in thunder. I accommodated myself to the Olympian uproar and shared in a play that would have delighted Jove and Mars. I had got beyond that mean where the soul of a man swings like a pendulum from fear to indifference, and from indifference to fear. In danger I am never indifferent, but I find that I can readily adapt myself to the moods and tempers of my environment. But all men have some restraining influence to help them in hours of trial, some principle or some illusion. Duty, patriotism, vanity, and dreams come to the help of men in the trenches, all illusions probably, ephemeral and fleeting; but for a man who is as ephemeral and fleeting as his illusions are, he can lay his back against them and defy death and the terrors of the world. But let him for a moment stand naked and look at the staring reality of the terrors that engirt him and he becomes a raving lunatic.

The cannonade raged for three hours, then ceased with the suddenness of a stone falling to earth, and the ordeal was over.

As the artillery quietened the men who had just come into our trench plucked up courage again and took their way back to the front line of trenches, keeping well under the cover of the houses in Loos. In twenty minutes' time we were left to ourselves, nothing remained of those who had come our way save their wounded and their dead; the former we dressed and carried into the dressing-station, the latter we buried when night fell.

The evening came, and the greyish light of the setting sun paled away in a western sky, leaden-hued and dull. The dead men lying out in the open became indistinguishable in the gathering darkness. A deep silence settled over the village, the roadway and trench, and with the quiet came fear. I held my breath. What menace did the dark world contain? What threat did the ghostly star-shells, rising in air behind the Twin Towers, breathe of? Men, like ghosts, stood on the banquettes waiting, it seemed, for something to take place. There was no talking, no laughter. The braziers were still unlit, and the men had not eaten for many hours. But none set about to prepare a meal. It seemed as if all were afraid to move lest the least noise should awake the slumbering Furies. The gods were asleep and it was unwise to disturb them . . .

A limber clattered up the road and rations were dumped down at the corner of the village street.

'I 'ope they've brought the rum,' somebody remarked, and we all laughed boisterously. The spell was broken, and already my mate, Bill Teake, had applied a match to a brazier and a little flame glowed at the corner of a traverse. Now was the moment to cook the hen which he had shot that morning.

As he bent over his work, someone coming along the trench stumbled against him, and nearly threw Bill into the fire.

''Oo the blurry 'ell is that shovin' about,' spluttered Teake, rubbing the smoke from his eyes and not looking round.

'It's the blurry Colonel of the London Irish,' a voice replied, and Bill shot up to attention and saluted his commanding officer.

'I'm sorry, sir,' he said.

'It's all right,' said the officer. 'If I was in your place, I might have said worse things.'

Bill recounted the incident afterwards and concluded by saying, "'E's a fine bloke, 'e is, our C.O. I'd do anythink for him now.'

CHAPTER 13

A PRISONER OF WAR

A star-shell holds the sky beyond
Shell-shivered Loos, and drops
In million sparkles on a pond
That lies by Hulluch copse.

A moment's brightness in the sky,
To vanish at a breath,
And die away, as soldiers die
Upon the wastes of death.

'There'll be some char [tea] in a minute,' said Bill, as he slid over the parapet into the trench. 'I've got some cake, a tin of sardines and a box of cigars, fat ones.'

'You've been at a dead man's pack,' I said.

'The dead don't need nuffink,' said Bill.

It is a common practice with the troops after a charge to take food from the packs of their fallen comrades. Such actions are inevitable; when crossing the top, men carry very little, for too much weight is apt to hamper their movements.

Transports coming along new roads are liable to delay, and in many cases they get blown out of existence altogether. When rations arrive, if they arrive, they are not up to the usual standard, and men would go hungry if death did not come in and help them. As it happens, however, soldiers feed well after a charge.

Bill lit a candle in the German dug-out, applied a match to a brazier and placed his mess-tin on the flames. The dug-out with its flickering taper gave me an idea of cosiness, coming in as I did from the shell-scarred village and its bleak cobbled streets. To sit down here on a sandbag (Bill had used the wooden seats for a fire) where men had to accommodate themselves on a pigmy scale, was very comfortable and reassuring. The light of the candle and brazier cast a spell of subtle witchery on the black walls and the bayonets gleaming against the roof, but despite this, innumerable shadows lurked in the corners, holding some dark council.

'Ha!' said Bill, red in the face from his exertions over the fire. 'There's the water singin' in the mess-tin; it'll soon be dancin'.'

The water began to splutter merrily as he spoke, and he emptied the tea on the tin which he lifted from the brazier with his bayonet. From his pack he brought forth a loaf and cut it into good thick slices.

'Now some sardines, and we're as comfy as kings,' he muttered. 'We'll 'ave a meal fit for a gentleman, any gentleman in the land.'

'What sort of meal is fit for a gentleman?' I asked.

'Oh! a real good proper feed,' said Bill. 'Suthin' that fills the guts.'

The meal was fit for a gentleman indeed; in turn we drank the tea from the mess-tin and lifted the sardines from the tin with our fingers; we had lost our forks as well as most of our equipment.

'What are you goin' to do now?' asked Bill, when we had finished.

'I don't know that there's anything to be done in my job,' I said. 'All the wounded have been taken in from here.'

'There's no water to be got,' said Bill. 'There's a pump in the street, but nobody knows whether it's poisoned or not. The nearest well that's safe to drink from is at Maroc.'

'Is there a jar about?' I asked Bill, and he unearthed one from the corner of his jacket. 'I'll go to Maroc and bring up a jar of water,' I said. 'I'll get back by midnight, if I'm not strafed.'

I went out on the road. The night had cleared and was now breezy; the moon rode high amongst scurrying clouds, the trees in the fields were harassed by a tossing motion and leant towards the village as if seeking to get there. The grasses shivered, agitated and helpless, and behind the Twin Towers of Loos the star-shells burst into many-coloured flames and showed like a summer flower-garden against the sky. A wind-mill, with one wing intact, stood out, a ghostly phantom, on a rise overlooking Hulluch.

The road to Maroc was very quiet and almost deserted; the

nightly traffic had not yet begun, and the nightly cannonade
was as yet merely fumbling for an opening. The wrecks of
the previous days were still lying there; long-eared mules
immobile in the shafts of shattered limbers, dead Highlanders
with their white legs showing wan in the moonlight, boys in
khaki with their faces pressed tightly against the cobblestones,
broken wagons, discarded stretchers, and derelict mailbags
with their rain-sodden parcels and letters from home.

Many wounded were still lying out in the fields. I could
hear them calling for help and groaning.

'How long had they lain there?' I asked myself. 'Two days,
probably. Poor devils!'

I walked along, the water jar knocking against my legs. My
heart was filled with gloom. 'What is the meaning of all this?'
I queried. 'This wastage, this hell?'

A white face peered up at me from a ditch by the roadside,
and a weak voice whispered, 'Matey!'

'What is it, chummy?' I queried, coming close to the
wounded man.

'Can you get me in?' he asked. 'I've been out for – oh! I don't
know how long,' he moaned.

'Where are you wounded?' I asked.

'I got a dose of shrapnel, matey,' he said. 'One bullet caught
me in the heel, another in the shoulder.'

'Has anybody dressed the wounds?' I asked.

'Aye, aye,' he answered. 'Somebody did, then went off and
left me here.'

'Do you think you could grip me tightly round the shoulders if I put you on my back?' I said. 'I'll try and carry you
in.'

'We'll give it a trial,' said the man in a glad voice, and I flung
the jar aside and hoisted him on my back.

Already I was worn out with having had no sleep for two
nights, and the man on my back was heavy. For a while I
tried to walk upright, but gradually my head came nearer the
ground.

'I can't go any further,' I said at last, coming to a bank on
the roadside and resting my burden. 'I feel played out. I'll see
if I can get any help. There's a party of men working over there.
I'll try and get a few to assist me.'

The man lay back on the grass and did not answer. Probably
he had lost consciousness.

A Scotch regiment was at work in the field, digging trenches; I approached an officer, a dark, low set man with a heavy black moustache.

'Could you give me some men to assist me to carry in wounded?' I asked. 'On each side of the road there are dozens –'

'Can't spare any men,' said the officer. 'Haven't enough for the work here.'

'Many of your own countrymen are out there,' I said.

'Can't help it,' said the man. 'We all have plenty of work here.'

I glanced at the man's shoulder and saw that he belonged to 'The Lone Star Crush'; he was a second-lieutenant. Second-lieutenants fight well, but lack initiative.

A captain was directing work near at hand, and I went up to him.

'I'm a stretcher-bearer,' I said. 'The fields round here are crowded with wounded who have been lying out for ever so long. I should like to take them into the dressing-station. Could you give me some men to help me?'

'Do you come from the Highlands?' asked the captain.

'No, I come from Ireland,' I said.

'Oh!' said the officer; then inquired: 'How many men do you want?'

'As many as you can spare.'

'Will twenty do?' I was asked.

I went down the road in charge of twenty men, stalwart Highlanders, massive of shoulder and thew, and set about collecting the wounded. Two doors, a barrow and a light cart were procured, and we helped the stricken men on these conveyances. Some men were taken away across the Highlanders' shoulders, and some who were not too badly hurt limped in with one man to help each case. The fellow whom I left lying by the roadside was placed on a door and borne away.

I approached another officer, a major this time, and twelve men were handed over to my care; again six men were found and finally eight who set about their work like Trojans.

My first twenty returned with wheeled and hand stretchers, and scoured the fields near Loos. By dawn fifty-three wounded soldiers were taken in by the men whom I got to assist me, and I made my way back to the trench with a jar full of water. Wild, vague, and fragmentary thoughts rioted through my mind, and

I was conscious of a wonderful exhilaration. I was so pleased
with myself that I could dance along the road and sing with
pure joy. Whether the mood was brought about by my success
in obtaining men or saving wounded I could not determine.
Anyhow, I did not attempt to analyse the mood; I was happy
and I was alive, with warm blood palpitating joyously through
my veins.

I found a full pack lying in the road beside a dead mule
which lay between the shafts of limber. The animal's ears stuck
perkily up like birds on a fence.

In the pack I found an overcoat, a dozen bars of chocolate,
and a piece of sultana cake.

I crossed the field. The darkness hung heavy as yet, and it
was difficult to pick one's way. Now I dropped into a shell-
hole and fell flat on my face, and again my feet got entangled
in lines of treacherous trip-wire, and I went headlong.

'Halt!'

I uttered an exclamation of surprise and fear, and stopped
short a few inches from the point of a bayonet. Staring into
the darkness I discerned the man who had ordered me to halt.
One knee was on the ground, and a white hand clutched the
rifle barrel. I could hear him breathing heavily.

'What's wrong with you, man?' I asked.

''Oo are yer?' inquired the sentry.

'A London Irish stretcher-bearer,' I said.

'Why are yer comin' through our lines?' asked the sentry.

'I'm just going back to the trench,' I said. 'I've been taking a
wounded man down to Maroc.'

'To where?' asked the man with the bayonet.

'Oh! it seems as if you don't know this place,' I said. 'Are
you new to this part of the world?'

The man made no answer, he merely shoved his bayonet
nearer my breast and whistled softly. As if in reply to this
signal, two forms took shape in the darkness and approached
the sentry.

'What's wrong?' asked one of the newcomers.

'This 'ere bloke comes up just now,' said the sentry, pointing
the bayonet at my face. ''E began to ask me questions and I 'ad
my suspicions, so I whistled.'

'That's right,' said one of the newcomers, rubbing a
thoughtful hand over the bayonet which he carried; then he
turned to me. 'Come along wiv us,' he said, and, escorted by

the two soldiers, I made my way across the field towards a ruined building which was raked at intervals by the German artillery. The field was peopled with soldiers lying flat on waterproof sheets, and many of the men were asleep. None had been there in the early part of the night.

An officer, an elderly man with a white moustache, sat under the shade of the building holding an electric lamp in one hand and writing in a notebook with the other. We came to a halt opposite him.

'What have you here?' he asked, looking at one of my captors.

'We found this man inquiring what regiment was here and if it had just come,' said the soldier on my right who, by the stripes on his sleeve, I perceived was a corporal. 'He aroused our suspicions and we took him prisoner.'

'What is your name?' asked the officer, turning to me.

I told him. As I spoke a German shell whizzed over our heads and burst about three hundred yards to rear. The escort and the officer went flop to earth and lay there for the space of a second.

'You don't need to duck,' I said. 'That shell burst half a mile away.'

'Is that so?' asked the officer, getting to his feet. 'I thought it – Oh! what's your name?'

I told him my name the second time.

'That's your real name?' he queried.

I assured him that it was, but my assurance was lost, for a second shell rioted overhead, and the escort and officer went again flop to the cold ground.

'That shell has gone further than the last,' I said to the prostrate figures. 'The Germans are shelling the road on the right; it's a pastime of theirs.'

'Is that so?' asked the officer, getting to his feet again. Then, hurriedly, 'What's your regiment?'

Before I had time to reply, three more prisoners were taken in under escort; I recognised Pryor as one of them. He carried a jar of water in his hand.

'Who are these?' asked the officer.

'They came up to the sentry and asked questions about the regiment,' said the fresh escort. 'The sentry's suspicions were aroused and he signalled to us, and we came forward and arrested these three persons.'

The officer looked at the prisoners.

'What are your names, your regiments?' he asked. 'Answer quickly. I've no time to waste.'

'May I answer, sir?' I asked.

'What have you to say?' inquired the officer.

'Hundreds of men cross this field nightly,' I said. 'Working-parties, ration-fatigues, stretcher-bearers and innumerable others cross here. They're going up and down all night. By the way you duck when a shell passes high above you, I judge that you have just come out here. If you spend your time taking prisoner all who break through your line' (two fresh prisoners were brought in as I spoke) 'you'll be busy asking English soldiers questions till dawn. I hope I don't offend you in telling you this.'

The officer was deep in thought for a moment; then he said to me, 'Thanks very much, you can return to your battalion.' I walked away. As I went off I heard the officer speak to the escorts.

'You'd better release these men,' he said. 'I find this field is a sort of public thoroughfare.'

A brigade was camped in the field, I discovered. The next regiment I encountered took me prisoner also; but a few shells dropped near at hand and took up the attention of my captor for a moment. This was an opportunity not to be missed; I simply walked away from bondage and sought the refuge of my own trench.

'Thank goodness,' I said, as I slid over the parapet. 'I'll have a few hours' sleep now.'

But there was no rest for me. A few of our men, weary of the monotony of the dug-out, had crept up to the German trench, where they amused themselves by flinging bombs on the enemy. As if they had not had enough fighting!

On my return they were coming back in certain stages of demolition. One with a bullet in his foot, another with a shell-splinter in his cheek, and a third without a thumb.

These had to be dressed and taken into Maroc before dawn.

A stretcher-bearer at the front has little of the excitement of war, and weary hours of dull work come his way when the excitement is over.

CHAPTER 14

THE CHAPLAIN

The moon looks down upon a ghost-like figure,
Delving a furrow in the cold, damp sod,
The grave is ready, and the lonely digger
Leaves the departed to their rest and God.
I shape a little cross and plant it deep
To mark the dug-out where my comrades sleep.

'I wish I was in the Ladies' Volunteer Corps,' said Bill Teake next day, as he sat on the fire-step of the trench and looked at the illustrated daily which had been used in packing a parcel from home.

'Why?' I asked.

'They were in bathing last week,' said Teake. 'Their picture is here; fine girls they are, too! Oh, blimey!' Bill exclaimed as he glanced at the date on the paper. 'This 'ere photo was took last June.'

'And this is the 28th of September,' said Pryor.

We needed a rest now, but we still were in the trenches by the village, holding on and hoping that fresh troops would come up and relieve us.

'Anything about the war in that paper, Bill?' someone asked.

'Nuthin' much,' Bill answered. 'The Bishop of — says this is a 'oly war . . . Blimey, 'e's talkin' through 'is 'at. 'Oly, indeed, it's 'oly 'ell. D'ye mind when 'e came out 'ere, this 'ere Bishop, an' told us 'e carried messages from our wives, our fathers an' mothers. If I was a married bloke I'd 'ave arst 'im wot did 'e mean by takin' messages from my old woman.'

'You interpreted the good man's remarks literally,' said Pryor, lighting a cigarette. 'That was wrong. His remarks were bristling with metaphors. He spoke as a man of God so that none could understand him. He said, as far as I can remember, that we could face death without fear if we were forgiven men; that it was wise to get straight with God, and the blood of Christ would wash our sins away, and all the rest of it.'

'Stow it, yer bloomin' fool,' said Bill Teake. 'Yer don't know what yer jawin' about. S'pose a bishop 'as got ter make a livin' like ev'ryone else; an' 'e's got ter work for it. 'Ere's somethin' about parsons in this paper. One is askin' if a man in 'oly Orders should take up arms or not.'

'Of course not,' said Pryor. 'If the parsons take up arms, who'll comfort the women at home when we're gone?'

'The slackers will comfort them,' someone remarked. 'I've a great respect for slackers. They'll marry our sweethearts when we're dead.'

'We hear nothing of a curates' regiment,' I said. 'In a Holy War young curates should lead the way.'

'They'd make damned good bomb throwers,' said Bill.

'Would they swear when making a charge?' I inquired.

'They wouldn't beat us at that,' said Bill.

'The holy line would go praying down to die,' parodied Pryor, and added: 'A chaplain may be a good fellow, you know.'

'It's a woman's job,' said Bill Teake. 'Blimey! s'pose women did come out 'ere to comfort us, I wouldn't 'arf go mad with joy. I'd give my last fag, I'd give – oh! anything to see the face of an English girl now . . . They say in the papers that hactresses come out 'ere. We've never seen one, 'ave we?'

'Actresses never come out here,' said Pryor. 'They give a performance miles back to the R.A.M.C., Army Service Corps, and Mechanical Transport men, but for us poor devils in the trenches there is nothing at all, not even decent pay.'

'Wot's the reason that the more danger men go into the less their pay?' asked Teake. 'The further a man's back from the trenches the more 'e gets.'

'Mechanical Transport drivers have a trade that takes a long apprenticeship,' said Pryor. 'Years perhaps –'

''Aven't we a trade, too?' asked Bill. 'A damned dangerous trade, the most dangerous in the world?'

'What's this?' I asked, peeping over the parados to the road in our rear. 'My God! there's a transport wagon going along the road!'

'Blimey! you're sprucing,' said Bill, peeping over; then his eye fell on a wagon drawn by two mules going along the highway. 'Oh, the damned fools, goin' up that way. They'll not get far.'

The enemy occupied a rise on our right, and a machine gun hidden somewhere near the trench swept that road all night. The gun was quiet all day long; no one ventured along there before dusk. A driver sat in front of the wagon, leaning back a little, a whip in his hand. Beside him sat another soldier . . . Both were going to their death, the road at a little distance ahead crossed the enemy's trench.

'They have come the wrong way,' I said. 'They were going to Loos, I suppose, and took the wrong turning at the Vallé Crossroads. Poor devils!'

A machine gun barked from the rise; we saw the driver of the wagon straighten himself and look round. His companion pointed a finger at the enemy's trench . . .

'For Christ's sake get off!' Bill shouted at them; but they couldn't hear him, the wagon was more than a quarter of a mile away from our trench.

'Damn it!' exclaimed Bill; 'they'll both be killed. There!'

The vehicle halted; the near-side wheeler shook its head, then dropped sideways on the road, and kicked out with its hind legs; the other animal fell on top of it. The driver's whip went flying from his hands, and the man lurched forward and fell on top of the mules. For a moment he lay there, then with a hurried movement he slipped across to the other side of the far animal and disappeared. Our eyes sought the other soldier, but he was gone from sight, probably he had been shot off his seat.

'The damned fools!' I muttered. 'What brought them up that way?'

'Wot's that?' Bill suddenly exclaimed. 'See, comin' across the fields behind the road! A man, a hofficer . . . Another damned fool, 'im; 'e'll get a bullet in 'im.'

Bill pointed with his finger, and we looked. Across the fields behind that stretched from the road to the ruined village of Maroc we saw for the moment a man running towards the wagon. We only had a momentary glimpse then. The runner suddenly fell flat into a shell-hole and disappeared from view.

'He's hit,' said Pryor. 'There, the beastly machine gun is going again. Who is he?'

We stared tensely at the shell-hole. No sign of movement . . .

''E's done in,' said Bill.

Even as he spoke the man who had fallen rose and raced forward for a distance of fifty yards and flung himself flat again. The machine gun barked viciously . . .

Then followed a tense moment, and again the officer (we now saw that he was an officer) rushed forward for several yards and precipitated himself into a shell-crater. He was drawing nearer the disabled wagon at every rush. The machine gun did not remain silent for a moment now; it spat incessantly at the fields.

'He's trying to reach the wagon,' I said. 'I don't envy him his job, but, my God, what pluck!'

''Oo is 'e?' asked Bill. ''E's not arf a brick, 'ooever 'e is!'

'I think I know who it is,' said Pryor. 'It's the Roman Catholic chaplain, Father Lane-Fox. He's a splendid man. He came over with us in the charge, and he helped to carry out the wounded till every man was in. Last night when we went for our rations he was helping the sanitary squad to bury the dead; and the enemy were shelling all the time. He is the pluckiest man in Loos.'

'He wanted to come across in the charge,' I said, 'but the Brigadier would not allow him. An hour after we crossed the top I saw him in the second German trench . . . There he is, up again!'

The chaplain covered a hundred yards in the next spurt; then he flung himself to earth about fifty yards from the wagon. The next lap was the last; he reached the wagon and disappeared. We saw nothing more of him that day. At night when I went down to the dressing-station at Maroc I was told how the chaplain had brought a wounded transport driver down to the dressing-station after dusk. The driver had got three bullets through his arm, one in his shoulder, one in his foot, and two in the calf of his leg. The driver's mate had been killed; a bullet pierced his brain.

The London Irish love Father Lane-Fox; he visited the men in the trenches daily, and all felt the better for his coming.

Often at night the sentry on watch can see a dark form between the lines working with a shovel and spade burying the dead. The bullets whistle by, hissing of death and terror; now and then a bomb whirls in air and bursts loudly; a shell screeches like a bird of prey; the hounds of war rend the earth with frenzied fangs; but indifferent to all the clamour and tumult the solitary digger bends over his work burying the dead.

'It's old Father Lane-Fox,' the sentry will mutter. 'He'll be killed one of these fine days.'

CHAPTER 15

A LOVER AT LOOS

The turrets twain that stood in air
Sheltered a foeman sniper there;
They found who fell to the sniper's aim,
A field of death on the field of fame –
And stiff in khaki the boys were laid,
To the rifle's toll at the barricade;
But the quick went clattering through the town,
Shot at the sniper and brought him down,
In the town of Loos in the morning.

The night was wet, the rain dripped from the sandbags and lay in little pools on the floor of the trench. Snug in the shelter of its keep a machine gun lurked privily, waiting for blood. The weapon had an absolutely impersonal air; it had nothing to do with war and the maiming of men. Two men were asleep in the bay, sitting on the fire-step and snoring loudly. A third man leant over the parapet, his eyes (if they were open) fixed on the enemy's trench in front. Probably he was asleep; he stood fixed to his post motionless as a statue. I wrapped my overcoat tightly round my body and lay down in the slush by a dug-out door. The dug-out, a German construction that burrowed deep in the chalky clay of Loos, was crowded with queer, distorted figures. It looked as if the dead on the field had been collected and shovelled into the place pell-mell. Bill Teake lay with his feet inside the shelter, his head and shoulders out in the rain. 'I couldn't get in nohow,' he grumbled as I lay down; 'so I arst them inside to throw me a 'andful of fleas an' I'd kip on the doorstep. Blimey! 'tain' arf a barney; mud feathers, and no blurry blanket. There's one thing certain, anyhow, that is, in the Army you're certain to receive what you get.'

I was asleep immediately, my head on Bill's breast, my body in the mud, my clothes sodden with rain. In the nights that followed Loos we slept anywhere and anyhow. Men lay in the mud in the trenches, in the fields, by the roadside, on sentry, and out on listening patrols between the lines. I was asleep for about five minutes when someone woke me up. I got to my feet, shivering with cold.

'What's up?' I asked the soldier who had shaken me from my slumber. He was standing opposite, leaning against the parados and yawning.

'There's a bloke in the next dug-out as 'as got wounded,' said the man. ''E needs someone to dress 'is wound an' take 'im to the dressin'-station. 'E 'as just crawled in from the fields.'

'All right,' I replied. 'I'll go along and see him.'

A stairway led down to the dug-out; an officer lay asleep at the entrance, and a lone cat lay curled up on the second step. At the bottom of the stair was a bundle of khaki, moaning feebly.

'Much hurt?' I asked.

'Feelin' a bit rotten,' replied a smothered voice.

'Where's your wound?'

'On my left arm.'

'What is your regiment?' I asked, fumbling at the man's sleeve.

'The East Yorks,' was the reply to my question. 'I was comin' up the trench that's piled with dead Germans. I couldn't crawl over them all the way, they smelt so bad. I got up and tried to walk; then a sniper got me.'

'Where's your regiment?' I asked.

'I don't know,' was the answer. 'I got lost and I went lookin' for my mates. I came into a trench that was crowded with Germans.'

'There's where you got hit,' I said.

'No; they were Germans that wasn't dead,' came the surprising reply. 'They were cooking food.'

'When was this?' I asked.

'Yesterday, just as it was growin' dusk,' said the wounded man in a weary voice. 'Then the Germans saw me and they began to shout and they caught hold of their rifles. I jumped over the trench and made off with bullets whizzin' all round me. I tripped and fell into a shell-hole and I lay there until it was very dark. Then I got into the English trenches. I 'ad a sleep till mornin', then I set off to look for my regiment.'

While he was speaking I had lit the candle which I always carried in my pocket and placed it on the floor of the dug-out. I examined his wound. A bullet had gone through the left forearm, cutting the artery and fracturing the bone; the blood was running down to his finger tips in little rivulets. I looked at the face of the patient. He was a mere boy, with thoughtful dark eyes, a snub nose, high cheekbones; a line of down showed on a long upper lip, and a fringe of innocent curling hairs straggled down his cheeks and curved round his chin. He had never used a razor.

I bound up the wound, found a piece of bread in my pocket and gave it to him. He ate ravenously.

'Hungry?' I said.

'As a 'awk,' he answered. 'I didn't save nothin' today and not much yesterday.'

'How long have you been out here?' I asked.

'Only a week,' he said. 'The regiment marched from — to here. 'Twasn't 'arf a bloomin' sweat. We came up and got into action at once.'

'You'll be going home with this wound,' I said.

'Will I?' he asked eagerly.

'Yes,' I replied. 'A fracture of the forearm. It will keep you in England for six months. How do you like that?'

'I'll be pleased,' he said.

'Have you a mother?' I asked.

' No, but I've a girl.'

'Oh!'

'Not 'arf I aven't,' said the youth. 'I've only one, too. I don't 'old with foolin' about with women. One's enough to be gone on, and often one is one too many.'

'Very sound reasoning,' I remarked sleepily. I had sat down on the floor and was dozing off.

The officer at the top of the stair stirred, shook himself and glanced down.

'Put out that light,' he growled. 'It's showing out of the door. The Germans will see it and send a shell across.'

I put the candle out and stuck it in my pocket.

'Are you in pain now?' I asked the wounded boy.

'There's no pain now,' was the answer. 'It went away when you put the dressing on.'

'Then we'll get along to the dressing-station,' I said, and we clambered up the stairs into the open trench.

The sky, which was covered with dark grey clouds when I came in, had cleared in parts, and from time to time the moon appeared like a soft, beautiful eye. The breezes held converse on the sandbags. I could hear the subdued whispering of their prolonged consultation. We walked along the peopled alley of war, where the quick stood on the banquettes, their bayonets reflecting the brilliance of the moon. When we should get as far as the trench where the dead Germans were lying, we would venture into the open and take the high road to Maroc.

'So you've got a girl,' I said to my companion.

'I have,' he answered. 'And she's not 'arf a one either. She's a servant in a gentleman's 'ouse at Y—. I was workin' for a baker and I used to drive the van. What d'ye work at?'

'I'm a navvy,' I said. 'I dig drains and things like that.'

'Not much class that sort of work,' said the baker's boy. 'If you come to Y— after the war I'll try and get yer a job at the baker's . . . Well, I saw this 'ere girl at the big 'ouse and I took a fancy to 'er. Are yer much gone on girls? No, neither am I gone on any, only this one. She's a sweet thing. I'd read you the last letter she sent me only it's too dark. Maybe I could read it if the moon comes out. Can you read a letter by the light of the moon? No . . . Well, I took a fancy to the girl and she fell in love with me. 'Er name was Polly Pundy. What's your name?'

'Socrates,' I said.

'My name is plain Brown,' the boy said. 'Jimmy Brown. My mates used to call me Tubby because I was stout. Have you got a nickname? No . . . I don't like a nickname. Neither does Polly.'

'How does your love affair progress?' I asked.

'It's not all 'oney,' said the youth, trying to evade a projecting sandbag that wanted to nudge his wounded arm. 'It makes one think. Somehow, I like that 'ere girl too well to be 'appy with 'er. She's too good for me, she is. I used to be jealous sometimes; I would strike a man as would look at 'er as quick as I'd think of it. Sometimes when a young feller passed by and didn't look at my Polly I'd be angry too. "Wasn't she good enough for 'im?" I'd say to myself; usin' 'is eyes to look at somethin' else when Polly is about –'

'We'll get over the top now,' I said, interrupting Brown. We had come to the trench of the dead Germans. In front of us lay a dark lump coiled up in the trench; a hand stretched out towards us, a wan face looked up at the grey sky . . . 'We'll speak of Polly Pundy out in the open.'

We crossed the sandbagged parados. The level lay in front – grey, solitary, formless. It was very quiet, and in the silence of the fields where the whirlwind of war had spent its fury a few days ago there was a sense of eternal loneliness and sadness. The grey calm night toned the moods of my soul into one of voiceless sorrow, containing no element of unrest. My mood was well in keeping with my surroundings. In the distance I could see the broken chimney of Maroc coal-mine standing forlorn in the air. Behind, the Twin Towers of Loos quivered, grimly spectral.

'We'll walk slowly, Brown,' I said to the wounded boy. 'We'll fall over the dead if we're not careful . . . Is Polly Pundy still in the gentleman's house?' I asked.

'She's still there,' said the boy. 'When we get married we're goin' to open a little shop.'

'A baker's shop?' I asked.

'I s'pose so. It's what I know more about than anythink else. D'you know anything about baking . . . Nothing? It's not a bad thing to turn your 'and to, take my tip for it . . . Ugh! I almost fell over a dead bloke that time . . . I'm sleepy, aren't you?'

'By God! I am sleepy, Jimmy Brown,' I muttered. 'I'll try and find a cellar in Maroc when I get there and have a good sleep.'

The dressing-station in the ruined village was warm and comfortable. An R.A.M.C. orderly was busily engaged in making tea for the wounded who lay crowded in the cellar waiting until the motor ambulances came up. Some had waited for twenty-four hours. Two doctors were busy with the wounded, a German officer with an arm gone lay on a stretcher on the floor; a cat was asleep near the stove, I could hear it purring.

Mick Gamey, one of our boys, was lying on the stretcher near the stove. He was wounded in the upper part of the thigh, and was recounting his adventures in the charge. He had a queer puckered little face, high cheekbones, and a little black clay pipe, which he always carried inside his cap on parade and in his haversack on the march – that was of course when he was not carrying it between his teeth with its bowl turned down. Going across in the charge, Micky observed some half a dozen Germans rushing out from a spinney near Hill 70, and placing a machine gun on the Vermelles-Hulluch road along

which several kilted Highlanders were coming at the double.
Gamey took his pipe out of his mouth and looked on. They
were daring fellows, those Germans, coming out into the open
in the face of a charge and placing their gun in position.

'I must stop their game,' said Mick.

He lit his pipe, turned the bowl down, then lay on the damp
earth and, using a dead German for a rifle-rest, he took careful
aim. At the pull of the trigger, one of the Germans fell headlong, a second dropped and a third. The three who remained
lugged the gun back into Loos churchyard and placed it behind
a tombstone on which was the figure of two angels kneeling
in front of 'The Sacred Heart'. Accompanied by two bombers,
Mick Gamey found the Germans there.

'God forgive me!' said Mick, recounting the incident to the
M.O., 'I threw a bomb that blew the two angels clean off the
tombstone.'

'And the Germans?' asked the M.O.

'Begorra! they went with the angels . . .'

A doctor, a pot-bellied man with a kindly face and an innocent moustache, took off Brown's bandage and looked at me.

'How are things going on up there?' he asked.

'As well as might be expected,' I replied.

'You look worn out,' said the doctor.

'I feel worn out,' I answered.

'Is it a fact that the German Crown Prince has been captured?'
asked the doctor.

'Who?'

'The German Crown Prince,' said the man. 'A soldier who
has just gone away from here vows that he saw Little Willie
under escort in Loos.'

'Oh, it's all bunkum,' I replied. 'I suppose the man has had
too much rum.'

The doctor laughed.

'Well, sit down and I'll see if I can get you a cup of tea,' he
said in a kindly voice, and at his word I sat down on the floor.
I was conscious of nothing further until the following noon. I
awoke to find myself in a cellar, wrapped in blankets and lying
on a stretcher. I went upstairs and out into the street and found
that I had been sleeping in the cellar of the house adjoining the
dressing-station.

I called to mind Jimmy Brown, his story of Polly Pundy;
his tale of passion told on the field of death, his wound and

his luck. A week in France only, and now going back again to England, to Polly Pundy, servant in a gentleman's house. He was on his way home now probably, a wound in his arm and dreams of love in his head. You lucky devil, Jimmy Brown! . . . Anyhow, good fortune to you . . . But meanwhile it was raining and I had to get back to the trenches.

CHAPTER 16

THE RATION PARTY

In the Army you are certain to receive what you get.
— Trench Proverb.

A rifleman lay snoring in the soft slush on the floor of the trench, his arms doubled under him, his legs curved up so that the knees reached the man's jaw. As I touched him he shuffled a little, turned on his side, seeking a more comfortable position in the mud, and fell asleep again. A light glowed in the dug-out and someone in there was singing in a low voice a melancholy ragtime song. No doubt a fire was now lit in the corner near the wall, my sleeping place, and Bill Teake was there preparing a mess-tin of tea.

The hour was twilight, the hour of early stars and early star-shells, of dreams and fancies and longings for home. It is then that all objects take on strange shapes, when every jutting traverse becomes alive with queer forms, the stiff sandbag becomes a gnome, the old dug-out, leaning wearily on its props, an ancient crone, spirits lurk in every nook and corner of shadows; the sleep-heavy eyes of weary men see strange visions in the dark alleys of war. I entered the dug-out. A little candle in a winding sheet flared dimly in a niche which I had cut in the wall a few days previous. Pryor was sitting on the floor, his hands clasped round his knees, and he was looking into infinite distances. Bill Teake was there, smoking a cigarette and humming his ragtime tune. Two other soldiers were there, lying on the floor and probably asleep. One was covered with a blanket, but his face was bare, a sallow face with a blue, pinched nose, a weak, hairy jaw, and an open mouth that gaped at the rafters. The other man lay at his feet, breathing heavily. No fire was lit as yet.

'No rations have arrived?' I asked.

'No blurry rations,' said Bill. 'Never no rations now, nothink now at all. I 'ad a loaf yesterday and I left it in my pack in the trench, and when I come to look for't, it was gone.'

'Who took it?' I asked.

'Ask me another!' said Bill with crushing irony. ''Oo ate the first bloater? Wot was the size of my great grandmuvver's boots when she was twenty-one? But 'oo pinched my loaf? and men in this crush that would pinch a dead mouse from a blind kitten! Yer do ask some questions, Pat!'

'Bill and I were having a discussion a moment ago,' said Pryor, interrupting. 'Bill maintains that the Army is not an honourable institution, and that no man should join it. If he knew as much as he knows now he would never have come into it. I was saying that –'

'Oh, you were talkin' through yer 'at, that's wot you were,' said Bill. 'The harmy a place of honour indeed! 'Oo wants to join it now? Nobody as far as I can see. The married men say to the single men, "You go and fight, you slackers! We'll stay at 'ome; we 'ave our old women to keep!" Sayin' that, the swine!' said Bill angrily. 'Them thinkin' that the single men 'ave nothin' to do but to go out and fight for other men's wives. Blimey! that ain't 'arf cheek!'

'That doesn't alter the fact that our cause is just,' said Pryor. 'The Lord God of Hosts is with us yet, and the Church says that all men should fight – except clergymen.'

'And why shouldn't them parsons fight?' asked Bill. 'They say, "Go and God bless you" to us, and then they won't fight themselves. It's against the laws of God, they say. If we 'ad all the clergymen, all the M.P.s, the Kaiser and Crown Prince, Krupp and von Kluck, and all these 'ere blokes wot tell us to fight, in these 'ere trenches for a week, the war would come to an end very sudden.'

Pryor rose and tried to light a fire. Wood was very scarce, the paper was wet and refused to burn.

'No fire tonight,' said Bill in a despondent voice. 'Two pieces of wood on a brazier is no go; they look like two crossbones on a 'earse.'

'Are rations coming up tonight?' I asked. The ration wagons had been blown to pieces on the road the night before and we were very hungry now.

'I suppose our grub will get lost this night again,' said Bill. 'It's always the way. I wish I was shot like that bloke there.'

'Where?' I asked.

'There,' answered Bill, pointing at the man with the blue and pinched face who lay in the corner. ''E's gone West.'

'No,' I said. 'He's asleep!'

''E'll not get up at revelly, 'im,' said Bill. ''E's out of the doin's for good. 'E got wounded at the door and we took 'im in. 'E died . . .'

I approached the prostrate figure, examined him, and found that Bill spoke the truth.

'A party has gone down to Maroc for rations,' said Pryor, lighting a cigarette and puffing the smoke up towards the roof. 'They'll be back by eleven, I hope. That's if they're not blown to pieces. A lot of men got hit going down last night, and then there was no grub when they got to the dumping ground.'

'This man,' I said, pointing to the snoring figure on the ground. 'He is all right?'

'Dead beat only,' said Pryor; 'but otherwise safe. I am going to have a kip now if I can.'

So saying he bunched up against the wall, leant his elbow on the brazier that refused to burn and in a few seconds he was fast asleep. Bill and I lay down together, keeping as far away as we could from the dead man, and did our best to snatch a few minutes' repose.

We nestled close to the muddy floor across which the shadows of the beams and sandbags crept in ghostly play. Now the shadows bunched into heaps, again they broke free, lacing and interlacing as the lonely candle flared from its niche in the wall.

The air light and rustling was full of the scent of wood smoke from a fire ablaze round the traverse, of the smell of mice, and the soft sounds and noises of little creeping things.

Shells travelling high in air passed over our dug-out; the Germans were shelling the Loos Road and the wagons that were coming along there. Probably that one just gone over had hit the ration wagon. The light of the candle failed and died: the night full of depth and whispering warmth swept into the dug-out, cloaked the sleeping and the dead, and settled, black and ghostly, in the corners. I fell asleep.

Bill tugging at my tunic awoke me from a horrible nightmare. In my sleep I had gone with the dead man from the hut out into the open. He walked with me, the dead man, who knew that he was dead. I tried to prove to him that it was not quite the right and proper thing to do, to walk when life had left the body. But he paid not a sign of heed to my declamation. In the open space between our line and that of the Germans the dead man halted and told me to dig a grave for him there. A shovel came into my hand by some strange means and I set to work with haste; if the Germans saw me there they would start to shell me. The sooner I got the job done the better.

'Deep?' I asked the man when I had laboured for a space. There was no answer. I looked up at the place where he stood to find the man gone. On the ground was a short white stump of bone. This I was burying when Bill shook me.

'Rations 'ave come, Pat,' he said.

'What's the time now?' I asked, getting to my feet and looking round. A fresh candle had been lit; the dead man still lay in the corner, but Pryor was asleep in the blanket.

'About midnight,' said my mate, 'or maybe a bit past. Yer didn't 'arf 'ave a kip.'

'I was dreaming,' I said. 'Thought I was burying a man between the German lines.'

'You'll soon be burying a man or two,' said Bill.

'Who are to be buried?' I asked.

'The ration party.'

'What!'

'The men copped it comin' up 'ere,' said Bill. 'Three of 'em were wiped out complete. The others escaped. I went out with Murney and O'Meara and collared the grub. I'm just goin' to light a fire now.'

'I'll help you,' I said, and began to cut a fresh supply of wood which had come from nowhere in particular with my clasp-knife.

A fire was soon burning merrily, a mess-tin of water was singing, and Bill had a few slices of bacon on the mess-tin lid ready to go on the brazier when the tea came off.

'This is wot I call comfy,' he said. 'Gawd, I'm not arf 'ungry. I could eat an 'oss.'

I took off the tea, Bill put the lid over the flames and in a moment the bacon was sizzling.

'Where's the bread, Bill?' I asked.

'In that there sandbag,' said my mate, pointing to a bag beside the door.

I opened the bag and brought out the loaf. It felt very moist. I looked at it and saw that it was coloured dark red.

'What's this?' I asked.

'Wot?' queried Bill, kicking Pryor to waken him.

'This bread has a queer colour,' I said. 'See it, Pryor.'

Pryor gazed at it with sleep-heavy eyes.

'It's red,' he muttered.

'Its colour is red,' I said.

'Red,' said Bill. 'Well, we're damned 'ungry any'ow. I'd eat it if it was covered with rat poison.'

'How did it happen?' I asked.

'Well, it's like this,' said Bill. 'The bloke as was carryin' it got 'it in the chest. The rations fell all round 'im and 'e fell on top of 'em. That's why the loaf is red.'

We were very hungry, and hungry men are not fastidious.

We made a good meal.

When we had eaten we went out and buried the dead.

CHAPTER 17

MICHAELMAS EVE

It's 'Carry on!' and 'Carry on!' and 'Carry on!' all day,
And when we cannot carry on, they'll carry us away
To slumber sound beneath the ground, pore beggars dead and
gone,
'Till Gabriel shouts on Judgment Day, 'Get out and carry on!'

On Michaelmas Eve things were quiet; the big guns were silent, and the only sign of war was in the star-shells playing near Hill 70, the rifles pinging up by Bois Hugo, and occasional clouds of shrapnel incense which the guns offered to the god they could not break, the Tower Bridge of Loos. We had not been relieved yet, but we hoped to get back to Les Brebis for a rest shortly. The hour was midnight, and I felt very sleepy. The wounded in our sector had been taken in, the peace of the desert was over the level land and its burden of unburied dead. I put on my overcoat, one that I had just found in a pack on the roadway, and went into a barn which stood near our trench. The door of the building hung on one hinge. I pulled it off, placed it on the floor, and lay on it. With due caution I lit a cigarette, and the smoke reeked whitely upwards to the skeleton roof which the shell fire had stripped of nearly all its tiles.

My body was full of delightful pains of weariness, my mind was full of contentment. The moon struggled through a rift in the clouds and a shower of pale light streamed through the chequered framework overhead. The tiles which had weathered a leaden storm showed dark against the sky, queer shadows played on the floor, and in the subdued moonlight, strange, unexpected contrasts were evoked. In the corners, where the shadows took on definite forms, there was room for the imagination to revel in. The night of ruination with its soft moonlight and delicate shading had a wonderful fascination of its own. The enemy machine gun, fumbling for an opening, chirruped a lullaby as its bullets pattered against the wall. I was under the spell of an enchanting poem. 'How good, how very good it is to be alive,' I said.

My last remembrance before dozing off was of the clatter of picks and shovels on the road outside. The sanitary squad was at work burying the dead. I fell asleep.

I awoke to find somebody tugging at my elbow and to hear a voice which I recognised as W.'s, saying, 'It's only old Pat.'

'What's wrong?' I mumbled, raising myself on my elbow and looking round. The sanitary diggers were looking at me, behind them the Twin Towers stood out dark against the moon-light. Girders, ties and beams seemed to have been outlined with a pen dipped in molten silver. I was out in the open.

'This isn't half a go,' said one of the men, a mate of mine, who belonged to the sanitary squad. 'We thought you were a dead 'un. We dug a deep grave, put two in and there was room for another. Then L said that there was a bloke lying on a door inside that house, and in we goes and carries you outdoor and all. You're just on the brink of your grave now.'

I peeped over the side and down a dark hole with a bundle of khaki and a white face at the bottom.

'I refuse to be buried,' I muttered, and took up my bed and walked.

As I lay down again in the building which I had left to be buried, I could hear my friends laughing. It was a delightful joke. In a moment I was sound asleep.

I awoke with a start to a hell-riot of creaking timbers and tiles falling all around me. I got to my feet and crouched against the wall shuddering, almost paralysed with fear. A tense second dragged by. The tiles ceased to fall and I looked up at the place where the roof had been. But the roof was gone; a shell had struck the centre beam, raised the whole construc-tion as a lid is raised from a teapot, and flung it over into the street . . . I rushed out into the trench in undignified haste, glad of my miraculous escape from death, and stumbled across Bill Teake as I fell into the trench.

'Wot's wrong with yer, mate?' he asked.

I drew in a deep breath and was silent for a moment. I was trying to regain my composure.

'Bill,' I replied, 'this is the feast of St Michael and All Angels.

I've led such an exemplary life that St Michael and All Angels in Paradise want me to visit them. They caused the sanitary squad to dig my grave tonight, and when I refused to be buried they sent a shell along to strafe me. I escaped. I refuse to be virtuous from now until the end of my days.'

''Ave a drop of rum, Pat,' said Bill, uncorking a bottle.

'Thank you, Bill,' I said, and drank. I wiped my lips.

'Are we going to be relieved?' I asked.

'In no time,' said Bill. 'The 22nd London are coming along the trench now. We're going back to Les Brebis.'

'Good,' I said.

''Ave another drop of rum,' said Bill.

He left me then and I began to make up my pack. It was useless for me to wait any longer. I would go across the fields to Les Brebis.

The night grew very dark, and heavy clouds gathered overhead. The nocturnal rustling of the field surrounded me, the dead men lay everywhere and anyhow, some head-downwards in shell-holes, others sitting upright as they were caught by a fatal bullet when dressing their wounds. Many were spread out at full length, their legs close together, their arms extended, crucifixes fashioned from decaying flesh wrapped in khaki. Nature, vast and terrible, stretched out on all sides; a red starshell in the misty heavens looked like a lurid wound dripping with blood.

I walked slowly, my eyes fixed steadily on the field ahead, for I did not desire to trip over the dead, who lay everywhere. As I walked a shell whistled over my head and burst against the Twin Towers, and my gaze rested on the explosion. At that moment I tripped on something soft and went headlong across it. A dozen rats slunk away into the darkness as I fell. I got to my feet again and looked at the dead man. The corpse was a mere condensation of shadows with a blurred though definite outline. It was a remainder and a reminder; a remnant of clashing steel, of rushing figures, of loud-voiced imprecations – of war, a reminder of mad passion, of organised hatred, of victory and defeat.

Engirt with the solitude and loneliness of the night it wasted away, though no waste could alter it now; it was a man who was not; henceforth it would be that and that alone.

For the thing there was not the quietude of death and the privacy of the tomb, it was outcast from its kind. Buffeted by the breeze, battered by the rains it rotted in the open. Worms feasted on its entrails, slugs trailed silverly over its face, and lean rats gnawed at its flesh. The air was full of the thing, the night stank with its decay.

Life revolted at that from which life was gone, the quick cast it away for it was not of them. The corpse was one with the mystery of the night, the darkness and the void.

In Loos the ruined houses looked gloomy by day; by night they were ghastly. A house is a ruin when the family that dwelt within its walls is gone; but by midnight in the waste, how horrible looks the house of flesh from which the soul is gone. We are vaguely aware of what has happened when we look upon the tenantless home, but man is stricken dumb when he sees the tenantless body of one of his kind. I could only stare at the corpse until I felt that my eyes were as glassy as those on which I gazed. The stiffness of the dead was communicated to my being, the silence was infectious; I hardly dared to breathe.

'This is the end of all the mad scurry and rush,' I said. 'What purpose does it serve? And why do I stand here looking at the thing?' There were thousands of dead around Loos; fifty thousand perhaps, scattered over a few square miles of country, unburied. Some men, even, might still be dying.

A black speck moved along the earth a few yards away from me, slunk up to the corpse and disappeared into it, as it were. Then another speck followed, and another. The rats were returning to their meal.

The bullets whistled past my ears. The Germans had a machine gun and several fixed rifles trained on the Vallé crossroads outside Loos, and all night long these messengers of death sped out to meet the soldiers coming up the road and chase the soldiers going down.

The sight of the dead man and the rats had shaken me; I felt nervous and could not restrain myself from looking back over my shoulder at intervals. I had a feeling that something was following me, a Presence, vague and terrible, a spectre of the midnight and the field of death.

I am superstitious after a fashion, and I fear the solitude of the night and the silent obscurity of the darkness.

Once, at Vermelles, I passed through a deserted trench in the dusk. There the parapet and parados were fringed with graves, and decrepit dug-outs leant wearily on their props like hags on crutches. A number of the dug-outs had fallen in, probably on top of the sleeping occupants, and no one had time to dig the victims out. Such things often happen in the trenches, and in wet weather when the sodden dug-outs cave in, many men are buried alive.

The trench wound wayward as a river through the fields, its traverse steeped in shadow, its bays full of mystery. As I walked through the maze my mind was full of presentiments of evil. I was full of expectation, everything seemed to be leading up to happenings weird and uncanny, things which would not be of this world. The trench was peopled with spectres; soldiers, fully armed, stood on the fire-steps, their faces towards the enemy. I could see them as I entered a bay, but on coming closer the phantoms died away. The boys in khaki were tilted sandbags heaped on the banquette, the bayonets splinters of wood sharply defined against the sky. As if to heighten the illusion, torn ground-sheets, hanging from the parados, made sounds like travelling shells, as the breezes caught them and brushed them against the wall.

I went into a bay to see something dark grey and shapeless bulked in a heap on the fire-step. Another heap of sandbags I thought. But no! In the darkness of the weird locality realities were exaggerated and the heap which I thought was a large one was in reality very small; a mere soldier, dead in the trench, looked enormous in my eyes. The man's bayonet was pressed between his elbow and side, his head bending forward almost touched the knees, and both the man's hands were clasped across it as if for protection. A splinter of shell which he stooped to avoid must have caught him. He now was the sole occupant of the deserted trench, this poor, frozen effigy of fear. The trench was a grave unfilled . . . I scrambled over the top and took my way across the open towards my company.

Once, at midnight, I came through the deserted village of Bully-Grenay, where every house was built exactly like its neighbour. War has played havoc with the pattern, however: most of the houses are shell-stricken, and some are levelled to the ground. The church stands on a little knoll near the coal-mine, and a shell has dug a big hole in the floor of the aisle. A statue of the Blessed Virgin sticks head downwards in the hole; how it got into this ludicrous position is a mystery.

The Germans were shelling the village as I came through. Shrapnel swept the streets and high explosives played havoc with the mine; I had no love for a place in such a plight. In front of me a limber was smashed to pieces, the driver was dead, the offside wheeler dead, the nearside wheeler dying and kicking its mate in the belly with vicious hooves. On either side of me were deserted houses with the doors open and shadows brooding in the interior. The cellars would afford secure shelter until the row was over, but I feared the darkness and the gloom more than I feared the shells in the open street. When the splinters swept perilously near to my head I made instinctively for an open door, but the shadows seemed to thrust me back with a powerful hand. To save my life I would not go into a house and seek refuge in the cellars.

I fear the solitude of the night, but I can never ascertain what it is I fear in it. I am not particularly interested in the supernatural, and spiritualism and table-rapping is not at all to my taste. In a crowded room a spirit in my way of thinking loses its dignity and power to impress, and at times I am compelled to laugh at those who believe in manifestations of disembodied spirits.

Once, at Givenchy, a soldier in all seriousness spoke of a strange sight which he had seen. Givenchy Church has only one wall standing, and a large black crucifix with its nailed Christ is fixed to this wall. From the trenches on a moonlight night it is possible to see the symbol of sorrow with its white figure which seems to keep eternal watch over the line of battle. The soldier of whom I speak was on guard; the night was very clear, and the enemy were shelling Givenchy Church. A splinter of shell knocked part of the arm of the cross away. The soldier on watch vowed that he saw a luminous halo settle round the figure on the Cross. It detached itself from its nails, came down to the ground, and put the fallen wood back to its place. Then the Crucified resumed His exposed position again on the Cross. It was natural that the listeners should say that the sentry was drunk.

It is strange how the altar of Givenchy Church and its symbol of Supreme Agony has escaped destruction. Many crosses in wayside shrines have been untouched though the locality in which they stand is swept with eternal artillery fire.

But many have fallen; when they become one with the rubble of a roadway their loss is unnoticed. It is when they escape destruction that they become conspicuous. They are like the faithful in a storm at sea who prayed to the Maria del Stella and weathered the gale. Their good fortune became common gossip. But gossip, historical and otherwise, is mute upon those who perished.

CHAPTER 18

BACK AT LOOS

The dead men lay on the shell-scarred plain
Where death and the autumn held their reign –
Like banded ghosts in the heavens grey
The smoke of the conflict died away.
The boys whom I knew and loved were dead,
Where war's grim annals were writ in red,
In the town of Loos in the morning.

The ruined village lay wrapped in the silence of death. It was a corpse over which the stars came out like funeral tapers. The star-shells held the heaven behind Loos, forming into airy constellations which vanished at a breath. The road, straight as an arrow, pitted with shell-holes and bearing an incongruous burden of dead mules, dead men, broken limbers, and vehicles of war, ran in front of us straight up to and across the firing line into the France that was not France. Out there behind the German lines were the French villagers and peasantry, fearing any advance on our part, much more even than the Germans feared it, even as much as the French behind our lines feared a German advance.

The indefatigable shrapnel kills impartially; how many civilians in Loos and Lens have fallen victims to the furious 75s? In France the Allies fight at a disadvantage; a few days previously a German ammunition depot had been blown up in Lille, and upwards of a hundred French civilians were killed. How much more effective it would have been if the civilians had been Germans!

Our battalion was returning to the trenches after a fortnight's rest in H—, a village in the rear. We had handed over the trench taken from the Germans to the 22nd London Regiment before leaving for H—. In H— we got a new equipment,

fresh clothing, good boots and clean shirts; now we were ready
for further work in active warfare.

We were passing through Loos on the way to the trenches.
What a change since we had been there last! The adaptive
French had taken the village in hand; they had now been there
for three days. Three days, and a miracle had been accom-
plished. Every shell-crater in the street was filled up with
dead horses, biscuit tins, sandbags and bricks, and the place
was made easy for vehicle traffic. Barricades, behind which
machine guns lurked privily, were built at the main crossings.
An old bakery was patched up and there bread was baked
for the soldiers. In a cellar near the square a neat wine-shop
displayed tempting bottles which the thirsty might purchase
for a few sous.

The ease with which the French can accommodate themselves to any change has been a constant source of wonder to
me. In Les Brebis I saw roofs blown off the village houses
at dawn, at noon I saw the natives putting them on again; at
Cuinchy I saw an ancient woman selling *café-au-lait* at four
sous a cup in the jumble of bricks which was once her home.
When the cow which supplied the milk was shot in the stomach
the woman still persisted in selling coffee, *café noir*, at three
sous a cup. When a civilian is killed at Mazingarbe the children of the place sell the percussion cap of the death-dealing
shell for half a franc. Once when I was there an old crone
was killed when washing her feet at a street pump. A dozen
or more percussion caps were sold that day; every *garçon* in
the neighbourhood claimed that the aluminium nose-cap in
his possession was the one that did the foul deed. When I was
new to France I bought several of these ghastly relics, but in a
few weeks I was out trying to sell. There was then, however, a
slump in nose-caps, and I lost heavily.

The apt process of accommodation which these few incidents may help to illustrate is peculiar to the French; they
know how to make the best of a bad job and a ruined village.
They paved the streets with dead horses; drew bread from
the bricks and stored wine in the litter that was Loos. That
is France, the Phoenix that rises resplendent from her ashes;
France that like her Joan of Arc will live for ever because she
has suffered; France, a star, like Rabelais, which can cast aside
a million petty vices when occasion requires it and glow with
eternal splendour, the wonder of the world.

The Munster Fusiliers held a trench on the left of Loos and they had suffered severely. They had been in there for eight days, and the big German guns were active all the time. In one place the trench was filled in for a distance of three hundred yards. Think of what that means. Two hundred men manned the deep, cold alley dug in the clay. The shells fell all round the spot, the parados swooped forward, the parapet dropped back, they were jaws which devoured men. The soldiers went in there, into a grave that closed like a trap. None could escape. When we reopened the trench, we reopened a grave and took out the dead.

The night we came to relieve those who remained alive was clear and the stars stood out cold and brilliant in the deep overhead; but a grey haze enveloped the horizon, and probably we would have rain before the dawn. The trenches here were dug recently, makeshift alleys they were, insecure and muddy, lacking dug-outs, fire-places, and every accommodation that might make a soldier's life bearable. They were fringed with dead; dead soldiers in khaki lay on the reverse slope of the parapet, their feet in the grass, their heads on the sandbags; they lay behind the parados, on the levels, in the woods, everywhere. Upwards of eleven thousand English dead littered the streets of Loos and the country round after the victory, and many of these were unburied yet.

A low-lying country, wet fields, stagnant drains, shell-rent roads, ruined houses, dead men, mangled horses. To us soldiers this was the only apparent result of the battle of Loos, a battle in which we fought at the start, a battle which was not yet ended. We knew nothing of the bigger issues of the fight. We had helped to capture several miles of trenches and a few miles of country. We brought our guns forward, built new emplacements, to find that the enemy knew his abandoned territory so well that he easily located the positions of our batteries. Before the big fight our guns round Les Brebis and Maroc were practically immune from observation; now they were shelled almost as soon as they were placed. We thrust our salient forward like a duck's bill, and our trenches were subject to enfilade fire and in some sectors our men were even shelled from the rear.

Our plan of attack was excellent, our preparations vigorous and effective, as far as they went. Our artillery blew the barbed wire entanglements of the first German trench to pieces; at the second trench the wire was practically untouched.

Our regiment entered this latter trench where it runs along in front of Loos. We followed on the heels of the retreating Germans. Our attack might have been more effective if the real offensive began here, if fresh troops were flung at the disorganised Germans when the second trench was taken. Lens might easily have fallen into our hands.

The fresh divisions coming up on Sunday and Monday had to cope with the enemy freshly but strongly entrenched on Hill 70. The Guards Division crossed from Maroc in open order on the afternoon of Sunday, the 26th, and was greeted by a furious artillery fire which must have worked great havoc amongst the men. I saw the advance from a distance. I think it was the most imposing spectacle of the fight. What struck me as very strange at the time was the Division crossing the open when they might have got into action by coming along through the trenches. On the level the men were under observation all the time. The advance, like that of the London Irish, was made at a steady pace.

What grand courage it is that enables men to face the inevitable with untroubled front. Despite the assurance given by the Higher Command about the easy task in front of us, the boys of our regiment, remembering Givenchy and Richebourg, gave little credence to the assurance; they anticipated a very strong resistance, in fact none of them hoped to get beyond the first German trench.

It is easy to understand why men are eager 'to get there', as the favourite phrase says, once they cross the parapet of the assembly trench. 'There', the enemy's line, is comparatively safe, and a man can dodge a blow or return one. The open offers no shelter; between the lines luck alone preserves a man; a soldier is merely a naked babe pitted against an armed gladiator. Naturally he wants 'to get there' with the greatest possible speed; in the open he is beset with a thousand dangers, in the foeman's trench he is confronted with but one or two.

I suppose 'the desire to get there', which is so often on the lips of the military correspondent, is as often misconstrued. The desire to get finished with the work is a truer phrase. None wish to go to a dentist, but who would not be rid of an aching tooth?

The London Irish advance was more remarkable than many have realised. The instinct of self-preservation is the strongest in created beings, and here we see hundreds of men whose

premier consideration was their own personal safety moving
forward to attack with the nonchalance of a church parade.
Perhaps the men who kicked the football across were the most
nervous in the affair. Football is an exciting pastime, it helped
to take the mind away from the crisis ahead, and the dread
anticipation of death was forgotten for the time being. But I
do not think for a second that the ball was brought for that
purpose.

Although we captured miles of trenches, the attack in several
parts stopped on open ground where we had to dig ourselves
in. This necessitated much labour and afforded little comfort.
Dug-outs there were none, and the men who occupied the
trenches after the fight had no shelter from shell-splinters and
shrapnel. From trenches such as these we relieved all who were
left of the Munster Fusiliers.

The Germans had placed some entanglements in front of
their position, and it was considered necessary to examine their
labours and see what they had done. If we found that their
wire entanglement was strong and well fastened our conclu-
sions would be that the Germans were not ready to strike, that
their time at the moment was devoted to safeguarding themselves from attack. If, on the other hand, their wires were light,
fragile and easily removed, we might guess that an early offensive on our lines would take place. Lieutenant Y. and two men
went across to have a look at the enemy's wires; we busied
ourselves digging a deeper trench; as a stretcher-bearer I had
no particular work for the moment, so I buried a few of the
dead who lay on the field.

On our right was a road which crossed our trench and
that of the Germans, a straight road lined with shell-scarred
poplars running true as an arrow into the profundities of the
unknown. The French occupied the trench on our right, and a
gallant Porthos (I met him later) built a barricade of sandbags
on the road, and sitting there all night with a fixed rifle, he
fired bullet after bullet down the highway. His game was to
hit cobbles near the German trenches, from there the bullet
went splattering and ricochetting, hopping and skipping along
the road for a further five hundred yards, making a sound like
a pebble clattering down the tiles of a roof. Many a Boche
coming along that road must have heartily cursed the energetic
Porthos.

Suddenly the report of firearms came from the open in front, then followed two yells, loud and agonising, and afterwards silence. What had happened? Curiosity prompted me to rush into the trench, leaving a dead soldier half buried, and make inquiries. All the workers had ceased their labour, they stood on the fire-steps staring into the void in front of them, their ears tensely strained. Something must have happened to the patrol, probably the officer and two men had been surprised by the enemy and killed . . .

As we watched, three figures suddenly emerged from the greyness in front, rushed up to the parapet, and flung themselves hastily into the trench. The listening patrol had returned. Breathlessly they told a story.

They had examined the enemy's wire and were on the way back when one of the men stumbled into a shell-hole on the top of three Germans who were probably asleep. The Boches scrambled to their feet and faced the intruders. The officer fired at one and killed him instantly, one of our boys ran another through the heart with the bayonet, the third German got a crack on the head with a riflebutt and collapsed, yelling. Then the listening patrol rushed hurriedly in, told their story and consumed extra tots of rum when the exciting narrative was finished.

The morning country was covered with white fog; Bois Hugo, the wood on our left, stood out an island in a sea of milk. Twenty yards away from the trench was the thick whiteness, the unknown. Our men roamed about the open picking up souvenirs and burying dead. Probably in the mist the Germans were at work, too . . . All was very quiet, not a sound broke the stillness, the riot of war was choked, suffocated, in the cold, soft fog.

All at once an eager breeze broke free and swept across the parapet, driving the fog away. In the space of five seconds the open was bare, the cloak which covered it was swept off. Then we saw many things.

Our boys in khaki came rushing back to their trench, flinging down all souvenirs in their haste to reach safety; the French on our right scampered to their burrows, casting uneasy eyes behind them as they ran. A machine gun might open and play havoc. Porthos had a final shot down the road, then he disappeared and became one with the field.

But the enemy raced in as we did; their indecorous haste equalled ours. They had been out, too. One side retreated from the other, and none showed any great gallantry in the affair. Only when the field was clear did the rifles speak. Then there was a lively ten minutes and a few thousand useless rounds were wasted by the combatants before they sat down to break-fast.

'A strategic retreat,' said Pryor. 'I never ran so quickly in all my life. I suppose it is like this every night, men working between the lines, engineers building entanglements, covering parties sleeping out their watch, listening patrols and souvenir hunters doing their little bit in their own particular way. It's a funny way of conducting a war.'

'It's strange,' I said.

'We have no particular hatred for the men across the way,' said Pryor. 'My God, the trenches tone a man's temper. When I was at home [Pryor had just had ten days' furlough] our drawing-room bristled with hatred of some being named the Hun. Good Heavens! you should hear the men past military age revile the Hun. If they were out here we couldn't keep them from getting over the top to have a smack at the foe. And the women! If they were out here, they would just simply tear the Germans to pieces. I believe that we are the wrong men, we able-bodied youths with even tempers. It's the men who are past military age who should be out here.'

Pryor was silent for a moment.

'I once read a poem, a most fiery piece of verse,' he continued: 'and it urged all men to take part in the war, get a gun and get off to Flanders immediately. Shame on those who did not go! The fellow who wrote that poem is a bit of a literary swell, and I looked up his name in "Who's Who", and find that he is a year or two above military age. If I were a man of seventy and could pick up fury enough to write that poem, I'd be off to the recruiting agent the moment the last line was penned, and I'd tell the most damnable lies to get off and have a smack at the Hun. But that literary swell hasn't enlisted yet.'

A pause.

'And never will,' Pryor concluded, placing a mess-tin of water on a red-hot brazier.

Breakfast would be ready shortly.

CHAPTER 19

WOUNDED

If you're lucky you'll get killed quick; if you're damned lucky you'll get 'it where it don't 'urt, and sent back to Blighty.
— Bill Teake's Philosophy.

'Some min have all the damned luck that's agoin',' said Corporal Flaherty. 'There's Murney, and he's been at home two times since he came out here. Three months ago he was allowed to go home and see his wife and to welcome a new Murney into the wurl'. Then in the Loos do the other day he got a bit of shrapnel in his heel and now he's home again. I don't seem to be able to get home at all. I wish I had got Murney's shrapnel in my heel . . . I'm sick of the trenches; I wish the war was over.'

'What were you talking to the Captain about yesterday?' asked Rifleman Barty, and he winked knowingly.

'What the devil is it to you?' inquired Flaherty.

'It's nothin' at all to me,' said Barty. 'I would just like to know.'

'Well, you'll not know,' said the Corporal.

'Then maybe I'll be allowed to make a guess,' said Barty. 'You'll not mind me guessin', will yer?'

'Hold your ugly jaw!' said Flaherty, endeavouring to smile, but I could see an uneasy look in the man's eyes. 'Ye're always blatherin'.'

'Am I?' asked Barty, and turned to us. 'Corp'ril Flaherty,' he said, 'is goin' home on leave to see his old woman and welcome a new Flaherty into the world, just like Murney did three months ago.'

Flaherty went red in the face, then white. He fixed a killing look on Barty and yelled at him: 'Up you get on the fire-step and keep on sentry till I tell ye ye're free. That'll be a damned long time, me boy!'

'You're a gay old dog, Flaherty,' said Barty, making no haste to obey the order. 'One wouldn't think that there was so much in you; isn't that so, my boys? Papa Flaherty wants to get home!'

Barty winked again and glanced at the men who surrounded him. There were nine of us there altogether; sardined in the bay of the trench which the Munster Fusiliers held a few days ago. Nine! Flaherty, whom I knew very well, a Dublin man with a wife in London, Barty a Cockney of Irish descent, the Cherub, a stout youth with a fresh complexion, soft red lips and tender blue eyes, a sergeant, a very good fellow and kind to his men . . . The others I knew only slightly, one of them a boy of nineteen or twenty had just come out from England; this was his second day in the trenches.

The Germans were shelling persistently all the morning, but missing the trench every time. They were sending big stuff across, monster 9.2 shells which could not keep pace with their own sound; we could hear them panting in from the unknown – three seconds before they had crossed our trench to burst in Bois Hugo, the wood at the rear of our line. Big shells can be seen in air, and look to us like beer bottles whirling in space; some of the men vowed they got thirsty when they saw them. Lighter shells travel more quickly: we only become aware of these when they burst; the boys declare that these messengers of destruction have either got rubber heels or stockinged soles.

'I wish they would stop this shelling,' said the Cherub in a low, patient voice. He was a good boy, he loved everything noble and he had a generous sympathy for all his mates. Yes, and even for the men across the way who were enduring the same hardships as himself in an alien trench.

'You know, I get tired of these trenches sometimes,' he said diffidently. 'I wish the war was over and done with.'

I went round the traverse into another bay less crowded, sat down on the fire-step and began to write a letter. I had barely written two words when a shell in stockinged soles burst with a vicious snarl, then another came plonk! . . . A shower of splinters came whizzing through the air . . . Round the corner came a man walking hurriedly, unable to run because of a wound in the leg; another followed with a lacerated cheek; a third came along crawling on hands and knees and sat down opposite on the floor of the trench.

How lucky to have left the bay was my first thought, then I got to my feet and looked at the man opposite. It was Barty.

'Where did you get hit?' I asked.

'There!' he answered, and pointed at his boot which was torn at the toecap. 'I was just going to look over the top when the shell hit and a piece had gone right through my foot near the big toe. I could hear it breaking through; it was like a dog crunching a bone. Gawd I it doesn't 'arf give me gip!'

I took the man's boot off and saw that the splinter of shell had gone right through, tearing tendons and breaking bones. I dressed the wound.

'There are others round there,' an officer, coming up, said to me. I went back to the bay to find it littered with sandbags and earth, the parapet had been blown in. In the wreckage I saw Flaherty, dead, the Cherub, dead, and five others disfigured, bleeding and lifeless. Two shells had burst on the parapet, blew the structure in and killed seven men. Many others had been wounded; those with slight injuries hobbled away, glad to get free from the place, boys who were badly hurt lay in the clay and chalk, bleeding and moaning. Several stretcher-bearers had arrived and were at work dressing the wounds. High velocity shells were bursting in the open field in front, and shells of a higher calibre were hurling bushes and branches sky-high from Bois Hugo.

I placed Barty on my back and carried him down the narrow trench. Progress was difficult, and in places where the trench had been three parts filled with earth from bursting shells I had to crawl on all fours with the wounded man on my back. I had to move very carefully round sharp angles on the way; but, despite all precautions, the wounded foot hit against the wall several times. When this happened the soldier uttered a yell, then followed it up with a meek apology. 'I'm sorry, old man; it did 'urt awful!'

Several times we sat down on the fire-step and rested. Once when we sat, the Brigadier-General came along and stopped in front of the wounded man.

'How do you feel?' asked the Brigadier.

'Not so bad,' said the youth, and a wan smile flitted across his face. 'It'll get me 'ome to England, I think.'

'Of course it will,' said the officer. 'You'll be back in blighty in a day or two. Have you had any morphia?'

'No.'

'Well, take two of these tablets,' said the Brigadier, taking a little box from his pocket and emptying a couple of morphia pills in his hand. 'Just put them under your tongue and allow them to dissolve . . . Good luck to you, my boy!'

The Brigadier walked away; Barty placed the two tablets under his tongue.

'Now spit them out again,' I said to Barty.

'Why?' he asked.

'I've got to carry you down,' I explained. 'I use one arm to steady myself and the other to keep your wounded leg from touching the wall of the trench. You've got to grip my shoulders. Morphia will cause you to lose consciousness, and when that happens I can't carry you any further through this alley. You'll have to lie here till it's dark, when you can be taken across the open.'

Barty spat out the morphia tablets and crawled up on my back again. Two stretcher-bearers followed me carrying a wounded man on a blanket, a most harrying business. The wounded man was bumping against the floor of the trench all the time, the stretcher-bearer in front had to walk backwards, the stretcher-bearer at rear was constantly tripping on the folds of the blanket. A mile of trench had to be traversed before the dressing-station was reached and it took the party two hours to cover that distance. An idea of this method of bringing wounded away from the firing-line may be gathered if you, reader, place a man in a blanket and, aided by a friend, carry him across the level floor of your drawing-room. Then, consider the drawing-room to be a trench, so narrow in many places that the man has to be turned on his side to get him through, and in other places so shaky that the slightest touch may cause parados and parapet to fall in on top of you.

For myself, except when a peculiar injury necessitates it, I seldom use a blanket. I prefer to place the wounded person prone on my back, get a comrade stretcher-bearer to hold his legs and thus crawl out of the trench with my burden. This, though trying on the knees, is not such a very difficult feat.

'How do you feel now, Barty?' I asked my comrade as we reached the door of the dressing-station.

'Oh, not so bad, you know,' he answered. 'Will the M.O. give me some morphia when we get in?'

'No doubt,' I said.

I carried him in and placed him on a stretcher on the floor.

At the moment the doctor was busy with another case.

'Chummy,' said Barty, as I was moving away.

'Yes,' I said, coming back to his side.

'It's like this, Pat,' said the wounded boy. 'I owe Corporal Darvy a 'arf-crown, Tubby Sinter two bob, and Jimmy James four packets of fags – woodbines. Will you tell them when you go back that I'll send out the money and fags when I go back to blighty?'

'All right,' I replied. 'I'll let them know.'

CHAPTER 20

FOR BLIGHTY

The villa dwellers have become cave-dwellers.
                                        – Dudley Pryor.

The night was intensely dark, and from the door of the dug-out I could scarcely see the outline of the sentry who stood on the banquette fifteen yards away. Standing on tiptoe I could glance over the parapet, and when a star-shell went up I could trace the outline of a ruined mill that stood up, gaunt and forbidding, two hundred yards away from our front line trench. On the left a line of shrapnel-swept trees stood up in air, leafless and motionless. Now and again a sniper's bullet hit the sandbags with a crack like a whip.

Lifeless bodies still lay in the trench; the blood of the wounded whom I had helped to carry down to the dressing-station was still moist on my tunic and trousers. In a stretch of eight hundred yards there was only one dug-out, a shaky construction, cramped and leaky, that might fall in at any moment.

'Would it be wise to light a fire?' asked Dilly, my mate, who was lying on the earthen floor of the dug-out. 'I want a drop of tea. I didn't have a sup of tea all day.'

'The officers won't allow us to light a fire,' I said. 'But if we hang a ground-sheet over the door the light won't get through. Is there a brazier?' I asked.

'Yes, there's one here,' said Dilly. 'I was just going to use it for a pillow, I feel so sleepy.'

He placed a ground-sheet over the door while speaking and I took a candle from my pocket, lit it and placed it in a little niche in the wall. Then we split some wood with a clasp-knife, placed it on a brazier and lit a fire over which we placed a mess-tin of water.

The candle flickered fitfully, and dark shadows lurked in the corners of the dug-out. A mouse peeped down from between the sandbags on the roof, its bright little eyes glowing with mischief. The ground-sheet hanging over the door was caught by a breeze and strange ripples played across it. We could hear from outside the snap of rifle bullets on the parapet . . .

'It's very quiet in here,' said Dilly. 'And I feel so like sleep. I hope none get hit tonight. I don't think I'd be able to help with a stretcher down to the dressing-station until I have a few hours' sleep . . . How many wounded did we carry out today? Nine?'

'Nine or ten,' I said.

'Sharney was badly hit,' Dilly said. 'I don't think he'll pull through.'

'It's hard to say,' I remarked, fanning the fire with a newspaper. 'Felan, the cook, who was wounded in the charge a month ago, got a bullet in his shoulder. It came out through his back. I dressed his wound. It was ghastly. The bullet pierced his lung, and every time he breathed some of the air from the lung came out through his back. I prophesied that he would live for four or five hours. I had a letter from him the other day. He's in a London hospital and is able to walk about again. He was reported dead, too, in the casualty list.'

'Some people pluck up wonderfully,' said Dilly. 'Is the tea ready?'

'It's ready,' I said.

We sat down together, rubbing our eyes, for the smoke got into them, and opened a tin of bully beef. The beef with a few biscuits and a mess-tin of warm tea formed an excellent repast. When we had finished eating we lit our cigarettes.

'Have you got any iodine?' Dilly suddenly inquired.

'None,' I answered. 'Have you?'

'I got my pocket hit by a bullet coming up here,' Dilly answered. 'My bottle got smashed.'

Iodine is so necessary when dressing wounds. Somebody might get hit during the night . . .

'I'll go to the dressing-station and get some,' I said to Dilly. 'You can have a sleep.'

I put my coat on and went out, clambered up the rain-sodden parados and got out into the open where a shell-hole yawned at every step, and where the dead lay unburied. A thin mist lay low, and solitary trees stood up from a sea of milk, aloof, immobile. The sharp, penetrating stench of wasting flesh filled the air.

I suddenly came across two lone figures digging a hole in the ground. I stood still for a moment and watched them. One worked with a pick, the other with a shovel, and both men panted as they toiled. When a star-shell went up they threw themselves flat to earth and rose to resume their labours as the light died away.

Three stiff and rigid bundles wrapped in khaki lay on the ground near the diggers, and, having dug the hole deep and wide, the diggers turned to the bundles, tied a string round each in turn, pulled them forward and shoved them into the hole. Thus were three soldiers buried.

I stopped for a moment beside the grave.

'Hard at work, boys?' I said.

'Getting a few of them under,' said one of the diggers. 'By God, it makes one sweat, this work. Have you seen a dog about at all?' was the man's sudden inquiry.

'No,' I answered. 'I've heard about that dog. Is he not supposed to be a German in disguise?'

'He's old Nick in disguise,' said the digger. 'He feeds on the dead, the dirty swine. I don't like it all. Look! there's the dog again.'

Something long, black and ghostly took shape in the mist ten yards away and stood there for a moment as if inspecting us. A strange thrill ran through my body.

'That's it again,' said the nearest digger. 'I've seen it three times tonight; once at dusk down by Loos graveyard among the tombstones, again eating a dead body, and now – some say it's a ghost.'

I glanced at the man, then back again at the spot where the dog had been. But now the animal was gone.

An air of loneliness pervaded the whole place, the sounds of soft rustling swept along the ground: I could hear a twig snap, a man cough, and in the midst of all the little noises which merely accentuated the silence, it suddenly rose, long-drawn and eerie, the howl of a lonely dog.

'The dirty swine,' said the digger. 'I wish somebody shot it.'

'No one could shoot the animal,' said the other worker. 'It's not a dog; it's the devil himself.'

My way took me past Loos church and churchyard; the former almost levelled to the ground, the latter delved by shells and the bones of the dead villagers flung broadcast to the winds of heaven. I looked at the graveyard and the white head-stones. Here I saw the dog again. The silver light of a star-shell shot aslant a crumpled wall and enabled me to see a long black figure, noiseless as the shadow of a cloud, slink past the little stone crosses and disappear. Again a howl, lonely and weird, thrilled through the air.

I walked down the main street of Loos where dead mules lay silent between the shafts of their limbers. It was here that I saw Gilhooley die, Gilhooley the master bomber, Gilhooley the Irishman.

'Those damned snipers are in thim houses up the street,' he said, fingering a bomb lovingly. 'But, by Jasus, we'll get them out of it.' Then he was shot. This happened a month ago.

In the darkness the ruined houses assumed fantastic shapes, the fragment of a standing wall became a gargoyle, a demon, a monstrous animal. A hunchback leered down at me from a roof as I passed, his hump in air, his head thrust forward on knees that rose to his face. Further along a block of masonry became a gigantic woman who was stepping across the summit of a mountain, her shawl drawn over her head and a pitcher on her shoulder.

In the midst of the ruin and desolation of the night of morbid fancies, in the centre of a square lined with unpeopled houses, I came across the Image of Supreme Pain, the Agony of the Cross. What suffering has Loos known? What torture, what sorrow, what agony? The crucifix was well in keeping with this scene of desolation.

Old Mac of the R.A.M.C. was sitting on a blanket on the floor of the dressing-station when I entered. Mac is a fine singer and a hearty fellow; he is a great friend of mine.

'What do you want now?' he asked.

'A drop of rum, if you have any to spare,' I answered.

'You're a devil for your booze,' Mac said, taking the cork out of a water bottle which he often uses for an illegitimate purpose. 'There's a wee drappie goin', man.'

I drank.

'Not bad, a wee drappie,' said Mac. 'Ay, mon! it's health tae the navel and marrow to the bones.'

'Are all the others in bed?' I asked. Several hands work at the dressing-station, but Mac was the only one there now.

'They're having a wee bit kip down in the cellar,' said Mac.

'I'll get down there if you clear out.'

'Give me some iodine, and I'll go,' I said.

He filled a bottle, handed it to me, and I went out again to the street. A slight artillery row was in progress now, our gunners were shelling the enemy's trenches and the enemy were at work battering in our parapets.

A few high explosives were bursting at the Twin Towers of Loos and light splinters were singing through the air. Bullets were whizzing down the street and snapping at the houses. I lit a cigarette and smoked, concealing the glowing end under my curved fingers.

Something suddenly seemed to sting my wrist and a sharp pain shot up my arm. I raised my hand and saw a dark liquid dripping down my palm on to my fingers.

'I wonder if this will get me back to England,' I muttered, and turned back to the dressing-station.

Mac had not gone down to the cellar; the water bottle was still uncorked.

'Back again?' he inquired.

'It looks like it,' I replied.

'You're bleeding, Pat,' he exclaimed, seeing the blood on my hand. 'Strafed, you bounder, you're strafed.'

He examined my wound and dressed it.

'Lucky dog,' he said, handing me the water bottle. 'You're for blighty, man, for blighty. I wish to God I was! Is it raining now?' he asked.

'It is just starting to come down,' I said. 'How am I to get out of this?' I inquired.

'There'll be an ambulance up here in a wee,' Mac said, then he laughed. 'Suppose it gets blown to blazes,' he said.

'It's a quiet night,' I remarked, but I was seized with a certain nervousness. 'God! it would be awkward if I really got strafed now, on the way home.'

'It often happens, man,' said Mac, 'and we are going to open all our guns on the enemy at two o'clock. They're mobilising for an attack, it's said.'

'At two o'clock,' I repeated. 'It's a quarter to two now. And it's very quiet.'

'It'll not be quiet in a minute,' said my friend.

I had a vivid impression. In my mind I saw the Germans coming up to their trench through the darkness, the rain splashing on their rifles and equipment, their forms bent under the weight which they carried. No doubt they had little bundles of firewood with them to cook their breakfasts at dawn. They were now thanking God that the night was quiet, that they could get into the comparative shelter of the trenches in safety. Long lines of men in grey, keeping close to the shelter of spinneys sunk in shadow; transport wagons rumbling and jolting, drivers unloading at the 'dumps', ration parties crossing the open with burdens of eatables; men thinking of home and those they loved as they sat in their leaky dugouts, scrawling letters by the light of their guttering candles. This was the life that went on in and behind the German lines in the darkness and rain.

Presently hell would burst open and a million guns would bellow of hatred and terror. I supposed the dead on the fields would be torn and ripped anew, and the shuddering quick out on the open where no discretion could preserve them and no understanding keep them, would plod nervously onward, fear in their souls and terror in their faces.

Our own men in the trenches would hear the guns and swear at the gunners. The enemy would reply by shelling the trench in which our boys were placed. The infantry always suffers when Mars riots. All our guns would open fire . . . It would be interesting to hear them speak . . . I would remain here while the cannonade was on . . . It would be safer and wiser to go than stay, but I would stay.

'Is there another ambulance besides the one due in a minute or two coming up before dawn, Mac?' I asked.

'Another at four o'clock,' Mac announced sleepily. He lay on the floor wrapped in his blanket and was just dozing off.

'I'm finished with war for a few weeks at least,' I muttered. 'I'm pleased. I hope I get to England. Another casualty from Loos. The dead are lying all round here; civilians and soldiers. A dead child lying in a trench near Hulluch. I suppose somebody has buried it. I wonder how it got there . . . The line of wounded stretches from Lens to Victoria Station on this side, and from Lens to Berlin on the other side . . . How many thousand dead are there in the fields round there? . . . There will be many more, for the battle of Loos is still proceeding . . . Who is going to benefit by the carnage, save the rats which feed now as they have never fed before? . . . What has brought about this turmoil, this tragedy that cuts the heart of friend and foe alike? . . . Why have millions of men come here from all corners of Europe to hack and slay one another? What mysterious impulse guided them to this maiming, murdering, gouging, gassing, and filled them with such hatred? Why do we use the years of peace in preparation for war? Why do men well over the military age hate the Germans more than the younger and more sober souls in the trenches? Who has profited by this carnage? Who will profit? Why have some men joined in the war for freedom?'

Suddenly I was overcome with a fit of laughter, and old Mac woke up.

'What the devil are you kicking up such a row for?' he grumbled.

'Do you remember B—, the fellow whose wound you dressed one night a week ago? Bald as a trout, double chin and a shrapnel wound in his leg. He belonged to the — Regiment.'

'I remember him,' said Mac.

'I knew him in civil life,' I said. 'He kept a house of some repute in —. The sons of the rich came there secretly at night; the poor couldn't afford to. Do you believe that B— joined the Army in order to redress the wrongs of violated Belgium?'

Mac sat up on the floor, his Balaclava helmet pulled down over his ears, and winked at me.

'Ye're drunk, ye bounder, ye're drunk,' he said. 'Just like all the rest, mon. We'll have no teetotallers after the war.'

He lay down again.

'I know a man who was out here for nine months and he never tasted drink,' I said.

Mac sat up again, an incredulous look on his face.

'Who was he?' he asked.

'The corporal of our section,' I replied.

'Well, that's the first I've heard o',' said Mac. 'He's dead, isn't he?'

'Got killed in the charge,' I answered. 'I saw him coming back wounded, crawling along with his head to the ground like a dog scenting the trail.'

Sleep was heavy in my eyes and queer thoughts ran riot in my head. 'What is to be the end of this destruction and decay? That is what it means, this war. Destruction, decay, degradation. We who are here know its degradation; we, the villa dwellers, who have become cave dwellers and make battle with club and knobkerry; the world knows of the destruction and decay of war. Man will recognise its futility before he recognises its immorality . . . Lines of men marching up long, poplar-lined roads today; tomorrow the world grows sick with their decay . . . They are now one with Him . . . Yes, there He is, hanging on the barbed wires. I shall go and speak to Him . . .'

The dawn blushed in the east and grew redder and redder like a curtain of blood – and from Souchez to Ypres the poppy fields were of the same red colour, a plain of blood. For miles and miles the barbed wire entanglements wound circuitously through the levels, brilliant with star-clusters of dewdrops hung from spike, barb and intricate traceries of gossamer. Out in front of my bay gleamed the Pleiades which had dropped from heaven during the night and clustered round a dark grey bulk of clothing by one of the entanglement props. I knew the dark grey bulk, it was He; for days and nights He had hung there, a huddled heap; the Futility of War.

I was with Him in a moment endeavouring to help Him. In the dawn He was not repulsive, He was almost beautiful, but His beauty was that of the mirage which allures to a more sure destruction. The dew-drops were bright on His beard, His hair and His raiment; but His head sank low upon the wires and I could not see His face.

A dew-drop disappeared from the man's beard as I watched and then another. Round me the glory of the wires faded; the sun, coming out warm and strong, dispelled the illusion of the dawn; the galaxy faded, leaving but the rugged props, the ghastly wires and the rusty barbs nakedly showing in the poppy field.

I saw now that He was repulsive, abject, pitiful lying there, His face close to the wires, a thousand bullets in his head. Unable to resist the impulse I endeavoured to turn His face upward, but was unable; a barb had pierced His eye and stuck there, rusting in the socket from which sight was gone. I turned and ran away from the thing into the bay of the trench. The glory of the dawn had vanished, my soul no 'longer swooned in the ecstasy of it; the Pleiades had risen, sick of that which they decorated, the glorious disarray of jewelled dew-drops was no more; that which endured the full light of day was the naked and torturing contraption of war. Was not the dawn buoyant, like the dawn of patriotism? Were not the dew-decked wires war seen from far off? Was not He in wreath of Pleiades glorious death in action? But a ray of light more, and what is He and all with Him but the monstrous futility war . . . Mac tugged at my shoulder and I awoke.

'Has the shelling begun?' I asked.

'It's over, mon,' he said. 'It's four o'clock now. You'll be goin' awa' from here in a minute or twa.'

'And these wounded?' I asked, looking round. Groaning and swearing they lay on their stretchers and in blood-stained blankets, their ghastly eyes fixed upon the roof. They had not been in when I fell asleep.

'The enemy replied to our shellin',' said Mac curtly.

'Ay, 'e replied,' said a wounded man, turning on his stretcher. ''E replied. Gawd, 'e didn't arf send some stuff back! It was quiet enough before our blurry artillery started. They've no damned consideration for the pore infantry . . . Thank Gawd, I'm out of the whole damn business . . . I'll take damn good care that I . . .'

'The ambulance car is here,' said Mac. 'All who can walk, get outside.'

The rain was falling heavily as I entered the Red Cross wagon, 3008 Rifleman P. MacGill, passenger on the Highway of Pain, which stretched from Loos to Victoria Station.

THE END

KU-449-310

Dylan Moore has worked as a magazine editor, comprehensive school teacher, refugee support worker and chip shop counter assistant. His first book was *Driving Home Both Ways*, a collection of travel essays; his journalism has appeared in *Lonely Planet, Vanity Fair, Times Educational Supplement* and on BBC Radio 4. He is a Hay Festival International Fellow.

Newport Community Learning & Libraries

X051237

The item should be returned or renewed by the last date stamped below.

Dylid dychwelyd neu adnewyddu'r eitem erbyn y dyddiad olaf sydd wedi'i stampio isod.

Newport
CITY COUNCIL
CYNGOR DINAS
Casnewydd

Bett

WD

To renew visit / Adnewyddwch ar
www.newport.gov.uk/libraries

Three Impostors
3 Woodville Road,
Newport,
South Wales,
NP20 4JB

www.threeimpostors.co.uk

First published in 2021

Text © Dylan Moore
Cover design by Marc Jennings
Layout by Tomos Osmond

Printed and bound by Y Lolfa,
Talybont, Ceredigion, SY24 5HE

ISBN 978-1-8380628-1-1

For every copy of *Many Rivers to Cross* sold, a donation will be made
to the Sanctuary project, Newport.

For Eyob, for Mustafa,
and for seventy million and more

& in loving memory of
Leonard Innocent (1942 - 2020)

Contents

It is us today,
it will be you tomorrow.

Haile Selassie,
speech at the League of Nations, 1936

YOU ARE HERE

Your finger hovers over the red dot, reaching out like the one on the ceiling of the Sistine Chapel. You touch it as if checking in, as if registering your fingerprint, as if the cold, rain-streaked surface somehow confirms the truth of this bold claim – as if you have arrived.

'You are here.' In the undertow of your own breath you whisper the phrase and inside your ears it sounds like the shirr of a wave washing over a shallow shore. There is something comforting, definitive in monosyllables. You find these English words easy to say. Quietly, you repeat them. 'Here,' you say again, palm against the map, disbelieving that this city, scratched out before you on a square of aluminium, is really where you are, where you have, despite everything and everyone, washed up.

Beyond the red dot the city spreads like a bloodstain, as if somebody punched it in the mouth of its river. Its docks and reens, pills and wharves give way to stunted little terraces and scraps of inner city park. Further out, roads curve into crescents and cul-de-sacs and housing estate ring-roads. The map stops short of the mudflats and saltmarsh, the woods and hills that surround the city, ancient places that would, if only you could see and feel them, evoke memories of home.

Breaking Point

*There comes a point where we need to stop just
pulling people out of the river. We need to go
upstream and find out why they're falling in.*

Archbishop Desmond Tutu

A single photograph would come to symbolise the story, splashed across the front page of the local evening paper the day after the vigil. The picture shows a man with a distinctive blend of features, somewhere between Africa and Arabia, crouching near a three-bar railing, the gentle suggestion of a wave in its curve inwards from the riverbank. His jacket is slightly too big. Its folds hang from his languid limbs, creating contours and shadows. Behind him in soft focus, another man stands, hands on hips – an expression both of anger and despair – as if he wants to act on this, avenge the universe, but knows the futility of shaking a fist at the sky.

The crouching man seems lost, trapped in the torture chamber of his own mind. The whisper of a first moustache across his upper lip is tightened in the pained expression that plays across his gaunt, haunted, features. The long, delicate fingers of his right hand grip tight curls of oil-black hair. His left forearm rests on his knee, right hand dangling loose like a hurried sketch of a hanging. The limp leg of its index finger inadvertently points to the picture within the picture: a black and white portrait of his friend; relaxed, smiling, in happier times. Slipped inside a polythene document wallet and sellotaped between the second and third bars of the railing, in this picture the friend is wearing the leather jacket that had been discovered at the foot of the bridge; black leather, warm with damp, pockets empty but for a biro, ink run dry.

Other photographs begin to form an anatomy of grief: a pale-faced girl dressed head-to-toe in black – hijab, coat and jeans – leans in toward a tall white woman with wavy chestnut-coloured hair and a flowing mustard cardigan. A shorter woman in a jumper and jeans wipes a tear from her cheek, sleeve pulled down over her hand. A mild-looking man with a grey beard and a collared shirt looks on, the bright pink coat of a child folded over his arm.

In another image, a group of men – East Africans in their teens and twenties, the oldest in their early thirties – form a tribe in jeans and trainers. It is a kind of uniform, a kind of camouflage, too. In ones and twos, you wouldn't notice these young men walking down the street, disguised by their nonchalance, separated by their headphones, but here they are, gathered, and despite their disarray you would not hesitate to call them a community.

They studiously avoid the camera, heads bowed, hands clasped in prayer or desperation. Some stare at the screens of their mobile phones, as if answers might be found on social media timelines, or text messages from friends in distant places. Others stare into the middle distance. There are no ashes to be scattered, only the absence of one man accentuated by the presence of all these others. And the earth to which he would be returned lies five thousand miles upstream. There can be no meaning to a friend lost in a foreign river.

Once he saw it, David could not stop looking at the picture spread across the gleaming screen of his iMac. In his head he could already see it on the front of the paper. The minute hand was already edging toward four in the afternoon, and he felt the familiar daily pressure at his temples. Think of a headline. Recently he had favoured the one-word summary, partly as stylistic choice, but also – he admitted to himself now – out of laziness. And here he was, struggling – even for a single word.

He was, he realised, glancing at the clock again, singularly unable to summarise the emotion on the face of the young man in the picture, powerless to predict how a reader might empathise or understand. He tried to pillage the rickety filing cabinet in his brain, forty-nine years on the planet, the last twenty-five spent here – at a daily paper run from an industrial unit next to a carpet warehouse – looking through the bins of people's lives, their parochial melancholy triumphs, the moments of weakness that broke them and sent them to suicide or prison or up to no good. Come on, David, he thought, as he often did: file your copy, file and forget. This was the business, after all, of printing tomorrow's fish-and-chip wrapping.

But this picture had pulled him up short, he had to admit. The posture of this crouching man, brought low by grief and bewilderment, was at once familiar and strange. It was the juxtaposition that demanded his attention. A private tragedy played out in public, a foreign story on his home patch. That was, he began to realise, staring still at the gloaming screen, what it was that didn't compute. This was a story from a land so far away from the experience of his readers, of himself, it may as well be mythical. This tragedy did not belong here, and it was beyond expectation – beyond his remit, even – to think of a headline.

David knew the bare facts of the story, the ones that had already been picked up and repeated by the nationals. Missing presumed drowned. Personal effects found near the foot of the Transporter Bridge. Originally from Ethiopia. A failed asylum seeker. Friends called him a gentle soul. A man called Aman Berhane.

As he continued to study the anguished faces of the mourners at the vigil, the clock still ticking away, dusk descending slowly beyond the vertical pull-blinds at the window, David alighted upon what it was that frustrated him about quick-fire daily reportage. Over a couple of decades, through junior reporting and sub-editing, then as deputy, now as editor, David had grown expert at producing copy, explaining the who and the what, the when and the where, but he had it now: he couldn't explain the why.

Sometimes the why was wrapped up in the what. *Scrapped Tolls Boost Local Economy. County Celebrate Cup Win. Bypass Cancelled to Save Wetlands*. But this one wouldn't fit on an A-frame board. Maybe he would pitch it to the *Guardian*'s Long Read. He still dreamt of becoming a real journalist one day.

'Shit happens,' said Sean from Sales, walking past David's computer screen. And Sean from Sales was right, of course. It had become their mantra, particularly when there was a difficult story. *Toddler Loses Battle With Leukaemia. Drug Dealer Sentenced for Machete Attack. Steelworks Closure – 500 Jobs Axed.* Shit happens.

But this? David looked hard at the photo. This kind of shit was supposed to happen somewhere else. In the gaping space on his screen that was waiting for tomorrow's headline, David typed the single word WHY and three question marks, deleted two of them and then increased the font size to as large as was remotely sensible. He hit publish before he could think again.

In the car, Radio 4 carried the story of a government minister forced to resign over the creation of a hostile environment. At the traffic lights, David waited for a Slovak Roma family with seven or eight kids to cross the road, a blur of double pushchairs and zigzag runners in fur-lined hoods. Outside the kebab shop on the main road, he watched a group of Kurdish teenagers smoking cigarettes, each with one leg up against the window or one hand down the front of tight grey jogging bottoms tapered at the ankles to accentuate the branded tongues of trainers. Among them local youths stood sentry over mountain bikes. And in their North Face jackets zipped to the jugular, there was nothing to tell between them except the contrast between the dead-straight fringes on the locals and the studied coiffing of Kurdish hair.

David thought about Sean, who had voted Leave. He imagined his colleague standing in front of that notorious billboard – Breaking Point – and realised he had reached his own point of no return. He had refused to be drawn into conversations about the national news for over a year now, an increasingly untenable position for the editor of the local newspaper in a city that had overwhelmingly voted for Brexit.

He had his wife to thank for the lack of people opening their mouths at the photocopier. He'd lost count now of the times he had felt the conversation subside when he'd walked into the office. His staff knew better than to talk to a man with a black wife about too many Poles and Romanians. And the comment threads were full of it, too. David rued the day his paper's parent company had insisted he open up the website to public opinion. It was as much as he could take sometimes, to wade through the bile. It had become a job in itself, moderating the comments, but most of the ill-informed, poorly spelled dross seemed to slip through anyway, making David wonder sometimes why he continued to bother writing anything at all above the line. Facts made little difference to opinions.

When had he missed it, the point where his city had changed? It used to be solid Labour – warm, working class and open hearted. When his wife had gone to vote in the referendum, even the woman crossing names off the electoral register had laughed, within earshot as she was leaving: 'I bet she voted Remain!'

Claudie's father had come over from the Caribbean, not on the Windrush in '48, but not long after, on a different boat. Claudie had never known the name of it, nor even been interested to learn, because what did it matter to her half a century later having been born and bred here? But that woman at the polling station and all this talk of Windrush on the news had made her want to know more. At least the name of the ship.

He suffered with dementia now, her father, and it was doubtful she'd be able to get a straight answer anyhow. She'd expressed it to David one night when they were lying in bed and talking, for once, rather than staring at their phones, her watching Netflix with headphones in and him scrolling through the *Guardian*. She didn't know anything about her roots, she'd said.

And Claudie felt sure that, even though David had seemed to be only half-listening at the time, it was fuelling something in him lately, a dissatisfaction that left him coming home from work tired and irritable. Maybe it was finally time to give up news, she'd said, try something else.

David knew secretly that Claudie was right. News had become, to him, a kind of addiction. He'd reached that age where people are set in their ways, stuck in jobs or marriages they hate, or struggling with debts or drink or gambling or drugs. At least, thought David, I don't have those kinds of problems. Perhaps that's why he liked the news, too, preferred it to novels and films. People in the news had problems that were far bigger than David's, and far bigger than anyone's he knew. It gave him a sense of perspective and proportion, a reminder of how quiet and insignificant his life was, measured out in box-set dramas early in the week, the quiz at the Alex on a Thursday and an alternating Chinese or Indian on Fridays. Saturday they'd visit his parents in Cardiff or Claudie's mum down the road, or on a special occasion – birthdays, anniversaries – they'd get the train and stay overnight in London. Sundays he'd read the papers in bed or go for a jog while Claudie was in church or up at the Home dropping in on her father. Children had been a conversation for a while, but the mild disappointment had died away quietly, much like his dreams of proper journalism. He was content.

Claudie was cooking mutton, the aroma of Mr Brown's seasoning detectable from the front porch. 'Hello!' David shouted through the house, a large red-brick terrace built in the dying decade of the nineteenth century, back when the city had been a small engine of industry during Britain's imperial pomp.

'It'll be ready now in a minute,' Claudie shouted back. 'I'll call you to finish the rice.' David smiled at Claudie's perfect mix; local dialect and an inherited attitude to time, an encapsulation of South Wales Caribbean. Now in a minute might be any time this evening. He collapsed onto the sofa and dug into the space between cushion and armrest where he knew the remote would be.

On *Channel 4 News* a beach was strewn with orange life vests. David thought he recognised it from their holiday in Sicily a few years earlier, Claudie soaking in some Vitamin D while he walked the *Godfather* trail. Another migrant boat had gone down in the Med. Scores had drowned. The reporter was talking about the new government in Italy and an end to rescue missions, the difficult conditions at sea, organised criminals in Libya. As she continued to narrate, pictures flashed up: desperate refugees being rescued from boats. And apart from how exhausted and scared and desperate they looked, what David noticed was how much each one looked like the grieving man on the front of tomorrow's paper, and the missing man in the picture.

Fragments of poetry came into his mind. Teeming masses. Huddled something something shore. Wretched refuse. Emma Lazarus. Information stored under General Knowledge, ready for Thursday's quiz. And now the thought gnawed at him again: he knew who, what, where, when – facts – but he knew nothing of *why*.

In the hallway, he reached for his coat and untangled a long tassel-fringed scarf from its hook in the cupboard under the stairs. He met Claudie coming through the dining room to call him, apron fixed over a fluffy woollen jumper with a big heart on it and the Welsh word *Cwtch*, two sets of cutlery in her hand.

'Can you save me some mutton?' he asked, and kissed her.

'Where are you going, love?' she called as he opened the front door, letting in a cold blast of air and the sound of sirens from the street.

'I'm not sure,' said David, gesturing not to worry, a mixture of determination and wonder at himself.

As she watched him go, Claudie smiled to herself mysteriously.

David parked at the edge of the city centre where the chain stores cease and the pawn shops begin. He walked past the bookies and credit union, two mobile phone repair shops and a hostel for the homeless, a dilapidated church and the sort of Wetherspoons where people queue like it's the doctor's or post office. Charity shops, nail salons, a butcher, and a row that would have been empty if it hadn't been reclaimed for local arts projects, a valiant attempt to halt the city's seemingly terminal decline.

Crossing the square, he realised it had been months, maybe even years, since he had come to this part of town on foot.

'You alright, mate?' he was asked, almost immediately. A rake-thin girl in her early twenties. 'Up to anything?'

'Fine thanks,' said David, politely, the stench of her desperate poverty making him feel embarrassingly middle class. He took a sideways glance at her, furtively, anxious not to make eye contact. Pretty, but her hair was greasy and her collapsed cheeks covered with silver glitter.

'Want any business?' she said. Just like that. David had to check himself, repeat the question in his head, process the request.

'No, no thank you,' he said, feeling a sudden, unnecessary pang of guilt. One of his reporters had done an investigation about prostitution in the area that had interested, briefly, the national press; the salaciousness of underage girls servicing kerb-crawlers and long-distance lorry drivers in the road behind Lidl had the broadsheets wringing their hands and the red-tops licking their lips, but apart from further reputational damage to the city's poorest district, very little was done.

A moment's silence, awkward for him, nothing to her, and then: 'You wouldn't have a couple of quid, then, would you then, mate?'

David dug in his pocket, retrieved a crumpled fiver, wondering at himself as he handed it over, wordlessly, then continued down Commercial Road with that mix of interest and caution usually reserved for a foreign city.

As a young man, he had occasionally frequented the pubs down here, emboldened by the frisson only youth and the phrase 'the docks' could bring. It was here he had met Claudie, literally bumping into her as she came out of a midweek prayer meeting at the church and he stumbled out of one of the pubs, a cigarette dangling from his hand. She was beautiful, he apologised, and they each made secret promises to themselves to stumble upon each other at a similar time the following week.

Now all the pubs had been closed down, and immediately David thought of the Specials song. Everyone had sung 'Ghost Town' together. Back then it was that simple, or it seemed to be. Your mates were mostly white; a few were black, and they had the best records and the best weed; some of the kids at school were Asian, one or two might be Chinese, but they ran the cornershops and takeaways, didn't come out drinking or play football. They were part of the scenery.

Now as he continued past closed-down pubs, closed-down supermarkets and grand-looking buildings that looked like they might have been something important back when this really was a commercial road, he wondered at just how multicultural the area had become. David noted the names of the takeaways, tried to match them – pub quiz style – to the correct country. Turkey featured prominently. Anatalya Falafel, Izmir Kebab. Odessa Restaurant and Grill. Black Sea coast. Ukraine? Sometimes there was a geographically sequential stretch. Beirut Grill, Lebanon. Falafilo House, Syria perhaps? Babylon Barbers. Not a takeaway, but Iraq. Then there would be little blips, oriental outposts that predated the kebab's domination. Shanghai Chef, Taiwan House. Doner and Shish competed like Sunni and Shi'a, and there was a potential nuclear stand-off as the Lahore Curry House and Little Bombay faced each other down across the road.

David thought his way around the globe and noted the lack of American or Mexican food. You'd have to go back into town for that, although there was USA Nails, which seemed mainly to be staffed by Vietnamese. Then there was the Afro Hair Centre, where Claudie occasionally went to buy 'products'; Global Mini-Mart; Polski Sklep; a row of Slavic flags.

It felt good to be on assignment, a secret mission he had set for himself. But outside the Habesha Restaurant, David hesitated. For a start, he couldn't exactly place the country, even though this was the address he had found in the report on the missing boy.

The inside was obscured by flashing signs: he read 'Open' in English, recognised 'Halal' in Arabic. Above the door the name of the restaurant was curled into yet another script that David didn't know. Suddenly his pub-quiz general knowledge felt very parochial. Laminated cards tacked to the inside of the windows detailed highlights of the menu. David recognised some of the items: Chicken, Omelette, Spaghetti. Others he could imagine: Spiced Bread with Rice and Curry, Marinated Lamb. Others still were a complete mystery, despite being accompanied by photographs. What was Laham Ziar? Saltah? Ful Medames? On the door, he was surprised to note a food hygiene rating of 4, and then, rebuking himself for his prejudice, opened the door.

Inside, there were just three tables, which had been pushed together so that everyone could eat communally. He recognised the gathering, the same crowd as the vigil. The man whose photograph had swallowed half of David's afternoon looked like he'd not slept in days. David had stared at his picture so long, he felt like he knew him. But to Solomon, who announced himself now, David was a stranger.

'Hello – my name is Solomon,' was an invitation for David to explain himself. He felt a curious warmth from the Africans present, but the locals looked at him suspiciously. Maybe they knew who he was.

'I'm David,' he said. 'David McCarthy. I'm the editor of the *South Wales...*' He stopped, feeling a frost descend. 'I'm not here professionally,' he said, his tone suddenly almost pleading. 'Obviously,

I heard about what happened' – he wondered about using the young man's name – 'what happened with Aman – and I wanted to pay my respects. I couldn't be at the vigil this afternoon, but I saw the pictures, and –.'

David was running out of words. He couldn't – not really, not fully – explain why he was here, because he didn't know. 'If I can do anything to help...' he finished, more a generalised sentiment of sympathy than a genuine offer.

Solomon studied this strange white man still wearing his coat, glasses off-centre, brogues scuffed, scarf askew. He seemed windswept and unsure, and for the moment those things made him seem worth a modicum of trust.

'Sit down,' he invited, indicating the only remaining empty chair. 'We are about to eat.' Encouraged by the nods of those around him, he sat and – ever the journalist – performed a surreptitious headcount, looking from face to face, making mental notes. At the Last Supper, there had been thirteen including Jesus before Judas made his getaway; here, there had been twelve until they had to shuffle up to make room for him.

It made David feel like a kind of Judas-in-reverse, a traitor sneaking uninvited through the back door; an interloper, sitting in the empty chair that should have been Aman's.

Four large silver platters arrived, each spread with what looked like a giant pancake, pockmarked with air bubbles like crumpets. The Africans ate silently, fingers working easily, ripping small sections from the edges, using them to scoop the various foodstuffs that one of the women was ladling on top. Bright orange lentils. Spicy, finely chopped meat. A yellowish dhal.

'This is *injera*,' Solomon explained, for the benefit of those who had not eaten it before, and David took comfort that he was not the only one for whom this whole experience was new. Eating communally, with your hands. Already he felt a bridge had been crossed.

The short white woman who had worn the jumper and jeans at the vigil was now in a flower-print dress and a cardigan. She passed him a can of Coke, which David was glad to open, just to give his hands something else to do.

'I'm Leah,' she said and smiled. 'I run the Diversity Project.' David returned the smile, though he felt a pang of guilt that he had not met Leah before. She'd received an MBE a couple of years previously for her work with homeless people and had been on the front of the paper. He wondered whether to congratulate her, decided it was too late, and promised himself he'd get out of the office more in the new year.

'When did you last see Aman?' she asked. It was not an unreasonable question, given that he was here.

He was grateful that in his silence, Graham, the grey-bearded man, sitting on his left, took up the question. He'd apparently seen Aman last at a pottery class in the arts centre, just a few days before. Aman had refused to make a pot, instead expertly crafting a clay goat. 'It looked real,' said Graham. 'It made me realise how much time he must have spent with the animals as a boy. He talked about how he had grown up looking after his father's livestock. It was much more interesting than making a pot.'

Leah had last seen him at the Diversity Project, the day before he went missing. He'd gone in to ask for help posting a parcel. She'd sent one of the volunteers down to the post office with him, and was kicking herself now because they'd come back without a receipt or any record of the address where the parcel had gone.

'If we just knew where that parcel had gone, and what was in it, and who it was addressed to, we might know what Aman was thinking,' she said. 'On that day.'

As they ate, the conversation oscillated between reflective silence and these snippets of insight into a life. The Africans fell into talking their own language. David asked and Leah said it was Amharic, the script above the door. 'Habesha is how Ethiopian and Eritrean peoples are referred to in Arabic,' she explained. She lowered her voice: 'It's also a way of glossing over differences between them. There's a few different languages and ethnic groups here, actually.'

She pointed out a set of drawings on the wall, each depicting a different tribe, slightly different features, a vague sense of national costume. Tigray, Amhara, Oromo, Sidama. David studied them and decided that he couldn't tell the difference. 'A bit like saying we're from the British Isles, rather than distinguishing Welsh, Scottish, Irish, Cornish?' he asked.

'Or European!' said Leah.

'Exactly!' David enjoyed the connection he had made with Leah. Knowing she was enjoying his company and that she was a good person made him feel like a better person himself. He wondered if she knew Claudie, from church circles perhaps. Probably.

Another painting was mounted on a panel of wood and reminded David of Byzantine religious murals. He remembered Ethiopia had an Orthodox Church, although this picture was an entirely secular scene. Three men sat chatting in sandals and white robes while a young woman with intricately braided hair looked on, smiling as she poured coffee into small white cups on a silver tray. Over a coal fire, another woman ground out the coffee beans in a large black pot. Behind her on a shelf were stacked various pots and urns and other vessels.

As coffee arrived in the real world, David's thoughts drifted away. He thought of his brother out in Torrevieja, with his day-late *Daily Mail*; bacon, egg and chips; cupboards stacked with Heinz beans and Custard Creams. He had realised what this place was, the Habesha Restaurant: an attempt to create a little piece of home in an alien land. And out there beyond the window was the worst Britain had to offer: poverty and prostitution and people who wanted foreigners to go back to their own country.

The coffee kept him awake that night. Senses heightened, David's mind replayed the events of the day: the photograph and the question he'd posed on the front of tomorrow's paper; the tang of alcohol and desperation on the breath of the prostitute; the warm spice of the sauce that came with the *injera*; the sweet bitterness of the coffee; the poems and prayers that followed; exchanging mobile numbers with Solomon; the cold walk back to the car, and parting company with Leah; the sight of the Transporter Bridge lit up against the sky at the end of Commercial Road. He had to admit: he'd rarely felt more alive.

And calmed by the rise and fall of Claudie's gentle snore, in the soft blue light from his phone David only faintly surprised himself as he tapped into Google: 'Flights London to Addis Ababa.'

Mudcrawlers

By a lonely harbour wall
she watched
the last star falling

The Fields of Athenry

It was *mild*, the day we went to the Wetlands. I am trying to learn these British expressions. The weather is so changeable here. One minute it can be sunny and the next it is giving hailstones. Some people say it is like *four seasons in one day*. But if the weather is just dull and it is not warm but not too, too cold, and if the sky is just plain white with cloud, I have learned to say that *it is mild*. British peoples, they talk about the weather a lot.

'Good morning, Selam,' says Leah. 'Well done for remembering your raincoat. You never know when the weather is going to turn.' I like Leah. She has very good heart. She has a lot of time for the asylum people.

I get into the minibus and sit by Asha. Asha is from Sri Lanka, and she doesn't speak very, very much, so I like sitting *beside* her because it means I don't have to talk.

Sometimes if I sit by a British, or especially if it is someone from my country, then I feel like I have to talk even when I don't feel like talking. With Asha, you can just sit in silence and drink coffee, no problem. Sometimes when you talk, that is when your problems begin. Even the simple questions. What is your name? Where are you from? Why did you...? I am too, *too* tired of talking about these things.

This is why people like the Diversity Group. They are not like Home Office, where you must talk again, again about every problem in your life, and then they say you are a liar. With Diversity, you can just drink coffee and talk about things like *mild*. Learn a little bit of English and sometimes forget about your life.

Today the forgetting is going for a walk, in a place called Wetlands. Leah has told us to wear strong shoes and a raincoat if we have one. From the word Wetlands, I think it is the ground not the sky that should be wet. But in Wales I don't take chances. At any minute it can rain.

On the minibus, Leah tells us more about the place. 'The Wetlands is a place where the nature is perfect for birds to live,' she says. 'We call it a natural *habitat*.' I like the way Leah talks. Her voice goes up and down like a very beautiful song. She uses the simple words, and slowly, so that many people can understand. On this one minibus, we have Rojîn from Kurdish, and Bakhita from Iran, Asha from Sri Lanka and Fatima from Somali. Me, Ethiopia and Lemlem, Eritrea. Some people's English is very good, but some others can only say *yes* and *no*, *hello* and *thank you*.

It is a trip for only women. Sometimes we do some trips together with the men, but mostly it is better if just the ladies because we are more relax. Even though today I am missing Aman, I am glad because even with Aman I would have to talk, and there are many things I don't want to tell, even to him. *Especially* to him.

'We are going to a Centre that looks after birds,' explains Leah. 'There are lots of different types of birds that come to the Wetlands because they can find shelter, and food. Because it is the autumn, some of the birds are getting ready to fly to Africa, where it will be warmer for the winter.' After ten minutes talking like this, we are coming to the edge of city. We drive past factories and warehouses and a big place where they are building new houses and then all of a sudden it is green. After that there are fields. I begin to breathe different, clean, clean air. And then finally I can smell the soil from the animals.

The only thing different to my home life is there is too much electricity here. Wetlands is a beautiful place with birds and trees and water, but also there is big power station and turbines spinning in the strong wind. I look out of the minibus at the pylons. They walk through the peaceful countryside like army, and I think about those birds – Leah says they are called *swallows* – flying high above the earth without passports or papers, free to come and go to the places where they will be warm.

At the Wetlands we meet Rory. He is a short man, just a few centimetres taller than me, around fifty years old, something like that, and his soft beard is grey with bits of ginger. I am fascinated by red hair, but I have learned to call it *ginger*, and not to ask people about it if I just met them. Rory wears a checked shirt and a dark blue baseball cap that looks like it has lived on his head for many years.

'Good morning ladies, I'm Rory,' he says. His voice sings like Leah's, but there is also something flat in his throat that sounds like steel, a kind of roughness that is also friendly. If I was a British, I could probably explain where his accent was from. I have learned that the Welsh people and English people can tell from which town somebody is coming only by listening to their voice, but for me sometimes they can not tell even that I have come from Africa. All they know from my voice is that I am not from here, so lots of times I try not to speak. Maybe then people will think I am one of the black persons who has been born and grown in this country, and they won't bother me with questions or words like *immigrant*.

'I hope you enjoy the walk today,' says Rory. 'It's a beautiful place to be, and it's great to get outside in the open air.' I can agree with Rory about this, but what he says next is wrong: 'And it's a lovely sunny day.' Then he adds: 'For Newport.' A few people laugh, so I think he may be joking, but I am not sure. I want to tell him it is more like *mild*, but he is talking again. Rory does not stop talking for nearly an hour.

'What we are walking along now is the Wales Coast Path,' he says, pointing to a small blue and yellow sign hidden in the *hedgerow*. 'Wales is a small country, but it has many miles of coastline. If you were to walk that way, it wouldn't take you long to reach England. But if you were to walk the other way,' Rory says, turning himself around and pointing into the west, 'you'd need to walk a total of eight hundred and seventy miles to reach the border with England again.'

He takes a stick and scrapes the rough outline of a map in the mud beneath our feet. 'Some people says Wales looks like a pig's head,' he tells us. From the shape he has drawn, we do not understand. None of us are from place with many pigs. 'To reach England this way,' he says, 'you'd need to head west, and then north, looping all the way around here, Cardigan Bay.' He points with his stick. 'And then east again. So, which way do we want to go?'

Rory doesn't wait for answer. He starts to walk to west. 'We don't want to go to England, do we?' he says. 'We want to go to Newport!'

Sometimes I am not sure whether Welsh people are joking when they say bad things for England. When there is rugby matches they do it more and more. It is very confusing humour. In my country, there are too, too many problems now with people saying they are Oromo, or they are Amhara, or they are Tigray, or they are the real Ethiopians or other people not want to be Ethiopians. Nobody is joking when they say these things, and many, many people killed.

I don't want to think about these things but it is good because we are all a little, little out of breath, and Rory keeps talking. We climb steep stone steps and then standing in a place we can see the coast ourselves. Last time I saw the sea I was being rescue, in small, small boat. But this is different. It is more like big brown river than deep blue sea. Here the water is flat and in pale, pale light, even the ripples on the water look grey.

We stand above the place where the water meets the land, and look across at gentle hills and rows of houses on the opposite side. 'Can you see the big H in the distance, there?' asks Rory, pointing. 'That's the Severn Bridge, the border with England. And this path passes right underneath it.' We all look at it across the water, hard to see against the white of the cloud.

Later, when we have walked together a little distance down the path to what he tells us is mouth of river Usk, Rory asks us if when we are walking we ever think about whose footsteps came before ours. All the time Leah tells me I should *just concentrate on putting one foot in front of the other*, so the answer really is no, but Rory makes us think about it.

When we come to a gate, he stops and we wait for Fatima and Bakhita to *catch up*. 'All this,' says Rory, pointing out across the water, 'was once land. After the last ice age, and the glaciers melted, the whole area became flooded with water. But once upon a time it was grazing land. Thousands of years ago, people brought their animals here to eat the grass. Out there, we have found the footprints of aurochs – like a big cow, deer, wolves, and, of course, birds.'

Rory very seem like teacher. I like the way he explains what was here before. I imagine animals he mentioned in a huge grassland stretching across the place we can now see just mud. A little distance further, a Coca-Cola can is floating like a tiny boat, bright red colour turned mild.

'Thirty years ago,' says Rory, 'there was a big storm, and after they cleared away the debris, a trail of footprints were discovered. Scientists have proven that the prints were made over six thousand years ago, during a period known as the Mesolithic, or the Middle Stone Age.'

Fatima frowns, thinking about what Rory has told us. 'How could they know if these footprints were not made last week?' she wonders.

'Carbon dating,' says Rory, as if you only have to ask one question and he will talk for another five minutes about any subject. He tells us wait where we are, on the safe side of the wall along the path. He goes the other side and brings a little, little mud between his finger and thumb.

Rory holds it up. 'This mud is special – *estuarine clay*. Inside this mud you can find peat deposits – soil – from six thousand years ago.' Rory talks about science, and secrets that are thousands of years old, about how this man who walked across the mudflats out toward the sea had *splayed* toes that show he was walking with no shoes, about how the impressions made by the soles of his feet became baked in hot, hot weather as the world warmed up after the ice age, about how the prints became filled with peat, about how many, many years later that storm washed away materials covering those footprints.

I wonder how if these people in the *Mesolithic* could not keep their secrets, how we possibly keep ours. I begin to worry about my own secret, hidden for now inside my own body. I look up at the clouds, which have started turning grey. I know a storm is coming.

'My ancestors walked across here too,' says Rory, turning back so we are again walking toward the Wetlands Centre, and his voice changes. He talks quiet, quiet. Some of his words are lost on the wind. He pulls at the peak of his baseball cap and rubs the side of his beard. Some of the ginger hairs show in sunlight.

'My name, my surname – my family name,' he says, 'is Mahoney. It's Irish.' He spells it out: M-A-H-O-N-E-Y. To me this says Ma Honey, sounding like a sweet mother in a story for children, but Rory pronounces it *Maarrnnee*. He can't help being like a teacher, asking questions. 'Does anybody know why there are so many Irish people in Newport? Local people, I mean – Welsh people, with Irish blood.'

I look at Leah, expecting that because she is a *local*, she will be the one to give Rory the answer. But when she *catches my eye*, she just gives a small shrug with one shoulder to tell me she is learning too.

'In the mid 1840s,' says Rory, 'there were a series of terrible famines in Ireland. The potato crop failed and millions of people were left to starve. Hundreds of thousands died and hundreds of thousands left the country. It was a national trauma.' As Rory talks I look at the other women, and try to imagine what they are thinking. It seems like it is not just Rory's voice that has *gone quiet*. Fatima is staring out into the place where the footprints were discovered. Rojîn is looking at her own feet. Lemlem is looking at me.

'Many of them washed up in Glasgow, or in Liverpool, or in Cardiff,' continues Rory, pointing out the next bay around the coast. 'But the ships' captains would be fined if they were caught bringing *paupers* into the country. So they would dump them here, in the mud of the Usk. Many people died, from fever and famine. Others were able to walk ashore, and went straight to the workhouse, still covered in this mud, where they might be lucky to be given a cup of soup. They called them...' Rory stops and changes his words. 'They called *us*... mudcrawlers.' Almost whispering now. 'For obvious reasons.'

High above us, the dark sky bursts into birds. Some thousand starlings swirl in wind, following one and then another leader, travelling in circles and then in lines, forming shapes like clouds. When we stop to watch, I can tell Leah is wanting us to enjoy the peace. Diversity bring us to places like this so that we can forget about the voices in our heads and the noise of guns and the letters from the Home Office. For a short moment I think I see in the shapes the birds are making a foot with splayed toes, a pouring of soup, and then the tiny kicking legs of a baby. But the birds move quickly, so I can't tell.

At the coffee shop, I sit next to Asha, hoping I will not have to talk. Leah visits the tables, smiling and asking if we want some tea or coffee, saying that don't worry it's from the Diversity. I nod quietly and say *coffee*. I don't know because I am not looking at Leah's eyes, but something is telling me that she knows the secret inside of me. When the teas and coffees come, carried on a tray by a young teenager, and everybody has finished talking about milk, shaking the little sugar packets one by one into their cups so that the drinks taste sweet, Leah comes to sit next to me. People from my country taking many, many sugars. Leah doesn't say anything at first. She doesn't need to, because she is so, so good at talks like this.

I am watching the tiny pieces of air floating around on the top of my coffee. It is not like the strong, black coffee from my country, it is a milky one with too many bubbles, looking like soapy water.

'You are very quiet today, Selam,' says Leah. 'Is there anything you would like to talk to me about?' For a little while I stare into my cup. The bubbles are circling around each other like a mating dance. And then I look up at her face, which looks very kind, and I say: 'Yes Leah, there is something.'

And because I am a woman, and she is a woman, and because we understand each other very well, I think I know that she knows what is the secret inside of me.

And because Leah is Leah, she knows what to do. So she doesn't say anything else. Just underneath the table, she reaches to my hand and holds it still.

After a long time looking out of the windows, watching the birds swooping and flocking and moving in a *murmuration*, she says in a low voice: 'I will come to the doctors with you. Don't worry about anything, Selam, I will arrange an appointment.' Outside the window the starlings look like someone has thrown a handful of seeds into the wind.

'Thank you,' I say, my voice catching at the back of my throat. 'Thank you, Leah.'

And then, because she says something British, I find my lips curling into small smile, at least little bit of hope. 'Don't mention it,' Leah says, and squeezes my hand.

On the way home in minibus, the atmosphere is like celebration. We have been taken out of our lives for a little while. Watching the freedom of those birds has been good for our souls, like a kind of going to church, but outside and it doesn't matter what religion you are. Here you don't have to make a confession of your sins, or listen to long prayers; you can just be in nature and talk to God.

Rojîn starts singing a Kurdi song, and although none of us know the words or understand the language, we begin to clap. Leah smiles when she sees me clapping. Then Bakhita starts a song from Farsi language and then Lemlem sings something song from Eritrea. I understand little, little Tigrinya. It is about home.

Then the rain that has been promising all afternoon begins its drumming on the windows of the bus. Rojîn asks Leah to sing a song from Wales. Rory takes it over in a booming voice like from the bottom of a cave. Afterwards he tells us that on Sunday evenings he sings in a choir for only men. It is nice to hear a Welsh man sing. Rory tells us the words are asking God for a clean heart. 'It's from a time long ago, when many, many Welsh people would go to chapel and church, not like today.'

As he sings I close my eyes and see many women in white shawls standing on the green of a mountainside. And then my phone rings. I answer it and learn that Aman is missing. And in that moment, everything has changed.

HOSTILE ENVIRONMENT

In the theatre café, only one table is occupied. A man sits with an Americano. It's black; the miniature milk-jug that came with it sits untouched. His jacket is black, too, leather with a turned up collar. Blue jeans. White trainers – brand new, Puma brand. He scrolls a social media timeline, white background, blue stripe flecked with a single red dot, a notification. Gently, he applies an index fingertip to the screen.

Jawar Mohammed has added a new video. He presses again.

'Are you here for the pottery class?' someone asks, but he doesn't hear.

Outside gulls whirl and wheel in the salted breeze, squawking noisily, shitting and gobbing, mobbing an unidentified predator. The wind-rippled river is almost still, downstream current and upstream tidal influx held in temporary suspension. A wall of glass offers a wide-angle vista on the avian drama. Angular architecture speaks the language of regeneration. Across the water, the new flats and houses rise like children's drawings, their windows simple squares, roofs zigzagging the underside of the clouds.

The cries of the gulls are drowned by the thickness of the glass, the low hiss of the coffee machine, the echo of chatter from the gallery. Another train slides into town across the bridge. Cars continue to glide. A cyclist rolls along past the new flats. The river continues to flow.

The footage is filmed shakily on a mobile phone. Uniformed men – police or army – are raiding a house, beating men with sticks. There is a cruel nonchalance to the violence, a kind of unspoken pleasure. Three uniformed thugs in military boots drag an unarmed teenager from a doorway and throw him to the floor. He flops like a rag doll, powerless. The only sounds are chaotic shouts from off-screen, heavy breathing from whomever is filming. A truck pulls up. More men, more swinging of sticks, more kicking. Then shots are fired. A crowd that had gathered – to watch, to help, to bear witness – scatters like scraps of paper. The boy is lifted into the truck. Off screen again, a sharp intake of breath.

The man presses the home button decisively, the phone defaulting to its neat rows of glowing icons. He frowns, unhooks the buds from his ears. The white of their trailing wires stands out against the black of his jacket and the brown of his skin.

A white man has appeared behind him again, gently touches his shoulder this time. 'Are you here for the pottery class?'

The black man stares, attempts a thin smile. 'Yes,' he says. 'My class here.'

Outside, a single kittiwake takes off downstream.

The
Feast of Saint Mike

Isn't this how all places once began? With refugees stopping at a river, a beach, a crossroads, and saying, we'll just pause here for a bit. Put on the kettle, kill a chicken.

A. A. Gill, 'Refugee Camp Café'

'*Mani newi yihe*?' said the voice on the other end of the line. 'Who is this, please?'

A few short hours before, I had clasped Aman's hand in mine. We had bumped shoulders in that half-embrace whose contours were a regular reminder of home. Now his disembodied voice seemed distant, an echo of another time and place, the *djangal* I had left behind.

'Who is this, please?' he repeated, tone on the edge of pressing red.

I swallowed, and when seconds later my voice emerged I found it strangely choked. Elation, apprehension, relief and – *was it?* – a touch of regret.

The others in the lorry – four of us had made it through – studiously bowed their heads, hunching themselves into private thoughts, making like they had not heard or understood or shared the emotions that strummed and strangled my vocal cords into this sudden bum note.

'It's Solomon,' I managed to say. At the other end of the line, I heard Aman shout freely with joy.

Moments earlier, I had received a text message: *Welcome to the United Kingdom. Call & text EU and other EEA numbers & get online using your allowance at no extra cost here. It's then 3p/min 2p/SMS 1p/MB. Calls & texts are free to receive. Data use over 15GB but within your allowance incurs a surcharge of 0.50p/MB. For full charging info call +447770171717.*

It was not the way I had expected to be welcomed to The

Promised Land, olive branch delivered not by a dove but by Lycamobile.

'We made it!' I said.

The sound of Aman's laughter brought him, and the camp, momentarily closer. I could hear other voices in the background, other East Africans gathered around his phone, celebrating our success. I could picture the scene easily because I had spent nine months there in The Jungle, and perhaps every four or five days there were some Ethiopians and Eritreans we had come to know who made it to the UK.

Every time somebody reported a success we made a little party, gathered around a phone with cups of warm chai, maybe some dry biscuits. And when we weren't celebrating, we might see other groups around the camp cheering good news too. It was a strange kind of World Cup for climbing fences and jumping onto lorries, allowing small, small victories for countries that had never qualified for football. Afghanistan, Kurdistan, Syria, Sudan, Eritrea.

It was the Sudanese who had given us the idea for the Church. In the cold wet north European winter, men from the *wadis*, the dried up riverbeds of Darfur, had organised communal tents where people could go to pray. Walking back to our shelter, a wooden shack with a plastic sheet nailed through bottle-tops to make a roof, raincoats zipped around our faces and ankle deep in mud, we saw neat rows of trainers outside these little mosques, and Aman began to talk about how we might do something for our people too.

'Man, I didn't recognise your number,' he was saying now, and as he did I was wondering about our friendship. Through the project of constructing the Church we had become like brothers. From those first conversations between ourselves through talking with the volunteers from the French Catholic Mission and later with the priest from the Orthodox Tewahedo Church in Paris; from a crazy dream in a refugee camp, we had mobilised people from England to bring wooden beams to make the structure, people from France to bring sheets of metal to make the roof, and our people from Ethiopia and Eritrea to come to worship. Our Church could accommodate up to four hundred people at a time.

Then came the international press. I did interviews with CNN, the BBC, Al-Jazeera, and charged the journalists a fee so that we could buy a generator to power a microphone and lights. All we had wanted was somewhere to gather, somewhere to worship, a little piece of dignity amid the dirt of the camp. Now we were famous. The Parish of Saint Michael's in The Jungle became a symbol of hope.

'I'm not *Plus Trente-Trois* any more,' I told Aman, 'I'm *Plus Forty-Four*. I'm going up in the world, mate.'

The others in the lorry – Sami, Aklilu and Mo – stifled their giggles, listening to me interspersing Amharic with French and English, high on adrenalin and the enormity of our success. Endorphins swam in our eyeballs. Thin beams of light poured through the square we had cut into the thick red tarpaulin covering the cargo bed, and we all sat like Jonahs in the whale, hunkered between boxes of fish in the cool of the dawn.

We had left The Jungle at midnight, walking an hour and a half to the train station, away from Security at the port. At three in the morning I had lain beneath cold steel rails in the oil-black darkness, listening to the vibrations of trains along the tracks and the rise and fall of my own breath. 'Please God,' I had prayed, 'don't let any dog find me.'

As I related the story now to Aman, trying not to leave out any details, I became conscious that this was a story I would tell again and again. The more times you try and fail to cut through the fences, to enter the station, to avoid the police, to board the train undetected, the more you realise it is the details that make the difference between life and death. 'There is Devil in the detail, but the Angel is there too,' I tell him, knowing that he will understand.

It is Michael for whom we named the Church, the Archangel who led the Israelites to freedom as they wandered through the desert, waiting to cross the Red Sea.

I lower my voice, and on the other end of the line, Aman moves away from the little party of celebrants. He is going to sit in the Church, he tells me. And as he trudges through the mud, zigzagging through The Jungle, heading toward the cross at the top of Saint Mike's, I relay my experience, providing the instructions for his border crossing.

'The most important thing is that you go as a group. To succeed, you have to help each other. And each time, you get a little bit further. You have to notice where the cameras are, where the police hide themselves...' For the last five or six months, Aman has thought about nothing but the Church and providing for others, so I find myself relating the most basic of information. 'You need one person to cut the wires so you can squeeze through the fences.'

'Where do I get the cutters?' he asks.

So innocent. I laugh and wonder how he got this far. 'Aldi,' I tell him, and then: 'Don't pay any more than twenty-one euros. And you have to be like a snake. The only place in the train station where you can't be detected – by the cameras or by the police – is beneath the rails. You have to avoid the cameras to get to the platform, jump down onto the tracks and slide yourself underneath until the train arrives above you. Then slide along like a snake until you find the gap between the carriages.'

From beneath the rails, I imagine the lights I have seen from the platform: red and gold and green. On our flag, green is a reminder of African land; here it gives the train the signal to move off toward England. But everything is dark, and instead we must listen for the three long blasts of the klaxon, like waiting for the ram's horn to blow and the walls of Jericho to fall.

Three times I mimic the sound of the train's klaxon whistle down the phone to Aman. 'As soon as the third blast sounds, you don't have even one second to lose. If you want to keep your life, and get onto the train, you must stand up straight away, and quickly hang on to something.'

As I jumped up, two or three policemen saw me and came running down the platform. They must have seen Aklilu and Sami and Mo too, hanging onto loops of metal at the backs of the carriages for all their lives were worth, but it was too late for the police. They run after the train like Egyptians chasing the Israelites into the Red Sea, shouting *allez allez allez*, long batons swinging at their waists like spokes splintering from the wheels of chariots.

As the train gathers speed, the policemen who have made our lives hell in the camp become navy-blue dots in an impressionist painting as continental Europe disappears into soft focus like an evaporating cloud of tear gas.

I know it is a turning point in my life.

I cannot stop myself from smiling, and before the *gendarmerie* disappear from view altogether, I actually wave.

I cradle the memory. Like a newborn baby, now just a few hours old, I know it will be with me for the rest of my life. Like any story, I know the details will change with each retelling, but even if one day I have children and grandchildren, there will always be time to recall that wave at the police. Goodbye Jungle, goodbye France.

The lorry stops and suddenly the others go quiet. Above us the square of light has darkened, and from the shadows we hear a burst of laughter, a clanking sound, loud voices speaking English quickly. I gesture to the others, holding the index finger of my left hand to my lips and my phone in the air with my right. I draw it across my neck in a cut-throat gesture. We've been told by those who have gone ahead that in the ports they have scanners that can detect mobile phones, body-heat, even breathing. Four phone signals and four little clouds of carbon dioxide in a lorry full of dead fish would be a giveaway, and after all it has taken to get here – the train and the tunnel, the months of waiting in The Jungle, and before that the deserts and the seas, the border crossings in escape from our own countries – it would be a travesty if we were detected now. In the port, they can refuse you entry, but once you are beyond it you can claim asylum, and the endgame is in sight.

As we wait, eyes closed, willing our own hearts to stop beating in the long silence, I rehearse my story in my head. I know that in the near future I will sit across a desk from a stranger who will require me to recite every detail of my life, and how it was I came to leave my country. I imagine the room will have blank walls and a very small window. In fact, in my mind's eye the only difference between the room of interrogation and the inside of this lorry is the absence of fish.

I think about the question that started it all. *If there is no corruption, why are we still poor?* I think about the time I spent in prison for writing that article, for asking a simple question about our coffee industry, the second largest in the world, only behind Brazil. I think of my editor, still in jail, and all the magazines that have been closed down. I think about the concrete floor of my cell, the mosquitoes and the cockroaches.

When I open my eyes, the lorry is moving quickly. Aklilu climbs the stacks of fish boxes toward the bright again square and announces that we are in England. We take turns to poke our heads out of the cargo-bed like meerkats emerging from the sand, blinking wide-eyed into the pale light of morning. Outside the wind feels cold and the cars are driving on the left.

After all of the waiting, in the camp and under the rails and in the back of this lorry, a kind of impatience overtakes us. We exchange hugs and shoulder-bumps of delight, and then the others begin to make telephone calls. Each of them has a relative living in England: a brother who made it through Calais a couple of years ago; an aunt who has lived here since the time of the Derg; a cousin working as a university professor in London. I listen to them making arrangements, talking about beds waiting for them in cities called Plymouth and Leeds, and the repetition of this word *Croydon*, the place we must all attend in the next few days, to report our presence here, to hasten our claims for asylum and finally be free of our pasts. When this lorry stops, I will be on my own.

And then the lorry stops. The lorry stops and we wait. And the lorry does not begin to move for what seems like a very long time.

And then we crawl out of the square and see green hills and trees and feel the cold wind blowing across the motorway. Before we crawl along the roof of the lorry, scampering down like squirrels and then walking, calmly, away from the trailer and the unwitting driver who has been our saviour, I take a look through his side window. At the rear of the cab, beneath a flag – a red dragon walking across a green field – there is a small door beyond which the driver is sleeping, unaware of our presence until the time when he will discover the small square cut into the roof of his cargo-bed tarpaulin.

I am sorry for that.

When I step down from the lorry, the others have already disappeared. And here I am afraid to speak. I do not know the country. I do not know the people. I do not know the culture. If I ask somebody if they have seen another man who looks like he is from my country, or *what is the time* or *how can I speak to police*, how do I know that they might not say that *I don't know you*?

I look around. There is a petrol station and a supermarket and some places to buy food and a place called Days Inn, which looks like a kind of hotel with grey square windows and rows of solar panels across its roof.

From the edge of where the cars are parked, near some empty wooden benches nailed to empty wooden tables, I stand in the wind and watch the local people. They get out of cars and into cars. They stretch their arms and legs and roll their necks. They take babies and small children out of special seats in the backs of the cars. They walk into the building with their hands in their pockets and come out holding cups of coffee in paper cups with plastic lids and rings of corrugated cardboard to stop their fingers getting too hot. They walk toward the building, away from the building. I watch them eating French fries with their fingers, baguettes and burgers out of cardboard boxes, pastries out of paper bags. I watch them sip coffees and swig from slim red Coca-Cola cans with metal ring-pulls, observe the children drinking juice from cartons with tiny plastic straws.

I look at their pale faces, scrunched against the weather, and think how strange it is that they do not know that I am here.

Behind the low brick building with its rows of light-up logos advertising supermarkets, motels and fast food chains there is a low wooden rail and beyond it a thick hedge. Bushes and saplings have been planted to screen off the shops from the motorway. I walk briskly, swinging my arms as if I have just stopped my car because I want a coffee. I head across the car park diagonally, across the path of those going in and out of the building. I am heading toward the border rail.

I crouch in the bushes and my heart rate slows. I think of the words I said on the phone to Aman. You have to be like a snake. I listen to the hum of traffic from the road beyond the trees and look at the bright lights of the petrol station, green and white and yellow. Months in The Jungle have made life in the bushes seem normal. You have to be also like a jackal.

I think about the red jackals that live in the Bale mountains in the south of my country. They say there are only a few hundred remaining. In my language, we call him the *walgie* – the trickster. To survive in the wilderness, you have to be a trickster.

But now the terrain has changed. Later, I will phone Aman once more, and add to his instruction manual. To survive here, in car parks and petrol stations and supermarkets, you have to be a human.

I take off my trainers – handouts from the volunteers in Calais – and pull off my jeans, caked in dry mud from the fields of northern France, stained by oil from a British lorry and torn by the fence erected by the governments of two countries already separated by a channel of water. From my jacket, I fish out the things I need. Phone, notebook, pen. My small wooden cross dangles on a string. I hang it around my neck, touch the cross and whisper: 'Please Jesus, no more being like a snake. No more jackal, no more *walgie*. I want to be a human now.'

And I emerge, cold but clean. The jogging bottoms I have worn beneath my jeans make me feel free, as if those border crossing jeans can be left in the past. I cross the car park thinking about Lot's wife, and make it to the service station without turning into a pillar of salt.

Inside the building I follow the signs for the Gentleman toilets, and spend as long as I dare sitting in a cubicle, collecting my thoughts. I need to report myself to the police as soon as I can. This will help, people have said, with an asylum claim. But first I need to wash, and I need something to eat. On the inside of the door, somebody has written in marker pen: *SMASH CAPITALISM!* And someone else has added a sticker that says *Yes Cymru*.

Outside the cubicle, the lights shine brightly on the white tiles. I press the shiny silver tap on the red button where it says *Caution Hot Water* and splash my face, rub the heat of the running water into the creases in my neck and into the curls of my hair. I close my eyes for what feels like a long time, and when I open them I see in the mirror that I am standing next to another African man.

At first I think it is Sami or Aklilu or Mo, but this man is smartly dressed. He wears a shirt, ironed and pristine in midnight blue, and the gold band of a wedding ring on his finger. He is around forty years old and his face looks confident and calm. As he washes his hands with careful movements, lathering the liquid soap, I study his clothes in the mirror. I see the sharp pleats of his trousers and the polished shine of his shoes.

The man places his hands palms down into a drier that warms them like pieces of toast with a blast of warm wind. I study and mimic his movements, hoping that what I see in the mirror is an apparition of myself in the future. I place my hands into the toaster too, and think about his wedding ring. I wonder if his wife is from here or from home. I wonder who has ironed his shirt. Does his wife iron his shirts, or does he have a maid? How much does he earn in a year? Does he have a nice house? He must have his own car, to be here at this motorway services. Maybe he can take me to Croydon?

I follow the man past a vast communal sink and a vending machine selling condoms, sex pills, toothbrushes and mints. A few steps behind him in the tiled corridor, we reach the place where the women separate from the men, and I mutter a *salaam*, my voice croaking desperately. It is a question more than a greeting, an enquiry.

When the man turns his eyes on me I worry desperately that he is Kenyan or Jamaican or just a British person who just happens like the rest of humanity to trace his ancestry back to the Rift Valley.

But in his brief reply I hear the accent of Addis Ababa.

He looks at me quizzically and then decides to speak in English. 'Can I help you at all?' His language is polished, so good it sounds like he's from a film.

'Yes please,' I say, replying in kind, finding myself hoping that he thinks I speak good English. 'I have just arrived.'

Outside the toilets, we stand for a moment near some machines. One is for taking cash out; others are for putting cash in. A young white man in a white tracksuit and Adidas baseball cap is muttering at one while the lights flash, dancing across the screens of the gambling machine, a mesmerising whirl of reds and yellows and greens. An older man stands next to him in a red and black checked shirt, occasionally glancing sideways at the pair of us. He has close cropped hair receding backwards from the temples so that the front half of his head is bald. His eyes are slightly bloodshot and his face is the colour of fresh-cut pork.

In the moment we stop to watch, three spinning wheels arrive at a stop. Seven, and then seven, a brief pause before a third seven lands and a waterfall of gold coins gush into the tray, making a noise like thunder. It is his lucky day.

'Do you need some breakfast?' says the Ethiopian. He glances at my wooden cross. 'Today is the Feast of Saint Michael. We should be celebrating.'

I look up at the backlit pictures of food above the breakfast counter. There seems to be nothing but bacon, which we will not eat, even on feast days. Behind us, a toy car has space for a child to ride with two cartoon pigs, a big one with a pink dress and a little one with a blue t-shirt. I wonder if the Ethiopian has started eating bacon and sausages, and how long he has been in the UK. 'I just need some water and coffee,' I say.

'Don't worry,' he says, understanding my thoughts. 'I will order the vegetarian option.'

I don't understand, but anyway sink into a long cushion in front of the little room where the lucky man is one by one putting all of his winning pound coins back into the machines. My back and limbs are taut like wire. I have grown unused to comfort and the seat is soft. And I am tired, so tired.

When the Ethiopian rises to join a small queue at the counter, I place my phone on the table, and see a message has come through from Aman. I swipe to open it and see a picture of him smiling, a pair of wire cutters in his hand. He is holding out the label so that I see there is a Special Offer: €15.

I am still smiling at the picture when the Ethiopian returns with our breakfasts. My face betrays the fact that I can barely believe the size of the plates, nor the different foods piled up. Fried eggs, toasted breads, mushrooms, small triangles of fried potato, a grilled tomato, some beans in orange sauce. 'I am sorry,' he says in Amharic, 'this is a small portion.'

At first I don't think he is joking, but then I see the look on his face. Coffee comes mixed with hot water in cups the size of bowls for food. It is hard to lift the handle with one hand. The Ethiopian continues to regard me with interest, as I pick up my knife and fork, make the sign of the cross, and begin to dismantle the food. He works his knife and fork slowly and carefully, cutting chunks of food to sizes that will fit into his mouth. I continually fight an urge to pick things up. It is the first time I have used a knife and fork for months, and I am glad when the Ethiopian uses our traditional method for some of the food, tearing morsels of toast and dipping them in the egg-yolk with his hands.

When our plates are clean, he looks at me comically and says: 'Truly, this was the Feast of Saint Mike.'

As we begin the drive to Croydon, my new friend stops to fill the tank with petrol. His name is Berhanu. I watch him through the window of the petrol shop with his smart shirt and haircut, paying with his credit card. And then from the passenger seat of his Mercedes I see the gambling man walking across the car park in his checked shirt toward his lorry, my lorry. I think of those three sevens landing in a row, and as he takes a seat in his cab in front of that big red dragon, I wonder if the lucky lorry driver is not the Archangel Michael himself.

Leave to Remain

A la porte,
les sauvages

Nicolae Titulescu,
at the League of Nations, 1936

Mike rises from his chair to demonstrate how he had wielded the iron bar. Beer sloshes tempestuously in his pint glass. He grabs a pool cue lying idle on the faded blue baize, waves the thick end in the air like a club. 'Like this,' he says. 'You have to be harsh or they won't fucking move.'

The top end of the pub is pretty empty; it often is these days. Bottom end, a few families are out for meals, blissfully unaware of Mike's histrionics beyond the partition. Quietly they peruse the choices printed beneath the brewery logo and cartoon flames on big laminate menu cards: steaks, burgers, buttermilk chicken. The cards are stacked in order of size – Mains, Drinks, Desserts, Kids – behind miniature buckets containing the cutlery and napkins, the ketchup and the mayonnaise.

Stepping back toward the fire escape to get maximum purchase on his swing, Mike is making the most of his small audience. 'Otherwise you'll have them crawling everywhere,' he says. Each utterance brings with it a wild swipe, as if from a man driven crazy by an insect that refuses to be swatted. 'In the cargo bed. Under the wheel arch. On the bloody roof. I even found one cheeky fucker in my cab!'

Gethin laughs at the thought of a migrant hiding in Mike's cab, peeking out from under his bedclothes, trying not to be seen, but John Mod is having none of it. 'Where's David?' he's asking, desperate to get off the subject of migrants before their friend arrives for the quiz. When David was there, Gethin and Mike would lay off the subject, out of respect for David's wife.

John Mod had asked them about it once, why they would say certain things, give their honest opinions about something when David wasn't there, and then when he was they'd stick to arguing the toss about football or – their favourite pastime – reminiscing about their school trip to the outdoor pursuits centre at Storey Arms, or the time they had burned down a tree by attempting a campfire just beneath their treehouse, or the time their Under-13s football coach had kicked a ball in anger away down the sports hall and straight into the basketball hoop – safe territory fast becoming the only thing the whole gang of them truly had in common.

'Out of respect for his wife,' Mike had said, as if it was somehow respectful to hold the view that someone who was born in Newport should go home to an island they couldn't even afford to visit on holiday, a country they had never been to, as long as you held the opinion behind their husband's back.

At the time – this was a good few years ago, before the refit – John Mod had simply shaken his head and drained the remainder of his pint, letting his frustration ring out in the sound of his glass brought to rest on the bar with a less than subtle degree of extra force. Mike would barely have noticed, would have turned away and started chirping to somebody else about something else, and it would have been forgotten. These were the days before it was all on the front of the papers every day, and you couldn't so much as set foot in the pub without somebody starting a conversation about it.

'Listen, John, I've got nothing against immigrants. If they're coming here to work, then good luck to 'em.' Mike jabs a finger toward the door of the pub, out across the main road toward the housing estate. 'As far as I'm concerned, there's enough lazy twats down there don't want to work.' Mike shoves his hand down the front of his jeans, attempting parody, the way the nippers on the estate carried on. *'Got a lighter, bro? Go in the shop for me, brah? I need me some dank, brurve.* But there's one thing I can't stand and that's rudeness.'

John looks about to interject, but thinks better of it, takes a gulp from his pint, lets it blow out his cheeks like mouthwash.

'All I'm saying,' says Mike, 'is *speak English*. How hard can it be?'

John swallows. 'You're a hard man to please,' he mutters, giving his head a little shake, then cranes his neck around Mike's ample frame to see the umpteenth replay of a shot hitting the side netting.

'He's right,' says Gethin, keen to get a word in. 'I'm telling you the truth now, right. It'd melt my heart if just one of them – just once – could look me straight in the eye as they get off the bus, and just say *Cheers Drive* like everyone else.'

'Like a local,' says Mike.

'Just *be* like a bloody local,' says Gethin. 'Come and have a drink.' He makes a wide-armed gesture toward the rest of the pub, flashing the three feathers tattooed beneath the hair on his forearms, as if he were the very spirit of generosity and welcome.

'Ah, but what's a local?' says Mike, warming to the theme, face already ruddy with a two-pints-of-Strongbow glow. He sweated like a bastard these days when he was drinking, and went to the toilet about three times a pint too, according to the others, which was a bit of an exaggeration but not much. 'How many people here in the pub right now went to Saint Gabe's?'

'Well, that's a bit narrow, isn't it?' said John, who had, just like the others, attended the local Comp. 'You can't just include people who went to our school.'

'Alright, alright – anyone we know counts then, boys, alright? Anyone we know or *know of*, anyone with *roots* in the area.'

At the far end of the bar, people started to filter in for the quiz, draping coats over the backs of chairs, shuffling up from the carpeted section with its dining tables and American-style booths. It's a different kind of crowd these days: groups of young lads who only have a couple of pints because alcohol might disagree with their protein shakes or foul up their Fitbit. They all look the same with their close-cropped hair smarmed full of product, the angles of their jawlines and sideburns as tight as their t-shirts, laughter somehow contrived, a kind of controlled rowdiness. They are, of course, showing off to the kind of women who have begun to frequent that end of the bar: big-hooped earrings and denim shirts hanging out over jazzy leggings; hair dyed blonde with visible dark roots; sipping flavoured gins from glasses the size of goldfish bowls. The wood-effect floor in front of the bar area marked a kind of neutral zone before the partition and the step up to the top end, past the fruit machines in the corner where the boys traditionally huddled, the floor here tiled in mock flagstones to give the impression of some cosy country inn. There was even a fireplace – a cavity wall with a huge cast-iron grate filled with logs – but it was never lit because there was no real chimney.

The refit was all for show; it was a chain pub pretending to be a real pub. Behind the bar there was rough wooden cladding inset with plain white tiles, rustic looking but brand spanking new. Long shelves of the more traditional spirits – Jameson, Smirnoff, Captain Morgan – stood in front of a long mirror alongside the oversized perfume bottles containing all the new gin concoctions for the goldfish bowls. The Carling, Strongbow and John Smiths triumvirate that had previously been the pub's entire on-tap offer had been supplemented, not only by Coors Light, San Miguel, Peroni, Guinness and Strongbow Dark Fruits, but by several tall fridges stacked full of craft ales in brightly coloured bottles. And cans were the latest thing, little cans like Coca-Cola tins, flavoured pale ales and alcoholic pop.

But the thing Mike really objected to was the coffee machine. 'If you want coffee, go to a fucking café,' he was fond of saying, particularly in earshot of people from the new-builds, the latest clientele who just popped in for an after work cappuccino or mocha with a little almond biscuit set on the saucer in a cellophane wrap. To make matters worse, it wasn't even proper coffee, the barmaid just pressed a button and waited for it all to pour out, all-inclusive of a pathetic little dribble of milk. But Mike's protestations only brought him funny looks. It wasn't his pub these days.

There were places down the road that Mike could have frequented instead if he was so keen to avoid coffee machines, pubs that were still as rough as they had always been, places you definitely wouldn't be able to get a fresh slice of bloody lime, but the Alex had always been his local. Hell, it had been his old man's local when Mike himself was just a kid pretending to be Kenny Dalglish, kicking a ball about in the beer garden until it started going dark and the adults told him to go home. So he just didn't see why he should be the one to move.

Sometimes he'd come to the pub on his own. He'd spend half an hour pushing pound coins into the fruit machine, trying to match horseshoes and harps, shamrocks and pints of Guinness while a light-up leprechaun laughed in mockery at his insubstantial winnings and incremental losses. And then Mike would mutter darkly about how he had been pushed into the corner of his own pub, glaring across the demilitarised zone of laminate between the mock flagstones and the carpet. From the partition wall hung a big chalkboard – 2 MAINS *for* £9.99 *all day* MONDAY to FRIDAY – and when the so-called restaurant was full of diners Mike imagined it an invisible Checkpoint Charlie, a demarcation line between those like him, born and brought up in the terraces running down the hill, and those who had moved in recently to the new-build estate where it used to be warehouses, where when they were kids he and the boys rode their bikes, built dens and played football until their mams called them in for tea.

'Do you recognise any of these fuckers?' he was saying now.

'They're all regulars,' said John.

'Regulars, yes, but are they *locals*?' said Mike. 'They might turn up here every Thursday. They might even win the fucking quiz every week. But are they *locals*?' Mike was on one tonight, thought John. Big-mouthed and dangerous, spoiling for something. He'd been watching too much *Question Time*. John had known Mike since their first day at school and had never known his childhood friend to take more than a passing interest in politics. But since his declaration before the last election, that for the first time in his life he would not be voting Labour, Mike had been a pain in the arse. If you listened to Mike, every other person who walked up to the bar was a potential strain on the NHS.

It was Kaycey who came to the rescue. 'Two pound each, guys,' she was saying. A big-boned girl, hair tied up in a bun the size of half a loaf of bread, she was collecting the quiz money in a pint glass, handing out pens and a sheet of paper with badly photocopied pictures of celebrities that the teams had to identify.

Mike took a big slurp from his pint. 'Kaycey, love – what's the difference between a regular and a local?' he asked her.

The girl curled her big paint-on eyebrows. 'Do you have your two pounds, Michael?' she asked.

He dug in his pocket theatrically. 'Regulars turn up every week,' he said, dropping the first coin into the jar. He left a pause and then let the second pound clink into the glass, as if it proved something significant. 'But locals belong here.'

Kaycey walked off toward the diners' end of the pub, diamante-encrusted iPhone peeking out of the tight space in her jeans' back pocket.

'I'm sure she fancies me,' said Mike.

It didn't help that he was on his own so much. Mike's working life meant long drives down to Bari on the east coast of Italy, sleeping alone in his cab, and nowadays running the gauntlet at Calais, keeping an iron bar under his seat to scare off illegals. Gethin was married with two daughters, now almost Kaycey's age, but his days were even more monotonous: driving the same old bus routes up and down the city's arterial roads, pulling in and out of the bus station, the only variation in whether the time of day meant he should travel clockwise or anticlockwise around the housing estate. Only on his every third week Saturday shift would he get as far as Cardiff, the motorway that Mike was sick of feeling like a treat to Gethin, a chance to put his foot down.

At least John had his own taxi, a little bit of agency, deciding when he would go on and when he'd clock off, a little bit of variety in where he got to go, although invariably it was local journeys. Very rarely did anyone in this city want to go very far afield. And on the weekends, John ran the record stall in the indoor market, from where he took the name everybody knew him by. But John Mod was heavily subsidised by his night shifts in the taxi and the pies and pasties and sausage rolls his wife sold in the next aisle over. It was a hobby, really.

What none of them ever mentioned was why they'd agreed in the first place to make a thing of meeting up to do the quiz at the Alex every week.

They had come up with the idea on the way back from Wootton Bassett, the day John had driven them all there in his taxi to see Gareth's body repatriated.

It was as much as anybody could take, seeing someone you had grown up playing mob with, knocking doors and running off with, sharing your first joint with, being wheeled out of a plane draped in a Union Jack.

People had lined the streets in silence, and the boys had all watched it again when they got home, on the news. In the privacy of their own homes, each of them had cried. John remembered being at the barbers and seeing Gareth's picture there on the coffee table, on the front of the *Mirror*, alongside all those other lads, and then reading about where each of them was from: Burnley and Hartlepool and Mansfield and Braintree, towns just as crap as Newport, where people signed up for the army, just like Gareth had done, for something to fucking do.

Gethin didn't talk about it, tried to just carry on, driving his bus up and down Chepstow Road like he was training to be the Karate Kid; *bus up, bus down*. David, the brainy one, what had happened to him? He seemed unhappy at the *Argus* these days, as if a local paper wasn't enough for him; he wanted to change the world. And was it then that Mike had started his thing about Muslims? John couldn't remember now. Maybe he'd always had that streak in him, and Afghanistan had just riled it all up. Mind you, thought John, to be fair to Mike, he had it in for most people these days.

'These fuckers can turn up every week for the next twenty years,' he was saying now. 'Far as I'm concerned, they'll never be local.' He gestured across the empty chair, where Gareth would have been sitting if he was home off tour. 'And I'll tell you why. Look at those pictures behind me.'

The way he didn't turn, just gave a little flick of his balding head, Mike had obviously been thinking about this. Behind him was a row of black-and-white photographs in gold frames. Beneath plasma screens permanently turned to the sports channels and in the light of the multi-coloured glow of fruit machines and illuminated beer-taps, the photographs faded into the wallpaper. There was the High Street, at once familiar and completely alien, served by trams, peopled by women in lace bonnets and men in flat caps, shopfronts obscured by awnings. There was the steelworks, where all of their fathers had worked. And there, centre-stage above the fireplace, beneath three former footballers in suits talking animatedly around a curved table, was the Transporter Bridge, that symbol of their city.

'This is a docks town,' said Mike. 'It runs in our blood. How many of our old men worked down there, in the fucking fog and grime? Look at these fuckers. How many of them have done a real day's work in their lives?'

John surveyed the competition at the table opposite. They were, in truth, an ordinary looking bunch. The markers of social separation were subtle indeed. A couple of them wore glasses. One of the men had a beard that had clearly been oiled and slightly longish hair, swept up on top of his head into a little knot. One of the women had a little nose-stud. One of them had earphone wires dangling from the open collar of his shirt, which to Mike's way of thinking had too many buttons undone. One of them – and this was the clincher for Mike, fucking unforgivable – was wearing brown leather moccasins that looked like they'd come from somewhere like John Lewis, with *no socks*.

'White collar workers,' said Mike finally, dragging out the initial letters of each word as if he was going to explode into expletives. Gethin laughed, but it was nervous laughter, the kind of laugh you give to a man like Mike when he's in one of these moods.

When David arrived, he was with a black fella. 'Just in time for your round, Mac,' said Mike, his greeting every time he saw David. Both men smiled as Mike stole a sideways look at Solomon, who didn't look like the kind of black man he thought might be alright. He didn't look like Claudie, David's wife, or people who had grown up here after their parents or grandparents moved here from Jamaica or wherever. He had a different kind of look about him, properly African, like the migrants in Calais, the ones who threw bricks across the road in front of his lorry, the ones who were giving him stress.

As David handed him his Strongbow, tall, golden, fizzing with gas, John noticed Mike glancing over at the pool table where he had laid down his makeshift club.

When the quiz began, Mike shouted wrong answers in ironic attempts to put the other teams off.

'Who succeeded Queen Victoria on the English throne?'

'Henry the Eighth!'

'Which was the first British football club to win the European Cup?'

'Newport County!'

'Shut up now, Mike,' John was saying as the questions ascended the gradient of difficulty, the team from the new-builds whispering intensely, questioning each others' answers, working collaboratively in a way which for his team seemed now to be impossible.

Solomon sat impassively through all of this. It was all new to him: the pub; the drinks; the quiz; the way Mike was behaving, like a teenager with a receding hairline. He looked at the giant metallic letters that ran the full length of the bar, in front of the mirrors and the optics, each inset with a series of light-bulbs that back home would have comprised the sum total of a household's annual electricity consumption. *ALEXANDRA DOCK*, it said. He wondered who Alexandra was, and why the pub was named after a place where ships set down their anchors.

Lost in these thoughts, he didn't notice the way Mike was looking at him – the look of a man trying to work out where he had seen somebody before. 'Come on mate, do you know this one?' the man was saying now, referring to a question about a Hollywood actor called Morgan Freeman.

'Give it a rest, Mike,' David was saying. Solomon hadn't known David for very long at all, but he trusted his friend not to abandon him to the red-faced man's seemingly unending barrage of queries.

'Where you from then, butty – you *local*?' had been his opening gambit. In different circumstances, Solomon might have appreciated the chance to explain where he was from, and even why he'd had to leave, but on this occasion he was grateful that the quiz questions seemed more important to the rest of the team than the interrogation Mike was attempting to organise. And he knew some of the answers, too.

'Who was the first black Bishop of Cape Town?'

'Desmond Tutu.'

'Set up in 1920, which organisation was a forerunner of the UN?'

'League of Nations.'

'In which of the four gospels does Jesus *not* say it is easier for a camel to pass through the eye of a needle than for a rich man to enter heaven?'

'Not a clue,' says John. 'Do you know this one?'

'You should do,' smiles Solomon, 'he has the same name as you.'

'What phrase, meaning *Shame be to him who thinks evil of it* features alongside *Dieu et mon droit* on the coat of arms of the United Kingdom?'

'I don't know this one,' Solomon admits.

'Who's got a pound coin?' asks David. 'It's on the pound coin. Is it? There it is. *Honi Soit Qui Mal y Pense*. Never noticed that before!'

'Which Irish folk ballad features the story of a man transported from County Galway to Botany Bay for stealing corn to feed his family?'

'Fields of Anfield Road,' says Mike. 'What's the original called?'

'Athenry,' says David.

'Which Italian island, off the coast of Tunisia, is home to a sculpture called The Door to Europe?'

There is a silence. Then Solomon clears his throat and says: 'Lampedusa'. Nobody asks him how he knows.

Kaycey comes around and collects the papers, and this time John goes to the bar. Solomon is amazed at the size of the beer glasses and the increasing speed with which they are emptied. It has been a long time since Solomon drank a lot of alcohol, and then it was small bottles and slowly. He is struggling to keep up, but something tells him that acceptance depends on his keeping pace. David is subtly covering costs for both of them, but there seems to be no question of his being able to sit out a round. He sips and sips.

When the results are announced, a reverent hush descends on the Alexandra Dock. Solomon hadn't really noticed the volume of the rock music that had been playing in the background. The other men's voices raised over it had seemed loud enough anyway because of the beer they had been drinking. Now Kaycey builds the tension a little bit, announcing the scores in reverse order. The quiz is a tie between their team and the group opposite.

Kaycey pushes a button on her iPad, where all the pre-set questions are online, another aspect of modernity that might have annoyed Mike if he hadn't been concentrating so hard and more than slightly drunk.

'Which line,' enunciates Kaycey carefully, 'formed the boundary between occupation zones on the Korean peninsula, later becoming the border between North and South Korea?'

It is Solomon's big moment. He knows it, for sure, and listening to the group – whispering furiously but not settling on an answer – he knows he must be the one to proffer it before the other team jump in. He clears his throat. 'The thirty-eighth parallel,' he says.

'He's right,' says David. 'That's it.'

Kaycey confirms it and the other team give a polite round of applause. John and Gethin share a high five. Mike shoots David a look, as if to say where have you found this immigrant from the arse end of nowhere, who has just waltzed in and, after all these weeks of our losing to those *white collar workers*, won us the fucking quiz. He gets up to go to the toilet.

When Mike returns, still fiddling with his zip, the boys have got a round of shots in with the winnings and Solomon is being introduced to the concept of a whiskey chaser. Gethin asks a supplementary question: how many whiskeys did Dylan Thomas drink before his death in New York, to which Mike replies: 'Eighteen – and I think that's a record!' Solomon thinks these men have performed this ritual before. They tip their heads back and drink, slamming tiny glasses on the table.

Meanwhile, David and John are asking him how he knows about the thirty-eighth parallel and before he can think about it too much he is telling the story of his grandfather. 'He had only one lung. He used to say his lungs were like North Korea and South Korea. One was destroyed by a chemical bomb, and the other was what kept him breathing until he was eighty-nine years old. Throughout his life, the Korean Embassy paid school fees for me and hospital treatment for him.'

'How come?' says John. 'Korea's a bloody long way from – where is it – Ethiopia?'

Solomon's face has a serious expression. 'Do you know about the Kagnew Battalion? When North Korea invaded the South in the 1950s, our Emperor Haile Selassie was reminded of what happened to us in the 1930s – when Mussolini invaded our country – and so he sent over three thousand men, from his own Imperial Guard, to be part of the United Nations soldiers.'

David, John and Gethin look impressed. 'The Kagnew are famous,' says Solomon, 'because they never gave an inch of ground, and although some were sadly killed or injured, not one Ethiopian soldier was captured in the whole period of the war.'

'What do you do for work then?' says Mike, not accusing exactly, but wanting to bring the conversation back to the present, maybe to check what kind of an immigrant this Solomon is, that he isn't a strain on the NHS.

John looks at David apologetically, seems on the verge of stepping in, telling Solomon he doesn't owe Mike his life story, but the newcomer is already answering.

'Care.'

'You what mate?'

Solomon repeats himself: 'Care. I work in a care home, for the old people.'

Mike is surprised. 'What, like wiping shit and that?'

'To be honest,' says Solomon, 'I didn't expect, when I came to this country, to be working in Care. In fact, in our country, we don't have such kinds of things.'

'What do you have?' asks Mike, a little blindsided.

'Our old people are looked after in the family, so it was kind of a shock to me when I came here and I discovered that there are special places where old people can be looked after. It's kind of amazing what you do in this country, the way you look after those people who have given so much for their country, the generation who fought in the war.'

Mike, for once, is listening rather than talking, and David smiles broadly at John as Solomon continues, the whiskey chaser no doubt aiding his fluency. 'I like to talk to the people about what they know. Maybe I connect better with the older generation because I was brought up by my grandfather. My parents passed away when I was young. So I became used to listening to the stories of the old people. My grandfather explained why my school fees were paid by the Embassy of South Korea. It was to thank him for his service, for wearing the blue helmet. Without my grandfather's lost lung, I would never have had an education, would never have become a journalist, would never have got into the kind of trouble that has brought me here. Without this story, we never would have met.'

'Fair play,' says Mike, for once at a loss for words, 'fair play.'

In the car park, the team from the new-builds are getting into their cars; half of each couple are designated drivers. John is calling a mate from his taxi firm to take his team home for a discounted rate, but the sudden rush of cold and damp after the warm stale air of the pub has a strange effect on Solomon, a hot flush of fever across his sweaty brow. His guts churn and he feels warm bile tickling the back of his throat. When he opens his mouth, vomit gushes like a river. He looks up, queasily observes the drizzle streaking through the sulphurous glow of the lamp that lights a picture of the transporter bridge, swinging in the wind on the sign for the pub. He is ashamed of his own weakness, deeply embarrassed in front of his new friends.

But that's when Mike grabs hold of him affectionately, calls him 'Kagnew', and despite his own uneven gait, holds Solomon up so his back is straight.

'See this man,' announces Mike to their departing opponents. 'This is what I call a local!'

Misericordia

Let salt winds punch our faces and your coast-guards
pluck us from the water like oily birds!

Alemu Tebeje Ayele,
'Greetings to the People of Europe!'

Just because I am an immigration officer doesn't mean I haven't got a heart. It's just that – what you have to understand – is that this is a two-way street.

You don't trust me. Of course, I understand that. No, no – please don't try to pretend that you do. It is quite natural. And perhaps – and I already know this too – you have been *told* not to trust us.

You have to understand, also, I have been doing this job for a long time. Not like this young man next to me. I can see the way you are glancing at him, nervously, and you're quite right to feel that way, because the truth is that he is almost as anxious as you.

Like you, he's a young man on an island very far from home. Before he took this job he was a ski instructor, apparently. Maybe you can't see his background the way I can, a certain type of wealth evident in the smooth bronze of his skin, the sun-bleached blond of his hair, the chunky silver bracelet of his watch.

This is his first mission here to the island. His only prior experience of border control was sitting in an office at an airport – Frankfurt am Main – watching live footage of people walking past the sign that says *Nothing to Declare*. But you – you have Something to Declare, don't you?

You have a Story. Well, he has a story too – he told me some of it last night – though it's not like yours. I'm not trying to compare your life experiences, you understand, but we all – each of us has a story. The important thing is how we tell it, whether we stick to the truth.

This other young man – yes, it's distracting the way he clicks his pen – was born and brought up in Luxembourg, a small town called Schengen. Right at the heart of Europe, where France meets Germany. Yes, it's the same one where the agreement was signed, the one that allows free movement. The signing ceremony took place on a boat – *can you believe that?* – because the tripoint, the exact place where Luxembourg meets its neighbours, is in the middle of a river.

He was telling me about it yesterday while we waited at our accommodation, before the WhatsApp message came through and we set off down toward the port to come and collect you.

You know, last night, just as you were being rescued from the sea, we were sitting *al fresco* at a little table on our balcony, playing cards. It's ironic, isn't it? There you were risking your life to reach Europe, and this fellow from Schengen couldn't summon the courage to bluff through a busted flush. He didn't win a single hand.

We weren't drinking beer, I must say that. Normally, a group of us will sit on the balcony, we'll watch the sun go down with a couple of chilled Peronis. There's a lot of waiting around, and you have to do something to pass the time. We'd been told by our bosses earlier in the day not to consume alcohol. It was more than likely a boat may be coming in. Your boat. But the Sicilian lemonade is so refreshing you might almost never want beer again. You will have heard of the famous Mediterranean diet? Olive oil, sun dried tomatoes, wild herbs, fresh fish. There are places in the south of Italy where the whole village lives to be a hundred years old! And these are the comforts and freedoms it is my job to help protect. You understand that, don't you?

Would you like a coffee? Of course you would. Coffee comes – *doesn't it?* – from your country. Yes, it is good coffee. The Italians like it strong. You like it even stronger? I will take your word for it, though I can't imagine how strong that must be!

We have some croissants here, too. Please, pass them around. We will all eat breakfast together. Young Herr Schengen seems to be frustrated already, but don't mind his grumpy mood. Like you, he hasn't had much sleep. And it will be me who will take charge of the conversation here. Make sure you have exchanged some words with our interpreter. He is my friend, but he's your friend too because he speaks your language.

Amharic is not your first language? Petros tells me you are Oromo, but that you speak Amharic perfectly. It is your national language, right? The interview will be conducted through English and Amharic. Would you be surprised to learn that English is not my first linuage? You have not heard of Cymraeg, or even of Cymru? Well, let me tell you that before I began doing this job, I had never heard of Afaan Oromoo. And you have thirty-five million speakers!

We are all on neutral territory.

I know you will have been through some difficult experiences, some hard things. I understand that these are difficult to talk about sometimes. But I want to encourage you to speak openly. Tell me the truth.

I know that you want to stay in Europe. You want to have breakfast every day like this? Strong Italian coffee, these rich buttery croissants from France. And look – this jam has come from Spain. Petros, can you pass him the knife? Spread it like this.

It's very important, if you want to stay in Europe, that you tell us the truth from the beginning. I know that you won't want to talk straight away. I know that maybe someone – perhaps it was one of those people who helped you to reach this island – maybe they told you not to talk to us at all. That's okay, I understand that, even if young Herr Schengen here is showing his frustration already. The way he is clicking the top of his pen over and over is starting to grate on me, too, and I do not like the way he is looking around the room.

When we step outside together later to go over what you tell us, to discuss next steps, and so that Petros here can enjoy a cigarette in the sunshine, I will be talking to him about the importance of establishing trust by making eye contact, the way we are now, even if you still look at me with so much suspicion.

Let me tell you, while you are enjoying your coffee, while you are tearing your croissant into small pieces with your fingers and chewing them very slowly, while you are waiting for Petros to translate what I am saying into Amharic, let me tell you a little about last night from how I saw it.

The WhatsApp came at two in the morning. We had already been told that a boat had been seen, that some people had been rescued. I took my grab-bag – a bottle of water, facial mask, antiseptic gel, pad and pen – and drove down to the port with Herr Schengen here beside me. I couldn't tell whether he was a little sullen or half-asleep or a little bit of both. We don't wear uniforms, you'll understand, because we don't want you to think that we're police. There are enough police already.

Quayside was a beehive. Everybody scurrying about preparing for your arrival. So many agencies it was difficult to know who was in charge, but overall I was impressed with the efficiency of the Italians. *Polizia di Stato* and the *Guardia di Finanza*, the state police and what they call the finance police – customs. The *Guardia Costiera* – the coast guard – were there too. It's a good job I have a little Italian, or the whole situation might have been even more bewildering.

On top of the various law enforcement agencies you had all the NGOs – the non-governmental organisations – all trying to do their best to help. And then there's the reporters and the press photographers, all trying to get into position with their cameras, telescopic lenses pointing out toward the cold, dark sea.

I know that for you it may be different, but for someone like me – or someone like young Herr Schengen here – those of us brought up in Europe, we can only compare this kind of experience to being on the set of a film. All those cameras! And then, as if in response to a clapperboard, you arrived.

And we could see from the shore – all of us, scores of white faces illuminated by searchlights on the quayside – as soon as your boat came into view, the whole three hundred and sixty degrees of the boat occupied by scores of black faces. At first all I could see was that everybody on board was African. Only as you came closer did the diversity strike me, the mix of peoples from right across the Sahel, from Conakry to Hargeisa.

When you have seen such boats come in before, you begin to be able to anticipate responses to those initial questions: names, places of origin, dates of birth. Bereket, Hasan, Mamadou. Asmara, Kano, Ouagadougou. And the classic: first of the first, oh one.

You want to know why the police had guns last night when we took down your names and countries? It's an understandable question, and I'll try to answer as best I can.

We have to have what we call a controlled environment. What we have to try to find out first is what happened in the boat. If we are going to be able to help you to the best of our ability we need the facts. Fresh information is the best. We know that one among you was the driver. Somebody must have been in charge of the motor, somebody must have had a compass.

We also know that you will be protecting each other, or afraid to tell us who it was who was taking the vessel out into danger, or who it was that organised such a reckless voyage. Many people have told me already that they couldn't see – they were too far away, or there were too many people on the boat – but we simply can't believe the ones who say that the navigator used the stars. The sky was covered completely in cloud last night!

And I know there are other things that happened in the boat that will be difficult for you to talk about.

I know that you do not remember the details about what happened last night because when the boat arrived you were unconscious. That is why I am talking about what I remember. It's only fair – *is it not?* – that I provide you with the facts about what happened before, and as you were stretchered from the boat. What I need you to do is to give me the facts about how you came to be on the boat in the first place. What happened in Libya, and how you came to be in Libya to begin with. Is that okay? Don't mind Herr Schengen, it is his job to make notes, and I will be checking them later to ensure he has been listening attentively, to make sure he does not make mistakes that may disadvantage your asylum claim should you choose to make one. I assume you will be making such a claim?

I have to say I was impressed by the way you were treated by the medical staff as you stepped off the boat, each of you helped onto dry land with the hand of another. What you will not have seen from your position on the stretcher is the way that very discreetly they lifted your t-shirts, just a very quick glance at your stomach. I am no doctor, so I am not sure what signs they are looking for, but they can tell immediately if there is a problem that means you must be transferred to the hospital, and many people sadly arrive with illnesses they have picked up on the journey, through dehydration or malnutrition, the way you have all been packed together, each from a different country and then packaged up like sardines.

What I noticed first, as many of you stepped onto the island, was the lack of shoes – very few of you had anything at all on your feet. And as we expect, anything of value has been stripped away. In fact, some of my overzealous colleagues can get a little bit carried away. If they see a wedding ring, they think they may have found a trafficker, as most of the migrants will have had any personal items of any worth removed, stolen from them in Libya, or used in part payment for the journey at a much earlier stage.

And so as I stood and watched you all being taken away, the multiple ironies were not lost on me. I watched as volunteers from the *Misericordia* gently wrapped each of you in golden foil as if restoring to you the wonders of your continent: the indescribable wealth of Mansa Musa or the glories of the Pharaohs.

And the way that each of you walked away toward the waiting coaches, one following another with stiff, robotic movements, sheets of shimmering foil draped from your necks like flags, it was as if you had just finished a marathon, which in a way I suppose you had.

I know that people from your part of the world are among the best marathon runners on earth. That was something else I thought about. Feyisa Lilesa crossing the finish line at the Rio Olympics, silver medal achievement overshadowed by the crossed arms gesture he made as he crossed the line. A symbol of your Oromo protests?

Yes, you are smiling now because you know that I know this gesture. I cross my arms above my head, like this. As if I am in chains. This is part of your story, right?

We followed the coaches in our cars, up the winding road on the hill toward the centre of the island, to what we call the Hot Spot, the reception centre. We waited patiently for the doctors to see you first, observing each of you as you sit for the first time in a line, under the canopy.

Many people were injured, suffering lacerations in the legs. Sadly – and you will know this yourself – some people had already passed away by the time the rescue ship reached the shore. And I should let you know, in the hospital another four people did not wake up this morning. Two with hypothermia, two with unexplained wounds.

I am sorry there's no air conditioning in here, although I imagine this heat is far worse for me than it is for you. Petros seems quite relaxed about it, shirtsleeves rolled and just the one button undone beneath his collar. You'll excuse me for wearing a polo. Schengen by contrast looks like he's going to explode. You've never seen a human being that colour? White people turn red when they spend too long in the sun. Mad dogs and Englishmen, they used to say. Herr Schengen must be the mad dog.

When the time for separation comes, what I notice more than anything, more even than the brothers and sisters clinging to each other, or the way the young children hold fast to their mothers' legs, is how the women cannot look you in the eye. I hate to think what has happened to make each one of them so wary.

You remember the lady you saw when you came to consciousness? She would have been one of the doctors from the *Confraternite di Misericordia*. They are a volunteer organisation that runs an ambulance service here in Italy. *Misericordia* means Mercy. No, if I'm honest with you – *and I have to be honest with you, right?* – I don't think she would remember you.

They were very busy last night. It may well be that she helped to save your life, but there were scores of others. Even when compared to boats I have seen rescued before, I really don't know how so many hundreds were packed into that one small vessel made of rubber.

The one thing that I know will stay with me – for the rest of my life I will remember it – is that you were, all of you – *how can I describe it to be honest with you?* – surprised. Not surprised to be in – to have finally made it to – Europe, but surprised to be alive.

You have finished your coffee. I'm glad you enjoyed it. Can you hear the sincerity in my voice? I have been trained, you see. My lack of sudden movement is also a part of my training. And the way I hand you this bottle of water, the way I keep hold of it for a split second too long. I'm making you aware of my generosity.

Be thankful you're not reliant on old Schengen, here. He seems to have lost interest, doesn't he? The way he's looking at the ceiling like that, as if he's praying for a fan, or imagining one into existence.

Please, don't blame him. He's not unlike a lot of people in the world. He's thinking about his own comfort and convenience. This is not how he imagined he'd be spending the summer; it's not what he signed up for. Baking alive in a portacabin with no windows and no breeze.

It's not what you had in mind, either, is it – *let's be honest* – when you climbed aboard that rubber boat? Or let's go further back, when you left your country. The clicking of Herr Schengen's pen, the dry heat, the drops of sweat at the nape of your neck, my white face staring at you from behind these glasses and beneath this baseball cap. Be honest, this is not what you thought about when you dreamed of Europe.

So if I ask our friend here to go and take a little walk, to take a break from staring at the ceiling and to get some fresh air, will we make a start? That's good.

So now, Aman Berhane, twenty-sixth of the third, nineteen ninety-five, now that the clicking of the pen has stopped, please can you tell me how did you come to leave Ethiopia?

YOU ARE MARVELLOUS

Hi, I'm Lucy, says the pop-up banner, *I'm almost 3.2 million years old but am walking fully upright.* And so you look at the picture of this skeleton breezily introducing herself as your ancestor. It feels like a strange kind of date.

Further in, the exhibition switches to third person. *Some 3.18 million years ago, Lucy's body was slowly sinking in the mud of a lake. Fossilisation was the beginning: this admirable process preserved her bones from destruction until scientists discovered them in 1974.* The editor in you makes you want to point out that admirable is probably not the word the translator was looking for, and rearrange the syntax, but the guard is watching you keenly. A gun lies snug between his hand and his hip.

The museum is quiet. In Europe, Lucy would be swarmed, you think. Crowds would queue and surge, as for the Mona Lisa or Rosetta Stone. Here in Africa – in Addis – there are more pressing matters; maybe the locals have had enough of being followed by men in uniforms.

You stop to read about Lucy's pelvis and how it is different from that of a chimpanzee. *Australopithecus afarensis* it says. You think about the guys who found her. You know they called her Lucy after the Beatles song. You imagine these young archaeologists with moustaches, long hair and baseball caps and it's like someone drops a needle in your head. They had been working out in Hadar, in the

Afar triangle. Now these fossils, laid out in a modest glass case, give reason for the whole of humanity to trace its origins here.

The Advent of Modern Humanity says the next board, introducing maps of million-year migrant flows with the certainty of arrows. Your fingers trace each line fanning out from East Africa to the Fertile Crescent and then on – north, east and west across the Eurasian landmass. We are all migrants, you think. We always have been.

Upstairs, Haile Selassie's throne is roped off but hardly inaccessible. A portrait of His Imperial Majesty is mounted on the wall behind it. A middle-aged emperor dressed in a grey military coat, bearded chin jutting outwards as the sky darkens. Africa's bulwark against European imperialism, you have read, but himself an emperor. A subjugator of his subjects.

You look at the other portraits that surround the throne in this simple gallery. On the plane you were reading up on Ethiopian history, and you feel proud to have identified Tewedros II, 'the barefoot emperor', symbol of Ethiopian unity. The upper row of portraits recedes into history, severe faces under crowns that denote the Solomonic dynasty, the country's claim to Biblical majesty. But you notice Haile Selassie is abutted by the man who organised his death. Mengistu Haile Mariam, chairman of the Derg, architect of the Red Terror. Then there's Meles Zenawi, who overthrew the communists in 1991.

You try and fail to imagine an equivalent rogues gallery in another nation on earth. Surely there is no museum in Moscow that places portraits of the Tsars in line with Lenin and Stalin, Gorbachev and Yeltsin with Vladimir Putin. As if each successive strongman is part of an unbroken tradition, rather than a reality of coups upon coups and violent repression.

The guard follows you as you ascend the stairs to the modern art – women weaving baskets, the continent of Africa shaped like a tree, abstracts, histories. A local patron passes, shoots you a funny look and then tries to start a conversation. He tells you that in Ethiopian religious art, the good guys have two eyes and the bad guys are shown in profile, so they only have one. The guard follows you through to the exit, where you are thankful for the lack of a gift shop.

Outside Lucy's Restaurant, in the shade of a tree, you order a coffee. A taxi arrives, and your driver tells you that the new prime minister is opening up the palace grounds to the public. It's all part of bringing the country together. How long, you think, before he's afforded a painting on the wall inside?

Out loud, you change the subject. 'What did you think of Lucy?' the driver wants to know. You haven't decided yet, but you know that even standing proudly upright she was tiny. A child.

And you prefer the girl's Amharic name: *Dinknesh* means 'You are marvellous'. And she is.

THE GREAT RIFT

That day we sat on the seawall, a miles-long barrier of concrete raised above the level of the fields. Selam had brought with her a packet of chips wrapped in thick sheets of white paper. We dangled our feet over the edge of the wall like children, enjoying the feeling of being close, although our coats were thick and the wind was strong.

The tide was out and beneath us the flats stretched out toward the distant river like a desert. It was as if I saw the past in diorama. The way the mud had been shaped by the water – its gentle inclines, rivulet trickles and the pock-mark footprints of the wading birds – made it seem like we were inside a satellite looking down at the earth.

When I told Selam what I was thinking she laughed and shook her head as if she was talking to a crazy person, so I didn't tell her that from here it seemed to me that Wales was the coast of Africa, and that the other side of the wide river where we could see the houses of England in the glinting sunlight was Europe.

Instead I let her speak and she told me the place was called Somerset. I heard it as *summer set*, like the disappearance of the sun or the end of the season, and so I suggested we stay until the time that it would start to go dark.

Moisture had come right through the paper that wrapped the chips and so we opened the packet to release the steam while bits of wet paper floated into the wind like ash. It wasn't raining exactly, but the wind was strong and kept changing direction, and every now and again it would contain little droplets of water that you couldn't tell if they had come from the sky or the sea. In the distance we could see the bridge, wide H-shaped stanchions supporting miles of cables holding two countries together.

Downwind and downriver a flag was waving – flashes of green and white, a dragon with a tongue of fire. For a moment, I considered talking about flags, and nations, but I can't bring myself to mention politics when it might jeopardise love.

Instead I sighed, and lowered my shoulder hoping Selam might rest her head while we waited for the sun to go down. A group of birds crossed the sky in formation, making a V, taking turns to lead.

When we were full from eating chips, we scattered the remainder for the gulls. That was the last time I ate chips with Selam.

A Baptism of Dust

The responsibility lies not just with telling the story of the individual refugee but with laying the blame, or at least the assessment, with these larger forces – these countries, militaries, exploitative bodies that forced the production of all of these refugees in the first place.

Viet Thanh Nguyen

What could be more fitting than the indignity of a *faranji* face down in the dust of Addis Ababa?

I try to imagine how the fall would have appeared to passers-by. A white man in smart trousers and collared linen shirt, tumbling forwards, helpless, arms and legs splayed, prostrate across what should have been the pavement.

In the *Lonely Planet* I had read about the con men who work the streets of Addis, and their various tricks. Pickpockets working together, one grabbing your ankles while another rifles your pockets; or invitations to coffee ceremonies in people's homes where you're held to ransom for upwards of fifteen hundred birr. The one I liked the idea of least was a ruse where someone 'accidentally' spits on your clothing, and then makes an elaborate show of apologising and wiping you down, all the while going through your pockets. What irony then. Walking too quickly because I thought I was being followed, tripping, falling, sprawling, glasses flying from my face and out toward the traffic. And as some local women came rushing to my assistance, it appeared as if I, after all, might be the conman.

What was I doing here, anyway – a refugee in reverse – looking for a man I had never met, without even really knowing why?

In my prostrate position, I was conscious of the chunky silver bracelet of my watch, the way its hour hand still pointed to London Time.

I fully expected my fall to be followed by an opportunistic mugging, but all around me pedestrian traffic continued. Sandals, dusty leather shoes, imitation branded trainers and the occasional pair of bare feet all had places to go. With bodies moving among tuk-tuks and taxis, minivans and donkeys, in Addis there's no time or space to stop. My contorted limbs became as out of place and useless as a modern art sculpture at the centre of a roundabout. Perhaps worse than being trodden on or having my pockets picked, people simply walked around me.

So as I stretched out a hand toward the stony kerbside with its loose and broken concrete tiles to retrieve my glasses, I thought about all the other outstretched hands I had seen, the ones I had studiously ignored: desperate wild-eyed beggars tapping on taxi windows with twisted or truncated arms; brazen street-girls with their high-pitched *give me just one dollar*; demon-voiced addicts lying half-clothed under road bridges like dead cats.

I have not turned a blind eye to the hassle and the hustle, but neither have I crossed to the other side, naturally I suppose preferring comfort and luxury back inside the hotel with its high fences and armed guards, a cool, calm oasis of the global north amid the heat, dust and noise of the south.

And then I see a face. Framed by a royal blue hijab, the woman's smooth dark skin and long features make her look more Somali than Ethiopian, but I am no expert on ethnicity in a country with more than eighty tribes.

'Okay?' she says, her voice high-pitched and the question-tone of her voice an implication that I am not. Face down in the African dust, I struggle to respond. I take a breath – leaded petrol – look dazedly at my thankfully unbroken spectacle lenses, and cough.

I sense the woman wants to help me up, but without making physical contact. Her kind face looms in my blurred vision.

'Okay sir, I help you, no problem,' she says.

I open the fragile arms of my glasses and fix their tortoiseshell frames onto my face, looping the delicate golden arms behind my ears. Even they seem out of place here, designer shapes speaking subtly of wealth and privilege.

'Come, I help,' says the woman, and I prop myself onto an elbow, clamber to my feet.

There is pain in my knees. I cannot tell if it is grazing, bruising, bleeding, or some of all three. My navy blue trousers, crisply pleated, have turned beige with dust. I attempt to rub it away, dust myself down, but the balls of my thumbs sting too. I open my palms and stare blankly at purple flecks of broken skin where my hands saved my face from the broken pavement.

'Come,' says the woman again, and she touches very slightly the cloth gathered at my elbow where earlier I had rolled my sleeves. Gathering the suit jacket I had been carrying, folded over my forearm, I feel a sticky damp heat at my armpits and am grateful for the sudden shade of the plastic sheeting which covers her roadside stall.

No more than double the size of a red telephone box, on one side the woman has squeezed a small row of low stools for customers; on the other, two upturned plastic buckets cut in half allow her to sit at the level of a crouch, level with a metal bowl of roasting coffee beans. A thin piece of corrugated iron forms the back wall, glinting in the sun like a piece of kitchen foil; its faded paintwork in the colours of the national flag is half-heartedly decorated with stickers: Che Guevara, Bob Marley, Tewedros II. All else is plastic sheeting, held with angled pieces of stick hardly adequate for the purpose.

'Welcome, welcome,' the woman says as if inviting me into the front room of her home, the way people living in terraced cottages in the Valleys used to keep one room for best. 'Sit down, please.'

I set down my jacket on the nearest stool, then lower myself onto the one furthest from the street, and find I am still not quite in the shade. Unable to bend my knees, my legs continue to protrude into the path of passers-by. 'Leg up, please,' says the woman, indicating I should rest it on one of the other stools. I think about her loss of custom while she attends to this careless *faranji* and rue that my travel insurance policy probably does not cover this kind of impromptu medical care.

Another woman, from a stall next door – its eclectic wares include candles, disposable lighters, laminated paintings of the saints and plastic combs – is fussing with a bottle of water.

'No problem, please,' says the first woman, implying that navigating around my outstretched size ten brogues is the least of people's problems. Probably those who walk these streets often are far more careful than a man who has managed to cause himself injury tripping over a stone no bigger than a tennis ball.

'Drink water,' the woman says, taking the bottle from her friend and lifting a plastic wrapper from the lid with her fingernail.

'Thank you,' I say, realising as I open my mouth that this is the first time I have responded verbally.

I twist off the top and allow the cool of the water to gush into my dry throat like the waterfalls at Lake Tana I have been reading about in the guidebook. At a place called Gish Abay lies the source of the Blue Nile, a place that drew the Scottish explorer James Bruce in the late eighteenth century, but which had hosted missionaries from Spain as early as 1618. I splash a little water into the palms of my hands where the skin is stinging, rub a little onto my brow and neck. Amazing how we still tell stories about places that pretend as if the whole world was virgin territory until Europeans arrived. Missionaries from Spain in the second oldest Christian country in the world!

Even the way I will tell this story when I return home – my fall into the dust and the way this woman appeared to help me out – will cast me in the starring role, and the three million inhabitants of Addis Ababa, the same number of people as spread across the whole of Wales, will be mere supporting artists, overshadowed by my foolish exploits.

I take a deep breath, much-needed oxygen mingled with the dust of the street. 'Thank you,' I say again, and smile. 'It's very kind of you to help me. That was quite a trip!'

'Very danger!' says the woman, pointing at the stones and pieces of broken tile lying haphazardly in the dust, incredulous perhaps that I had failed to note them earlier.

As I return to the task of dusting down my trousers, much more gingerly than before, she asks me: 'You from America?'

'No,' I say, 'I'm from Wales.' I let the familiar blank look play itself out across her features, a passing cloud of unrecognition, and then add: 'In the UK, next to England.'

'Ah, English!' Her face lights up with a smile, and I let it pass. 'My sons is gone to England.'

She pokes at the smoking coffee beans with the backside of a spoon, wanting to talk, perhaps wondering how much to tell.

'Too many problems here,' she says. 'Very, very problem. Better life in England?' Her tone perches on the border fence between statement and question, as if she wants me to confirm to her that her sons made a right decision, subtle hints of her fear that England has its problems too.

'How many sons?' I ask.

'Four,' she says, and begins moving coffee cups across a tray in illustration. 'First boy, Hirpho, left many years ago – when my husband still alive. We lived outside city, small town – Shashamane – take four hours by bus.'

She moves one cup away from the other five, as if it is Hirpho flying the nest, leaving the family home. Her fingers are reluctant to set it down, to let it go. I am not sure if she means the other side of the tray to represent her hometown, or the place where her son might be living now. 'My husband sold forty sheep and forty goats to raise the money for this passage. In those days, easier. People you paid didn't demand more, more money then. Forty sheep, forty goats and my eldest son was in Sweden.'

The woman looks down at the cups, wondering what she has started, knowing she must finish the story. She finally lets go of the first cup. For the moment, the far side of the tray is Sweden. I imagine this beautiful dark-skinned boy with his mother's features, sitting at the edge of a glass-blue Scandinavian lake surrounded by the silence of a forest that stretches beyond the Arctic Circle, and wonder if there is anywhere on earth he could have ended up that would be more different to Addis.

'Second boy, Gadisa,' the woman continues, 'things were getting more difficult. Government they took away my husband into prison.' She moves a cup off the tray altogether, setting her husband down amid the dust and broken concrete, as if removing a captured piece from a chessboard. 'I needed the boys to help at home. We had many sheep, many goats. But after my husband taken, things very, very danger for my boys.' She takes up another cup, and holding Gadisa in her left hand and a third boy, Gameda in her right, she explains: 'My husband in prison. These boys do everything to help Liberation Front. Putting up posters, organising meetings, sometimes marches; sometimes moving, hiding things. I ask less and less. Government soldiers start coming to our house, looking for boys. In the end, we decide sell the farm, send Gadisa to Europe; sell the house, send Gameda to Europe. Very, very expensive now. Agent people can make a lot of money. But my sons safe, at least.'

'Where are they now?'

She looks down at the cups for a moment, contemplating. 'Gadisa in England, place called Glasgow.' I smile as she sets down the cup, imagining her son walking around Glasgow, telling people he is pleased to have made it to England. I am sure he has been corrected by now.

The smile fades, though, as she sets down the second cup. 'Gameda, I am not sure. I have not heard anything about him for two years now. He was in Libya, but the agents they asked for Europe, more money.'

I try to think of something to say, to fill the sudden silence. I test my leg, bend the knee slowly so that my foot is out of the street.

Cars continue to honk their horns and teenage boys continue to lean out of the windows of blue and white minivans, shouting the local names of destinations. I recognise *Bole, Bole, Bole!* because that is the name of the airport.

'It must be hard for you,' I say, 'with them gone away.'

'They send me some monies,' she says, 'sometimes. No survive just selling coffee.' She pushes the cup that has come to represent her youngest son toward me, and then holds the coffee pot six inches above it, expertly pouring a trail of thick, steaming black liquid into the white china receptacle. For a few seconds the aroma catches in my nostrils, blocking out the petrol and dust, and its scent recalls upmarket coffeehouses in Cardiff's Edwardian shopping arcades. For a brief moment I am thinking about low-level lighting, wood and metal interiors, hessian coffee sacks stapled to the walls, and the word Ethiopia in san serif capitals on a retro letterboard, along with Sumatra and Guatemala, other places the customers have never been.

'Life always very hard for a mother,' says the woman. 'Where our children go, no matter. Opposite side of street, other side of world. Always still you lose your children.'

She doesn't ask if I want sugar, just spoons it in. 'Better your children have good life,' she says. 'Too much suffer, hard life like this.'

I sip the coffee – piping hot, sweet and powerful. My senses heightened, I begin to drink in the surroundings. Men with beards lying hopeless at the gates to a big church, stalls selling brightly-coloured religious artworks, goatskins painted with angels and saints; piles of bibles, metal crosses, incense. As I lose myself in observation, the woman returns to her job. '*Kaffe, kaffe, kaffe,*' she calls out, into the babble of the street.

I wonder about her fourth son, the one she hasn't mentioned, and before I can think too hard about it I find myself saying, 'What about your youngest boy? Where is he now?'

The woman begins rummaging in the folds of her robe, and

eventually brings out a grubby, dog-eared piece of thin photographic paper. The image is in black and white. A teenage boy with close-cropped hair and a gap in his teeth, a collared shirt suggestive of school.

'His name is Tuji.'

The swift reaction of my tear ducts takes me by surprise.

She stuffs the photo back into the folds of her robe without looking. 'I not hear now for many weeks. Sometimes his phone no credit. Very expensive in Europe to give calls.'

Back at the hotel, I take a long shower. Hot water gushes from the ceiling of the wet-room, bigger than the woman's stall. I step out onto a textured white bath mat, unhook the robe from its hanger, untie the belt and wrap its fluffy warmth around my aching body. All the dust of Addis has been washed away, and along with it the troubles of Ethiopia and all the global south.

I lie on the king-sized bed, press a button on the remote control and flick through news channels with the sound down. CNN, BBC, Al-Jazeera. There is a weather forecast for the whole of Africa. It's raining in Cape Town and Lagos, but most of the continent looks dry and sunny. Back home, Liverpool have won 2-0. I roll across the foot-thick mattress, propping myself against the giant headboard with three super-soft pillows, press 9 on the phone and ask Room Service to bring me two cold beers. Yes, the local Saint George is fine.

Whatever I do, I can't stop thinking about the woman, her kindness at the roadside, the hardship of her life, her love for her sons, and the whereabouts of that boy in the photo.

I listen to the wail of the priest through a tannoy outside, the Orthodox call to prayer little different from Islam in its wailing insistence, its unapologetic fervour. I close my eyes but still see white-shawled women making their way to church with slow, purposeful steps; the bustle of young men going to and fro, if not to work then to somewhere they can make money somehow; the occasional tram across the new incongruous Chinese-built elevated railway. Something about this country is moving inside of me like the wings of a dove.

The beers arrive. I go to the door and let in a young lad with a jazzy shirt that speaks subtly to the Western view of a generic 'Africa'. He presents two bottles on a tray covered in a red cloth, thick as the carpet of Emperor Haile Selassie the First. He won't just let me take them. Instead he places a paper doily on the glass-topped coffee table in the room, sets down a napkin and makes an elaborate show of lifting off the bottle top with a fancy opener, a small cloud of gas escaping like vapour from a holy spring. Then he sets down a glass and pours perfectly at an angle to avoid the creation of froth.

'Is everything okay, sir?' he asks.

I want to say no. I want to say that this little tableau we have created is the perfect expression of global inequality. I want to scream, and ask him what has happened to Aman? But I just say yes, meekly, and dig in my pocket for a generous tip to assuage my first-world guilt. A hundred birr later he has gone, and I am alone with Saint George.

The patron saint of England is revered in Ethiopia as a talisman who helped them defeat the Italians. The Battle of Adwa in 1896 occupies a place in the national imagination equivalent to the Battle of Britain. Plucky defence of the realm against evil invaders, the country united in the face of a foreign enemy.

Now, it seems, in both places national mythologies are falling apart. And as fewer people subscribe to the dominant narratives, those who cling to the old stories become more virulent in their views, more entrenched in their singular visions of what it means to be Ethiopian, what it means to be British. Fewer and fewer people fit the mould, and tiny cultural fissures become deep rifts.

An ashen-faced Theresa May appears on the screen, the latest gargoyle falling from the gothic façade of the Palace of Westminster. I don't need the crawler at the foot of the screen to tell me the headlines from home. Even billed as Breaking News, they form a series of epitaphs for the British State, the death of a nation narrated by women in high-neckline single-colour dresses and silver-haired men in suits standing with microphones outside white marquees on a temporary village green planted with competing flags and populated by red-faced people shouting slogans into the wind.

I look at Saint George on the beer bottle, text in English and Amharic, the label damp with cold. The saint is depicted as a medieval knight in armour; famously, he is slaying a dragon. I scroll Wikipedia on my phone, smiling to note that going by the Western calendar, the Battle of Adwa happened on Saint David's Day.

Front desk has advised not to go out alone on foot, but after my trip this afternoon, I figure that if I do get pickpocketed or swindled or spat on and jostled like the *Lonely Planet* says, it's the least I deserve for having the means to order cold beer on a red carpet, and for possessing – in the hotel safe – a burgundy passport and crisp white boarding pass that will see me back in the Alex for the quiz in under half a day. I resolve at least to cross the road.

Outside the museum, a languid security guard gives me a quick frisk, a formality at the entrance to any building worth entering here. While he does so, he smiles a welcome and asks if I am English. This time, I decide to resist. 'Cymro,' I say, and leave it at that.

Enough of defining oneself by your next-door neighbours, propping up other people's ignorance, bearing the weight of other peoples' empires. I'm not here to make money, save souls, or search for the source of the Nile.

'Holiday?' asks the guard, unperturbed by my sudden one-man revolution.

'No,' I say. 'I'm looking for someone.'

Satisfied I don't have a bomb strapped to my belt or knives

tucked into my socks, he ushers me forward. 'I hope you find them, sir,' he says. 'Welcome to the Red Terror Martyrs' Memorial Museum. We are run by survivors of the Terror and are able to operate solely with your generous donations.'

Inside I'm assaulted by carefully curated images of horror. A photograph of Ethiopia's most celebrated emperor is displayed next to the outstretched arms of a starving peasant. Further in, there's an outsized version of a famous photograph in which Haile Selassie is walked from his palace to a waiting Volkswagen Beetle that will drive him to his execution. In a glass cabinet, a military helmet from the early seventies carries a slogan that echoes only too resonantly in the present day: *Ethiopia First*. And then come the pictures: rows upon rows of profile photographs depicting just some of the millions who died at the hands of the Derg.

Paintings by survivors show beatings, hangings, piles of twisted bodies next to soldiers' nonchalantly swinging guns.

Another room, and a pile of earth is representative of the many mass graves that the era produced. In small glass cases, where many museums might display bits of broken pottery, here, accompanied by pictures and some personal effects, are the bones of the vanquished: boxes of ribs, piles of tibias and fibulas, stacks of skulls. Blinking into the sunlight of late afternoon, I decide that I have seen enough. It is time to go home. And it is only then that I see the statue.

NEVER EVER AGAIN reads the simple inscription, English capital letters shouting its imploring slogan beneath the Amharic. Above the words, three women – mothers, we presume – are cast in bronze and dissolved in sorrow, eyes closed, faces covered in streaks of tears. They might be called despair, dignity and hopelessness.

And the middle one is holding a jacket: symbol of all this country's missing and disappeared and dead, then, now and forever, and a reminder – to me – of the man I am looking for, a man whose jacket sent me here.

Back to Africa

A people without the knowledge of their past history, origin and culture is like a tree without roots.

Marcus Garvey

I had never heard of Shashamane, but it turns out that's where my father wants to be buried. The first time he started muttering it under his breath – *Shash-a-man-e, Shash-a-man-e* – I just thought it was him talking patois, telling me to shush. I said, Dad, I'm being as quiet as I can.

I was cleaning his room in the Home, dusting off some of the photographs he often no longer recognises. I suppose I harboured a vague hope that if I rearranged them this would turn out to be one of his better days, that he would see them anew. I mounted them onto the blankness of the wall, made sure the glass was sparkly clean.

I had even been to that place in the corner of the big Tesco that specialises in retouching old photographs and blowing them up to bigger sizes. But clarity and size made no difference. Dad's hippocampus itself was pixelated. And for me the saddest part was not that he frequently struggled to remember but that it was only since his synapses snapped that I had started taking a genuine interest in his past.

Just as years ago I wouldn't have wanted to sit around talking about the old days, now I didn't want to discuss his catheter or his Care Plan or be locked into a circular conversation about where I'd hidden his cigarettes. Now that Dad was rooted in one place – a reclining chair in the corner of this high-ceilinged room with its single window looking out over a rectangle of grass – I developed an overwhelming desire to reconnect, not only with Dad but with my own past.

My father's memory comes and goes, but as it recedes so does my whole world. Lately I've started to feel like I'm trapped inside one of those science fiction things where people start fading out of photographs until someone does something about it to change history. I want to be the heroine, the one to stop the rot in my father's brain, stop the present becoming the past, I want to save the only connection I have to the places I have never stopped seriously to consider.

It started – this feeling – like a lot of things I suppose, with the Windrush. Just that word being on the news all of the time. Not the ship itself, nor the scandal, but the word itself. The way its associations whispered a warm breath of tropical wind through my own autumnal brain. Suddenly it made me feel very cold, a creeping sense of being out of place in a city I had lived in my whole life.

'Tings are gettin' very cold here in Hingland,' my father had taken to saying, even when the carers had turned his heating up to full blast so that we might as well have been sitting somewhere in the West Indies. Perhaps the phrase was some echo of that first winter he'd spent down the docks – Tiger Bay in Cardiff, in the dying days of the fifties – when the taps were frozen with ice and before he realised that his new home was called Wales.

Windrush. Windward. Leeward. I found myself mumbling words under my breath as I rearranged his meagre belongings, the way my father had with *Shash-a-man-e*. I didn't even know the difference between the chains of islands, and so I asked my father. Most days he couldn't tell me the name of his new carer – although he did make a point of saying he was a black man, a simple fact that seemed to make him extremely happy – but he could tell me about the Caribbean. Much better for me to focus his ailing mind on the past, and the things that he knows, than trying to ask him again where he'd put the remote so I could turn the volume down.

'You don't need it turned up to a hundred to watch the snooker, Dad. They don't even commentate much, and you can see the score by there.'

'We come from the Leeward Islands,' he said, returning anyway to what I had asked him earlier, his voice disembodied, like a tape recording from some oral history project.

I loved the way that he'd said *we*. My whole life has been spent uttering the phrase *I was born here* as a point of pride, a badge of honour, something that made me somehow more legitimate, but now there was nothing I wouldn't give to have been born *over there*, even if I couldn't name all of the islands let alone remember them.

From his single bookshelf – how few things you end up with when you're put into a Home – I pull down an atlas that has belonged to my father since its publication – I check the date – in 1960. The year after he arrived in what he thought of then as the Mother Country, and a decade before I was born.

This was the first expensive item he bought after he got taken on as a docker, loading and unloading ships in the port of Cardiff.

'Before the shipping containers,' he used to tell me, in the days when he lived back at home with Mum. 'Now the Chinese dem, they can fill these things like Lego boxes, and nobody needs dockers. I lost my job to the shipping containers and that's when I had to start on the building sites.'

Now when I ask him why he bought an atlas, of all things, it takes him a little while to respond. I have to listen first to how he was paid five pounds a week, and how he sent three pounds back home to my mother, how one pound covered his living expenses and the remaining pound was *pocket money*. I have heard the same story so many times – the figures have been on a loop in recent weeks – but I smile and nod until he finishes outlining the uses of his pocket money, the costs of cigarettes and beer and bets on the horses, a little bit lost and a little bit won playing dominoes down in the Seaman's Social Club, where you didn't need to worry about white people. And then I ask him again, and he says he bought the atlas because he needed it to show people where he was from.

I look for the page with the wide Caribbean Sea, and find it on a page labelled South America: North. Despite the yellowing at the edges of the paper, the sea remains a deep blue. I run Dad's finger along the chains of islands, reciting their names like a litany: 'Guadeloupe, Antigua and Barbuda, Saint Kitts and Nevis, Saint Martin.' He often can't remember what he has had for lunch, but he is able to repeat my incantation. 'Dominica, Martinique, Saint Lucia, Saint Vincent, Grenada.'

'You have some cousins in Grenada.'

'Where were you born?' I ask, wanting the whole story before he is taken away forever.

'I was born on Antigua but we moved over to Saint Kitts. I grew up eating fresh fish.' He laughs. 'I never saw a frozen fish until I came to this country. The British people dem, they like to tink that they discovered this and they invented that, and turned the whole world red. Dem say the sun never set on the British Empire. But it was the Portuguese dem who discovered the trade winds when they went sailing off down the coasts of Africa.'

And that's how we get on to Shashamane. My father muttering restlessly about how it was the place where the children who had been taken out of Africa as slaves would one day return. He made it sound like a mystical place, an El Dorado or Shangri-La, a place where people of African descent from all over the world could return to the continent and live in peace and harmony, growing vegetables, living off the soils of Africa.

'Dad,' I joked, 'have you been smoking some of that old Bob Marley stuff?'

He laughed out loud, the kind of raucous laughter I remember as a soundtrack to my childhood, a laugh that made the ornaments rattle. The house was always full in those days, full of love and honky tonk piano and the peal of my dad's laughter and the aroma of my mother's mutton, rice and peas.

'Nah man,' he says, 'you knows I never touched that stuff.'

My father flicks through the atlas distractedly, looking for the right page but failing to make sense of the coloured shapes floating in the pale seas. 'What was it like when you came to Cardiff?' I ask, edging him back to familiar territory.

'To a lot of the local people I was just another darkie, come from somewhere else to take their job. I got called all sorts of names you wouldn't want me to mention again. But some of the people was nice and welcoming.' I feel guilty that I'd never really known, never really considered how hard it must have been when my father first arrived.

Inside the cover he has scrawled his full name with a sharp pencil – Moses Anthony Charles. That's the name that appears on the birth certificate he has never had access to, burned in a fire at the National Library of Saint Kitts and Nevis, the reason that in all these years he has never been home. It's a name rarely used, except on official forms.

I lay the big book flat on the surface of the biggest table in my father's nest of three and regret that we have not done this more often. In the spring he will turn eighty. Outside, a smattering of rain blusters against the window and I watch the security cameras shaking in the wind. For once I am thankful for the heating turned up, even at the end of summer.

Last time we looked at the atlas together I might have been perched on his knee as he turned the pages and taught me the names of countries, long Caribbean vowel sounds that I learned to contract into the local accent at school when the little white girls pulled at my braids. I look at the clock ticking on his mantelpiece. What happens, I wonder, to time. When you're young, nobody thinks to tell you how you'll never be that young and good-looking and carefree again.

There's a photo of our band next to the clock. Freshly dusted, we look great. Ragged around the edges in a cool way. It's shot in black and white and we're all posing against a red-brick wall behind the church on Commercial Road, girls larking about in chequered stockings, boys in suit jackets and pork pie hats. Someone – probably Martin – has scrawled a graffito with the name of the group behind us, only a little obscured by my impressive 'fro. *SKA'D 4 LIFE*.

There he is on the end. Poor Martin. My first proper boyfriend. Long before David. There he is, posing with his saxophone. Every time we think of him now, we say 'Poor Martin'. He was in David's form group at school. By the time he left the band and I'd bumped into David, Martin's life was already spiralling out of control. He moved on to bad stuff, hard stuff, and I certainly didn't feel like I knew him any more. David, to my surprise, took it badly when Martin disappeared.

It was the not-knowing, more than anything, was what he always used to say. If you find someone sprawled across a train track or hanging or drowned, you can do something with it, process the information, come to terms with it, hold a funeral, have some closure. When someone just walks out one day – disappears and never ever gets found – it's hard to take. Even now, whenever I see a call-out for a missing person in the back pages of the *Big Issue Cymru* or even a poster for a missing cat, I immediately think of Martin, and hear him riffing away on the sax. Mind, that boy could play.

In the silence, sixty years collapse. Six long decades during which my father has clung doggedly to the most set of his set ways, and in which the continent of Africa has changed beyond recognition. Its familiar shape spreads west and south in front of us over a double-page of the atlas. Dad runs his fingers absent-mindedly down the crease which runs the length of the continent, from Benghazi to Bloemfontein, still tinted pink as if dipped in the blood of names like Tanganyika, Northern Rhodesia and Bechuanaland. It's strange to think about it now, as his hand stretches across the continent, that neither my father nor I, nor any of our family, have ever set foot on African soil.

My father's fingers stretch toward the coast of West Africa, and countries newly independent when the atlas was printed, out of date before it reached the shops – Mali, Senegal, Côte D'Ivoire, Togo, Benin. And then he taps distractedly at Ethiopia, the only country on the map not to have been coloured by a key denoting European colonial powers. Blue for French West Africa. Green for the Portuguese lands of Angola and Mozambique. Purple for the Belgian Congo.

From Addis Ababa, right in the centre of the country, he traces south through the lakes of the Great Rift Valley with their evocative names – Koka, Ziway, Abijata, Shala, Langano – like something out of a book for explorers. And there at the crossroads is *Shashamane*. He whispers the word again, and then repeats it. Louder, insistent.

'This is where you want to be buried?' I ask him, more pleased that my father is remembering something than that the place exists or that my father wants its name written into his last will and testament.

'It's five thousand miles away!' I say, tapping the word into my phone and bringing up a more modern map next to pictures of some corrugated iron gates painted in red, green and gold. I click *Images* and Google brings up further photographs. I scroll through wide dusty roads, blue tuk-tuks, groups of men in bandanas holding assault rifles and smiling, Rastafarians in sunglasses, a child in a ragged Liverpool shirt.

'We need to arrange for me burial,' my father says, as if he were discussing the protocols around his laundry basket being taken away. And he repeats the name again. *Shash-a-mane*.

'Dad, you're not even dying!'

'The new man is from there,' he says.

'Which new man, Dad?'

'We were talking about the Rastafarians. Him says the Rastafarians are there in Shashamane just like they are everywhere over in Jamaica.'

I stop myself from asking more questions and let Dad talk on. His thoughts and words are garbled now, but he mentions Marcus Garvey and the phrase 'Back to Africa', says it's time to move on out of Babylon, and talks about the Emperor, calls him the King of Kings and Lord of Lords. I think if my mother was alive today she would box his ears with her tambourine for this utterance of blasphemy.

I wonder whether the black man carer who has put all these ideas in my father's head is not actually from Ethiopia. More likely he is from St Pauls or Handsworth or Brixton and he's trying to talk the old man into some kind of Rastafarianism. As Dad continues, I check the details again on my phone: *In 1948 Emperor Haile Selassie donated 500 acres of his private land to allow members of the Rastafari movement, Ethiopian World Federation and other settlers from Jamaica and other parts of the Caribbean to go to Africa... On his 1966 visit to Jamaica, Haile Selassie reportedly encouraged Rastafari leaders to repatriate to Shashamane, but stressed that there was still important work to do in liberating Jamaica.*

'I don't want to get laid to rest in Babylon,' Dad was saying now. 'I need to go back to my fathers' land.' It was a funny turn of phrase – the land of my fathers. It makes me think about Wales' national anthem.

'You'd have to go back a lot of generations before you had ancestors in Africa, Dad,' I said. 'Especially in Ethiopia. They didn't take slaves to the Caribbean from the east, they took them from the west.' I point to the atlas. 'Are you sure you don't want to be buried in Nigeria, or Ghana – or Cameroon?'

Just then there's a knock at the door, and the new carer's face appears around the corner of the door.

Dad's face lights up. 'Here comes the man I was talking about,' he says. 'Come and tell my daughter about the Conquering Lion of the Tribe of Judah.'

'Good afternoon,' says the man politely. 'My name is Solomon.'

Ten minutes later, I am an active participant in organising my father's repatriation.

THE LETTER

As he walks to a house which will never be his home, in a land that will never be his country, Aman jams his phone into the inside pocket of his leather jacket and his hands into his pockets.

His collar is turned up against the wind that whips along the grey side streets around the stadium. Through his headphones he listens to pop music from home, vibrato vocals. The disembodied voice of Hacaaluu Hundeessaa echoes in his ears as if these streets were the green fields of Oromia.

The house which is not Aman's house is in a street that will never be his street. Truncated by the railway-cutting, its asphalt ugliness is ended suddenly by a row of pebbledash bollards.

On the doormat that will never be his doormat is the only thing in this country that truly belongs to him. A letter. Behind a small rectangle of cellophane, an aperture in the recycled envelope, his name appears in capital letters. AMAN BERHANE.

Aman holds the letter for a moment, enjoying its physical lightness and the knowledge at least that it means he exists, that somewhere in an anonymous government office somebody has typed out his name, that whoever posted it through the door may have thought about him briefly.

He starts at the thin line where the flap of the envelope is stuck, picking at it with clay-lined fingernails. He knows that as this cheap recycled paper unfolds, so too will the rest of his life.

A decision has been made in a room he has never been to by a person he has never met and whose name he will never know. He looks at the UK Home Office logo with its crown and its shield and a confusing motto in another language he will never know, and wonders why the printing is askew; the address that is not his address slopes slightly uphill.

Aman's reading in English is slow, but he understands the letter despite its legalisms and jargon. He knows in his head he has the right of appeal, but he knows in his heart that he has reached the bollards at the end of the cul-de-sac.

And half a mile away, inside a kiln, a crack appears in a clay goat.

Exiles

Your neighbour knows you are alive but only you know how you are living.

Oromo proverb

I had been over at the industrial estate. Don't ask me what I was doing over there. I try not to think about it, but in any case it would keep me alive for another week. I spewed into a bush and had an appetite for once, I don't know why, and so I decided to walk back to the flat to have something to eat, a meal that would be neither midnight snack nor ridiculously early breakfast, but something in between. And I was just thinking about whether there was anything there except a piece of toast when I saw him, sitting on a bench by the Transporter Bridge, staring out at the river. And I'd been there so many times myself that I knew why he was there.

So I crossed the main road in the greyish half-light, watching the traffic lights changing from green to gold to red, even though there were no cars, nor vans, nor lorries to obey them, and I walked along the gravel path at the edge of the river so that he would see me approaching.

We had known each other for a little while now, after the first time I followed him out of the Global Food Centre and asked his name, mistaking his response for 'a man'.

'I know you're a man,' I had said laughing, a little bit gassed up, half a litre of vodka swinging wildly in my carrier bag, 'but what is your name?'

And he had smiled too, a bashful smile that made him seem like just a boy, and he explained to me gently and carefully in his faltering English that his name really was Aman. And the thing about him apart from that beautiful unexpected smile, the thing that made me just want to talk to him was that he looked me in the eye.

And so, unlike the men who paid to have me suck them off but couldn't look me in the eye, I didn't offer him any business like I'd planned.

And suddenly I was scared, so scared of frightening him away with my dilated pupils and smudged make-up and swinging vodka, so I didn't ask him any questions, I just talked.

'My name is Jasmine,' I said. 'My real name. I don't usually tell people my real name. People just call me Jazz. You know, like the music. My dad played the saxophone in a band, apparently. At least that's what my mum told me. Before she died.' Aman stared blankly, but at least there was eye contact.

'I live just around the corner by there, in a flat. I live with some other girls. Five of us and we're all from different countries. There's one girl from Romania, and we've got Slovakia, and another one from Albania, and another one from Nigeria.'

And he listened, really listened, as I stood there spouting this cant in the middle of the pavement while people pushed past with their thin plastic bags striped blue and white, chock full of dusty mangoes and bulbous pak choi, gnarly stubs of ginger and little glass jars of harissa paste, brightly coloured sacks of basmati and vacuum-packed flatbreads.

And in that moment I was transported far away from the grey pavements polka-dotted with chewing gum and the disused car park carpeted with shards of broken glass, and the council-planted shrubbery full of used needles and condoms, and the graffiti and the closed down shops.

'I never knew my dad,' I told this stranger, 'the saxophone player. He went missing when my mum was pregnant. And then when I was eleven, my mum died. Breast cancer.'

The carrier bag stopped swinging in my hand and a Bengali woman with a double pram asked me if she could get past and I said yes, and then I said: 'Do you come from another country?'

And he laughed and said: 'It's a long story, do you want a cup of coffee?'

And I said: 'Yes, because fucking hell I'm freezing standing here.'

And he frowned and said: 'Don't say *fucking*, it's not a nice word.'

And I said I hadn't thought about it like that.

So I would say we went back to his flat, but it wasn't a flat and it wasn't a house; he had a room. Aman lived in a house for asylum seekers and when we sat down at the table, he was embarrassed because the *guys* he shared the house with, and their acquaintances and acquaintances of acquaintances, had been using the whole surface of a big old-fashioned hexagonal antique coffee table as an ashtray. I found it strange the way he said *guys*, as if it was a word he had learned but that he knew was not quite right to describe the lack of intimacy he shared with those with whom he had been housed.

'Asylum seekers have no choice, you knows,' he told me, and I wondered if the way he spoke was bad English, or if he'd just picked up the local dialect quickly. 'You knows, you have no choice to leave your country, no choice who to pay to get you out, no choice how you get to here, no choice who you live with in your asylum house.'

Aman told me that he didn't like being in his room because he was sharing with a big man from Sudan who spent the whole night reading aloud from the Quran. 'I don't care if people believe something different God,' he reassured me, 'but when someone is loudly chanting when you are trying to sleeping, life it becomes impossible.'

'You knows it,' I said.

'And after the bomb in London, police came and questioned another man who is just come here, from somewhere, I think Iraq. This *guy* was just a *young guy* who had nothing to do with bombs and he never been in London. But it makes me have nerves all the time if the police is coming around knocking the door, and then these people come in, you don't know who they are.'

Aman asked me to wait while he cleared the ash from the table with a dried up disposable dishcloth that had been stuffed between the taps and a row of cracked white tiles by the kitchen window.

I looked out through the single pane of glass and shivered as the back door rattled. Beyond a dilapidated garden shed, the Swansea to Paddington roared across the embankment.

And then: 'Coffee?' he asked, kettle already tilted toward the sink.

'Please,' I said, surprised by that soft, low voice and how already I was beginning to miss it, even though we were still in the same room, the only two people in the house. It was that same feeling I'd had on the pavement outside of Global Foods, a fear that he would leave before we had even shared a cup of coffee, that his housemates would return, or that I would do something wrong or he'd find out some things about me to make him change his mind.

But he just said: 'Did you know that coffee comes from my country?'

He showed me the label on the brown paper bag that he had purchased in the Global Foods Centre. It said *Dark Ethiopian Yirgacheffe Arabica Coffee. Complex and Rich.* I didn't care to be honest about where the coffee had come from as long as it was going to be hot and wet, but I liked the way Aman's face grew animated at seeing these strange words on the sticker, so in the interest only of hearing more of his small, small voice I said, idly, 'I wonder who invented coffee.'

'There is a legend,' he said, gesturing for me to sit down, 'from my country, that it was discovered by a man called Kaldi.'

The aroma began to fill our nostrils, overpowering the pungent mildewed damp and the fusty odour of stale cigarettes that had greeted us in the hallway.

'Do you want milk and sugar?'

'One please,' I said, watching Aman spoon four generous

teaspoons of sugar directly from the bag into his own steaming mug.

'I am sorry,' he said, bringing our drinks in two charity shop mugs taken straight from the draining board, 'normally in my country we have a ceremony for drinking coffee. We roast the beans, and we have a special pot from which to pour it into cups.' He handed over my mug, which had a picture of Freddie Mercury in a white vest, holding his fist aloft in front of a vast crowd. 'Our cups are smaller than this,' he said.

His own mug was a deep shade of amber, decorated with the badge of the local football club. Its nickname, *Exiles*, was emblazoned across the side that I could see as he took his first sip. I wondered if he knew the word, and what it meant, how appropriate it was in this house for fugitives from the warzones of the world.

'Kaldi was a goat herder,' he said, 'from a place called Kaffa, a place where coffee grows wild.' Aman's soft voice grew into an incantation, as if this was a story he had told many times, or a story he himself had perhaps been told since childhood. His voice lent the story a timeless quality, as if, even if it were not technically fact, deeper mysteries and truths lay contained somewhere within. 'One day, when he was herding goats through highlands near a monastery, he noticed his goats behaving strangely. They were excited.'

I sipped from Freddie Mercury's outstretched hand and nodded an encouragement. 'They were excited about a bush with bright red berries. Kaldi tried these kind of cherries himself, and they made him more alert and awake. When he took them home to his wife, she said these berries were sent from heaven, and that he should share them with the monks at the monastery. But when he did so, one monk called them *the devil's work* and tossed them into a fire.'

'According to the legend, the *aroma*' – Aman tested the word – 'of the roasting beans was enough to give the berries a second chance, and so the monks took the coffee from the fire, and put them in water. Following some time, roasting coffee beans and mixing them with hot water became the morning ritual for the monks. It helped them stay awake for long times to complete their prayers.'

When he had finished the story, we sipped our coffee in silence. It was hot and strong and sweet and it was very quiet in the house, the only sound from another passing train. I imagined the landscape of East Africa, the way that Aman had described it. 'I would like to go to your country,' I said.

And in the smallest, saddest voice I had ever heard, he looked at me over the rim of his mug and said: 'So would I.'

The next time we met he showed me a poem he had written. I didn't understand any of it because it was in his language. The characters looked beautiful the way he had curled and looped them across the faint lines on the page. Every letter seemed to be doubled up as if to emphasise the sounds, and I loved the way his Adam's apple moved halfway through each word, as if he was gasping for breath.

When he read the poem to me, it seemed like a lot of the words in his language were like that; they started and stopped and started again and he must have thought I was weird because as he was reading my eyes were transfixed on the beauty and grace of his neck. Now it was me who avoided eye contact. He made me feel shy in a way that made me remember Primary School, the way we would all look down at our shoes when Mrs Mahoney had caught us doing something wrong.

I asked him what it meant and he told me a little bit of it, translating it into English very slowly in a soft voice, very quiet. His voice was always like that, as if somebody had stolen it.

I wish he had written it for me in English, because now I can only remember the last line: *Put on the kettle*. I liked the way he had said *put on the kettle* instead of *put the kettle on*. It wasn't like he was telling you to do something, the words just became something you wanted to do for him.

I asked him what the poem was about and he said it was about being on your way somewhere and only getting half way and then deciding that that was after all where you want to stay.

That morning when I walked along the gravel path by the gloom of the river, I saw that Aman was writing something again. I tried to imagine what I looked like to him, what he might think of me as I ambled toward him, framed by the colossal structure of the bridge. I was wearing boots that came over my knees and skin-tight jeans and a black strappy top with silver sequins, and my hair was greasy and blowing across my face in the drizzle. The thick kohl across my eyelids and the silver glitter on my face had smudged.

As I sat down next to him on the bench, he stuffed his notebook into the pocket of his jacket. He was in no mood to share his thoughts.

'What are you writing?' I asked him, my voice cracking.

He stared straight ahead, across the river where the grey-brown mud was specked with small white birds pecking for breakfast.

I moved my body so that the pale goosebumps of my stick-thin arms were touching the black leather of his jacket.

He didn't talk, and I didn't blame him. He knew where I had been, what I'd been doing.

My hand was shaking with the cold and with something else, some new nervousness that had entered me since I met this boy from a country where I'd learned the calendar was seven years behind the rest of the world. It was like he was a time-traveller, or come from a different planet. And in the moments when I was high or gassed up or daring to think about some kind of positive future, I had started to believe that Aman had come to Newport especially for me, a saviour sent to give me a second chance at life.

I fumbled in the pocket of my jeans to find the joint I had rolled earlier. Aman continued to stare into space. I struggled to get my lighter to spark, freezing fingers slipping on the flint wheel, joint dangling precariously from my trembling lips. Eventually I managed to get the tip to burn and dragged furiously at the homemade filter, filling my lungs with the drug's dank, scented warmth. I rested my head on Aman's shoulder and looked up at the sky framed by the enormity of the bridge.

And when I woke, he had gone.

I didn't know how many minutes or hours had passed, but I was laid out on the metal bench. Its cold bars had printed long red lines on my left arm, which was immobile from having slept with my bodyweight pressed against it. The remains of my joint lay smokeless in the wet grass. And as I came to consciousness, I realised he had covered me with his jacket.

Before he disappeared, this was one final selfless act. I imagined the way he had taken off his jacket, the way he would have tenderly ensured it covered my shivering limbs, the way – perhaps, and in this I know there is wishful thinking – the way that maybe he stroked my hair and planted a small kiss on my sleeping forehead before he went to the place where perhaps he knew always that he was heading.

I was there when the police arrived with their blue and white tape and I was there when all those people left their flowers. I was there when the reporters and photographers came and turned his name into a tragic footnote of the refugee crisis.

I could have told any of them where he had gone, but nobody asked me.

Many Rivers to Cross

river bridge
the distance
of my prayer

Paul Chambers

The first time I saw those white, white cliffs of England, I thought about my mother. The undulations of the land, the way the cliffs cascade and twist, reminded me of the fall and folds of her long white *kemis* on a Sunday. My mother is a beautiful woman. She is ageing now, of course, but she is strong, and dignified, and in her eyes you catch always a glimpse of what it must have been my father saw all those years ago. There is a little grey in the braids at her temples, but the thick hawser of her hair remains as crow-black as the day she came into the world.

My mother's face is the colour of coffee with milk, a few thick lines running like dried-up rivulets down her cheeks and across her forehead. I sometimes think it may be a mother's lot in life to worry, and the role of the son to provide the reasons. When I was young, my mother worried about being able to find the money to send me to school. When I was at school, she worried about who I was playing with and whether I was doing enough work. Then, when I was older she worried about whether I would obtain a place in university, and after that whether I would find a good job. These last two years, she has had to worry about whether I am still alive.

And because of those white, white cliffs of England, and these green, green fields of Wales, she doesn't have to worry any more. It is the promised land she has prayed for every time she puts on her white, white *kemis* on a Sunday, and every time she lays her head on her white, white pillow at night and cries.

And when the lorry stopped to refuel, on what I now know to be the M23, and we clambered from beneath the wheel arches

– Tuji and I – covered in tar and dust and oil and grime, like a pair of newborn twins greased in fluid, it was just as if we had been born again, into a new world where we might once again be met with a mother's warm embrace.

And we hoped, when those yellow-jacketed policemen picked us up and took us to the station, that this was England taking us to her bosom, allowing us to suckle just a little drop, just one small, small drop from this land of milk and honey.

But now I know my umbilical cord has been broken forever.

In the blank grey dawn I close my eyes and feel the lightness of the rain on my face. I allow myself to dissolve, atom by atom, disappearing into this foreign city the way the river dissolves into the sea.

I think about how the river began, a trickle of spring water on a mountainside where the rain rarely stops, and I try to recall the sweet thick honey taste, layers across my mother's fresh-baked flatbread

I think about each globule, a great gathering of streams rushing down slopes and into valleys meandering into rivers and remember the milk that came warm and fresh from my very own goat, drinking from a china mug as I dangled my legs from the back wall of my father's compound.

And I think of young boys packing small, small bags of food; young women rolling small, small rolls of dollars, dirty notes pushed into the space between their breasts and much more secret, sacred places too. These were the innocent days before we all knew much, much better that nothing in this world is really sacred. Everything is unholy.

And I remember the shadows of these women, and men lost in private thoughts behind shabby curtains in the back of a minivan heading for the border at Metema – which means the place of cutting. I remember the world reduced to the view from a wing-mirror: the crowded marketplace, men in their long white thobes, women covered in full Islamic dress in the souk at Gallabat, the end of Ethiopia and the beginning of Sudan.

I think of young men changing out of jeans and trainers, of our knees tucked under our chins in the back of a Toyota Hilux, the sapping heat of the sun and the wide blue sky of Khartoum. I think of the place where the Blue Nile flows into the White, and of backyard compounds in Omdurman. I think of tall men with cruel faces, cracking sticks across our shins to keep us in line.

I think about the heat and dust of the Libyan desert, a machine gun soaked in the sweat of my hands to protect our drivers from ISIS. And I think about bodies floating in crystal clear water, washing up on perfect white sands.

I think about naked lighter-flames held to fingertips, the burning of identities, the erasure of previous lives and an unattended hole in a security fence. I think about long lines for handouts of soup and clothing, uneven rows of worshippers, men in ill-fitting jackets and women wrapped in white shawls, the hot stench of humanity crowding into Saint Mike's.

I open my eyes and see the litter on the riverbank. Coca-Cola cans poke out of the mud like mole-rats. In the unkempt grass, silver gas bulbs lie disposed among the cigarette ends like miniature bombs. Gulls glide on the contradictory currents of wind, unsure whether to land.

In the Bible it says from dust we came and to dust we will return, but sixty percent of us is water. It is the water not the earth that is calling me now. All these rivers I have crossed in search of a land to provide me with some place where I can simply be, and all the time it was the water that was calling me.

When I was a young and rebellious boy, foolish and carefree as the young should be, my mother's wish was that I could stop chasing girls and apply to university. But in my life's journey I have learned that going to school is only a first step in an education. A man learns as much from going to prison as he does from going to university. And I have learned much, much more from the experience of being a refugee than I would if I had stayed at home. The earth itself has been my teacher, even in the most hostile environments.

I learned kindness in the desert. When they tossed human beings out onto the sands, left living people behind because they were too weak or because their relatives had not wired the money that had been demanded, this is when we learned to share.

When the journey began, we were almost fighting for the water, so much that the agents would use their sticks to make sure some people passed the bottles on. In Sudan, it was all long sips and resentful looks. By the time we reached Libya, we had – all of us without exception – learned to know instinctively who was weaker than whom, who needed a fraction more water than ourselves if they were to make it to the next stop. Nobody wanted to see the strangers with whom we had all shared the journey carelessly abandoned to the heat and dust.

I learned to love in the most unexpected places. I learned to love God in the Jungle camp near Calais. Even when I was hungry and cold, for months I thought of nothing but how we could make sure our people were welcomed to the camp, that they had a little food and something warm to wear and that they had a place to pray for protection. We, the wretched of the earth, building community on a scrap of land outside the port. While we built the church, others built mosques and barber shops and restaurants and libraries. We made a life there, for a while.

I learned gentleness volunteering in the kitchen of the Diversity Project. Leah used to tease me because of how gently I was peeling the potatoes. Very, very slowly, cutting their rough brown skins with a sharp, sharp knife to reveal the naked white creamy texture underneath. In those days I would tell her that I was careful because I did not want to create waste, I wanted to ensure everybody had a lot of potato to eat. But I think she knew that I chose to do my work slowly so that I could spend more time standing next to Selam, the quiet girl from my country who would smile shyly at me and say nothing as she cut into chunks the potatoes I had peeled and lowered them in batches in a small, small metal basket into the bubbling hot oil of the fryer. This is how I learned to love a woman.

And here in Newport I learned to eat fried potatoes with salt and vinegar and then to call them chips and later still to eat them with curry sauce or gravy. One day we even tried the chips with cheese and gravy. Leah said it was a tradition.

Selam and I, we went and sat on a bench by the river, in the centre of town near the theatre where I had been attending the pottery class for asylum seekers, beneath the big steel wave where the seagulls gather. I was not sure at first about the thickness of the food in my mouth that evening. But when we unwrapped the paper and lifted the lid of the carton to reveal the steaming pile of yellow cheese and chips, covered with the rich, meaty smell of the gravy, I was learning joy.

I was more than sure about the smile of Selam. She laughed at the expression on my face when Leah mentioned that first time that the local people sometimes ate cheese and gravy together with their chips. And through this kind of food and these kinds of people, I grew to love this place.

When people talk about love, they make it sound very grand, but when I realised I felt a kind of love for Selam, it was nothing like the posters for the movies. It was nothing dramatic at all. I just discovered that I liked to be near her. I liked to watch how serious her face grew when she was cooking. I liked to tease her about the mistakes she made when speaking English, hoping each time that she would respond to my jokes by grabbing me playfully by the arm, moving the back of her hand toward my face as if she was going to slap, which only sometimes she did.

And for a while we began to do what some people here call

seeing each other. We were not exactly betrothed as my mother might have wished, even though Selam is not the kind of girl my family would object to.

Things only became complicated by the situation with our papers. I sometimes think papers are the enemies of love. Papers are for officials, for governments and the authorities – they are not for you. When you are asked about your papers by the person with whom you are sharing a bed, and this becomes an important fixation, a daily interrogation, you know the world has finally gone crazy.

The letter from the Home Office was printed on recycled paper so thin that if you held it to the light you could read the text on the back of the letter without turning it over. But it was enough to come between us. Selam she told me that she could not build a house on the sand.

I feel the lightness of the rain on my face and the cold air of the breeze. I have melted into semi-consciousness, the way I was inside that rubber boat, squeezed between souls on the precipice of life, a place where I could hardly breathe. Again, I am lost in the darkness, screams and babies who wail and then stop. Again I hear the babble of Tigrinya mixed with Arabic, French, Amharic, Yoruba and the gurgle of a deflating boat. The hard metal of the bench sinks beneath me and becomes the slow, soft sinking of the rubber.

I remember the terrible silence after the infant screaming ceased, the way everybody avoided everybody else's eyes. Nobody said a word. And the sickening churn of saltwater in my dehydrated stomach.

I don't remember the precise moment when I realised we were not going to make it. By the time it came, I was too weak to fight it, too far gone to care. Only now do I appreciate that we must all have been less than a half hour from death by drowning. I only remember the cold of the water lapping at my arms as the rubber of the boat bobbed very gently, parallel to the waves. The engine spluttered and my soul surrendered to the vast graveyard of the sea.

And then a shadow came upon us, someone speaking in another language – I think it was English – and when I woke, there was a lady. A white lady dressed in white.

I did not know whether I was dead or alive, whether she was an angel or a doctor. And at that moment – as I lay still in the purgatory of that little island, floating like a rubber ring somewhere between Africa and Europe, between the hell of detention and the heaven of the beach, watching her tuck a strand of hair behind her ear as she blinked and gently gave me something I had been missing for months, a beautiful smile – I genuinely did not mind.

I open my eyes again, and here comes another woman I have loved, walking in the cool of the dawn between the Waterloo Inn and the West of England Tavern. The bones of her slight figure shiver with cold. She is nothing like my mother, nothing like the beautiful lady doctor of Lampedusa and nothing like Selam, but she has an honest soul.

And it is because of her that I change my mind. How can I give myself to the river after all these rivers I have crossed? How can I allow my mother to continue to wonder? How can I choose to die when life keeps claiming me for itself?

You Are Marvellous

Gwnewch y pethau bychain mewn bywyd
Do the little things you have seen me do

Dewi Sant / Saint David

Today was the best day of my life, but its beginning was *inauspicious*. There was no sign when I woke up late this morning that things were going to be any more *favourable* than usual. There was no milk in the fridge, so I had to chew through two slices of toast with I-Can't-Believe-It's-Not-Butter while the monkey on the chocolate cereal box looked down at me from the shelf, smiling in mockery.

Then we had to run for the bus, and the hood of my coat blew down in the wind and my hair got wet and my glasses ended up looking like a windscreen without wipers. And then because my mum was flustered from all the rushing, she took ages looking in her pockets for change.

The bus driver was a white man with a bald head and a round *midriff*, and while my mum was counting out the money, he kept looking at me and then at his big silver chunky watch. He had three feathers tattooed onto his arm, but you could hardly see them because his arms were so hairy. All the time the orange light was flashing to *indicate* that he was about to drive off, and as soon as my mum had ripped the ticket out of the machine he put his foot on the accelerator almost like he wanted us to go flying down the aisle.

As we fell into the seats that are supposed to be reserved for people with wheelchairs, I was thankful not to be seen by any kids from my school. Instead the bus was full of old men with thick glasses and flat caps and hair coming out of their noses and ears, and old ladies in beige or turquoise or cranberry coloured raincoats with *retractable* umbrellas and those shopping trolleys which look like laundry baskets on wheels. Mostly they are the kind of old ladies who normally say that they love my hair, as if they have never seen a black girl's hair before.

There are good things and bad things about your mum working in your school. One of the bad things is that you have to get there early because she starts work in the breakfast club. One of the good things is that sometimes you get to have a breakfast in the breakfast club.

And sometimes I'm allowed to go and sit quietly in my classroom, especially when it's raining. Mrs Mahoney says it's because I'm responsible. She says I can be trusted to get on with something sensible. I think sensible is the wrong word for it because usually I will go to the book corner and read, or sometimes I'll sit at my table and do a drawing. In my Word Book, 'sensible' is a *synonym* for 'boring', and Mrs Mahoney would hardly like me to say that reading and drawing are boring. In fact, I find them *captivating* and *utterly absorbing*. I become *entranced*. I lose myself in these *pursuits*.

But my favourite thing is writing, as you might be able to tell. Mrs Mahoney has been trying to encourage me. She says I've got a very impressive vocabulary. Once she said that one of my stories made me sound like I had swallowed a thesaurus. I wasn't sure whether to take this as a compliment, as what I think she might have meant is that I overuse unusual words.

What she may not understand is that when you are writing in a language that is not your mother tongue, all new words sound equally unusual. For example, I don't know whether *shy* or *introverted* would be a better way to describe my personality, but as I am also quite *precocious*, I have a *predilection* for the *polysyllabic*.

The bell rings and I see my class lined up outside. Everybody has remembered it's Saint David's Day apart from me. Ahmad and Ibrahim are wearing red rugby shirts with the three feathers from the bus driver's arm. Dawit is dressed up like a coalminer, with a real light on his white hard hat. He is turning it on and off so it shines in people's faces. Sergio has made a Davy lamp out of cardboard, like the ones we learned about in class last week. The girls have all remembered to wear the Welsh lady outfit, and standing there in a row with black hats and red cardigans they look like the soldiers who guard the Queen of England outside Buckingham Palace. This is probably the only time our school has been compared to Buckingham Palace. I am wearing black and red too, but that's because it's the school uniform.

I want to hide. I want to run home. I want to go back to Oromia, the homeland I have never seen. I don't mind that we can't afford an aeroplane, I will walk there if I have to. I will walk and walk until I can run and be wrapped in the arms of my grandmother in the village where my ancestors are buried.

I hide my uniform beneath my olive green coat that is too big for me and has fur around the hood.

'Betty.' I don't respond at first because I genuinely don't hear. I am lost in my thoughts. Daydreaming. Away with the fairies, whoever and wherever they are.

'Betelhem.' The second time I don't answer, it is because I'm afraid that if I make a sound I might cry. I might burst into so many tears that I would fill the river and the channel and the ocean and end up drowning everybody in the school.

I have visions of all of us floating in a sea of tears, all of my classmates, children from all over the world being carried away by the waves, gasping for breath as the playground *apparatus* disappears beneath a rising tide. First the slide and then the climbing frame and then the school itself. And then we all float downriver, losing sight of each other as even the Transporter Bridge vanishes and the world turns a greyish blue.

Miss Anwar doesn't say my name a third time, but I can tell that she is sitting next to me, even though I have zipped my coat up to the top and the furry bit that goes around the hood is mostly covering my face. I must look like a tortoise who has pulled his head inside his shell, a big green lump which you can't tell whether it's alive or dead.

In front of us on the desk is the piece of paper on which I have written something, and drawn a picture. In the picture, stick girls and stick boys with upside down smiles are floating down a river.

Somewhere way off in another part of the school, someone is ringing the bell. It is followed by the quiet noise of excited children lining up, and above them a teacher's voice, Mrs Mahoney saying *Dim siarad* more times than she would wish, and then saying 'Excuse me, children, I have said *dim siarad* more times than I would wish.' Then the shuffle of everybody going into the hall, the squeak of trainers on the parquet floor. Eventually it all goes quiet and the piano starts up. It is the song Mrs Jenkins taught us last week.

Then children singing: *Nid wy'n gofyn bywyd moethus, aur y byd na'i berlau mân*. It sounds so beautiful I nearly cry again. I close my eyes and try to imagine the scene in the hall. I imagine the big boys at the back, trying to make it look like they are sort of joking, but singing louder than anybody. *Gofyn wyf am galon hapus*. And I imagine the very little ones at the front, still not knowing the words but opening and closing their mouths like baby birds to make it look like they are singing. *Calon onest, calon lân*.

Calon lan yn llawn daioni, goes the chorus, *tecach yw na'r lili dlos, dim ond calon lan all ganu, canu'r dydd a'r chanu'r nos*. Someone put their hand up last week and asked Mrs Jenkins what it meant. 'A clean heart, a pure heart...' she said. And on the way out she called me *cariad*, which I know means love.

It's funny to think about it, really. We are children from more than fifty countries. Together we speak more than thirty languages. Mrs Mahoney always says it is something we should all be very proud of. 'Fifty countries and thirty languages. We're the most *diverse* school in a diverse city. And we should all be very proud of how we all get on with each other.' She always finishes these speeches saying: 'The United Nations could take a leaf out of our book.' Some of the older children would giggle because they had heard her say it so many times.

And here we are singing and celebrating in the one language none of us can speak properly. Not even the teachers. I've only ever heard Mr Watkins say '*tri, dau, un, dim siarad*' and '*hyfryd*'. He says '*hyfryd*' every time someone answers a question whether their answer is *lovely* or not. He even has a laminated piece of paper sellotaped to his desk so that he can copy the date. Today's date in Welsh is a kind of *palindrome. Dydd Mawrth, Mawrth 1*. Tuesday, March 1.

In the corridor is a map of the world with coloured pins in it to show where we have all come from. Dilara and Yasmin use the pins to stab each other in the neck while they are waiting in the lunch queue, but I always stop and look at it and wonder why the pieces of string that attach us all to Wales are straight lines, as if we'd all flown here like birds. Nobody travels in a straight line.

At the side of the map are some flags that Mrs Mahoney printed out. There's the Welsh dragon, of course, and the Union Jack. And lots of flags from around the world, some of the countries where people in our school come from like Poland and Turkey and Slovakia and Afghanistan. But some flags are missing, like mine.

The teachers never explained it to us, but one day I heard my mum's friend telling my mum that the Ethiopian flag was missing because there had been complaints and arguments about whether to use the old flag or the new flag or a different flag. The teachers had decided that there were too many arguments and they didn't want to offend anybody, so I think they took it down and put the Canada flag there instead, because no one in our school is from Canada. Hozan said they should have put the flag of Kurdistan, but they wouldn't because it isn't in the United Nations.

Since then, whenever Mrs Mahoney says that thing about the United Nations, I always think quietly to myself about Kurdistan, and Oromia, and all the countries that we come from that are not in the United Nations.

'You are marvellous,' says Miss Anwar finally, and somehow I find can breathe out. I poke my head forward a little bit, into the fur of my hood, like an animal coming out from its burrow after hibernating for the winter.

Miss Anwar holds the piece of paper out in front of us. 'We should enter this into the Eisteddfod,' she says softly, without looking at me.

I take the hood down and look at the shapes of the words on the page: different letters, different alphabets, and the title I have given it, in Welsh. *Afon* means River.

'How?' I say. My voice sounds small and far away, like it did when we went on the train to Barry Island with the Diversity Project, and Leah taught me how to hold a shell to my ear to hear the sea.

Mrs Mahoney had been very strict that we had to get all of our entries finished on Friday.

'I can post it in the box for you,' said Miss Anwar, 'if it's okay with you'.

I nod slowly, a little unsure but feeling like I'll regret it if I don't.

'You remind me of my mum,' said Miss Anwar suddenly, which is a very weird thing to say considering I'm eight years old and Miss Anwar is at least twenty-five which means her mum is probably about fifty.

'My mum was born here, in the same hospital as you. But when she was a little girl she never believed she belonged, because her mum and dad were *immigrants*,' Miss Anwar explained. 'From Bangladesh.' She said the word immigrants as if she didn't like it, as if she was only using the word because there was no choice, as if there was another word she wanted to use instead but as if that word was imaginary. I wondered whether there was a synonym for immigrants that would make us seem beautiful.

'Now, if you take your coat off, I've got something you can borrow.' Miss Anwar went over into the cloakroom and didn't even look around to see whether I was going to take my coat off, so I kind of guessed that I should. It wasn't really like I cared what was in the carrier bag or what I was going to be allowed to borrow, but I didn't want her to be disappointed.

When she came back she was holding a *shawl*, a square piece of cloth that was chequered red and black, a little bit like *tartan* but not as fancy. She folded it diagonally and then *draped* it around my shoulders. And then, like a magician pulling a rabbit from a hat, Miss Anwar put her hand inside the crumpled Aldi bag and pulled out a tall black hat with beautiful white lace around the brim. White ribbons dangled from each side so that you could tie it under your chin.

'Put it on,' said Miss Anwar, so I did. 'There we are,' she said, 'you look like a proper little Welsh girl.'

I smiled.

Before we went into the hall, Miss Anwar went over to the windowsill and took one of the daffodils that was shining out of Mrs Mahoney's vase, and cut its stem with a pair of scissors. Then she got a safety pin from the drawer and pinned it to my shawl.

The hatch was a little wooden window where you could see through from the canteen into the main school hall, and I could see my mum standing there with some of the other dinner ladies, Mrs Powell and Mrs Akhtar and Mrs Hussein.

I didn't really know what to expect because this was my first Eisteddfod in the Juniors. In the Infants, we only came up to the hall for the singing. But this time there was an *elaborate* ceremony that Mrs Mahoney took a long time explaining. In fact, while Mrs

Mahoney was talking I kept looking at my mum to make sure she understood at least a bit of what Mrs Mahoney was saying and to make sure she wasn't going to get bored. But my mum just kept on smiling and looking kind of interested and proud. I can usually tell what my mum is feeling, but this time her face was happy, but also just a little bit *inscrutable*.

'What you are about to witness, *blantos*,' said Mrs Mahoney, using a Welsh word for children, which she always did even when it was not Saint David's Day, 'is a very old and traditional ceremony.' She paused, to create a dramatic effect, and then continued: 'There are records that versions of this ceremony date back to at least 1176. That's well over eight hundred years.'

As Mrs Mahoney was speaking, some of the Year Sixes shuffled up on stage. They were dressed in white robes and carried cardboard swords wrapped in silver foil to make the blades look real. They looked a little bit like the priests in the Ethiopian Orthodox Tewahedo Church. I wondered whether the Welsh people were also one of the lost tribes of Israel, like the Ethiopians.

'Now,' said, Mrs Mahoney, 'before we can begin, there's an important question to ask. Musa is going to ask a question, and we are all going to answer together.'

Musa is in Year Five. I know him from the Christmas Party for refugee kids that I went to last year with my mum, at the church on the hill in the centre of town. He's from Sudan. As Musa walked forward slowly looking extremely *introverted*, Mrs Mahoney kept talking.

'The question is this,' she said, pronouncing her words carefully. '*A oes heddwch?* It means: is there peace? Unless there is peace, we cannot continue with the ceremony, we cannot chair the Bard.'

Musa walked up to the front with his head bowed, wearing a proper *jellabiya*, a white Sudanese robe. In a big voice, as if he had been practising, he said: '*A oes heddwch?*'

It was the loudest and clearest I had ever heard him say anything.

Musa spoke English in a whisper, with a heavy accent, as if to emphasise that he would prefer to be speaking Arabic, but he spoke the Welsh language perfectly.

'*Heddwch!*' chanted all of the Juniors together, using the same voice we use for phrases like '*Bore da, Mrs Mahoney!*' with an exaggerated lilt that makes us all sound far more Welsh than we are.

'*A oes heddwch?*' said Musa again, this time emphasising the questioning tone.

'*Heddwch!*' we shouted, a few of the boys in the back row straining themselves with such enthusiasm that Mrs Mahoney gave them one of her scowls that meant that if they did it like that again she'd probably say something about the high jump.

'*A oes heddwch?*' said Musa a third time.

And this time, when all the children responded, by saying the word *heddwch* like that, just as rhythmic but a little bit softer than before, I did feel very peaceful. It was a nice word, and I didn't even wonder about its synonyms. Instead I thought about translations. Peace. *Salaam.*

And then Mrs Mahoney said: 'There is one competition that is more important than all of the others that we've given prizes for this morning. More than painting, more than pottery, and maybe just about the same as music, the Welsh people value poetry. *Gwlad beirdd a chantorion.* We sang it earlier, didn't we? *Land of poets and minstrels.* Minstrels were like wandering singers. So you see, this is the Land of Song, as we said earlier, but it's also the Land of Poetry, the Land of Poets.'

As Mrs Mahoney was talking and talking, for some reason I started to get nervous. My mum was still looking through the hatch. Miss Anwar was still looking through the box where we'd posted my poem.

'Does anybody know the Welsh word for a poet?' Mrs Mahoney was asking, and nobody was answering. The big boys at the back and the baby birds at the front were getting fidgety.

'The word is *bardd*,' said Mrs Mahoney, emphasising the soft *dd*. 'What's the word in English?'

Aisha put her hand up. Everybody in my school knows Aisha. 'It's Bard, Miss,' she said, 'like Shakespeare, the Bard of Avon.'

'*Da iawn*, Aisha. Very good. Well done. *Ardderchog*.' Mr Watkins would have said *hyfryd*.

'That's right,' Mrs Mahoney continued. 'And we are about to discover who is the Bard of Pillgwenlly.'

For a moment, I thought she was going to tell us all again about W. H. Davies, the supertramp poet who had been born in the Church House pub, around the corner and across the road, and how we should all go and look at the blue plaque, and how it was always worth taking a minute out of your day to stand and stare.

But she didn't. She said: 'The winner is Little Starling...'

She said it so quickly that I didn't remember that last week when we had learned about and chosen our secret names, I had thought about our trip to the Wetlands with the Diversity Project, when my mum had told me that the first time she felt me kicking inside her was also the first time she'd seen a *murmuration* of starlings.

So Mrs Mahoney turned the piece of paper over in her hand. 'Well done, Betty Berhane, Year Three.' My throat went dry.

There was a brief pause because most of the Juniors probably didn't know who I was. They were probably expecting a Year Six or at least a Year Five to be the Secret Bard.

But there I was. Eight years old and about to be chaired as the bard of Pillgwenlly.

Finally the hall burst into applause.

Mrs Jenkins started playing the piano, and a group of older children played along on recorders. Four big boys from the back row had the job of carrying a big wooden chair on to the stage.

Mrs Mahoney said '*Da iawn*, Little Starling, *bendigedig*. Betty, you are the youngest winner of the Bardic Chair we have ever had. It's the first time ever that a Year Three has been the winner, and I know that Miss Anwar is very proud. And so is somebody else.'

I was only half listening to what Mrs Mahoney was saying because I was looking over at the hatch. My mum had *momentarily* disappeared, but now she was back and clapping like everybody else. Mrs Mahoney looked at my mum and smiled, and my mum was trying to pretend not to cry.

'Would you like to read your poem?' said Mrs Mahoney. She said it in a voice that was gentle, but also *implied* that in the circumstances I kind of had to, and Miss Anwar *simultaneously* passed me the piece of paper.

I stood up from the Bardic Chair where the kids with swords had made me sit, and imagined that I had my furry hood around my head so nobody could see me.

First Musa was asked to do the questions again, and nobody was frowned at for shouting this time, and then I did a little cough and read my poem in the loudest voice I could, which trust me was not very loud.

For the rest of the day I had kids coming up to me to say 'Congratulations!' and to tell me they really liked my poem. A couple of Year Sixes even invited me to sit to eat packed lunch with them. I shared my grapes and they gave me Maltesers.

But all of this is not even the best reason that today was the best day ever. The very best thing didn't happen in school. It wasn't something that happened in front of everyone. Nobody clapped and nobody wiped a little bit of tears out of the corner of their eye and pretended that I didn't notice. In fact, nobody noticed anything at all, except me, because there was nothing to notice for anyone else because it was just my mum acting normal.

It happened on the way home. As we got off the bus, my mum lifted her head up, looked right into the driver's face and smiled. And then she said it. 'Cheers, Drive.'

THE EYE OF THE NEEDLE

Your left palm opens against the jamb of the open door, fingers splayed wide as you try to make sense of the monument. You touch it as if the detritus it depicts is real; as if the shoes, broken pieces of pottery, foreign objects left behind were abandoned by some ancient empire – Carthage, Rome, Byzantium – as if it really is a gateway to Europe, rather than an incongruous piece of modern art stranded on a godforsaken beach seventy miles from the coast of Tunisia.

'Mare Nostrum,' you say, naming and inadvertently claiming the whole expanse of water on behalf of the peoples of the continent behind you. Under your breath you whisper the phrase again and in your head you are chanting Latin verbs in a cool classroom near the bank of the river Moselle. There is something strange in the way you find these words so easy to say.

'Mare,' you say again, two syllables, palm against the door, tracing its etymologies through the other languages you speak – mer and Meer, zee and sea.

Beyond the door, the whole thing glistens like the horizon of heaven, as if the phrase 'let there be light' has been uttered just this morning and all the languages of the world set upon the waves.

But something in the cloudless sky, the rising shimmer of the morning's heat, the gentle lapping at the shore – something feels too good to be true. You know you are not here for a holiday, not even a working holiday as you first supposed when you filled the online form.

And when at last your eyes come to rest on what it is that spoils the view, although your mouth becomes dry your natural overwhelming disbelief is so strong you do not even realise that the thumb of your right hand is still moving up and down, clicking the top of the pen that you have been holding fast to all the morning long.

There, face down in the sand is the body of a nameless, stateless child, so tiny you cannot tell if it is a boy or a girl.

Afterword

THE OTHER AS MIRROR:
Disrupting the Formula of Refugee Narratives

According to the United Nations' refugee agency, an unprecedented 79.5 million people are currently displaced from their homes (2019). Sometimes presented as a singular narrative, this disparate, complex global crisis gives rise not only to the myriad stories of displaced individuals but also to those left behind, new encounters in host communities and the many people whose lives are 'crossed' along the way. There can be very few people left on the planet who have not been impacted in some way by this age of mass migration.

Many Rivers to Cross, a work of fiction, follows a single specific migration route 'backwards' – from Newport, Wales to Shashamane, Oromia – with the intention of exploring how creative writing complicates, calls into question and counters the dominant tropes of migrant-journey narratives; to explore what it might mean to 'use' existing stories that 'belong' to real people in fiction rather than journalism; and what literary work might uncover about the condition of exile, to better enable understanding of specific *sending* and *receiving* contexts in Ethiopia and the UK.

In a febrile time of polarisation at both ends of this route, with political instability in the Horn of Africa driving increased outward migration, and heated debate about immigration fuelling political crises in the United Kingdom, media narratives often conform to simple formulae. Asylum seekers are refugees fleeing persecution or illegal immigrants seeking economic advantage. In each case, a simple response is urged: either the refugee must be pitied and provided for, or the migrant must be resented and resisted. Having volunteered and worked with asylum seekers and refugees from a huge variety of countries and backgrounds, part of the impulse to write the stories that became *Many Rivers to Cross* was my desire to explore the complicated nature of the territory.

Originally planned as documentary nonfiction reliant on verbatim testimony from interviews with refugees, the work morphed into what I have come to claim as a 'composite novel', a cycle of stories which cohere to – I hope – bring greater nuance to refugee narratives through the employment of this polyphonic form. Through the writing I discovered first hand that in seeking radical empathy with the 'other', you necessarily discover something about yourself; through writing about other peoples, nations, cultures, languages and identities, you discover new ways of seeing and understanding your own. But what also emerged was the importance of telling a story from multiple perspectives, to acknowledge complex realities but also to overcome the ever-present danger of appropriation.

Many Rivers to Cross has its genesis in relationships forged during my time volunteering and then working at the Sanctuary project in Newport, south Wales, meeting and befriending asylum seekers and refugees who had been 'dispersed' to the city by the UK Home Office. The choice of Shashamane as terminus is bound up not only in its significance in Marcus Garvey's Back to Africa movement and its geographical position in the Great Rift Valley's 'cradle of humanity', but in its being the hometown of a friend. My aim to better understand the complexities of refugee stories arises from a desire to bridge the gap between my compulsion as a writer toward exile as idea and the lived experience of some of my interviewees, for some of whom it has been every bit as Edward Said described in his landmark essay on the subject: 'strangely compelling to think about but terrible to experience'.

The chasm between my thought and their experience is born of the global inequality described in *Globalisation: The Human Consequences* by Zygmunt Bauman, who writes that: 'freedom to move, perpetually a scarce and unequally distributed commodity, fast becomes the main stratifying factor of our late-modern or postmodern times'. And therefore however strong the personal connections we make, transnational friendships are always impacted by global structural inequalities. Whether volunteering or working at the Sanctuary project, I was always a white British passport-holder and the asylum seekers and refugees were – whatever their nationality or previous social status – now contained by labels imposed by nation states and supranational agencies.

The first problem of this writing therefore was to navigate these tiers of global stratification. Commenting on the way he uses his lived experience as a refugee in his writing, the Vietnamese-American author Viet Nguyen says: 'I cultivate that feeling of what it was to be a refugee, because a writer is supposed to go where it hurts, and because a writer needs to know what it feels like to be an other. A writer's work is impossible if he or she cannot conjure up the lives of others, and only through such acts of memory, imagination and empathy can we grow our capacity to feel for others.' But Nguyen is a *refugee writer*, I was to become a *writer of refugees*; the difference here, in terms of cultivating 'memory, imagination and empathy' is crucial.

The problem I faced is articulated perfectly in Chimamanda Ngozi Adichie's novel *Americanah*. The narrator says of the protagonist: 'she began, over time, to feel like a vulture, hacking into the carcasses of people's stories for something she could use'. This ethical dilemma lies at the heart of all writing that engages with the real world, especially transnational writing that transgresses national and experiential borders. There is a perpetual risk of appropriation. As much as anything else, therefore, *Many Rivers to Cross* is an exploration of how a writer can – ethically – engage with stories that belong to others.

A number of factors contributed to the gradual shift away from the non-fiction book I had originally devised. First, there was the practical restriction of participants' availability: many asylum seekers I had met at the Sanctuary project had 'moved on', either to other towns and cities, making face-to-face interviews more difficult, or in terms of lifestyle. After having been granted 'papers' – leave to remain in the United Kingdom – many refugees work long, unsociable hours as they seek to rebuild their lives by establishing a firmer financial foothold. This made arranging interviews practically difficult, and there was also a sense that participants, having started 'a new life', had much less appetite to revisit traumatic aspects of the past. Secondly, there was a realisation that the work was as much about myself, my own identity, family history, community and country as it was about refugees from Ethiopia or anywhere else.

The initial literary model for the project was *The Unwomanly Face of War*, Svetlana Alexeivich's creative documentation of Soviet women who fought in the Second World War. Structured as a collage of voices, the book allows the reader access to the voices of real people relaying their experiences to a writer whose role is akin to that of a curator: editing, shaping and sequencing individual stories that together amount to an epic work of literature, an alternative way of writing history. The unusual authorial position adopted by Alexeivich, close through use of first person but distant by dint of an implicit understanding that the writer is simply a kind of conduit – the stories 'belong' to those whose experiences are related – seemed an ideal navigation of stories that were not 'mine' in any experiential sense. Awarding Alexeivich the 2015 Nobel Prize for Literature, the committee described her 'polyphonic writings' as 'a monument to suffering and courage in our time', and I initially imagined that my work would do for migrants from the Horn of Africa what *Chernobyl*

Prayer had done for the nuclear disaster there and *Boys in Zinc* had done for the Soviet intervention in Afghanistan.

However, in addition to this preconceived model, my guiding principle for this creative research was to 'go upstream'. I was determined that the research would both feature and *be* a journey. Nathan Englander argues for an idea of writer-as-explorer: 'the only true way to expand your world is to inhabit an otherness beyond ourselves... Empathy is violent... tough... can rip you open. Once you go there, you can be changed'. Above all else, my intention for the writing was to make it an exercise in radical empathy, to go into uncharted waters: new literary and geographical territories and the internal lives of others.

The river as symbol, eventually integral to the title (borrowed from Jimmy Cliff), was born of two main factors: the centrality of the river Usk to Newport and its unusual two-way tidal flow, and a quotation ascribed to Archbishop Desmond Tutu. 'There comes a point where we need to stop just pulling people out of the river. We need to go upstream to find out why they're falling in.' This concept of an upstream journey had pertinence to the work I had been doing at the Sanctuary project during 2016 and 2017, where I had been involved in many senses with migrants who had reached the endpoint of their physical journey. We worked to improve the well-being of those who had already experienced trauma, often without understanding of the contexts that had led to their flight from their country of origin. But it also expressed something vital about practice-based research: if the writing was to achieve its aim – disrupting formulaic refugee narratives – it was going to be an uphill struggle where the ending (of any physical journey undertaken and the story itself) would not come into view until the research was almost completed.

Although conversations with refugees and others informed the content of the stories, reading around issues of displacement and exile was instrumental in informing the eventual choice of form. *War: What If It Were Here?* by Janne Teller disrupts the formula of the refugee narrative by imagining a world in which migrant flows are inverted. First published as an essay in a Danish magazine in 2001, and tilted against a similarly xenophobic context to the UK's contemporary debates about immigration, the book has now been translated into over twenty languages. In each version Teller reworks the content to meet the specificities of the context; for example, in the UK version, Britain finds itself at war with the Nordic countries and the protagonist flees to Egypt. This idea of an inverted journey clearly fit with my initial idea of tracing refugee journeys 'backwards' and seemed to offer genuine possibilities for breaking the mould.

This idea was further influenced by documentary photographer Michal Iwanowski's work *Go Home, Polish*, an artistic reaction to xenophobic graffiti in Cardiff. At a talk delivered at Bath Spa University, Iwanowski coined the phrase 'mother pole' to describe the centrality of one's mother in conceptions of home, underscoring what a participant had told me in the most emotional moment of his personal testimony; almost breaking down, words failed him as he tried to describe the pain of knowing, having watched many of his compatriots drown in the Mediterranean: 'all those mothers not knowing where are their sons and daughters'.

Given that ultimately the work became a kind of jigsaw that I had to puzzle out, the final piece of its construction in terms of form came with my introduction to the Mexican-American writer Antonio Ruiz-Camacho. I was attracted to the title of his collection of interrelated stories *Barefoot Dogs* because of its unconscious echo of the insult that inspired the Welsh insurrectionist Owain Glyndwr: 'what care we for these barefoot Welsh dogs' (a slur that finds an echo in 'mudcrawlers' as a word for Irish immigrants to the south Wales ports in the years following the Great Famine). Disparately set – in Madrid; Austin, Texas; and Palo Alto, California – each story relates to a central event: the brutal kidnapping, murder and dismembering of Jose Victoriano Arteaga, patriarch of a prominent upper middle class family in Mexico City. Together, the stories capture a range of perspectives on the horror of Mexico's drug war through focusing on its butterfly-effect fallout on those whose lives seemed to be removed or indeed cosseted from it.

In its tracing of individual lives, across borders and against the backdrop of a global concern, it is truly transnational writing. But what was most important for me was its form: a 'short story cycle' seemed the perfect canvas for my 'upstream journey', providing opportunity to construct a cross-section of the migrant journey landscape and a narrative that could leap nimbly and authentically across space and time: from Newport to Shashamane, via Calais and Lampedusa.

In the classic study of the genre, *The Composite Novel: The Short Story Cycle in Transition* by Maggie Dunn and Ann Morris, the authors define 'the composite novel' as 'a literary form that combines the complexities of a miscellany with the integrative qualities of a novel... a grouping of autonomous pieces that together achieve whole text coherence'. Such a versatile form would allow me to combine the polyphony of Alexeivich, the reverse story-arc of Teller and the central event/butterfly-effect fallout dynamic of Ruiz-Camacho – to create a work that might genuinely disrupt several of the classic tropes of migration literature.

Once I had discovered the most useful form for the work, the next challenge was to create a central event from which all plotlines would flow. I also needed a protagonist who would embody some universal aspects of the global 'refugee crisis' as well as the realities of the stories belonging to my project participants. As I searched for this central event – equivalent to the kidnapping in Ruiz-Camacho's *Barefoot Dogs* – two recent real-life tragedies involving asylum seekers in south Wales loomed so large in my mind that they could not be dismissed or ignored.

In 2018, Eyob Tesfera, from Oromia, drowned himself in Swansea Marina after his application for asylum was refused. I had not known Eyob, but attended an Irreecha meal where I met many of those who had been devastated by his death, local people as well as friends within the refugee community. Later that same year, Mustafa Dawood, from Sudan, died falling from a roof during an immigration raid on a car wash in Newport. Here were two bright young men who had travelled thousands of miles, risking their lives across deserts and seas only to die in tragic, needless circumstances in a foreign land.

But I soon found that finding the character of Aman – a victim of the refugee crisis – was not the key needed to unlock the aim of the writing. To disrupt the narrative formulas often applied to refugee stories, I had truly to work backwards. In an echo of the about-turn I had made in relation to form (from nonfiction to fiction), the discovery of the character of David – a journalist – proved the turning point in the writing. The 'refugee story' I wanted to tell was as much about *receiving* countries as those *sending* refugees, and David gave me the opportunity to adopt a point of view close to my own. In David's viewpoint, I could directly confer some of my own experiences onto the stories, a far more straightforward process than the complex ethical and emotional territory of 're-voicing' refugee narratives. He also provided the chance to explore some of the socio-political issues of the 'host' country: the complexities of Welsh identity, the migration histories of British port cities and – crucially, perhaps – Brexit, which as the constant news backdrop to the writing of the stories, inevitably weaved itself into the narrative.

Rather than simply 'channelling' the voices and views of refugees, as per the original intention, following the discovery of David, *Many Rivers to Cross* would now also include the perspectives of a sex worker, a lorry driver and an immigration officer. As the writing progressed, I came to feel that this diversity within the planned 'polyphony' of voices was absolutely vital to fully reflect the realities of refugees' lives. It was as important to have stories focalised through characters like Mike in 'Leave to Remain', Jasmine in 'Exiles' and the unnamed immigration officer in 'Misericordia' as it was to hear from Selam, Solomon or from Aman himself, especially in terms of fulfilling the aim of disrupting the formula of refugee narratives.

In *The Location of Culture* (1994), Homi K. Bhaba writes: 'The study of world literature might be the study of the way in which cultures recogni[s]e themselves through their projections of "otherness". Where, once, the transmission of national traditions was the major theme of world literature, perhaps we can now suggest that transnational histories of migrants, the coloni[s]ed, or political refugees – these border and frontier conditions – may be the terrains of world literature.' It is precisely through holding up Britain and Ethiopia like a pair of mirrors, and through interrogating transnational narratives, colonial histories and contemporary realities, that *Many Rivers to Cross* begins to open up spaces where cultures recognise themselves.

David's increasingly clear perception of his own (complicated) culture, crystallised in his Welsh-language claim to be 'Cymro' in 'A Baptism of Dust' is precipitated by the arrival of political refugees in his neighbourhood, a phenomenon he is less sure of being related to his own life in the collection's first story, 'Breaking Point'. The juxtaposition of David, 'white gaze' face down in the dust of Addis Ababa, with the unnamed child in the final fragment (deliberately reminiscent of Alan Kurdi, the Syrian-Kurdish three year old whose death made headlines around the world) is an attempt to bridge the gap between the comfortable Westerner and victims of the global refugee crisis.

But despite Aman's journey to Newport and David's to Addis, and the corresponding ones belonging to myself and my refugee-friends, we can never live inside each others' skins. Empathy is bounded by experience. Human beings can be exiled from each other as much as from a geographical home. But what these stories prove – maybe the most important thing – is that despite the global stratification that continues to divide us, our *degree of separation* has reduced. As played out here in fiction, in reality all our stories are interconnected. The power dynamics of colonialism are still in place, but everywhere and always the presence of the 'other' is disruptive.

Many Rivers to Cross, I hope, throws up many more questions than it answers. Perhaps ultimately its success or failure rests less on the disruption of migrant journey tropes and more on describing their net results. Bhabha writes: 'a willingness to descend into that alien territory... may open the way to conceptualising an international culture, based not on the exoticism of multiculturalism or the diversity of cultures, but on the inscription and articulation of culture's hybridity'.

In *Many Rivers to Cross* Aman's forced migration and David's upstream journey are both forays into 'alien territory' that necessarily involve exploration of multiculturalism and diversity, but the articulation of culture's hybridity comes most obviously in the final story. Although 'You Are Marvellous' depicts the multicultural character of a diverse community in a small city in south Wales, its rootedness in the language, culture and tradition of an ancient nation combines with a fresh perspective only made possible by the new arrival. Betelhem is a child not so much caught between two cultures as representing an entirely new one – one that nevertheless carries the cultural equivalent of genetic coding for multiplicity. The title – a reference to the English translation of *Dinknesh*, the Amharic name of 'Lucy', 'the first lady of humanity' – connotes the idea that such possibility has been inherent in all of us since the very dawn of time. Like the text itself, each lived experience is a palimpsest, able to be scraped clean, ready to be used again but always bearing traces of what came before.

Originality, then, might be a bridge too far, but the journey upstream into the terrain of the transnational, with its outroads of irreconcilable exile and the limitless possibilities of hybridity has been more than rewarding. As a displaced person or writer-explorer, the destination always offers another point of departure.

There are always more rivers to cross.

Acknowledgements and Thanks

The story behind these stories begins in my volunteering work at the Sanctuary project, run by members of Bethel Community Church in Newport. Thanks to Claire and Mark Seymour, and Sarah Croft, for your inspiration, and for allowing me to become part of the project's extensive family. Heartfelt thanks too, to all of the people I met during my time volunteering and working there – it was and is a privilege to walk alongside you in your journeys, and have you walk beside me in mine. I am particularly grateful to my friends Yohannes Obsi, Biniyam Birtukan and Denebo Wario for all the help you gave me in preparing this volume; thank you for sharing your stories and your expertise. It is your book too.

Diolch o galon also to Sian Melangell Dafydd for not giving up on having me study for the MRes in Transnational Writing at Bath Spa University. I feel very blessed to have been one of your final cohort. Thanks are due too to Bambo Soyinka for advice on what became the 'Afterword' and to Ian Gadd at the Global Academy of Liberal Arts for your enthusiastic support of my trip to Ethiopia. *Many Rivers to Cross* would have been a very different book without this opportunity. Thank you to everyone I met in Addis Ababa, at the university and around the city, particularly Fetene Regassa for glimpses behind the scenes. And to those others who helped – on and off the record – to give me an insight into some of the places most of us never get to, and would never wish to go.

Finally thank yous to the Three Impostors – David Osmond, Richard Frame and Mark Lawson-Jones – for believing in the book; to the ever-dependable Marc Jennings for another brilliant cover; and to Tomos Osmond for the layout. And, always, to my wonderfully supportive friends and beloved family – diolch yn fawr iawn i chi gyd.

Dylan Moore
Newport, Wales, 2021

For more books from Three Impostors please visit
www.threeimpostors.co.uk